TOUCH

Mark Sennen was born in Surrey, but spent his formative years in rural Shropshire where he learnt to drive tractors and worm sheep. He has been a reluctant farmer, an average drummer, a indolent Ph.D. student and a pretty good programmer. He lives with his wife and two children beside a Devon creek from where he tries to write full-time. *Touch* is his first novel.

Please visit www.marksennen.com for information on the DI Charlotte Savage series.

MARK SENNEN

Touch

AVON

This novel is entirely a work of fiction.
The names, characters and incidents portrayed in it are
the work of the author's imagination. Any resemblance to
actual persons, living or dead, events or localities is
entirely coincidental.

AVON
A division of HarperCollins*Publishers*
77–85 Fulham Palace Road,
London W6 8JB

www.harpercollins.co.uk

A Paperback Original 2012
1

Copyright © Mark Sennen 2012

Mark Sennen asserts the moral right to
be identified as the author of this work

A catalogue record for this book is
available from the British Library

ISBN-13: 978-0-00-751209-6

Set in Minion by Palimpsest Book Production Limited,
Falkirk, Stirlingshire

Printed and bound in Great Britain by
Clays Ltd, St Ives plc

MIX
Paper from
responsible sources
FSC **FSC C007454**
www.fsc.org

Writing is a solitary pursuit, but that doesn't mean a book is the result of just one person's work. So a big thank you to everyone who has helped me out along the way.

Special thanks must go to my agent, Claire Roberts at Trident, for lifting *Touch* from the virtual slush pile. Claire's office is on the thirty-sixth floor of a block on Madison Avenue, and whenever I'm on the phone to her I can't help but contrast my view of a muddy Devon estuary with her Manhattan vista, worlds apart, but it's never felt that way. Thanks also to Claire Bord, Caroline Hogg and everyone at Avon for having the faith to take DI Savage into print.

Joanne Craig offered emails full of encouragement and unrepeatable (and frankly libellous) jokes, while too-numerous-to-mention Twitterers and bloggers gave help and advice.

Extra special thanks to my daughters for putting up with a lost-in-his-head Dad and for character names and future book titles (*Blood*, anyone?). Finally, thanks to my partner, Gitte, whose understated assistance was, perversely, the push I needed to finish the book.

There are two worthy organisations that appear in *Touch* and they would appreciate your interest and support:

Devon Air Ambulance: www.daat.org

Dartmoor Rescue Group: www.dartmoor-rescue.org

For Sue and Michael

Prologue

When Harry was a child he lived at the top of the house. His little bedroom had been crammed under the eaves and had funny shaped walls, sloping ceilings and iron hooks in the beams to which you could tie things. Most of the year the temperature seemed glacial and when night fell he would go to bed fully-clothed and try to think himself warm. Then he would lie in the darkness listening to the noise of the water tank hidden behind one wall. He knew he wouldn't be able to sleep until he was sure nobody would come, but as long as the room stayed dark he didn't get afraid. The dark felt comforting. Safe. In the dark he became invisible. It was when the light came on he got scared.

Harry peered through the window into the gloom beyond the cracked glass. Nothing to see but black. Clouds hid the moon and stars and there were no streetlights, no cars or other signs of life. Not out here. Harry smiled to himself. He didn't get scared. Not anymore. He turned from the window and gazed across at the girl. She slouched in the chair dressed in the white underwear he had bought for her. She didn't say much, just sat unmoving, eyes wide. Her silence was understandable, after all they had been together for weeks and she didn't have much left to say. Still, he could tell by her demeanour she wasn't comfortable, that something wasn't quite right. Harry tutted to himself and shook his head. This would never do. He went over to the girl and reached out and touched her skin. Cold. Ice cold. Poor girl, no wonder the smile on her face had gone. He bent down and fiddled with the fan heater, turning the knob up a couple of notches. The fan whirred in protest but the air seemed a little warmer. He moved the heater and angled the air flow upwards so the warmth reached the girl's body. There, she looked almost happy.

Almost happy would do for him too, he thought. He didn't think it was much to ask. Years back he'd seen a woman lawyer talking on TV. 'There are human rights', she said. Those rights meant you could get stuff you didn't have. Stuff like happiness. It was the law. Written down. In books. You could go to court to get it. You could sue the council or the government and get damages. But now he knew there were easier ways.

Harry's ways.

He moistened his lips and pushed his tongue into the corner of his cheek and chewed for a moment, letting his eyes wander over the girl's body: pink toenails, delicate feet, shapely calves, not-too-thin thighs, rounded stomach, nice breasts, gorgeous long black hair . . . Nice. Very nice.

Her breasts were the best thing about her. Small and pert, the nipples pushing upwards through the white material of the bra. Towards God. As if thanking her creator for producing such a work of art. Harry considered the girl again. Overall she scored nine out of ten. Maybe nine point five. You would go a long way to find a better likeness.

Harry scratched the stubble on his chin. The nagging thought that had first come to him a few weeks ago returned. Things hadn't worked out as they should have. Not with this one. She was like an apple that was ripe on the outside but

2

rotten within. Full of worms and maggots, or perhaps hiding a wasp. Yes, a wasp. You would get stung if you bit into a piece of fruit with a wasp inside. He needed a girl who was clean and pure. Untouched.

A hint of a smile played on the girl's face for a moment. Was she mocking him or just feeling a little happier now the room had warmed up? Really it didn't matter. He could do whatever he wanted to her and she wouldn't mind because she loved him. He supposed he had made the same mistake when he had been a kid. He had let his parents do as they wished because he loved them, but they hadn't loved him. Ever.

Harry went back to the window and stared into the emptiness again. Nothing. For a minute or two his mood darkened, black, like the night. Thinking about the past did that because he had a whole bunch of memories he didn't want to recall. They still kept coming back to haunt him though, like a bad smell that crept up unnoticed. One moment you got a slight whiff in your nostrils and the next you were gagging on puke.

Harry scolded himself. It was stupid to dwell on the past. Futile. He looked at the girl again. She might not be right but that didn't mean they hadn't had some good times together. He smiled. Rapture would have to wait until the next one. For now he would just have some fun. He licked his lips and began to remove his clothing.

Chapter One

Detective Inspector Charlotte Savage woke with a sense of loss and sadness. Numb. The way she always felt after the dream. The last nightmare had been months ago, but if anything that made the shock more acute. She rolled over to look at the bedside clock, groaned at the time, and then saw the message light on the phone blinking. She sighed as she sat up to swing her legs over the edge of the bed. She would play the message in a moment, but first she wanted to check on the children.

The morning light filtered into the house, the weak light of a stormy autumn day. Savage peered through the landing window into the garden where sheets of rain lashed down and saplings whipped back and forth in the wind. Beyond the garden the ground dropped to the sea where a mist of spray rose and fell with every wave that hit the shore. Farther away, out across Plymouth Sound, a couple of tankers and a navy supply vessel lay anchored behind the shelter of the mile-long breakwater that cut off the roadstead from the open sea. Huge rollers crashed over the breakwater rocks as the storm tried to batter the city into submission.

She climbed the stairs to the suite of rooms where the

kids slept and paused at the door to Clarissa's old room, now used as an office, and the familiar twinge down in the pit of her stomach returned. She closed her eyes for a moment and there, right on the edge of her consciousness, she heard the little *ding-ding* of a bicycle bell. When she opened her eyes she was almost tempted to go to the window and look out, thinking she might see Clarissa riding in circles on the patio. Silly. Life went on, things got easier, but they never got put right. She shook her head and went to check on Samantha and Jamie. Of course they were fine. Samantha beginning to wake, a tangle of red hair painting the pillow, her limbs akimbo and the bedclothes half on the floor. No doubt she would soon be protesting about having to get up and dressed. The scattering of teen mags, the posters on the walls, glitzy clothing and the mess on the floor said the room belonged to a fifteen year old. Savage had to remind herself that Samantha was only thirteen, still her baby girl for a few more years yet.

In the adjoining room the mess belonged to Jamie. He'd come along only six years ago, time that seemed to be measured in a mere blink. Unexpected, unplanned, it had surprised Savage how much she loved him. Not a love she'd had to grow and nurture like she had with Samantha and Clarissa, but an instant, protective love as powerful as it was scary. Savage moved over to the bed where Jamie lay curled in a tight ball, knees pulled up to his face, almost as she had left him the previous night. He reminded Savage of a hedgehog hibernating for the winter, protected from anything outside its own little world.

It was Sunday, so she would let them sleep some more. She would go downstairs and defrost some bagels, make tea, grab some orange juice, jam and butter and carry the whole lot to her bedroom where they could cuddle up and watch

6

the storm develop through the big window that looked out across the sea. When Pete was home they'd do the same, and Savage reckoned it was good to stick to the routine when he was away. Keeping the children sane and secure while he was on patrol was something they had both agreed was important. Groundwork, her own mother had called it. With strong enough roots a tree could stand any gale, she had once said.

Down in the kitchen the base station on the phone blinked. She pressed the button on the unit and the Irish lilt of DC Patrick Enders rang out. His upbeat tone wouldn't have been out of place introducing a programme on a children's television channel, but the grim contents of the message belied his cheerfulness: a woman's body had been discovered over at Wembury beach. As the DC recounted the details, Savage wondered what kind of tragedy this might represent and for whom. Was somebody somewhere waiting for a knock on the door to tell them what had happened to their loved one? Or – more depressingly – was the woman unloved and not missed? Enders didn't elaborate other than to say that a recovery operation was going to take place at the next low tide and Detective Superintendent Hardin had requested Savage attend.

She'd have to phone Stefan and ask if he would come round for a few hours to mind the kids. Sunday was supposed to be his day off, but looking out at the rough water in the Sound Savage didn't think he would be racing.

Finding Stefan had been a godsend for the family. They had discovered him one August morning down at the marina moping about waiting for the Fastnet Race yachts to finish. He was meant to have been crewing on one of the boats but had broken his arm the week before. Chatting to Savage he had revealed he was from Sweden and a primary school teacher by trade. Really though, he lived for sailing. One

7

thing led to another and two weeks later Stefan had been installed in the granny annexe as the family's unofficial au pair. Now, with Pete away commanding his frigate on an Atlantic voyage and Savage working long hours, having him around to help out made all the difference.

Savage deleted the message on the phone and then glanced at the fridge where a printout of the week's tides hung clamped in the jaws of a green and purple magnetic dinosaur. Low tide Devonport was eleven thirty-seven. She smiled to herself; still time enough for those bagels.

Rain continued to drive in from the southwest in bands and the low clouds threatened to roll back the daybreak. The drive from her house to Wembury, a village a few miles to the southeast of Plymouth, had been treacherous. Water lay everywhere and twice Savage had to brake sharply to avoid fallen branches that half-blocked the road. With some relief she pulled into the car park at the beach and stopped the engine. Now the sheer force of the wind became apparent and the car shuddered as a gust spilled up from the shoreline, the rain drumming the windows even harder. She remembered back to a spring day many years before when she and Pete had been to a friend's wedding at the church on the cliffs high above the beach. The view had been spectacular, with the sea looking an impossible holiday-brochure blue, sparkling in the bright, early sun. With the joy and laughter of the occasion the place had seemed like something close to heaven. In late October, with yet another deep Atlantic low moving in, nirvana lay out of reach, redemption impossible. Unless you were already dead, that was.

On the other side of the car park a huddle of uniforms stood next to the shuttered café. They were there to prevent people from going down to the beach or along the coast path. Not that they had anything to do. The blue and white tape they had strung up oscillated in the wind, achieving nothing much other than to catch the attention of the occupants of an arriving car, the kids in the back seats pressing their camera phones to the windows in the hope of capturing a glimpse of something sordid or shocking. An ambulance was parked next to the café too, its light strobing in the gloom, the crew standing at the rear with their fluorescent coats drawn around them.

Savage got out of the car and retrieved her waterproofs from the boot, both jacket and trousers, since the rain was near horizontal. The jacket tried to become a kite before she managed to zip it up and pull up the hood, stuffing wayward strands of red hair in at the sides and pulling the cords tight around her face. She walked across the car park and ducked under the tape held up for her by one of the bobbies.

'Morning, ma'am. You'll find a grim business down there.' The young officer's face appeared pale and drained of colour. Savage wasn't sure if that was because of the weather or what he had seen.

'Thanks. Nice day, huh?' Savage smiled at him. 'Who's attending?'

'DI Davies.' He spat the name as if he had dirt on his tongue. 'TAG are here as well. D section. With their bloody big RIB.'

The Tactical Aid Group provided operational support, with D section responsible for the marine side of things. Inspector Nigel Frey led the team, and as an officer she rated him highly. Like Savage and her husband he was a keen sailor and they'd raced each other many times out on the Sound, the inevitable disagreements that close-quarter yacht racing brought always resolved later over a pint. Pity about Davies though.

Savage nodded and walked down the path leading to the beach. Only it wasn't really a beach, just a strip of wet, grey sand surrounded by jagged rocks and half-covered by seaweed and a few plastic bottles, soggy chip wrappings and other debris. Popular with locals in the summer, and on fine winter days a good spot for walking the dog, today the place was deserted.

She continued across the sand, dodging windblown balls of foam that rolled along like tumbleweed swept down the street in an old Western movie. On the other side of the beach she had to clamber up onto a plateau of rock. The seaweed, slime and the spray in the air made progress across the rock difficult and twice she had to drop to her hands and knees. Eventually she reached a finger of sand threading its way into the plateau from the sea. She jumped down off the rock and approached the four men standing in a group: DI Philip Davies, DC Little John Jackson – one of Davies's cronies, and two white-suited CSI officers. Davies kept his back to her as she neared, a dig suggesting that even though he held the same rank as her he thought he was by far and away the superior detective. His attitude didn't bother Savage. Silly little boys played silly little games.

Davies turned in time so as not to appear too rude. He sneered at her from a rough, pocked face which had a nose that had been broken more than once.

'Charlotte, dunno what you think you are doing here?' He scratched at the two-day stubble on his chin, grey like his hair, and shook his head. 'This is murder. Not a few girls getting their knickers all soiled because they had a bit too much to drink and went home with the wrong guy.'

'Cut the crap, Phil.' Savage pushed past and looked into the sea where a couple of divers bobbed at the outer edge of a huge, rough chunk of concrete wall, a remnant of wartime defences. The waves here were smaller than back at the beach because a lee was formed by the Mewstone, a small island lying half a mile out to sea. At low tide the rocky ledges leading to the shore became exposed, providing some protection from the open ocean, but even so a heavy swell rocked the divers up and down and threatened to pulverise them against the concrete. Twenty metres offshore the dive support RIB manoeuvred back and forth holding station like a concerned mother hen. At the helm Nigel Frey raised one hand to wave at her. She waved back; the howling wind made conversation over that distance impossible.

Some sort of pipe, perhaps a metre in diameter, lay half-sunken in the churning water. It emerged from the concrete and ran out into the sea and the divers concentrated their efforts around its end. The swell covered and uncovered a submerged object trapped in the pipe, an expanse of black plastic and something pale, white and waterlogged.

'Low tide,' Davies explained. 'A fisherman spotted her late last night. What the fuck they were doing fishing out here at that time in this weather I don't know.'

'Her?'

'Can't see now but a few minutes ago you could. Long hair, tits, or what remains of them.'

Jackson tried to emulate Davies's sneer and muttered something that caused them both to laugh. Savage guessed what he had said was offensive, but a gust of wind snatched the words into the air, no doubt hiding a multitude of sins.

'Anyway they say she's a woman,' continued Davies, nodding at the divers. 'And I don't think she came down here for a picnic.'

One of the divers first swam and then walked to the shore where a CSI officer handed him some sort of tool resembling a giant pair of pliers. He waded back in and disappeared

11

beneath the surface, bubbles of air rising round the pipe and the water boiling in response to unseen movement.

'Huh?' Savage turned to the guy who had produced the tool.

'Bolt croppers,' the man said. 'She was wrapped in bin liners, bound with tape and then chained to the grating.'

'Grating?'

'There's a metal grille back in the pipe. About a metre in. The body is well jammed in the pipe now the tide has turned.'

The diver surfaced and flung the tool back to the beach and he and his partner began to wrestle the body from the pipe entrance and towards the shore. Using each wave for assistance they half-swam and then half-waded, dragging the inert mass behind them.

'Shit.' Jackson swallowed hard and turned away for a moment. Davies just smirked.

Between the strips of black plastic and silver tape the body appeared to be in a considerable state of decay. Crabs or friction had torn away vast swathes of skin and only puffy and bloated patches remained. Where the skin should have been pieces of stringy flesh and muscle had gone white in the water the way a boil-in-the-bag fish changes colour when you cook it. Shrimps and lice crawled across limbs, and the rotten lips parted to reveal a manic smile.

The divers had the body in the shallows now and it lay face up, the belly swollen with gas making it look like a stranded whale. As each wave came in to the beach it moved in the water, the arms and legs rising and falling like a floundering swimmer captured in slow motion. Now Savage could tell the corpse belonged to a woman but it was difficult to know much else since the water-wrinkled skin gave no clue as to her age.

With some difficulty, the divers, along with the CSI

officers, began to move the body out of the water and onto a waiting body bag. Savage stepped forward to make a closer inspection.

'Jesus, look at the hole in her head!' Jackson had moved closer too and Savage understood why he was regretting it. A lot of the hair on the scalp had gone and white bone was showing through. Just above the right temple was a neat, round hole about the size of a penny.

Savage noticed a flash of metal around the neck. A little cross on a silver chain. Blind faith had never appeared so pathetic, she thought.

'Could you?' she asked one of the white-suited CSIs, pointing at the cross.

He bent over and held the cross in his gloved hand, turning it over to reveal an inscription.

'RSO,' the CSI said.

'Rosina Salgado Olivárez,' Savage said. 'Our missing student.'

'Bugger. Hardin will be livid,' Davies grunted. He said nothing else. Just pulled his jacket collar up against the driving rain and stomped away, Jackson scampering after him like a terrier after its lowlife master.

Chapter Two

Love. Harry didn't understand why but he hadn't ever got much of it. Not from his parents anyway. The pet cat had been shown more affection. He remembered his mother cooing and feeding the kitten titbits from the dinner table. It always got a stroke, even when naughty. Harry just got beaten. He loved the little tabby, but he felt angry when it competed with him for attention. So he strangled it. He buried the corpse in the garden, marking the grave with a brick. Many months later, lonely and needing a cuddle, he lifted the brick and started to dig. He was surprised to find only the white bones of the skeleton remained. The cat's flesh had decomposed, the animal's soul seeping into the ether, forever beyond his reach. The discovery made Harry wonder how you preserved things, how you stopped the flesh you loved from rotting away. There didn't seem to be anything in his life other than decay.

Me, Harry. Me.

Trinny.

Her voice snapped him out of his half-slumber and he sat bolt upright, confused for a moment. He rubbed his eyes and shook his head, grasping at consciousness, trying to pull the tangled threads into some sort of order. A wan light slipped past the curtains and painted the room with the awful chill of reality.

Naughty Harry.

Yes, but there was no going back, not after what he had done to Trinny.

I didn't mind, Harry. I love you, just like all those years ago.

All those years ago back when he was a kid. There had always been a girl in the house to help out, a nanny or an au pair employed to do the chores his mother and father couldn't be bothered with. Those girls had been the only ones who loved him. He was sure they guessed about his parents too. In the dead quiet of the night they must have heard the screams and wondered what was going on. And even though they never said anything, in the mornings they saw the bruises as they held him and rocked him and dried his tears. In some small way that helped. Believing somebody cared made him feel he was worth something after all.

I still care, Harry. I really do.

Maybe they did care all those years ago, but they never stayed long. A few months at most and his father and his wandering hands became too much for them.

He was disgusting, Harry. Dirty!

So they left. Went. Decayed.

I left, Harry. Yes. But decayed? No. Never. You never forgot me and I never forgot you. I'm still here, am I not?

Yes, Trinny was still here. Part of his collection. His growing collection.

Harry? I'm the one. You want me, not the others.

True. He did want her. And he'd had her too. Many times. Not good. Not right. Shameful.

Shameful? Harry, you are wrong. Sex is beautiful. I mean the stuff you did to me last night . . . I loved everything. Every minute. Every inch!

Trinny's words ended with a dirty cackle. This was bad. She had become too much of a handful, not like he expected

15

her to be. He needed to deal with her once and for all. Trinny seemed to read his mind because her voice became serious with a scolding tone that sliced into his heart.

Harry, do you still love me? I mean like before, like back then?

He didn't know. He clenched his teeth and tried to hold back the saliva building in his mouth. But he should know, shouldn't he? It was his business to know. If he didn't know something he got a little edgy, panic set in and he began to breathe too fast and he didn't like that. He really didn't like that.

Harry?

He swallowed the spit and mucus and sucked in air. In, out, in, out, in, out. Last night he shut Trinny away. Downstairs. So he didn't understand why she was still pestering him. She wasn't the girl he was looking for because she was too dirty. She knew. He'd told her.

You did tell me. You called me a slut. And after you called me a slut you screwed me. How does that work?

He couldn't explain. It was too complicated.

Complicated?

Yes. Complicated. Trinny wouldn't be able to understand. Nobody understood. Nobody knew about being mad but him.

Yes Harry, you are mad. Not to mention bad and sad. You can't go around—

Harry couldn't stand the wittering any longer so he reached out and pressed the button on the clock radio next to his bed and Trinny's voice vanished beneath the local station's jingle. Top of the hour and the news. The usual regional mediocrity had been abandoned and the headline spewed out a tale of rape, violence and murder. The police had found a body of a woman down on Wembury beach.

He turned off the radio. Fast. Not good. Not good at all.

Carmel, Harry! Carmel is back! Yuk! I bet she doesn't look so pretty now.

Trinny sounded excited. Hysterical. But could it really be Carmel? Nausea began to rise within him like dirty water overflowing from a blocked toilet. He fought back the urge to vomit.

Carmel. You didn't get her, did you? She is lost forever now. Decayed.

He ignored Trinny and wondered if the story signified something. Carmel back from the dead. Telling him he was on the right track, but also reminding him that Trinny didn't compare to her. Couldn't be the one.

Harry, what do you mean?

He'd kept her because he hoped she would change. She had been fun at first. Cute, lovely, bubbly. But now she went on yapping and nagging. And she was dirty. Very dirty. He had slapped her a couple of times, but it hadn't made any difference. The simplest thing would be a clean break. Splitting up would be for the best. For both of them.

Harry! You bastard! I am your girl. Me. Not Carmel. She is dead. Rotting. Mitchell killed her. Remember?

Mitchell.

Harry didn't like to hear that name. Not after what Mitchell had done to Carmel.

Mitchell was your friend!

Mitchell had once been his friend, true, although Harry didn't really know what a friend was supposed to be like and he didn't want to ask Mitchell straight out in case he had got it all wrong. Still, Mitchell had been good to him. Kind. He had told him to stop taking the pills.

Bad idea, Harry. Those pills kept you normal, didn't they? Stopped you from seeing things?

Trinny's tone of voice was mocking, but she was right. The pills kept him cocooned in his own little world. Snug. The pills stopped the voices too. Like the doctor said they would. But the clever doctor smiled with too many teeth and had an arrogant manner along with a flash car and a pretty secretary who wore a skirt just short enough so when she bent over you could see the tops of her stockings. Harry liked the skirt even as he despised the man.

Who is the dirty one now, Harry?

It was always the same way with women. When they dressed like dolls with flesh poking out his eyes went wandering. Still, no harm done, he only took a little peek, a brief gaze at something forbidden.

There are things beyond looking, Harry. That is the problem.

Yes. A problem. One he blamed Mitchell for. Mitchell was out of control. Saturday nights. Drunk girls getting into trouble. Party time. Harry was disgusted with himself for playing Mitchell's games, but then disgust was becoming a habit now.

No, Harry? Why is that?

Mitchell let him touch the girls. Harry didn't want to at first. Later on he couldn't stop.

And then?

And then Mitchell went and killed Carmel which meant Harry didn't have any friends anymore.

Harry thought about Carmel. He hadn't liked her dying, hadn't liked it at all. Seeing the blood spoiling the girl's pretty hair made him angry. Pretty things should not be spoilt. They should be kept. Forever.

Like me!

No. Not like Trinny at all. He wouldn't keep Trinny forever. He needed to get shot of her and soon. Maybe even tonight. They would drive somewhere together and on the way he would tell her in the nicest possible manner. If he let her down gently perhaps she would forgive him. You had to be cruel to be kind, didn't you? A sad way to end their time together, but Trinny wasn't right. And anyway only yesterday he noticed she was no longer beautiful. Some of her skin had gone a bit saggy. That happened when you got older, but even so Harry didn't think he could make allowances. Not now. Not when there were others waiting their turn.

Chapter Three

Crownhill Police Station, Plymouth. Monday 25th October. 8.30 am

Davies had been right about Hardin's reaction, and the shit hit the fan first thing Monday morning. Savage had just grabbed a cup of coffee and taken it to the Major Crimes suite when it all kicked off.

The double doors crashed open and Detective Superintendent Conrad Hardin entered the room as if leading a drugs raid. Although unarmed and lacking a battering ram, his entrance could not have been more dramatic. With the muscles and build of a heavyweight street-fighter he had the language and temper to match. His face burned bright red and he looked as if he would explode as he barrelled onwards, pushing past anybody foolish enough not to move out of his way.

'Rosina Salgado Olivárez,' his voice boomed out, the delivery of the words sounding official, like a vicar performing a wedding ceremony or a judge addressing a guilty prisoner. The noise level in the room dropped to zero and Hardin marched forward holding a large sheet of paper in his hands. Savage hoped he would save his anger for the briefing of senior officers, scheduled to take place later that morning. Her hope was misplaced.

'What sort of fucking piss-taking amateur outfit are we running here?' Hardin sneered and slammed the piece of paper against one of the whiteboards, holding it up for everyone to see.

'A source emailed me the afternoon special the *Herald* are printing. An eight-page pull-out with the headline "Sex Crime City: Now It's Murder".'

Hardin looked around the room, his eyes picking out each individual, one by one. Savage drew breath, bracing herself for the next onslaught.

'This morning I've had the ACC on to me. He in turn has had the mayor, both city MPs, the university Vice Chancellor, some worm from the Foreign Office and, of course, the Chief Constable on the phone. To say he's not happy would be the bloody understatement of the year. Neither, you will not be surprised to learn, am I. Nor are the poor parents of Ms Olivárez or any of the other girls. We have a duty of care to the people who live in and visit this city, and in this case we have discharged that abysmally. How many of you have daughters at home?' Hardin stared at Savage again. 'Ask yourselves if you would be satisfied with our work. Go on askyourbloodyselves!'

Hardin turned and stomped out of the room.

'Phew!' Someone whistled. 'Wouldn't like to be here when he got out of bed on the *wrong* side.'

Savage didn't spot who made the comment, but it brought smiles to a few people's faces and a couple of the usual suspects began trading wisecracks. Savage could only think of her impending meeting, in her mind comparing it to a trip to a headmaster's office to receive a beating. Still, Hardin had every right to be angry because operation *Leash* had become a joke, and with one of the victims dead, farce now slipped into tragedy.

21

Earlier Savage had pondered the latest development on her drive to the station. Thirty minutes of typical Monday morning traffic had given her plenty of time to think. A drain had blocked on the eastern side of the Laira Bridge and the dual carriageway was reduced to one lane, vehicles crawling along and surging through the almost knee-high water. People sat in their cars looking miserable, and with the Olivárez girl dead Savage couldn't help feeling down too.

Twelve months ago operation *Leash* had been created after the police had linked a series of rapes together. Since then the rapes had continued, the victims always sharing the same characteristics of being under twenty-five and students, often foreign, picked up from clubs and bars in the heart of the city. A car ride took them from the centre to a large house where two or more men gang raped them. After being assaulted for several hours the women would be dumped somewhere in the suburbs and told if they kept quiet no further harm would come to them. The parting threat from the attackers made the *Leash* team suspect a number of victims remained too scared to report the crime. The girls were duped into leaving the safety of the clubs because their drinks had been spiked with gamma-hydroxybutyrate, otherwise known as GHB. The drug had a plethora of street names including the incident room's current favourite, Easy Lay. Savage considered the tag politically incorrect, but apt. In a last ditch attempt to reduce the number of attacks uniformed patrols had taken to giving out free drug detection kits and assault alarms. With thousands of students in the city the task was hopeless. The rapists seemed to be able to carry out their plans with a boldness and impunity that was becoming a personal insult to all concerned.

The inquiry occupied a huge proportion of Major Crimes's time, more time than desirable or necessary, as

Hardin had pointed out to the team last week. His latest brainwave was an undercover operation with as many bodies as could be mustered. They would sprinkle the clubs with officers posing as students, not as honey traps, but as discreet observers who might spot something as it happened. The Big Night Out, a name coined by some of the younger officers, was planned for Saturday and already the talk at the station was of what everyone would be wearing. Savage thought it was a waste of time: anyone over their mid-twenties would stick out and the chances of seeing anything in a crowded, noisy club were minuscule. Still, as Hardin had said, they were down to clutching at straws now. And if the Big Night Out did not produce a result then the next Monday morning he would be in a worse mood than ever and looking for a scalp or two to serve up to the ACC. Savage didn't think she would blame him for wanting to do that either.

With Hardin gone the noise in the room rose to full volume again with phones ringing, keyboards clattering and people bustling this way and that. At one of the whiteboards DC Enders scribbled some notes next to a new picture taped slap bang in the centre. Pride of place now rather than just one of the other nine victims. He looked up as Savage approached, his young face beaming out from beneath a dishevelled mop of brown hair. Enders always appeared to Savage more like a member of a boy band than a hard-working detective, but she couldn't fault his passion and enthusiasm for the job.

'Remind me of the unlucky girl's details again, Patrick,' Savage said.

'Rosina Salgado Olivárez, twenty-one, Spanish national, student, lived in a shared flat in Mutley. Raped eight months ago on fifteenth February, a Saturday night. Someone dropped her outside the entrance to Saltram Park first light Sunday morning. Unbelievably, considering the state she was in, she managed to walk all the way from there back to her flat. When she got in she collapsed and slept for the whole day. Told her housemate about the assault in the evening and the flatmate phoned it in.'

'What about the MO?'

'Matches the others. Complained of dizziness after a couple of drinks so she informed her friends she was going home early. In a bit of a muddle she goes outside and someone offers her a lift. She gets in the car and collapses unconscious. Next thing she knows she's tied to a bed and two men are raping her. After a few hours of hell she is untied, forced to take a shower and then she's dumped. That and the fact that the men used condoms meant no DNA. Just like all the others.'

Savage shook her head and sighed. Enders continued.

'Understandably, after we had interviewed her, she makes plans to return home to Spain. We accompanied her to the Santander ferry on the twenty-first February, she went through passport control and we heard nothing more until we were contacted by the Guardia Civil. It appeared as if she never returned to her home town of Zaragoza. Now we know why.'

'So the first question is why was she killed?'

'And the second is how on earth did she get back to Plymouth?' Enders asked.

'Exactly.'

Savage dragged herself up to Hardin's office and found DCI Mike Garrett and DI Davies waiting. As a Superintendent Hardin had the luxury of his own space even if he hadn't made much effort to personalise it. The obligatory picture of him in uniform at some event with his wife standing dutifully at his side sat on one side of a tidy desk. There was also a calendar of Greek islands on the wall – a year out of date – and a couple of P.D. James novels stuck in the bookcase alongside the law books and policing manuals. Hardly a home from home.

Savage took the seat next to Davies. He had managed a shave, but still looked rough. Garrett was as smartly turned out as ever, but the older detective wore a subdued expression, fresh lines of worry on his face. As the Senior Investigating Officer on operation *Leash* he would have received the sharp end of Hardin's tongue, Savage suspected. However, rant finished, the DSup had now come over all conciliatory. He even muttered some apology to Savage about his earlier behaviour.

'This bloody diet plays havoc with my mood. Have you ever tried chewing a stick instead of having a doughnut with your morning coffee?'

He held up a jar of real liquorice and offered it around. All present politely declined.

'According to my doctor the coffee must be decaf, lunch is to be salad, dinner is wholemeal bread and a light soup and if the wife offers kinky sex I am to refuse.'

Hardin had suffered a mild heart attack around six months before. Enders said it couldn't have happened to a nicer bloke. The quip got a big laugh, but made Savage think of her next medical and wonder what the doctor would say to her when he checked her blood pressure readings. Especially the way operation *Leash* was going.

'Right,' Hardin rubbed his hands together. 'I'm taking direct control of this operation, in effect assuming Mike's position as SIO in all but name. I know you have worked your butts off, but the results are disappointing to say the least.'

Too true, Savage thought, meeting Garrett's eyes and detecting discomfort behind his frown. With Hardin as SIO in all but name Garrett was stuffed. If the investigation went further downhill he would carry the can, if they got a result Hardin would take the credit. Win-win Hardin. Relegation Garrett.

Hardin started to elaborate on the different approach the team would be taking now he had taken charge.

'I just had a call from the officers attending the post-mortem. This is definitely a murder inquiry, and not a nice one.'

'Is there ever a nice one?' Garrett said.

'No, but this is brutal and nasty. The pathologist believes the girl may have been killed with a, let me see . . .' Hardin peered down at some notes. 'Ah yes, a captive bolt stunner. Otherwise known as a humane killer, although I think we can agree that Olivárez's death does not fall into a category one would call humane.'

'A cow killer?' Savage said.

'Yes. Whether that is useful information or not remains to be seen. All depends on who might have access to one.'

'A farmer or a vet?' Davies said. 'Seems the obvious line of enquiry.'

'Or an antique dealer,' Savage said. The others looked at her. 'I came across an old one in a shop once. People collect this sort of stuff and I don't think they require a firearms licence.'

'OK, so the weapon may have come from anywhere,' Hardin said. 'Let's get to the subject of catching these people. As you are all aware Big Night Out will be taking place on Saturday nights for the next four weeks. This will push us for bodies on other stuff, but until this is solved follow ups on some minor crimes are on standby. The overtime budget is going to go through the roof and there are going to be complaints, but I tell you something: if we don't catch these brutes by Christmas then it's not going to be a happy one. For any of us.'

Hardin ran through his ideas for the Big Night Out and the others chipped in with a few suggestions. Garrett thought they should include Friday nights as well since two of the girls had been picked up then. Hardin disagreed.

'The problem is manpower. Not enough to go round, I'm afraid. Right bloody fools we'd appear when an attack happens at a club we weren't covering because we were spread too thin. I can visualise the headlines on the Monday morning and my bollocks nailed to the ACC's desk by the afternoon.'

Garrett also wanted to step up uniformed patrols, but again Hardin disagreed.

'They'll only end up going somewhere else where there are no patrols and we will miss them completely.'

In the end they compromised on some increased presence in the city centre around a couple of clubs. That would be good publicity and provide some pictures for the papers and mean the operation could take a risk in not putting officers into those particular venues, leaving more free for the others.

The meeting concluded and Savage and Davies left, leaving Garrett with Hardin.

'Poor old fucker,' Davies said, shaking his head. 'Mike had high hopes of promotion next year. Been DCI for as long as I can remember.'

'Hardin's a wily devil,' Savage said. 'Because he's built like the proverbial brick outhouse people assume there is nothing up top, but you don't dare underestimate his cunning.'

Savage grabbed another cup of something resembling coffee from the canteen and went back to the Major Crimes suite where the talk had once again degenerated into who would be wearing what come Saturday night. Not much else was happening or was likely to, Savage thought. They would be very lucky if the body on the beach yielded any forensic evidence. The corpse had been lying in the water so long anything present would have degraded to beyond the point of being useful. What they needed was something distinctive about the girl's life that separated her from the other victims. Something to indicate why she was tracked down and killed when the other girls had been let go.

Savage went over to where DC Jane Calter sat at a desk trying to piece together some intel on the girl's movements in the days following the assault. Calter was young, mid-twenties, and like Enders her appearance didn't shout 'detective'. She wore her hair in a shoulder-length blonde bob and dressed right on the 'casual' limit of the recommended dress code. Today that was a black denim skirt and jacket and shiny black boots. With Calter though appearances were deceptive: she was hard as nails, ran marathons and some years back had won a national junior title at Taekwondo.

Calter looked up at Savage and started to explain that her task was a waste of time: the girl had no contact with anyone but her flatmate and police officers before she left for Spain.

'She spent some time at the Sexual Abuse Referral Centre, ma'am,' Calter said. 'The doctor examined her and a sexual offence liaison officer did her bit too. Then she went back to her flat and the SOLO stayed with her until she departed. I interviewed her several times over the next few days as we tried to make sense of what had happened and get a coherent statement. She was never alone.'

'And you accompanied her to the boat?'

'I did, ma'am. With DC Enders. At least we took her through check-in and passport control. She had a single

28

room on the boat and we know it was used. Her father is disabled and requires constant care so there was nobody to meet her at Santander and she was going to make her own way home to Zaragoza, but she seemed quite happy about that.' Calter paused for a moment before continuing, a noticeable trace of emotion in her voice. 'You know, I liked her. She was a strong girl, confident. The assault affected her badly but I sensed she would get over it. That she wouldn't let what happened go on to destroy the rest of her life.'

Calter didn't say anything more. She didn't need to, the inference was obvious: somebody else had destroyed Rosina Olivárez's life.

Chapter Four

Malstead Down, nr Buckfastleigh. Monday 25th October.
4.41 pm

Gordon Isaacs was fed up with people telling him he was lucky to be a farmer. Everyone said it must be great to have such a varied existence with all the changing seasons and different challenges. In reality, one day was very much like the next and in Isaacs's mind that meant today had been bloody awful. People didn't realise it was a hard life. Bloody hard work and no days off and no knocking off at five thirty and having a drink with some cute blonde in a posh wine bar.

It just wasn't fair.

Isaacs whacked the starter motor with the hammer once more, squirted a burst of EasyStart into the air intake and used his screwdriver to bypass the ignition. The Landrover spluttered a couple of times, backfired, and then burst into life, coughing a plume of black smoke from the exhaust in the process.

'About bloody time you useless heap of shit,' he said, slamming the bonnet down and lumbering round to the door. He swung a leg to try to kick his collie as it went to grab the hammer. The dog jumped out of the way and leapt up through the driver's door and across to the passenger seat.

'Look what you bloody done now!' Isaacs eyed the muddy prints all over the seats. He got in anyway and rammed the gearstick forward, flooring the accelerator. The Landrover slewed round in the mud and he pointed it out of the farmyard and down the rutted lane.

'Lil' acre, Fly. That's where we're off to.'

The dog yapped and panted. Now they were moving Isaacs didn't feel too bad either. He hated having to fix things because there were always two constants in any job he had to do: never enough time and never enough money. Earlier in the day the big Ford had got a puncture because the previous repair had been a bodge job rather than a new tyre. And now his neighbour, Peter Wright, had been on the phone to tell him he'd seen a couple of Isaacs's heifers pushing their way through the fence at the bottom of Little Acre. Isaacs had spent a frustrating fifteen minutes trying to start the Landrover which meant that the heifers had plenty of time to frolic in the winter wheat, ruining the freshly sown crop and trampling pounds off his bottom line. Which in the grand circle of life meant the next puncture repair would be yet another bodge and he'd never be able to afford a new Landrover.

His ongoing problems reminded him of an old song, 'There's a Hole in My Bucket', and he began to hum the tune to himself as his Landrover bounced along the lane down towards Little Acre.

'—dear Liza, dear Liza.' Liza in his case was Sandra and she was always nagging at him to sell up and get out. They weren't getting any younger were they, so what was the reason for carrying on? Since the house, barns and land must be worth well over a million there wasn't a good one. If they sold up they could buy a little place somewhere and stick the majority of the money in the bank. They would be able to take holidays in the sun, treat their grandchildren with more than just love and reward themselves for years of hard work. They'd never have to worry again.

'Bugger that, eh?' Isaacs said to the dog.

Stubbornness was one trait all farmers shared and Isaacs wasn't going to give up just yet. His mum and dad had both worked the land until it had them beat. Now Mum tottered around some nursing home with only dribble and memories for company, and Dad lay six foot under in the local church-yard. He owed it to his parents to carry on while he could. If one of his sons had been interested things might have been different, but no, they were too clever for that. Off to university and no stopping them either. Still, they couldn't be blamed. Who in their right minds would put up with what he had to endure?

He stopped the Landrover at the gate to Little Acre and got out. Down past the water trough several of the heifers were pushing against the fence. A whole section had given up the ghost and left a bloody big hole. The buggers were walking back and forth between Little Acre and the wheat without a by-your-leave or a 'Thank you Mr Isaacs for feeding us.'

Isaacs undid the gate, swung it open, got back in and ripped into the field. Brakes, out, close gate, in, foot to floor, the vehicle skidding sideways for a moment before the chunky tyres got a grip and the Landrover shot across the grass. Several of the heifers had seen him coming and, thinking they were in for some extra feed, they began to trot towards him. He whacked on the anchors a few yards from them and the vehicle slid to a halt. Then he jumped out, grabbed a piece of black plastic pipe from behind the seat and rushed at the bemused animals.

'Get the hell out of there!' He thwacked the pipe against his wellies and it made a satisfying sound and the rest of the herd moved away from the gap. Isaacs could now see that a ten-yard section of the fence had been flattened. Three stakes had been knocked over and the netting and barbed wire had been pulled down too. The mess was a morning's work to fix.

He sighed and walked through the gap into the corn field to round up any of the heifers still in there. Then he spotted the tracks.

Some bastard had driven into the field, the tyres crushing the green shoots and compacting the seedbed. Hang on. Some bastard had driven *through the fence* into the field. Then something about the gate to the lane struck him. The chain and padlock hadn't been there. In his rush to get into the field he'd failed to spot they were missing. A few months ago he had taken the precaution of securing all the gates to his land after a spate of rustling saw a couple of neighbours losing some stock. Fat lot of good it had done by the looks of things.

Two sets of tracks led into the field, curved to the left and ran down the edge. From the way the new green shoots were bent over it was obvious that one set marked the outward journey and one the same vehicle returning. Isaacs swore extreme vengeance on the perpetrators and stumbled into the field to look down the tramlines the tracks had made.

Thwack.

The pipe thudded into his welly again. A lone heifer who decided to see if Isaacs needed any help had second thoughts and skipped back into Little Acre. Isaacs stared at her for a moment to make sure she had got the message that he wasn't standing for any trouble today and then plodded off along the boundary of the corn field to see where the tracks led.

They went down the field's gentle slope towards the copse at the bottom, always keeping close to the edge and making light work of the heavy soil. Isaacs reckoned that this and the tyre size made it probable it was a 4x4 some kids had nicked from a rich townie. Maybe there was a sort of perverse justice in the world after all. The tracks stopped at the bottom of the field next to the copse and Isaacs saw the vehicle had turned round by reversing into a patch of scrub in the corner and had then gone back the way it had come. Strange. It didn't seem like the driving style of some drugged-up hooligans from a sink estate. On the other hand maybe they were so tanked up with cheap cider that they couldn't drive fast.

He peered into the woodland where the last of the day's light dappled patches of soft, green grass. A couple of years ago he had some pheasants in there. Was it possible someone had hoped to get a few birds? They were pretty ill-informed if that was the case. Still, it might be worth taking a look to make sure of things.

The rickety stile creaked as he climbed over it and Isaacs followed the narrow path that wound into the shadows. For a moment he felt uneasy. He wasn't sure why and he tried to put the feeling from his mind; it was stupid, he'd been down this way hundreds of times. As a kid he'd played here, built dens and won fantastic battles against the Germans or the Indians. Later on as a young man, he'd taken a neighbour's daughter here and they had got sweet on an old blanket. He was already engaged to Sandra then. And it had happened again, with others, after they were married too. In more recent years he'd raised pheasants down here, stalked foxes, thinned out some trees. So it *was* stupid. There was nothing here to be scared of. Despite that he wished he had his gun with him, but it was locked away in a cabinet back at the farmhouse. Once he had always kept it in the Landrover, ready to take care of a stray dog or to bag a rabbit for the pot. Bloody bureaucrats and their rules, they simply couldn't stop meddling.

He shook his head to clear the ridiculous thoughts from his mind and followed the path for thirty yards or so to where it led into a glade at the centre of which some lilies were trying hard to cling to their beauty. Isaacs stopped and breathed in the air. Closed his eyes and breathed again. Sweet smells, earthy smells, and then he remembered the neighbour's daughter on the blanket, her mild protestations, her 'no' which meant 'yes'. It was all so long ago now, yet the memory was still clear. And he realised why. There weren't many memories worth recalling anymore.

He opened his eyes and sighed. As he turned to go something caught his eye. Something in the long grass on the far side of the clearing. He stopped and stared and couldn't believe what he was seeing. Lying in the grass in among the dying nettles and brambles was a young girl. A shaft of light shimmered down through the misty air and illuminated her. Brown hair, angel face, a white cotton sheet covering her body. Isaacs gasped in a lungful of air and then put his hand to his mouth and let the air escape. He moved one step forward. A twig cracked under his right foot. The girl didn't move. He edged closer across the mossy glade and now he noticed her eyes were shut. Closer still and he could see her full lips parted in a half-smile that made his insides go all light and tingly. She was beautiful, so very, very, beautiful.

He stood over her now and still she didn't wake. He realised he was still holding the plastic pipe and now he used it to probe the white sheet.

'Excuse me, er, miss?' he said, but got no response. He hooked the edge of the sheet with the pipe and pulled it down, sweeping the covering from her body. Golden skin, white bra and panties, nothing else. Legs long and not too thin, round hips, curvy waist, pert breasts. In his younger days Isaacs and his mates had a word for girls like this. The word was ripe.

There was still no reaction from the girl and she lay still, an object of perfection frozen in time. He poked her again. Nothing. A slow chill began to creep across his shoulders and down through his chest. He stuck out his foot and pushed it against the girl's arm. It moved in response and fell back.

Isaacs chucked the pipe away into the bushes and knelt beside the girl. He put the back of his hand over the girl's face. No breath. He looked down at her chest. No rise and fall. He moved his hand down there and placed it over her left breast. No heartbeat. He slipped it inside her bra, cupping the breast in his hand. Still nothing.

The breast was cold, but the round fullness hit him like a sudden white heat. He pulled his hand back. The sensation shocked him, set off a troubled train of thought in his head, the pleasing beginnings of an erection in his trousers. He glanced around the clearing, and beyond into the depths of the copse. There was nobody. Nobody to tell. He reached out and touched the girl again. She was like ice. Cold, but pure. Then, without knowing quite why, Isaacs bent over and kissed the girl on the lips.

Chapter Five

Barbican Leisure Park, Plymouth. Tuesday 26th October.
10.47 am

The glitter balls sent light spinning round the room, the patterns morphing as they swept over the floor and walls. Calter and Enders bopped in the centre of the empty dance floor to an old Police number, the club manager's idea of a joke, while Savage skirted the edge making notes.

It was Tuesday morning and the three of them were checking out clubs in preparation for Hardin's Big Night Out operation and so far they'd done the White Rabbit on Breton Side and Annabel's next to the marina. Now their focus had turned to Oceana, a huge club situated on the Barbican Leisure Complex along with a multiplex and a Pizza Hut. The club had several different themed rooms and right now they were in an area that mimicked a seventies New York disco, complete with flashing multi-coloured floor panels and a mirrored ceiling. Savage had pages of notes covering exits, vantage points, possible numbers of clubbers and anything else she thought might be of use for the undercover officers who would be on the ground come Saturday night. Even so the venue would be a nightmare to cover, what with the separate dance floors, booths and private rooms.

At this time of the morning with the venues empty, they all had the same sterile atmosphere. Savage had to remind herself it was the clubbers who made a venue, the 'in crowd' who gave a place its unique vibe. She thought, rather wistfully, that she hadn't been part of any sort of vibe for a good number of years. With that in mind she beckoned Calter over.

'What sort of people come here then?' she asked.

'Kids, ma'am. Fifteen-year-old girls trying to pass for eighteen. Eighteen-year-old boys trying to look older than their mates so they can snare one of those girls. A few older guys ogling the goods. It's that sort of place.'

'You've been here?'

'Once or twice when everywhere else has been full or when I have been too drunk to be sensible.'

'Well, snared is a good word, Jane. Both Sally Becker and Tayla Patterson were enticed from this club. Looking around though I'm wondering how.'

'It's like the other venues, ma'am. You wouldn't believe the place when full. The club is heaving. Anything could happen.'

'Yes, but someone couldn't be *dragged* out could they? The door staff would notice at least.'

'They are more concerned with stopping people coming in than worrying about who is leaving, and if someone looks drunk or ill and about to throw up then I would imagine they would be only too pleased to see them go.'

The CCTV from the camera at the entrance had shown Sally Becker looking ill. She had left alone, staggering down the pavement, pissed out of her brain, whereas Tayla Patterson had been with a man wearing a hoodie who had almost had to carry her away. The bouncers hadn't remembered the couple, but then why should they? They would shepherd a thousand drunken people in and out of the club every weekend. A half-comatose girl being helped, or even coaxed, to the exit by a guy was nothing out of the ordinary. It went with the territory. Most of the girls would wake up the next morning with a bad head and some would have regrets, maybe even require a visit to the doctor for a pill. The victims in operation *Leash* came home with rope burns on their wrists and the rest of their lives to try to work out 'why me?'

'Ma'am?' Enders. He had glided over the dance floor to Savage and Calter in a pale imitation of John Travolta. 'You coming out clubbing with us Saturday?'

'Don't be daft. Those days are over. At least in this sort of place. I'll be attending tea dances before too long. Us oldies, and by that I mean anyone over thirty, will be walking the streets while you're busy enjoying yourselves.'

'Well, what about a quick one now, right here, you and me?'

'Message in a Bottle', the Police number, had ended and 'I Shot the Sheriff' echoed from the speakers. Savage smiled, another joke from the manager.

'A quick what, Constable?'

Savage never got an answer because her mobile rang. Hardin. He wanted her to return to the station. No explanation. Just get back. Fast.

Savage left Calter and Enders to scout the rest of the clubs on their list and returned to Crownhill. Hardin was waiting in his office, impatient but wearing a mood of quiet seriousness instead of anger. The frown creasing his forehead and narrowing his eyes made her suspect the worst and she was right.

The body of another girl had been found at Malstead Down, a village on the edge of Dartmoor, some twenty-five miles east of Plymouth. She was naked and had been left in a small wood and the corpse showed signs of sexual inter-ference. Hardin had recounted the facts as if he was telling her about a stolen vehicle.

'Malstead Down. Not right in the village, but nearby. Close enough to make me worried.'

'Worried?'

'The Chief Constable's mother-in-law lives in the area.'

'Not Jean Sotherwell, the dog mess woman?'

'Yes.'

Hardin's mouth drooped, but Savage couldn't stifle a half-smile. The Dog Shit Bitch, as she had become known, had provided the lower ranks with much amusement a couple of years ago. She had managed to manipulate the local papers and TV stations and mobilise what, at times, seemed like half the force on a crackdown on dog fouling in Devon beauty spots. Simon Fox – the CC – and his immediate subordinates had jumped on command. It had been quite a sight. This was altogether more serious, but Hardin was taking no chances.

'I don't want the media stirred up on this one if it turns out to be a murder. Lord knows where it may lead. They are going to link the killing with the Plymouth rapes and that will cause us all sorts of problems.' Hardin gnawed on his liquorice stick. 'I want you out at the scene pronto. My eyes and ears. You've got sensitivity. Some of the others think the word means a type of high-grade cannabis.'

Savage didn't know whether to be offended or pleased.

'What about *Leash*?' Savage asked. 'With the Olivárez body turning up I feel we are getting somewhere.'

Hardin shook his head. *Leash* would continue, of course,

40

and he would need everybody come Saturday night, but a third of the team were going to be seconded to the new inquiry.

'*Zebo* is the name. I will be pressing to get this ramped up, especially if it does turn out it is a sexual crime. We will be drafting in some of the local boys who have a better knowledge of the area, but the inquiry is to be based here at Major Crimes.'

Savage nodded. Hardin was under a lot of pressure, and if the Malstead body proved to be yet another sex crime he was right, the media would have a field day.

The morning had started out fine, but the rain soon pushed in from the west and by the time Savage set off for Malstead it was torrential. The journey took her to the east, first crossing the Plym where the estuary sliced through acres of mud, a few lonely bait diggers braving the elements in search of lug. Then up onto the A38 where the spray from the heavy lorries made the weather seem all the worse. As she headed along the dual carriageway, Dartmoor rose to her left, a foreboding presence at the best of times. Now, with low cloud scudding over the tors and shadows coalescing in the valleys, the moor appeared as dank and dismal as ever. Savage had history with the place and the two of them had never made up. Never would either.

The little village lay up in the hills not far from Widecombe in the Moor. At Buckfastleigh Savage turned off the A38 and negotiated a maze of lanes that became smaller and more winding as she climbed onto the edge of the moor. Only a few patches of the purple heather bloom remained and the procession of cars, to be found clogging roads all over Devon during the tourist season, was absent. For that reason Savage was driving a little too fast, a fact she had cause to regret when at one T-junction she turned left and had to drive into the hedge as a tractor bounced past, its driver laughing at her as he went by. The car had a couple of fresh scratches, but no other damage and Savage resumed her journey at a slower pace. Half a mile farther on a sign on a neat and well-trimmed verge announced she had arrived. A collection of houses you would be hard pushed to call a hamlet, let alone a village, hugged a small green with a single tree in its centre. At the far end a church lay nestled up against the open hillside. A noticeboard with the name St Michael's on proclaimed 'Jesus Loves You'. That was as maybe, but in the wet the building loomed grey and grim; the last sort of place you would go for solace. To the right of the church a uniformed officer stood blocking a narrow lane that wound its way along the edge of the moor. Savage slowed the car, lowered the window and showed her warrant card. The officer bent over.

'Carry on along here, ma'am. After a mile or so you'll get to a lay-by where you can park.'

Savage thanked the officer and drove on. To the left the moor towered upward, disappearing into mist and cloud. To the right a patchwork of fields cascaded downward to meet a line of trees marking a river. Beyond the trees the fields grew larger and Savage guessed the river marked the boundary between a small farm and a bigger one. A mile farther on several vehicles were pulled off the road on a grassy verge. She parked the car and struggled into her waterproof jacket, recalling Hardin's parting words to her.

'Charlotte, I don't need to tell you these are disturbing times. With these rapes, the Olivárez murder and now this. I want you to go softly softly on this one because believe me we are already up to our necks in the brown stuff. One wrong step and we might slip under. All of us.'

Hardin's words seemed appropriate as she stepped out of the car into a squelch of mud. The rain poured down and the cloud seemed even lower, threatening to engulf her in its chilly grip. All around, the hedgerows and trees were fading to brown and up on the moor the bracken had turned a light tan colour. Winter was coming, a cold and harsh one, if you believed the forecasters. Savage shivered at the thought. She didn't like the winter with its short days and long, dark nights. With Pete away life became difficult. The children went stir-crazy if they couldn't be outside, and even with Stefan to help out they were a handful. After they had gone to bed for the night Savage should have been able to relax, but she rarely could. She either had stacks of paperwork to complete or, worse, nothing to do but think. And that wasn't relaxing at all. In a month or so though life would change for the better: In December Stefan would be returning to his family in Sweden for Christmas, like he always did. But Pete was due back end of November. Touch wood.

The door of the car parked in front opened and a young man in his late twenties got out. Tall and athletic with gelled blond hair that shook off the rain like a duck's back, he stuck out a hand, his big, friendly smile concealing the reason they were both here.

'DC Craig Newlyn, ma'am. Totnes. I think you'll find the whole thing a little confusing.'

'Morning, Constable. Who discovered the body?'

'Found by a local farmer,' Newlyn said. 'He spotted the tracks in his field, figured they belonged to poachers or vandals, went down to investigate and bingo. Name of Gordon Isaacs. He owns the land around here. His farm is along the road a bit, up on the left.'

'What time?' asked Savage.

'Last night. Only he didn't alert us until this morning, said he had work to do.'

'What? Well that's not a good start.' Savage glanced back up the lane where the tower of St Michael's poked up through the mist. 'We will need to get statements from everybody in the village ASAP. TIE and all that.' Trace, Interview and Eliminate. Unlike when an incident occurred back in the city, the task didn't appear too arduous out here. With just a handful of houses in the village and everybody knowing everybody else it wouldn't be hard to collect statements and cross-reference them.

'We have got a couple of extra bods coming from Totnes, should be arriving soon.'

'Good stuff.'

'Ma'am, are you the SIO on this one?'

'No, that will be Detective Superintendent Hardin. I'm here for a first look. We've got a lot on our plates back in Plymouth.'

'So I've been reading,' Newlyn said.

'Yes, well, you know. Hardin is on his knees and praying this one can be cleared up without any fuss.'

'I don't think so, ma'am. Not from what I have seen.'

Savage shook her head. If possible she wanted to get to the scene, have a quick scout around and return to operation *Leash*. She didn't want to consider the alternative right now.

She let Newlyn get back in his car out of the rain and walked up the lane to where a white van straddled the tarmac, parked slap bang in the middle of the road as if acting as a windbreak. Behind the vehicle the crime scene manager was a guy she recognised but couldn't place and he clung to a large umbrella in the gusting wind. The rain slashed down as determined as ever and neither the van nor the brolly were doing much of a job protecting a white-suited CSI

44

kneeling on the verge in a gateway. The officer had placed a tape measure on the ground alongside some tyre impressions and footprints and was in the process of taking a couple of photographs. Next to the gate a section of fence had been removed to allow access without having to go through the original entrance. A line of blue and white tape snaked across the ground and led down the side of a grassy field marking out a path along which they could walk without disturbing potential evidence.

'John Layton,' the man held out his free hand as Savage approached. Layton was mid-thirties. Dark hair poked from beneath the brim of a Tilley hat and framed an angular face with an aquiline nose. The hat dripped water onto a tan-coloured Columbo-style raincoat. He pulled the scene log from a coat pocket for Savage to sign. 'Hardin said he was sending you.'

'He knows I enjoy a nice summer jaunt in the country,' Savage said, indicating the autumn storm howling overhead. 'What have you got there?' She gestured at the mass of mud at Layton's feet.

'Tyre prints and footprints. The whole thing is a bit of a mess because we have got the farmer's as well but we might get something. Lifted a couple of good fingerprints off the gate too.'

'Can I go down?' Savage nodded towards the tape running down the field.

'Sure. One of my guys and a couple of photographers are at the scene already.'

'Pathologist?'

'Stuck on the A38 somewhere.'

'If it's Nesbit he won't be happy.'

'It is Nesbit, and no he didn't sound too pleased when he called to tell me he was late.' Layton paused and looked down

45

at Savage's feet. 'The field is a complete bog. Got some wellies in the back of the van if you'd like?'

Savage said she would and Layton dug out a pair of yellow boots as well as the obligatory white coverall. Her feet slid around inside the over-sized boots, but as she walked down the side of the field she was grateful for them. The cattle had made much of the pasture a quagmire and the saturated ground oozed underfoot.

The tape ran down to where it was tied to a small aluminium step ladder the CSIs had put up to span the fence. A few metres farther on fence posts and netting lay in a flattened tangle and Savage noticed tyre tracks leading from the pasture into an earthy field where green shoots of wheat or some other crop poked up through the soil. The tyre marks crossed the neat tramlines of tractor tracks and curved left down towards a small patch of woodland at the bottom of the valley.

Savage climbed over the ladder into the next field and followed the tape again. As she neared the trees the clouds seemed to crowd overhead, darkening the sky even more. A stile led into the copse and to its right some more fencing had been removed. She walked through the opening into a little grove with towering old oak trees and slender young ash.

A sudden flash of harsh white light from a camera lit up a white crime scene tent and through the open end Savage could see a pale body lying like a sleeping nymph from a fairy tale. Two people stood next to the body on plastic stepping plates, one taking the pictures, the other with a small video camera. She recognised the photographer as Rod Oliver. His silver hair and craggy, weathered face showed he was getting on in years, but he knew his job. A year or so ago he had gone independent and filled in his spare time doing wedding shoots. Two more disparate sets of clients were hard to imagine. At the far edge of the clearing another figure in white combed the scrub with a long metal probe, teasing the long grass and nettles apart. Savage didn't go any closer but she could see the corpse belonged to a young woman, late teens or early twenties. White skin, no clothing, hands by her sides, legs apart. She didn't appear dead, just as if she was resting for a while. Her angelic face stared skyward towards heaven, but although the nakedness hit Savage like an electric shock, there was nothing else of note.

She looked around at the woodland. On a summer's day with a picnic and a family and laughter and smiles this would be an idyllic place. Today an autumn chill seeped from the ground and the wind whistled through the trees. The scrub and brambles appeared to be creeping into the clearing, trying to cover everything, to wipe out all traces of humanity and reinstate the wilderness.

Oliver noticed her and walked back along the row of stepping plates. As if reading her mind he told her what he knew.

'At first sight no obvious cause of death, although there is a strange cut mark on the belly. I would hazard a guess drugs are involved. Also, clever young Matt spotted a couple of indentations in the moss between her legs.'

Oliver introduced the pale-faced guy with the video camera as his assistant. Savage didn't think Matt looked young or clever, but when you went independent you would have to keep a tight rein on costs, she thought.

'There's a substance on the pubis and stomach resembling semen,' Oliver continued. 'I'd say somebody knelt and ejaculated over her. Although it's not my job to speculate, of course. Doc Nesbit will be able to confirm the drugs angle.'

47

He nodded back towards the edge of the copse where a figure in a full white coverall plodded their way.

'You've seen everything, Rod,' Savage said. 'You probably know more than half the guys in the business. And it is a business now, isn't it?'

'Yes, for me at any rate. Although I must admit I find it hard to put in an invoice after I have been to a scene like this. Doesn't seem right somehow.'

Savage knew what he meant. She often struggled with what the job involved, but with her the emotion didn't involve guilt about the money. Her own guilt was about how much she enjoyed the excitement. Not this bit of course, not the death and the misery, but the rest of the process; from not having a clue to having them bang to rights. Sometimes it seemed inexorable and unstoppable as if mapped out by some greater being and all she had to do was follow a path leading to the criminals. Savage didn't have much time for religion, but there was something comforting about the fact that right beat wrong and justice always prevailed. Well, nearly always.

Savage heard a cough behind her and turned to see Doctor Andrew Nesbit, the pathologist. His half-round glasses identified him as much as his slight stoop, which he claimed he had developed from bending over too many bodies. Nesbit was old-school and beneath the coverall Savage knew he would be wearing a tweed jacket and tie, an outfit in which he could be – and sometimes was – mistaken for a country doctor. He had a polite bedside manner, full of charm and grace, but this was lost on his patients since invariably they were dead.

'How's that little MG of yours, Charlotte?' Nesbit said.

'She's tucked up in my garage for the winter, thank you very much. Still costing me though. New sills done in the summer.'

'The AA badge must be the only thing you haven't renewed.'

'Very funny, Doc. But you are right, totting up the bills does make me feel like I have bought five cars' worth of spare parts.'

'What about your boat? I saw the picture in the paper back in the spring. You, Pete and the children.'

Savage remembered the *Herald* had done a feature on Pete before he set off for the South Atlantic, a photo shoot with the whole family on their tiny yacht. The journalist had been tickled pink by the contrast between helming the little coastal cruiser and commanding the oceangoing warship.

'Took the children out a few times in the summer, but managing the boat on my own is a struggle and I can't seem to persuade Stefan to join me. If he isn't cold, wet and leaning over at forty-five degrees he doesn't think he's sailing.'

'Samantha is growing up fast. And turning into the spitting image of you with all that red hair. Very beautiful.' Nesbit smiled, a twinkle in his eyes.

Savage blushed, even though she knew Nesbit's words were small talk intended to make everyone feel relaxed in a stressful situation.

'Ah, well.' Nesbit shrugged. Then he moved past Savage and walked over the stepping plates and into the tent to examine the body. 'I overheard you telling Charlotte about drugs,' he told Oliver as he bent over. 'No way I can confirm that here of course. And looking at the body now I'm not sure you are right about there being no sign of obvious trauma.'

Nesbit knelt, opened his bag, put on some nitrile gloves and took out a flat wooden spatula. He pressed the rounded end against the girl's stomach, opening the cut Oliver had pointed out.

'The incision on the abdomen is deep, the hole goes right in. Hasn't bled though. Strange.' He moved his hands up and touched the girl's breasts and then probed her right arm. 'The skin doesn't seem quite right either and there is an odd smell, more a fragrance.'

'Soap?' Savage suggested. 'Could she have been washed?'

'Possible, the skin is a bit puffy,' Nesbit paused. 'But there is something worrying me. Can't quite figure it out at the moment.'

'Do you think she was killed somewhere else?'

'Appears that way. Note the lividity in the buttocks and upper thighs? She was in a sitting position at or soon after death because the blood has pooled there. Quite unusual.' Nesbit looked around, eyes drinking in every little detail. 'No sign of a struggle taking place here, but I noticed several sets of footprints in the moss.'

Nesbit pointed towards the path and Savage spotted some indentations in the bright, green carpet, a trail leading to and from the girl's body. They would have to work out which belonged to the killer, which to the farmer, and which to the PC who had first attended the scene.

'Finished for the moment?' Nesbit asked Oliver.

'Yes, got a camera full, close-ups of all of her from tip to toe.'

'Good.' Nesbit took a digital thermometer with a remote probe from his bag and called across to the CSI. 'Can you help me, please?'

Nesbit instructed the CSI to roll over the body and then he bent and inserted the probe into the girl's rectum. While Nesbit did this Savage reflected on the fact that dignity and suspicious death were incompatible and that there would be far worse to come on the post-mortem table. Nesbit told the CSI to let the body lie flat again and he placed the thermometer display down on the ground. A few seconds later the unit beeped and Nesbit peered at the screen and muttered something Savage didn't catch.

'Doc?'

'Strange. The core body temperature is way below ambient which is . . . what? Eight, nine, ten? I'll measure it in a moment. Overnight I am sure it wasn't much lower, not with this weather coming in off the Atlantic. It's evident she has been dead for a day or two and kept somewhere colder.'

'We had frosty weather last week and into the weekend,' Savage said.

'Yes. Perhaps the body was outside in another location and was moved here. That would explain the low temperature.'

'There's no way this could be an accident, some kind of . . .' Savage wasn't sure how to finish the question, not even sure why she was trying to grasp for an explanation other than the obvious one.

'I can't tell that here can I, Charlotte? Given the sexual angle I wouldn't have thought this is anything other than murder, would you? Sorry. I know you need some luck at the moment. For this girl though it has all run out.'

Nesbit glanced at his watch and then pulled out a little voice recorder and mumbled something into the microphone. Then he stood up straight and was silent, a sombre expression on his face. Savage knew he wasn't religious, but it seemed as if he was waiting for someone to say a few words or for something to happen. As if on cue the church bell began to strike the hour.

Gordon Isaacs was the farmer who had discovered the body and even before she had met him alarm bells were ringing

51

in Savage's mind. Not reporting a minor car crash or a theft to the police might be understandable, but when you had found a naked and dead girl on your land such negligence was unfathomable.

Calter and Enders had arrived from Plymouth and they piled into Savage's car and drove up to Isaacs's farm to see what he had to say for himself. The holding stood alone with no near neighbours and the feeling of remoteness from the safe, modern world grew as they lurched along the concrete road leading up from the lane and climbed across open hillside to a huddle of barns and an old farmhouse. Three abandoned tractors and a multitude of rusting farm machinery lay either side of the track. Blue fertiliser sacks replaced windows in several of the barns, baler twine stitched holes in fences and nettle, dock and brambles vied for supremacy everywhere. The place looked more like the local tip than a farm. The only thing pretty was the view. The countryside rolled away to the south in a patchwork of fields, woodlands, hamlets and villages. Somewhere beyond lay the urban sprawl of Torbay, hidden in the murk that clouded anything more than a few miles distant.

'Look at that, ma'am.' Enders pointed to a bonfire where a blackened and bloated corpse of a sheep was smouldering on top.

'Devon-style barbie,' Calter said. 'Lovely!'

A house stood to their right as they entered the farmyard, a pretty cottage built of stone with a thatched roof half-covered with moss. To their left a crumbling brick barn was a Health and Safety nightmare with a broken asbestos roof that had been patched with rusty corrugated iron. Ahead a traditional byre was also dilapidated, but surely ripe for conversion.

They parked next to an old Landrover with an out-of-date tax disc and a cracked side window. As they got out Savage caught a whiff of burning sheep mixed with an odour of cow shit and silage and the smell clawed at the back of her throat as they picked their way through the mud to the farmhouse front door. Savage knocked, and as they waited she heard loud classical music from inside the house. And the sound of machine gun fire.

'Huh?' Savage cocked her head on one side, trying to make out the cacophony coming from within. It sounded like a TV set on maximum volume.

'*Platoon*, ma'am, the film, I recognise the theme,' Enders said. 'The DVD was free with the *Mail* a week or two back. I'd love to watch it again, but I don't get the chance to see what I want these days. The missus seems to think the kids prefer In the sodding Night Garden.'

'Sensible woman.'

'Funny thing to be watching when you've just found a dead body on your land,' Calter said.

The sound from inside stopped and a moment later the front door swung wide to reveal a short and rather portly man with a large reddened nose and a wheeze that came before he spoke.

'Yes?'

'Detective Inspector Charlotte Savage. Can we come in, Mr Isaacs? We need to ask you a few questions.'

'What more? I've had you guys trampling over my land, blocking the road so the feed lorry can't get up here, and now you? I've got work to do, not time for questions to answer.'

'You were watching a movie,' Enders said.

'None of your bloody business what I was doing, lad.' Isaacs paused. 'Anyway, the wife was doing the watching. She likes a good war film.'

As if to confirm what he said a figure appeared from the gloom inside and stood beside him. Mrs Isaacs had an appearance and stature not dissimilar to Mr Isaacs except her nose was dripping instead of red. She brought out a large stained handkerchief to deal with the drips and the tears running down her face.

'Willem Dafoe. He just got shot to pieces by the slanties. Always affects me that bit,' she sniffled. 'Anyway, come in won't you? If you wait for Gordon to ask you in you'll be standing on the doorstep 'til Santa gets here with pigs pulling his sleigh.' With that she turned and beckoned them in.

Savage made a gesture for Calter to stay outside and nose around while she and Enders followed the couple into the hallway. Newspaper was strewn across the floor and she was aware of her muddy footprints as she walked in. Enders nudged her and pointed down at the papers. *The Daily Mail*. She smiled and mouthed a silent 'good work'. To the left was a living room, cold and unused, the furniture adorned with white dust-covers. To the right a smaller room, a snug she guessed you would call it, was more welcoming. Two armchairs and a sofa were arranged around a hearth, the coals glowing red and orange. A corner held a little television screen, on it an explosion with the same colours as the fire was frozen mid blast.

'You'll have some tea?' Mrs Isaacs asked.

'Thank you. That would be great,' Savage said.

Mr Isaacs went over and slumped in the armchair nearest the fire, but made no invitation to Savage or Enders to sit. The two of them took the sofa and Savage began to ask about the discovery of the body. Mr Isaacs wasn't interested. He had explained to the response team what had happened

54

and was buggered if he was going to go through it all over again.

'The problem is you said you discovered the body last night and yet you didn't call us until this morning. I'm wondering why you took so long to phone us?'

'Work to do. Things to sort. Animals and the like. Farm's got to come first. Always has and always will. I still had loads of jobs to do and I thought if I called you lot I wouldn't get the chance to finish any of them.'

'The girl was dead, Mr Isaacs. Do you realise you committed an offence by not reporting the discovery straight away?'

'She wasn't going anywhere was she? I could see she was dead because I . . .' Isaacs paused and huffed. 'Well, I touched her. Had to. Didn't know, did I?'

'Didn't know what, Mr Isaacs?'

'I didn't know if she was dead. She might have been sleeping.'

'So when you realised she was dead, why didn't you call us? It was obvious a crime had been committed.'

'You'd know that, being police. I wouldn't. I'm a farmer. Just a farmer. Anyway, I see death all the time. It's not something alarming when you've got animals. Only yesterday I had to collect a ewe from down by the brook. Daft bugger had drowned herself, see? Brought her up here for disposal.'

'We've seen the sheep carcass. It's not legal is it? Burning them like that?'

Isaacs huffed again and started a rant on the European Union and politicians and how they knew bugger all about anything apart from lining their own pockets. Savage wasn't unsympathetic when it came to the government meddling in affairs they didn't understand, but the conversation was leading nowhere so she asked Isaacs if he had seen anyone yesterday, noticed anything suspicious, something out of the ordinary?

'If I had seen anyone on my land they'd have known about it, so no, I didn't see anyone.'

As Isaacs spoke Savage heard a tap, tap at the window and she turned to see Calter's face beaming through. Calter motioned at Savage to come outside. Savage left Enders to continue the questioning and let herself out of the front door.

'Over here, ma'am.' Calter stood by the corner of one of the barns next to a bulging, blue fertiliser sack.

Savage went over to join her, squishing through mud and God-knows-what on her journey across the farmyard.

'Something interesting?'

'Oh yes!' Calter held the sack open for Savage.

The sack bulged with various items of farm rubbish and at the top she could see a couple of syringes complete with needles along with an empty dispensing bottle. There were some wood offcuts, a few dirty rags, sheep daggings, bent nails, a length of rubber tubing, an old piece of rusty iron . . .

'My eyesight must be going, Jane, I can't see much of interest.'

Calter grinned and took a pen from her pocket. She poked one of the rags, looped it on the pen, retrieved it from the sack and held it out in front of Savage.

'Oh no.'

The material had a bit of dirt on, but now it was free from the rest of the bundle Savage could see it was no rag, it was too clean for that. The pure white cotton wafted in the breeze as if drying on a washing line.

'Girl's panties, ma'am. Sainsbury's own brand. The Isaacs don't appear to have any young children and they are a wee bit small for the Mrs.'

Savage heard a noise and looked round to see the farmhouse door open. Mrs Isaacs's shrill voice sang out across the mud.

'Milk and sugar, Inspector?'

Chapter Six

Harry lay on the bed feeling the alcohol slither through his veins and watching the ceiling rotate above him. The plaster ceiling rose with the bulb hanging on the twisted wire went one way and the corners of the room went the other. After a while they each slowed down and almost synchronised before going in opposite directions again. Stagecoach wheels in cowboy films came to mind. He closed his eyes to remove the dizzying effect, but that only served to make him think about what he had done and what he had become.

Harry thought it was the blood that pushed him over the edge. The blood from Carmel had poured over his hands warm and sticky, the metallic taste still there days later when he'd absent-mindedly bitten a nail. He'd washed and washed but in the end figured memories took more than just soap to erase. He also blamed the pills. They had done evil things to him he was sure. When he stopped taking them he had flipped. And that was Mitchell's fault.

He opened his eyes and watched the ceiling rose spin round again. Thought of roulette. Not Russian, the other type. Where you won stuff. He'd never won anything. That really didn't seem fair. He remembered the woman he had seen on the TV. The lawyer. She'd talked about fairness. Maybe he should try and get her phone number. He could give her a call. Maybe she could help. Maybe she even wore stockings.

Poor Harry, do you expect me to feel sorry for you?

Jesus, it was Trinny! Harry pulled a pillow over his head and chewed his tongue. He thought he had dumped her and shut her up for good, but somehow she was back. What the hell?

There is no peace, Harry. Not for you and not for me.

No, he understood that. Sunday night hadn't worked out as it should have and Trinny wasn't at peace because he hadn't been able to leave her where he wanted to. There had been too many people. Cars parked around the green, a huge pyre of burning pallets, hot drinks being served from the church and children running everywhere. A stupid bonfire night being held a few days early. In the end he found somewhere nearby. It was quiet and secluded, but at the time he thought it hadn't been right leaving her in the dark little wood.

Right? The whole thing wasn't right!

No, but his desire had been uncontrollable. Evil. Not his fault. Which was why he needed to find someone like the girls who had looked after him when he was a kid. The ones who held him close. He had never wanted them. Not like that.

Harry. Let me tell you about the birds and the bees. Something happens when you get older . . .

Harry ignored Trinny. When you got older you got wiser and when you got wiser you stopped taking the pills. It was then he started to see them. Everywhere. He would catch sight of Trinny at the bus stop. The lovely Carmel serving in Starbucks. Lucy crossing the road and running into college, the naughty girl late for a lecture no doubt. And it wasn't only those three, it was the others as well: Deborah, Emma

59

and Katya. It was a miracle how they had all appeared. The pills must have hidden them somehow, but they were there all along. Waiting.

Crazy Harry!

Crazy. Sure he was crazy, but he also knew what he was seeing. The trouble was that the girls on the street didn't look right. Bits of flesh poked out everywhere and they wore make-up. Not good. Not clean. But there was one place he'd worked where the girls knew how to care, how to cuddle, and from the clothes they wore Harry didn't think they were likely to be dirty either. He began to spot familiar faces there too. He'd go home and look at the old pictures and then he would begin his observations and tests. If the girls were really lucky he might take it one step farther.

Like you did with me?

Yes. He discovered Trinny some months back. She had been the first he had collected and he'd got it a bit wrong. There had been a misunderstanding.

And I was half naked. Was that a misunderstanding?

He wanted a few more pictures, wanted her dressed like he remembered.

Something else as well.

When her clothes slipped off he had seen the curves. He needed to touch them, feel them, stroke them.

Fuck me, more like.

No. That was the last thing he had wanted to do.

But you did.

Yes. Afterwards. When the girl had been quiet. When she had gone through the cleaning process and he knew she hadn't been right.

And all that was Mitchell's fault?

Mitchell had dragged him into his little circle of depravity

60

and from then on in he had been slipping downhill. Actually it was like he was plummeting now. Freefall. Groundrush.

Drag, Harry? I don't think the police would see it that way.

Of course they wouldn't. Because they wouldn't make allowances for his sensitivities. And the police didn't know Mitchell and his way of twisting everything to his own advantage. That was how Harry had got involved with him in the first place. Mitchell had spotted Harry on the Hoe with his camera and guessed what he was doing. He followed Harry into the shopping centre and watched him take upskirt shots on the escalators. Mitchell had confronted him and sprung his trap.

At least his time with Mitchell made him realise about the other type of girls. The sluts. The ones struggling on Mitchell's bed may not have been begging for it, but they knew the risks. They went out for the night with their flesh on display, just waiting to be touched.

Touched, Harry? They were raped.

Like he had been.

You expect sympathy? After what you have done?

Harry knew that it wasn't his fault, that somehow, somewhere, everything had got all mixed up. Wrong. Broken.

So what are you going to do to fix things, Harry?

That was a good question. Harry pondered it for a few minutes. He had tried to fix things with Trinny. Only that hadn't worked out and he'd had to get rid of her. There was also the little matter of Lucy.

Juicy Lucy! That slut! She makes me look like a nun.

Lucy had come back from the past the same way as Carmel and Trinny had so he had collected her too. He couldn't risk losing her in the way he had lost Carmel. Now she was tucked away downstairs. Safe. The sad thing was that she was just about the same as Trinny. Dirty.

I told you, Harry. And the new girl will be no different.

Emma. Sleeping upstairs.

Thinking about her made him smile. The time with her on Monday had been such fun. They chatted and joked like old friends. He suggested a drink and they talked some more. She laughed and giggled and giggled and laughed and began to get a bit confused. After that she started to look a little tired and he had offered to take her home.

She accepted.

Chapter Seven

Crownhill Police Station, Plymouth. Wednesday 27th October. 9.03 am

The vista from the operation *Zebo* incident room took in a line of white police vans and a few squad cars sitting on the car park. A crap view was no bad thing, Savage thought. At least all eyes would be on the job and not on the people walking past two floors below. Eight terminals, twice as many screens and a decent amount of spare desk space crammed into a few square metres. Cosy. DS Gareth Collier had been Hardin's choice for office manager and Savage approved of the way the setup had progressed so far. Collier, always a stickler for procedure, liked things neat, well organised and locked down tight. He looked like he behaved, and with his greying hair trimmed in a parade ground cut he resembled a regimental sergeant major as he prowled the office searching for unfiled scraps of paper or terminals which had been left unattended but not logged out of. Luckily he also had a great sense of humour. The opposing facets were a perfect match and ensured smooth progress and a happy team. One without the other made work either dull or frustrating, and if both were missing an investigation didn't stand a chance.

Gordon Isaacs was banged up in the custody suite at the

station in the centre of town and according to DS Darius Riley he was looking pretty miserable after an uncomfortable night brooding. Riley sat at a desk fussing over a crease in his expensive jacket and then fingering his collar where his black skin contrasted with brilliant white cotton. Savage knew the shirt would most likely be from an outfitter on Jermyn Street in London – Hawes and Curtis or Thomas Pink – rather than from the local M&S, which was the brand the other male detectives favoured. When Riley had arrived in Plymouth a year or so ago those officers old enough to remember the US TV show *Miami Vice* had taken to calling him Tubbs after the show's stylish detective. Riley had borne the practice with good humour until someone from Human Resources had got wind of it and panicked, detecting a lawsuit and headlines. Nicknames were now banned, the penalty a day on an attitude reorientation course.

Riley undid the button on his collar and made some comment about the central heating being way too high before explaining what they had on Isaacs.

'He has confessed to removing the girl's underwear and wan—, um, masturbating over the body, but swears blind he knows nothing else about her. For the moment we can do him under sexual offences section seventy. Turns out he's got previous though, sex with a minor, however it was over thirty years ago. He was in his late twenties, the girl fifteen.'

'The case was still on file?' Savage asked.

'No, he admitted it. There was no sexual offenders' register or anything like it at the time, but I found the original records. He got off with a suspended sentence because according to the judge – and you'll like this – there were extenuating circumstances. Different world back then but he's pretty ashamed of himself now. I think he is so terrified of what the wife is going to do to him he just wanted to come clean.'

'So to speak,' Calter said.

Savage had selected Riley and Calter for the initial interview. She had figured the combination of Riley, tall, black and disarming, and Calter, who in her own words described herself as a 'hard-nosed bitch', would unsettle Isaacs. In fact, the interview plan had gone a little astray because Mr Isaacs claimed he had a history of mental illness and was on medication. A check with his GP had confirmed the fact and they had to get someone along from Social Services to sit in as an appropriate adult. Still, Savage was pleased with the results even though they'd had to adopt a softer approach than she would have liked.

'What's your hunch, Jane?' Savage asked Calter.

'I'm not sure, ma'am. Why would he call us and tell us about the girl? Why would he leave her on his land in the first place? On the other hand, he's got previous and by assaulting the corpse he has put himself in the frame forensically.'

'You don't sound convinced though?'

'Anything is possible, but all in all I don't think he's seriously up for it. Not at this early stage anyway.'

'Really? If the sexual offence from thirty years ago had been committed today he'd be on the sex offenders list. That, and his mental condition, should make us look twice.'

'He's not right in the head, ma'am,' Riley said. 'One raisin short of a fruitcake, I'd say. When we asked him about the previous conviction he went off on some rant about how the whole world was becoming soft and filled with poofters and that we needed to get back to a time where men could be men and not ponce about like girls.'

'We've got the underwear to consider too, ma'am,' Calter

said. 'I mean if the knickers and bra didn't belong to the girl then where did they come from?'

When John Layton had arrived at the farm to collect the underwear he had shown Savage the clothing. Through the polythene of the evidence bag he folded the material, hunting for the label.

'Sainsbury's girls' range, ma'am. Suitable for a twelve to thirteen year old. They wouldn't be the right size for the victim.'

Now Savage thought about the underwear again. The knickers would fit her own daughter and although the young woman in the copse could have squeezed into them they didn't belong to her.

'But Isaacs has sworn he removed them from the girl,' Riley said. 'I can't see any reason for him to lie.'

'Unless he bought them to *put on* the girl,' Savage said. 'In that case he would want to remove the evidence after he'd had his fun.'

'Some sort of fetish?' Calter said, wrinkling her nose in mock disgust.

'Whatever. The search team are going over the farm at the moment in the hope of finding the rest of the girl's clothing. Come up trumps and we've got him. You two can have another go at him later this morning. Some extra pressure this time, please, I want him unsettled a little bit more. If that's possible.'

She could imagine poor old Isaacs squirming at the sight of his interviewers returning for a second round. A man like that, whatever he had done, had pride, and he wouldn't be comfortable with Riley and Calter squashing him underfoot.

'Ma'am?' Riley pointed to the terminal in front of him on which he'd pulled up a map of the area in a browser window. 'The underwear was from Sainsbury's, right?'

'Yes. So?'

'The closest supermarket to Isaacs's place would be the Tesco Megastore at Lee Mill, near Ivybridge. Sainsbury's is much farther away.'

'You are right. And the more I think about it the more I can't imagine Mr Isaacs trooping up and down the aisles searching for girls' knickers. I bet he doesn't even do any of the shopping, that would be Mrs Isaacs's job and she'd use the local shops. He'd be lost in a supermarket.'

'Well, if he didn't buy the underwear then he's out of the frame, isn't he?' Riley clicked the browser window shut as if that was the end of the matter and that further questioning of Isaacs would be pointless.

The immediate priority, apart from dealing with Isaacs, was to identify the girl. Often murder victims knew their killers, so establishing the victim's network could be the key to finding the murderer. Isaacs had said he had never seen her before he came across her in the wood, but if he was lying he would be in deeper shit than the muck in his farmyard.

A steady trickle of calls were coming into the incident room hotline about the girl and two officers logged the details into the system. DC Susan Bridge, an older officer recently transferred out of uniform, was raising actions on those calls, arranging for follow-up interviews or passing information to Savage if she wasn't sure further investigation was needed. She was spot on when she had asked if they weren't up against two problems at once.

'I mean, ma'am, that we have a sort of reverse missing person case as well as the murder,' she said. 'We need to find out who the girl is, but that is being coloured by the fact she is dead.'

She was right. Already there had been a fair number of

reports from people who claimed to know the girl, where she had been and what she had done. All of them, so far as the team knew, were plain incorrect. Well-meaning but misguided members of the public often did that sort of thing. They wanted a resolution to the story and the gaps were like missing an episode of *EastEnders*. In this case you couldn't catch up on iPlayer or ask your friends what had happened so your mind filled in the blanks for you.

'Ma'am?' Enders broke into her train of thought. 'I've got the results on screen.'

Savage had asked Enders to come up with a list of mispers reported in the last few weeks and now she went over to where he was sitting in front of a terminal navigating through the missing person register on the COMPACT MISPER system. Riley and Calter came over too and the three of them peered over Enders's shoulders at the screen.

'Four on my shortlist, ma'am,' Enders said as if announcing the winner of the Christmas raffle.

'Number one, Alice Nash. She's sixteen, from Ashburton, a town close to Malstead and just along the A38 from Buckfastleigh. There seems to be some real concern about her. She left her work place in Ivybridge and never boarded the bus to Ashburton. When her dad realised that she hadn't got her usual bus or the following two he called us. Some report of her possibly accepting a lift from—'

'Idiot!' Calter said, flicking the top of Enders's head with her hand. 'Read the date, Sherlock. She went missing Monday evening. Isaacs had found the body by then. Worrying for the parents, sure, but no way she can be our victim.'

Enders looked sheepish before carrying on.

'Lindsey Nation, nineteen, I can see it's not her. She's blonde, not dark-haired like the girl in the wood.'

Enders clicked through his list.

'Um, Jenny Smith?'

'No.'

'Simone Ashton?'

'No.'

'That's your lot from round here.'

'We need to widen the area or the timeframe or both,' Calter chipped in.

'Evidently.'

Enders went back to the search page where he changed some of the parameters.

'Still sticking to Devon and Cornwall, but extending the date range to six months.'

'That's long enough. The girl died in the last week or so.'

'Right.' Enders hit the return key and data filled the screen. 'Bloody hell. Eighty-four names.'

'I'll get some coffees, ma'am,' Calter said as Enders began to scroll through the results.

Savage nodded and examined the list. They had searched for females between the age of fifteen and twenty-five missing in Devon and Cornwall in the past six months and the results were staggering. The figures would be distorted by the fact that the area was a tourist destination: many on the list would have gone missing while on holiday and turned up later back on their own patch. The problem was nobody bothered to inform the police. Even so the number seemed high. Savage knew a couple of hundred thousand people went missing in the UK each year but she'd always mistrusted the figure. Most would turn up, but the official guidance set down in procedure was clear: if the investigator had any doubt then they were to think murder. Her thoughts were interrupted by Enders jabbing at the screen.

'Don't bother with the coffees, I've found her.'

It was too late as Calter had already gone, but Enders was

right. Savage looked at the record and the dead girl's face stared out at her. Kelly Donal, eighteen years old, enrolled on an Early Childhood Studies course at the university with a work placement at Little Angels nursery. Her address was listed as Beacon Park, Plymouth. She had been reported missing thirteen weeks ago.

Enders gave a quick précis of the notes.

'We have a report of an incident at the flat in the city that Kelly shared with a friend – this was the day before Kelly went missing – but by the time officers arrived it was over. According to the friend it was something to do with Kelly's glamour modelling. A guy had turned up demanding to see Kelly and she wouldn't let him in. There was a row in the street and a neighbour called the police. When they arrived a man known to them as David Forester was hanging about outside. He was allowed to leave when Kelly insisted she was not making a formal complaint. Forester had already received a conviction for ABH at the start of the year. Managed to avoid a custodial, got a Community Service Order instead. Before that he had a caution for possession. Let's see, yes, registered address is in North Prospect. A right swillyite by the sound of it.'

'If he's implicated there is going to be some serious press heat,' Riley said.

'Yes, but for once it won't be on us. Should have been banged up.'

'Go on,' Savage said. 'There's more.'

Enders continued reading from the notes.

'Seems like Kelly told the flatmate she was going to a friend's house for the weekend, something she often did. The next day was a Friday and the flatmate came back to find Kelly gone.'

'And she didn't worry because she thought she had gone away?'

'Precisely.' Enders pointed at the screen again. 'It wasn't until Monday evening that she called Kelly's parents to ask them if Kelly had been there. They said that they hadn't seen her and in turn called us.'

'Appears we did bugger all,' Riley said.

'They were told to call again at the end of the week and did so. Seems like then someone decided the girl had gone off to London modelling. She mentioned something about an agent to the flatmate and in the weeks before she had fallen out with her parents. Further investigation led to the incident being classified as low risk with a flag to review the case and reassess it at a later date. As of today it doesn't seem as if that has happened.'

Savage could understand why. The amount of resources needing to be deployed was not inconsiderable. They would need to get search teams into Donal's property, obtain the necessary permission to access landline and mobile telephone records and bank accounts, liaise with the Met to see if there was any evidence she had ever made it to London, check with the UK Border Agency as to whether she might have left the country ... Now those resources would be forthcoming, but Savage wondered if the officers on Kelly's case had been hesitant in taking the investigation to the next stage because of cost worries or if the error was down to negligence.

'This is all news to me,' Savage said. 'I think I was on holiday at the time.'

'You'd flown out to Brazil to meet your husband,' Riley said. 'I remember the sun, sea and sand on the postcard made us all depressed.'

'You shouldn't have transferred down here if you like the weather sunny and warm.'

'It was a little *too* hot in London, I was in danger of getting

71

burnt,' Riley said, without further explanation. 'Anyway, where does Forester fit into all this?'

'I'm on the case, Darius,' Enders said. He typed and clicked and the results of a new search for male mispers came up. He pointed to the screen. 'David Forester, twenty-nine, of North Prospect. Reported missing by his parents on the eighth of August.'

'Damn. Why didn't that get linked in with Kelly's case?' Savage said. The date was two weeks after Kelly's disappearance, but there should have been some sort of flag in the system to draw attention to the previous incident; a definite mistake on somebody's part.

'Someone missed the connection,' Riley said. 'For a mispers case it doesn't seem much of an oversight, but now we've got a body . . .'

'Exactly. Forester is now the prime suspect,' Savage said. 'Right, we need to generate some action points on this. One, get family liaison to inform Kelly's parents and arrange for formal identification of the body. Two, let's get the Beacon Park officers involved in the domestic and ABH incidents in, plus those on the Kelly mispers case, we need their input. Three, get a search team into Kelly's and Forester's properties. Four, re-interview Kelly's parents and her flatmate. Five, interview Forester's parents and employer.'

'He was unemployed,' Enders said, pointing to the screen again. 'Used to work at Tamar Yacht Fitters, but was dismissed after the conviction for ABH.'

'Still, might be worth a word. You and DS Riley will take that one and I'll see what I can get out of his parents. I also think we need to make an appeal for David Forester to come forward. This isn't a missing person inquiry anymore, it's murder. Let's ditch the interview with Isaacs and ask the CPS if they want to charge him with the sexual offence on the body. Then we can concentrate on Forester.'

'But taking Kelly all the way over to Malstead Down? Forester? We don't know much about him, but he doesn't seem the type to go to all that trouble.' Enders sounded sceptical, as if he didn't agree with Savage.

'Taking her over there might have seemed like a good way of misdirecting us. But first we find Forester and then let's see where we are. It is my guess he's our man.'

Chapter Eight

St Ives, Cornwall. Wednesday 27th October. 10.30 pm

The damp shirt stuck to DS Kevin Tatershall's skin as he shifted in his seat, trying to get comfortable. The heater had been going full-blast on the twenty-minute drive from Penzance but the fan hadn't dried him much and he was still soaking. The downpour had started first thing in the morning and he'd got wet on the walk to work. He'd just about got dry when DI Peters came across with a piece of paper and a nasty smile, which Tatershall guessed meant an assignment outside of the station. The run from the building to the pool car left him at square one all over again.

In St Ives the rain continued to fall. Cats, dogs and pretty much everything else tumbled from the sky, and lashings of water filled the roads with runoff. Tatershall didn't want to think about leaving the warm cocoon of the car and he pitied the tourists working their way up and down the streets with their odd shuffle, looking as if they were in harness rather than on holiday. They must be crazy to bother coming to Cornwall at this time of year.

'I wish I was a tumble dryer, I'd run my program through.' The soft, husky voice came from DC Kate Simbeck and she smiled as she continued her rhyme. 'I wish I was a tumble dryer, I'd dry your clothes for you.'

Simbeck didn't look too keen to get out of the car either, but apart from her long pony tail, which she wore on the outside of her over-sized Musto, at least she'd stayed dry. As they sat contemplating the rain the windows began to steam up and Tatershall drew a quick stick figure on the windscreen, completing the drawing with a hangman game gallows.

'That DI Peters?' Simbeck said.

'Yuppee doodah. Can't draw what I'd really like to do to him or we'd have the obscene publications law to deal with.'

Simbeck giggled and the noise and the way her cute little nose wrinkled caused butterflies in Tatershall's stomach. He wished they had parked somewhere a little more remote and he wasn't married with three kids. Maybe then she would say 'yes' if he asked her for a shag.

Driving somewhere remote wouldn't be a problem. Within five minutes they could be out of town. Within fifteen Tatershall knew dozens of places quiet enough. The wife and kids were more of an issue though, and the chance of a pretty twenty-something girl saying 'yes' to an early fifties guy like him were in the arena of having a winning lottery ticket. Of course, if he'd won the lottery he wouldn't be on some stupid mispers goose chase involving an elderly couple DI Peters had chosen to push his way. No, he'd be on a golden beach somewhere hot, rubbing suntan oil into Kate's glorious—

'Kevin?' Simbeck pointed out through a patch of window where she had smeared a circular hole in the condensation. A well-filled uniform stood some way up the street looking wet, miserable and not a little angry.

'Bugger.' Tatershall sounded the horn, wound down the window and waved at the PC. 'Over here mate.'

The PC jogged down the pavement, dodging umbrellas, baby buggies and a group of disgruntled tourists. The latter glowered at him as if the local police were responsible for the weather as well as crime. The officer arrived at the car puffing and leaned in, dripping rain and a palpable hostility.

'You're late. I was told half past.'

'You got the keys?' Tatershall ignored the jibe. 'Only I'd hate to have made a wasted journey.'

He heard Simbeck stifle a laugh which the PC didn't catch. The PC nodded and explained he had managed to track down a spare set held by a neighbour in case of emergency. The couple owned a gallery with a flat above, and it only became apparent they'd gone missing when the water company needed access to the rear of the property.

'I'd noticed the gallery was closed in July,' the PC said, 'which I thought a bit odd considering we were at the height of the season. I forgot about it until yesterday when the neighbour called about the water people. I went in with the neighbour to check the flat just in case. Nobody. Fridge empty, place clean, nothing untoward. Well, they have been gone four months now so I thought—'

'To call in the experts?' Tatershall heard Simbeck snigger again. 'You did right, lad. This sort of investigation can be incredibly complicated, but never fear, the Simbeck House Investigation Team Squad are here.'

The PC stared in the window, bemused, but Simbeck had abandoned any semblance of decorum and was laughing her head off.

Tatershall and Simbeck got out of the car and the three of them walked up the road to the gallery front. Tatershall glanced in, noting the usual watercolour rubbish typical of galleries all over the West Country.

'Shall we?' The PC opened a door next to the gallery

entrance and went into a small lobby, beyond which stairs led up to the flat. A fan of mail lay spread on the doormat and Tatershall told Simbeck to grab the letters and bring them up.

With the posh gallery below Tatershall had been expecting the flat to be something one step up from the grotty spaces often found above shops, but he was surprised by the luxury as he broached the top of the stairs. The interior of the place had been gutted to make a huge open plan area like something out of one of those TV makeover programmes. A floor-to-ceiling window in the rear wall of the property looked out over the town to Porthmeor Bay and even on a miserable day like today the view was stunning. The furnishings were expensive and the style more swish London riverside flat than an old couple's retirement home.

'In their seventies?' Tatershall said, shaking his head.

'Yes. From London. With money.' The words came out with resentment attached and Tatershall was tempted to stir the PC up some more, but Simbeck had arrived with the stack of letters.

'Quiet couple by all accounts,' the PC continued. 'Moved here ten years ago, but not many friends and no one who knows where they might have gone to.'

'Family?' Tatershall asked.

'None that we know of.'

'OK. You can leave it to us now, Constable, I've got your notes. We'll drop the keys back at the station when we've finished.'

The PC stared out of the window for a moment before grunting and making his way down the stairs, slamming the door as he left.

'That was a bit harsh, Kev. He was itching to stay out of the rain.'

'Yeah? Well, I've got to take my frustration out on someone haven't I? We've got plenty of stuff to be getting on with back home without having to come over here.'

'You wouldn't be moaning if it was a nice summer's day!'

'No, but it isn't a nice summer's day. That's the point and DI Peters knows it. I bet he is sitting back at the station with coffee, a plateful of doughnuts and a bloody big grin on his face.'

'Well, we are here now so we might as well get on with the job.'

Simbeck began sorting the letters on a white oak sideboard while Tatershall slouched into one of the chairs and took in the impressive view.

'Anything?' he said after a while, more out of hope than expectation.

'I've found a bank statement. Joint account.' Simbeck was leafing through the pages. 'Three months to the end of September. Regular stuff to start with, a supermarket, some other local shops. Then I've got a transaction at Tesco Lee Mill for forty quid exactly. Fifteenth July. Petrol.'

'Where the hell is Lee Mill?'

'No idea, but it's not round here.'

'Anything else?' Tatershall asked.

'A cashpoint withdrawal same day. Fifty pounds. Dartmouth.'

'Dartmouth? Well that's this one sussed. They're on bloody holiday! Case solved, closed, finito. I'll buy you lunch in the pub and then we can get back, and if you are a good girl I'll let you do the paperwork.' Tatershall struggled to push himself upright from the embrace of the soft leather sofa.

'I don't think so, sir. There are a couple more standing orders but no more EPS transactions. The cash withdrawal was over four months ago now. Since then nothing.'

'They are using the cash.'

'Fifty quid, boss? You're joking, right? Think about how far fifty quid would go if you were on holiday here. Can't see Dartmouth being much different.'

'Could be they lost the card and are using another bank account or a credit card.'

'Could be. But why, when you live here, would you go on holiday in Dartmouth? It's a hundred miles away, but not much of a change. And for four months? What would they be doing over there all this time? You are forgetting the gallery too. They wouldn't leave it unattended.' Simbeck was looking through the rest of the mail. 'I don't buy that. Call it women's intuition, superior detective ability or whatever you like, but I think something has happened to them. I don't think this story has got a happy ending. Here, look at this.'

Simbeck had opened another piece of mail and she walked across and handed the letter to Tatershall. At the top the blue NHS logo stood above the address for the Royal Cornwall Hospital in Truro. Below, the contents of the letter detailed a missed appointment at the Sunrise Centre.

'What's the Sunrise Centre?' he asked Simbeck.

'My gran was there, it's oncology. The big "C". Cancer.'

Tatershall let himself slump back in the sofa and stared out at the view again. Atlantic rollers surged into the bay to crash against the shore and the sandy beach looked nothing like it did in the summer, deserted and strewn with flotsam as it was. Farther out a fog was creeping in across the grey sea and Tatershall felt that the world had got just a little bit grimmer.

During a bad winter, snow covered Dartmoor for weeks burying everything but the dark granite tors beneath a rolling expanse of white. The tors stuck out like the proverbial and DS Darius Riley did too. Devon didn't do black. At first Riley hadn't much liked Devon either, but he hadn't had a choice in the matter. Up in London some people fancied burying him, not in snow, but six feet under. He had been undercover for the last year, deep in the heart of the organised crime gangs and, in the end, in deep shit because he had been blown out by a woman he'd got too close to. Escaping with just two cracked ribs from a nasty beating had been a bonus. After the inquiry into what had gone wrong moving had been the only option offered to him, and Plymouth at least promised something different from the high-intensity policing he'd been used to. And it was different. Once you ventured outside of the major metropolitan areas black officers were a rarity, and Devon and Cornwall Police followed the pattern. Less than one per cent of the force came from an ethnic minority background. That could make things difficult, but at least he wasn't in uniform. A black colleague had told him about Saturday nights on patrol in the town centre mopping up the idiots spilling out from the clubs. It didn't bear thinking about.

Even in CID Riley still encountered times when an undercurrent of racism bubbled to the surface. Just last week an old lady had looked twice at his warrant card before letting him into her house, and when she had made the tea she had brought out a multitude of different biscuits because 'I didn't know what kind you coloureds liked'. He supposed most people would have called her behaviour misguided but harmless. In Riley's view her words showed ignorance at best, blatant prejudice at worst.

On the other hand he didn't want to return to the Met nor would he have been allowed to. Since the move out west he'd got used to a more relaxed and less dangerous way of life. And, although it sounded clichéd, he sometimes sensed a genuine feeling of community he hadn't known in London.

At the moment community spirit was working against him and Enders. They were at Tamar Yacht Fitters talking to employees about David Forester and getting nowhere fast. As they wandered about the workshop and strolled along the pontoons they encountered no one willing to say much about Forester, good or bad.

Tamar Yacht Fitters stood on the banks of the river, just opposite Princess Yachts. A hangar with sliding doors big enough to accommodate a twenty-five-metre boat sat above a wharf with half a dozen pontoons crammed with gleaming white motor yachts. The location was no coincidence because Tamar were specialists at fitting out the huge gin palaces Princess produced. Gavin Redmond, the managing director, had a trim, athletic figure for his fifty-something years and his face still glowed with a tan gained from a summer on the water. He explained that for a buyer wanting more than the basics, they were the first choice.

'HD radar, security systems, underwater lighting, marine computers. You name it, we fit it.'

Redmond had shown them around a huge boat considerably more spacious than Riley's flat and many times as expensive. Back in Redmond's office, a smart new prefab in one corner of the yard, Enders seemed to be having a hard time understanding the market.

'So what you are saying is you spend a couple of million on a boat and then you've got to pay more for some extra goodies?'

'That's the long and short of it. Think of a boat like your house. You buy a nice new place so you need some nice new things as well, like an HD TV or one of those American-style fridges. The cost is peanuts compared to what you have paid

81

for the house. Same here. Or maybe you have bought a used boat a couple of years old. The equipment may be a bit last generation instead of next and you don't want your mates to think you are stingy. Basically boys love toys, and we provide those toys. For a price.'

'David Forester.' Riley brought the conversation back to the purpose behind their visit. 'Your employees don't seem very pleased to be asked questions about him. Any particular reason?'

Redmond sighed. 'Forester wasn't a pleasant type of bloke. He was a big hulk of a guy, liked a drink, a bit rough. Nobody wanted to get on the wrong side of him. Funny, when he first came to work here a few years ago he was OK, a bit shy even. However, in the last year he was here he became more difficult, and I must admit I was thinking we might have to let him go.'

'But you didn't?'

'Not at the time. He was good at his job. Not a bright kid, but he knew his way around computers and was a wizard at sorting out the CCTV and video stuff some people want on board. But then we had a little incident.'

'Go on,' encouraged Riley.

'Forester was installing a marine computer on a yacht and setting up the WIFI system. I discovered he had downloaded a porn movie to show to some of the lads here.'

'So? Looks like a bit of porn is about par for the course.' Riley pointed out a calendar on the wall with a picture of a big motor yacht and a babe. Bronze flesh lay across smooth contoured fibreglass and spotless teak and the viewer didn't have to guess if the girl's blonde hair was natural.

'This wasn't like that,' Redmond said. 'That's marketing. What Forester had downloaded disturbed me.'

'Kiddie stuff?'

'No. If it had been I would have sacked him, called you guys too. This was a woman tied up, beer bottle and worse. The content was probably nothing illegal assuming it was consensual, but it wasn't nice. The thing was, a load of them were watching at lunch time and one of the girls from the office came down to see what they were up to. She wasn't amused, mentioned the magic word "harassment" and threatened to go to a solicitor. One of those advertising in the local papers.'

'Ambulance chasers?'

'Those are the ones. Bloody tossers if you ask me.'

'So why didn't you dismiss him?'

'Couldn't prove he was the one. Other people had access to the yacht and none of the lads involved would say a word. Plus an audit of our own systems showed the practice of downloading porn was widespread, although mostly just the soft stuff.'

'Hence the reluctance of the others to talk much about it.'

Redmond nodded.

'You got it. We disciplined the lot of them and I gave the girl a promotion. She shut up after that. Clever lass, knows which side her bread is buttered. Anyway, once he got the ABH conviction it was the chance I needed to get rid of him and good riddance.'

'Was Forester popular?'

'He was a bragger and towards the end he seemed to have plenty of money to spend. People will listen to your stories if you buy them enough drinks. I'm not sure if he was what I would call popular though. For instance he bought this flash new motor, a big Shogun, and I think some of the lads were getting a bit jealous. He obviously hadn't purchased the car on the money we paid him, and rubbing your mates' noses in it doesn't tend to endear you to people.'

'Did you know if Forester had a girlfriend?' Riley asked.

'Heard him talking about one, sure. He couldn't tell the lads enough about her. Big tits, tight pussy, liked humping doggie style. Sorry about the language, his words, not mine. I thought the girl was all in his head myself.'

Riley pulled out the picture of Kelly and showed it to Redmond.

'Mind if I show this around, see if anyone here recognises her?'

Redmond went pale and swallowed hard.

'Bloody hell!'

'Mr Redmond?'

'The girl in the movie. The one with the beer bottle. It's her.'

'You sure?'

'Let's just say I never forget a face, shall we?'

Chapter Nine

Harry stopped washing the dishes and went to switch the radio off. He chewed his tongue while he mulled over the latest bulletin: the police had found Trinny. The news worried him, although Trinny wouldn't tell them anything. She might have a loud mouth, but she would keep it shut for him. Still, it might be sensible to stay away from town. At least for a while. To let things calm down. He would cancel some of his appointments, say he was sick. Which he was. Very. Anyway, he had the new girl to deal with. He couldn't leave her all on her own day after day. She would get lonely.

When he had got her back to his place she was already unconscious so he stripped her naked and laid her out to examine her. Perfection in a little over five feet. Beautiful. Mind you they all appeared so. At first.

Emma would be different, he knew she would. Just the name caused butterflies in his stomach.

Not her real name of course, but she wouldn't be using that again. Emma was her special name. Harry's name. He had written it in big letters on the first page of the luxurious black leather notebook he had bought for her. All the other pages remained blank. White, virginal and untouched. If things worked out between them he would write nice things in the book and they could look over it together. If things didn't work out he knew he had to write down all the nasty stuff he discovered. The nitty-gritty-shitty stuff that Emma didn't want anyone to know about: The dirty habits, the spots and blemishes, the bad language, the conceits, deceptions and lies, the broken promises, the filthy thoughts that came when she turned off the light, the . . .

Hell, he was getting ahead of himself. Emma hadn't been given a chance yet. He was condemning her without a fair trial.

Trinny had been given a fair trial. She had a chance but failed. Two whole weeks of cleaning and she had still been too desirable. Desire turned love into lust and flesh into the apple of corruption. The Bible said so and the Bible couldn't be wrong, could it? He recalled the leather-bound copy his mother had pressed into his hands every evening as she made him kneel next to the bed and pray. *God the Father, God the Son, God the Holy Ghost* . . . The unholy trinity of his family, his mother the ghost, ethereal both in her presence and in her pitiful attempts to control his father's cravings. All she could do was wash the sheets, wash her hands, repeat the mantra that 'your father loves you'. It didn't make sense but then neither did the Bible. *Suffer little children* . . .

Love, desire, lust. He remembered when he had been little Trinny held him and he felt nothing but warmth. When he held the new Trinny he wanted her. The sensation repulsed him. If you fucked somebody you didn't love them. He learnt that the hard way as a kid, and Mitchell showed him too. The lesson had to be applied to his search for his angel. Angels were pure. Spotless.

He walked back to the sink and plunged his hands into the foam. The water scalded, but it needed to be hot to eat away at the dirt. This was the second time he had washed the plates. Once more after this should be enough. Rinse, wash, rinse, wash, rinse, wash, rinse. Back at his flat in town he would simply run the dishwasher cycle a few times, but out here he had no mod cons so keeping things clean proved difficult.

Trinny hadn't been clean from the start but it wasn't her fault. Her boyfriend, a half-wit from the slums, contaminated her and the seed spread, decomposing her from within, spoiling her before Harry had ever met her. But Harry hadn't known about the boyfriend so he couldn't have guessed the trouble Trinny would cause.

The selection took longer with Lucy but it hadn't worked out perfectly with her either. He had made copious notes, observing her before he ever went near her, but always knowing a more hands-on approach would be needed. Satisfied everything looked right he collected her. Then he used the spy hole into the little room to watch some more as she went through his detox routine. Finally he examined her properly. He hadn't liked the procedure and neither had she. She screamed when he touched her. The problems started then.

Harry finished the plates, giving them a final rinse to make sure. Poor Lucy, she had failed. Like Trinny before her, she was not the one he wished to choose and she would have to leave as well.

Emma wouldn't be leaving though, she would stay. And hopefully she would live.

Chapter Ten

Yelverton, Devon. Wednesday 27th October. 11.30 am

Savage never liked meeting the parents. It wasn't that she had no sympathy for their plight; quite the opposite. She found she empathised with them all too easily, and that was a problem. She was glad in this case the news about Kelly had already been broken to Mr and Mrs Donal and that a family liaison officer would be present when she and Calter arrived for their meeting.

The village of Yelverton lay some five miles north of Plymouth and the drive up there offered fine views of Dartmoor off to the right, or rather it would have if low cloud hadn't been obscuring the tops. They reached the village early and parked in the car park on the green next to the cluster of local shops. If village life was supposed to be dying Yelverton must be the exception that proved the rule, thought Savage, since the place was buzzing. The Co-op and the delicatessen had a constant stream of people going in and out and there was a hairdressing salon, a pharmacy, a couple of estate agents and a garage as well. Calter seemed to read her mind.

'Too much money and time, ma'am.' Calter indicated the woman getting out of the royal blue Mercedes that had just pulled up next to them. The brand new car with white leather seats contrasted with the woman's grubby Barbour jacket and Hunter wellies. 'I bet she has a doctor husband who works at the hospital.'

'Lucky girl. Perhaps if you socialised somewhere other than Union Street you might get to meet one too.'

'Thanks, boss. I wondered where I was going wrong. You know it's my ambition to end up in Aga Saga country.'

'Really?'

'No!' Calter said, shaking her head and laughing. 'I couldn't stand living out here. All those people with bits of straw sticking out of their ears. Like Mr Isaacs, for instance.'

'I very much doubt if ninety-five per cent of the people in Yelverton know one end of a cow from another unless it's packaged up on the counter at Waitrose with a big label on top.'

'Wot, no Lidl? On my salary anything above a Scummerfields is a complete non-starter.'

Savage looked at the dashboard clock. Time to go.

'Come on,' she said, and they got out of the car and walked across to the row of houses where the Donals lived.

Greenbank Terrace stood well back from the main road, the tall three-storey Edwardian houses running down one side of an unmade-up track. The front gardens overlooked the trim village green, and several properties bore bed and breakfast signs having taken advantage of the prime location. Dartmoor View, the Donals' house, had a B&B sign outside too, only a board had been attached to the underneath which said 'No Vacancies'.

'A386 View would be a better name,' quipped Calter as they approached.

Savage started to remark that you might be able to see something from the top floor when the front door opened and Luke Farrell, the FLO, came out. Farrell had a boyish mop of straw-blond hair sitting above the type of face people called open and his welcoming smile never failed to lift the spirits. Hardin had labelled him a genius at family liaison because he somehow became the elder brother you never had or the caring grandson always ready to help out. His skill was providing the right amount of support without laying the sympathy on treacle-thick.

'Saw you coming, ma'am. I wanted a quick word before you went in.'

'What sort of state are they in, Luke?' As soon as Savage had asked the question she realised it was a stupid remark. Their daughter had been missing for three months and had now turned up dead. They weren't going to be overjoyed at meeting Savage and Calter, for sure.

'Mrs Donal – Cathy – has been hysterical, blames everything on Kelly's modelling. He's just brooding. Reactions typical of their gender. I have to warn you, though, Mr Donal is pretty disgusted with the police. He reckons if we had shown more interest when she first went missing then she might still be alive now.'

'He could be right.'

'With respect, ma'am, I wouldn't tell him that.'

'Don't worry, I won't.'

'I think the disgust with the police is a psychological projection. He's more disgusted with himself. Any anger he shows towards you is a coping strategy.'

'To cope with what, Kelly's death?' Savage asked.

'No, the guilt.'

'Guilt?'

'Yes. Beyond that which any parent might understandably feel. If Mr Donal hadn't encouraged Kelly in her modelling she might never had met Forester.'

'What? According to the DC who re-interviewed her flatmate, Kelly first met Forester at the Metropolis club in town. Are you saying Donal had something to do with this?' Savage turned to Calter. 'Why don't we know this already?'

'I'm not sure, ma'am.' Calter looked contrite and pulled out her notebook as if to double-check.

'Someone hasn't delved deep enough,' Farrell said. 'They did meet at the Metropolis but not at a club night. It was in the daytime. A camera club had hired the place for a meet and set it up as a mock pole-dancing venue. Kelly was one of the models.'

'What club was this?'

'Plymouth Snappers.' Farrell pointed at the rear of a Ford Galaxy parked in the road outside the house. A sticker in the rear window depicted a grinning cartoon shark holding a camera. 'Legit club, but they had a glamour section into some pretty risqué stuff.'

'And her parents approved of this?'

'Approved? Mr Donal suggested the shoot. He was at the club taking pictures.'

'Fuck!' It was Calter and she immediately put her hand to her mouth. 'Sorry, but he was her father. I wouldn't want my dad taking pictures of me half-naked with my boobs hanging out. And anyway I thought you said they didn't think much of what she was up to?'

'I said Mrs Donal didn't.' Farrell smiled as if he couldn't help but imagine Calter doing a bit of pole dancing. 'She didn't realise half of what was going on. She thought Kelly was only doing the usual kind of modelling. By which I mean with clothes on.'

'Thanks for the heads up, Luke,' Savage said. 'Good work and valuable information, it fits with what DS Riley found out at Forester's workplace. Turns out Forester had been

91

involved in producing at least one explicit video featuring Kelly Donal as the star turn. Shall we?' Savage indicated the door, and Farrell led the way over the threshold and into the neat hall with an imposing grandfather clock, polite little notices, a boot rack and a shelf of guidebooks.

Several photographs hung on the walls: an atmospheric shot of Dartmoor in the mist and rain, a stunning snowscape with a single set of footprints leading to the horizon, a beautiful beck with bluebells in the foreground. Each had neat little paper stickers in the bottom right corner with a price written on. The images weren't of Savage's favourite subject, but she imagined they would sell well to the guests.

Farrell led them down the hallway and stopped at a door which had a 'Private' sign on it. He knocked and entered. They went into a living room where Mr and Mrs Donal sat waiting. More photographs hung on the walls in here. Not landscapes though. Above the fireplace a huge print of a girl with big doe eyes stared into the room. She had sleek brown hair and the sort of figure many women would die for. And men might kill for. Savage averted her gaze and moved forward to greet the parents. Mrs Donal, a slight woman with brown hair like her daughter's but gone part grey, was slumped on a big white sofa and registered their presence with a mere glance. In happier times Savage guessed she would have been the perfect B&B hostess, busying herself with rustling up some tea and homemade biscuits. Mr Donal, on the other hand, did not behave like the perfect host as he sneered and leapt to his feet. He was late middle-aged, perhaps older, big and heavy-set and with a face like a round tomato, all red and glowing and ready to burst. He reminded Savage a little of Hardin.

'More police?' Donal said, not hiding his disgust and not offering his hand either.

'Detective Inspector Charlotte Savage. We just have a few more questions, Mr Donal.'

'A lifetime of questions. That's what I've got.'

'It's about Kelly.'

'Oh? I didn't think you'd come about Neighbourhood Watch, did I?'

'I'm sorry this is painful for you, Mr Donal, it is for all of us.'

'Painful? Painful! I have never really been hurt before. Not *really* hurt. Have you experienced the type of hurt I'm talking about, Inspector? The sort of pain that is nothing? Empty pain, agony at night when you put out the light and then worse when the sun streams in the windows the next morning.' Donal stood rocking on his heels.

Savage had known pain like that when Clarissa had died, but she didn't think telling Donal about it would do much good. Instead she started off with the usual stuff about how sorry the whole force was and offered their condolences and sympathies. The standard spiel sounded like crap and she found herself faltering halfway through. She felt Farrell's hand on her arm.

'They know all that, ma'am,' he whispered. 'They—'

'We just want you to catch the bastard who did this to our Kelly,' Mrs Donal blurted out, before the tears came and her head went down into her hands.

Farrell moved over and crouched by the chair and said something Savage didn't catch. He then stood and helped Mrs Donal to her feet and led her from the room.

'Sorry about that,' Mr Donal said. 'The wife has taken it bad. Kelly was our youngest, our little girl. Our other two children are older, flew the nest a while ago. Kelly was always the favourite, our little baby if you like, and well, the wife is . . . I mean, she's . . . well, I . . . she didn't much like—'

'She blames you, Mr Donal, is that what you are getting at?' Savage said, indicating the pictures on the walls. 'I am not surprised. I mean, Kelly was a beautiful girl, but there is more to her modelling career than this stuff, isn't there? The porn? Your daughter wrapped around that pole with a group of sad men baying for her to get her tits out. Can't say it is what I would want for my daughter, but each to their own, I suppose.'

'Boss,' Calter hissed. 'Shouldn't we wait for Luke—'

'That sort of thing doesn't leave much to the imagination does it?' Savage continued. 'And the trouble is for some of these men imagination is not enough. Jerking off to some image on their computer screens is OK for a bit, but in the end they always end up wanting what they can't have. Isn't that right, Mr Donal?'

'Ma'am!' Calter was louder now, urging Savage to stop. 'I really need to ask you to consider what—'

'Isn't that fucking right, Mr Donal? Does your wife know about the porn? Does she know about the videos? The stuff on the internet? What will she say if we ask her?'

'Of course she doesn't! For God's sake shut up, will you?' Mr Donal collapsed on the sofa, hands to his face.

Savage drew breath, aware of Calter staring at her open mouthed.

'Detective Constable? Was there something you wanted to say?'

'Er, no, ma'am.'

'Mr Donal.' Savage went over to the sofa and sat down beside him. Her voice quieter now she had said her piece. 'I don't like any of that stuff. I don't like seeing girls draped over cars. I don't like seeing female celebrities thinking that showing half their bodies off is necessary when all it does is show how thick they are. When I think of my own daughter,

I don't like the fact I can count female role models who deign not to get their kit off for some men's mag on the fingers of one hand. However, I never forget that whatever we, as girls and women, do, the men do the looking. And in the end the men commit the crimes. All of which means I'm going to try my hardest to get Kelly's killer. Whatever it takes.'

Mr Donal looked up, drew in a large breath and let it out, pursing his lips as if about to whistle, but instead making a long, tuneless hiss.

'It started so young,' he said, unburdening himself without prompting. 'Just family pictures, family snaps. But even years back we could see she was different. Then she was the carnival queen one year and a local photographer asked if she would pose for him. Of course I went along too, and that's how I began to get interested.'

'You took up photography?'

'I had dabbled before, but I bought a better camera and some studio equipment and joined the Plymouth Snappers. They saw my pictures of Kelly and wanted her for a shoot. For the first couple of years it was innocent enough stuff, fashion shots and the like. But she was growing up, filling out and soon some of the members were asking for more. Trouble was Kelly loved it, loved the attention, loved the fawning. When she was around fifteen there was a night where she was dressed in club gear, nothing outrageous, the sort of thing all young girls wear. Anyway, one member jokingly asked her to take off her top and she did. Just like that, bra and all. I should have stepped in and called a halt, but I didn't. As soon as she was sixteen she went topless legitimately and they couldn't get enough. We had glamour shoots with clubs visiting from all over the South West.'

Donal stopped and Savage heard the clock in the hall

tick-tocking, marking the silence. She struggled for what to say to a man who was happy to have other men leer at his daughter, but could think of nothing. After a moment Donal continued.

'I suppose you wonder at how I could stand it? Well, I can't explain. She was happy doing it and earning money. Plus it was tasteful at first, nothing you don't see in magazines or on the television. Trouble was they soon wanted more and Kelly wouldn't say no.'

'And you couldn't either?'

'If I had she'd have probably gone off and done it without me.' Donal looked across at the print of Kelly above the fireplace before turning back to Savage. 'Sixteen, Inspector. Legal to do almost anything. Another two years and she was lost to me whatever I did. I guess I wanted to cling on to something and by going along to those early shoots I knew she was safe and nothing untoward was taking place. At least that was how it was before she met Forester.'

'Which was at the Metropolis?'

'Yes. Back in the spring. An all-day shoot. Kelly was getting a couple of hundred quid net for it after we had paid a sum to the club management and something for equipment hire. The money worried me because Kelly was beginning to get used to it. She had already moved out and rented the place in Plymouth. She said it made it easier to get to college and to her work placement, but I thought she might drop her studies if too many rewards came her way. I think that was how Forester got to her.'

'Because you were not around?'

'Yes.' Donal's voice dropped to a whisper. 'And he promised her more money and other stuff too.'

'Drugs?'

'Yes.'

'For doing the videos?'

'Yes.'

'Which from what we have seen weren't quite so tasteful.'

'No.' Donal lowered his head and looked down at the floor and Savage let him brood for a moment.

'Was there anybody else she saw, apart from Forester?' she asked.

'What, you mean at the shoots?'

'No, I mean generally. Other men interested in her.'

'Oh, there were lots. If you are a woman who takes her clothes off for money you get interest. After a shoot my phone would ring red hot for the next few days. "Does Kelly do girl-on-girl, Mr Donal?"' Donal put on a weasel-like voice. '"Can she use her fingers for me, Mr Donal? For an extra couple of hundred?" They wanted to get as much flesh into their cameras as possible. You were right in what you said earlier, Inspector. It had got out of control, it had gone too far. Her innocence had gone.'

Donal glanced up at the big picture of Kelly and bit his lip. Savage wondered whether he thought it was all his fault the innocence had slipped away along with Kelly's clothing.

'What about other boyfriends?'

'I wish there had been, Inspector, but no, Forester would have killed them.'

'But he didn't seem to mind other men getting off on pictures or videos of her, did he?'

'Some men like that, owning something others can't have. Anyway, with Forester I reckon it was the money. Kelly was his way out. His way up.'

'He was hardly the next Mario Testino.'

'Forester wouldn't see it like that. You know how these estate kids are, they think they are the best at everything. Stupid, because he was an all round loser, a right scrote.

Poor Kelly got hooked on whatever crap he was peddling and look where she's ended up.'

At that point the living room door opened and Farrell came in with some cups on a tray.

'Mrs Donal has gone to have a lie down so I thought I would do the honours. Have I missed anything of importance?'

Calter opened her mouth as if she was about to say something, but Donal got there first.

'No, Luke, not really.' Donal was half-smiling now, but shaking his head at the same time. 'Only the sound of some birds flapping their wings.'

'Sorry?'

'Chickens. Coming home to roost.' The smile vanished from Donal's face and a tear rolled down the man's cheek.

Chapter Eleven

They drove back from Yelverton in silence. Calter stared out of the window, arms folded across her chest, and Savage just let her stew. The girl had to learn that real life situations differed from those encountered during training. Donal needed to be told. Maybe now the truth had been knocked home he might come to his senses and realise what he had done had, at least in part, led to Kelly's death. It wasn't going to be easy for him, but better to face up to the facts now than let them stew for the rest of his life.

Back in town Savage drove them through Beacon Park, where Kelly had lived, and then into the adjoining area of North Prospect. The place had a reputation for being rough and crime-ridden, filled with youths who liked nothing better of an evening than indulging their passion for a bit of anti-social behaviour. Thanks to the efforts of community workers and the police the reputation diminished a little every year. Nevertheless, the council had plans to transform the neighbourhood by demolishing half the properties and refurbishing the rest, despite the protestations of many of the residents. In Savage's eyes it didn't seem too bad; you would feel far more nervous walking through so-called good areas in London, and in the summer the place had an aura nearer to that of a leafy suburb than a location associated with high deprivation.

Appearances could be deceptive though, and in the mile or so distance from his parents' house in St Budeaux to his flat in North Prospect David Forester had moved down the social scale, hitting rock-bottom with a grotty place on the ground floor of half an old council semi. Cracks in the pebbledash, metal window frames crusty with corrosion and a pile of junk in the minuscule front garden didn't make it inviting, and inside was worse. Officers were trooping in and out with plastic boxes filled with what looked to Savage like rubbish.

'Evidence,' a member of the search team assured her. 'Mind you, the place is a complete tip. Cigarette butts ground into the floor, empty cans of coke, Stella, half-eaten Indians, McDonald's, pizza, you name it. And the whole thing nicely festering since it has all been sitting for a few months.'

'Lovely.'

'There's worse. Dog shit everywhere as well and a thousand flies swarming around. We couldn't figure out where they were coming from until the neighbour told us about Forester's dog.'

'Oh no.'

'Oh yes! A Staffy, as if you couldn't have guessed. We found the corpse in the spare room under the bed. It was mostly maggots. A neighbour said she heard barking but was too scared of Forester to do much.'

'Couldn't have happened to a nicer breed of dog,' Savage said.

'My gran kept Staffies,' Calter said. 'Me and my brother played with them when we were kids.'

'Well, if they get anywhere near my kids I kick first and ask questions later.'

Calter shut up and went even deeper into her sulk while Savage asked the team leader if they had found anything linking Forester to Kelly. He stood at the edge of the garden and sparked up a fag, leaning over the wall to ensure any ash dropped outside his search cordon.

'He's got a couple of computer screens and a keyboard in his bedroom, but no computer. There must be a base unit or laptop somewhere, but we haven't found it yet.'

'Anything else of interest?' Savage asked.

'A hundred grams of smack and some small bottles of liquid that could be GHB.'

'Really? Confirms he was a serious dealer then.'

'Looks that way. We also found his mobile phone and there are a hell of a lot of contacts. We'll download the address book and call logs and let you have them. Last call was made on the seventh of August.'

'A couple of days after Kelly was last seen.'

'Yup. And we found a *Mirror* dated the eighth on the kitchen table.'

'So they didn't disappear together then, we now know that at least. Let's see if his parents can shed any light on where he might be.'

Alice Nash came round in pitch black, a cloying darkness smelling of damp, mould and mildew. Her head hurt like crazy and she felt groggy.

That would be the alcohol then, idiot.

She remembered having drunk too much, *way* too much. After work? With a friend? The memory flickered somewhere in her mind but she couldn't quite grasp it. She reached out for the bedside clock to try and find out the time and her hand fumbled in the air. Nothing. No bedside table either, and as she groped farther – *ouch* – a wall. Now she realised she was lying on the floor. In her bedroom?

No, my room has a nice soft carpet with a couple of big sheepskins.

She felt the hard, wooden surface beneath her body, an uneven floorboard digging into her back. She shivered and hugged herself, touching the goose bumps on her arms and realising at the same time she was naked.

Naked!

An uncontrollable spasm shook through her whole body and she began to retch. Almost without thinking she put her hand down between her legs, but no, she wasn't sore there or anything, so she hadn't been raped.

She sat up and turned and saw a thin, horizontal glare of light at floor level. She blinked. The light came from a gap under a door perhaps two metres away and gave her some perspective. The slit cast a weak ray that fanned out across the floor and illuminated a space no bigger than a box room. The walls appeared to be rough plastered. An old house perhaps? That would explain the damp. But when she breathed in she detected a pungent aroma as well, a smell of something rotten. Next to her a mattress lay on the floor with no bed frame or anything.

Was I on that? Did I roll off in my sleep?

She eased herself across the floor and onto the mattress. Now she could see something on the mattress, a bulky, form-less shape. She put out a hand and discovered a duvet. She pulled it nearer and gathered the soft material around her, grateful for the warmth and the privacy.

Privacy from what? From whom?

She let out a little cry, involuntary; her instincts told her she should scream, scream at the top of her voice until someone heard, but she didn't.

He would have thought of that.

He? It must be a 'he' mustn't it? They always were. Apart from Rose West or the Myra woman who'd died in prison from cancer because they didn't ever let anyone like her out.

She wished she hadn't thought of that. Not just of those women, although the image of them was bad enough. It was also the thought of prison, being trapped in a small room and dying without ever knowing freedom again.

Hang on, who said you were in prison, stupid?

She shook herself and laughed at her wild imagination. Maybe she had crashed out at some party or dossed down in some student's room. She moved off the mattress and stood up, wrapping the duvet around herself like an over-sized toga. She walked over to the door and reached for the handle. The cold metal made a slight squeak as she pushed it down and tried to pull the door towards her.

It was locked.

They drove from North Prospect to the top end of St Budeaux, the nicer part, which wasn't saying much. However, on Waverley Road neat little bungalows and semis jostled for position and some care and attention had been paid to the properties by their owners. The line of mid-range cars – some new – parked on the road testified to the fact that the area had aspirations. Still on-street though, Savage noted. Only once you parked your car on your own land could you finally say you had arrived in true middle-class suburban heaven.

Number sixty-two had a tiny pond in the front garden and a black and white porcelain cat dipped a paw in the water, intent on catching one of the goldfish swimming under the dying lily pads. The house backed onto some woodland, almost a rural idyll, Savage thought. But not quite. When she and Calter got out of the car the roar of the traffic became all too apparent. The A38 lay the other side of the trees and the noise of the cars rushing down the hill towards the Tamar Bridge crossing into Cornwall was quite intolerable.

The bright red front door reeked of fresh paint and was opened by Mrs Forester, an overweight woman in her seventies. She held on to the door for support with one hand and with the other tried to button her mauve cardigan against the chill. The cardigan was loose-knit and the sleeves looked like they had expanded over the years to accommodate her pudgy arms and body to the extent that the garment now resembled a purple fishing net. She gave up fumbling with the buttons and accepted the need for further questioning with a weary nod of her head. Savage got the impression the woman had dealt with the police many times before.

She led them through into the lounge, a simple, neat little room, probably unchanged for decades. Apart from the huge flat screen TV standing half in front of the fireplace. Older houses hadn't been designed with such monstrosities in mind and it looked ridiculous.

'Present from David,' Mrs Forester said, noting Savage's interest. 'He was always good to me when he was around.' She nodded at the sole picture on the mantelpiece. A teenage boy in football kit, one foot on a ball, hands on hips. Defiant.

'Is that him?' Savage asked.

'Yes. Years ago.' The old lady smiled. Then her face turned sour. 'Before you lot started hassling him.'

Savage ignored the dig and began to ask about David's childhood. It soon became evident Mrs Forester was not

David's mother after all, rather she was his grandmother. Savage asked her how she had come to care for David.

'Clary, my daughter, had David when she was fifteen and still at home. By seventeen she had got bored with the baby and buggered off. We got the occasional letter for the first few years, then nothing. Don't even know where she is now.'

'So you had to bring up David all on your own?'

'Well, with my husband Vic, but he wasn't much help. He hit David hard enough but he never changed a nappy, never fed him, never read a bedtime book.'

Mrs Forester stared out of the bay window with a blank expression Savage had seen countless times before. The empty eyes almost always belonged to a woman, and Savage could usually sense regret and resignation in them. Regret at who the woman had married, resignation to their fate and the fact that Prince Charming was not about to rescue them.

'And David? Bringing him up must have been difficult.'

'Difficult! What would you lot know about difficult? Does your husband come home drunk and slap you around? Do the kids round you shoot cats with airguns? Do your neighbours fight on the street outside?'

'Mrs Forester, we are not here to judge you, we just want to find David.'

The old lady ignored Savage and carried on.

'Initiatives and targets then back to your nice house with a driveway and a bloody people carrier, I'll bet. Good school round the corner where the teachers can teach rather than spend their time searching the kids for knives or drugs.'

'We are police officers, Mrs Forester, we are not social workers or politicians. We are trying to find out what happened to David and Kelly.'

'Kelly? Oh, it's about her is it? I seen on the news she was dead. No one cared before, no one bothered about what had happened to my David.' The woman's eyes filled with tears and her head went down, a hand scrabbling in her sleeve for a handkerchief.

Savage made a gesture to Calter and the younger officer moved to comfort the old woman. Savage left the room and went back to the kitchen to see about rustling up a pot of tea. The kitchen was a surprise after the staid lounge: modern, everything clean and tidy. Through the window to the back Savage saw a pretty garden. You'd have to be deaf to enjoy sitting out on the patio, but the plants appeared well-tended and a lot of work had gone into laying out the lawn and the neat flowerbeds. Mrs Forester must be proud of it. Savage wondered if she could say the same about her grandson.

When Savage returned with the tea Mrs Forester had composed herself. She had suggested to Calter that they might like to see David's room.

'Room?' Savage asked. 'I thought he had a flat in North Prospect?'

'He does. But he only moved out three years ago and I've kept his room for him. He likes to crash here sometimes and he's still got his photo stuff up there so he's round a couple of times a week. Or rather, he used to be.'

'If you don't mind, Mrs Forester, it might be useful.'

'Not at all.' The old lady's face brightened for a moment. 'First on the left at the top of the stairs.'

Savage and Calter climbed the stairs and heard Mrs Forester call out after them. 'The pictures on the wall are all his own work. He's quite good with a camera. He was with a club you know?'

'Which club, Mrs Forester?' Savage called down.

'A photography club. I can't remember the name, but

it's in Plymouth. He used to go there before he got interested in video. After that he preferred to make movies.'

Calter mouthed a silent, 'Did he now?' to Savage as they entered the bedroom.

The single bed had a faded Chelsea duvet on it and football stickers covered the flat-pack off-white wardrobe and chest of drawers. Over to one side of a window that overlooked the back garden was a desk on which sat three flat screen monitors. A jumble of leads snaked down from the monitors to a computer base unit tucked away underneath. Calter moved to the desk and reached down to switch the unit on.

'Result, ma'am. You don't have three big screens connected to one machine just to waste your life on Facebook.'

Savage let Calter get on with searching the computer and scanned the pictures on the walls of the room. Poster-sized black and white prints of women, naked or partially clothed, dark shadows, pale skin, almost abstract and not in any way pornographic. They weren't even in that category called tasteful, which was merely an excuse for sad wankers to display them without appearing sexist. These were innocent, naturalistic and the women were not looking at the camera. They wouldn't have been out of place at a local gallery, except Plymouth didn't do such things very well. Take them up to Salcombe or Dartmouth though and the grockles swarming round the streets in the summer would snatch them up.

Mrs Forester was right, her grandson had talent. But that didn't square with what the manager of Tamar Yacht Fitters had told DS Riley. Savage looked at the pictures again. They were a world away from a sordid video of a girl shoving a beer bottle up between her legs.

'Password protected, ma'am.' Calter interrupted Savage's thoughts. 'I've tried the usual tricks but I can't get in. Have to take it to the lads in hi-tech crimes.'

'Right.' Savage was browsing through some CDs on a tall rack. Nirvana, Stone Roses, Radiohead, REM. Pretty standard fare for a kid who was a teenager a dozen or more years ago.

'What kind of twenty-something year old has a Chelsea duvet spread?' Calter asked. 'And all those stickers? They are the kind of thing an adolescent would have, not a young man.'

'You're a profiler now, are you? Chelsea bedspread equals criminal behaviour?'

'No, ma'am,' Calter giggled. 'A bit odd though.'

'I agree.'

Maybe David Forester hadn't grown much beyond a teen until something had changed him. Savage looked at some of the football stickers again. Stuck on the wardrobe was an entire set of the 2006 Premiership winning team. From the smiling faces of Lampard, Cole and Drogba to hardcore pornography, drug dealing and violence. In just a few short years.

Chapter Twelve

Derriford Hospital, Plymouth. Wednesday 27th October.
4.45 pm

The post-mortem on Kelly Donal had been scheduled for twelve thirty and DS Riley had been booked to attend. Savage said she would be along later. If being late had been her intention, missing the whole affair had not. Now that seemed possible because they got stuck nose to tail on the A38 not long after they left St Budeaux.

On the dual carriageway heading east cars sat nose to tail and according to their police radio the cause was a major RTC up ahead. Half a dozen ambulances and two fire engines blocked the road creating traffic chaos and leaving a good proportion of Plymouth in total gridlock. At one point even the air ambulance buzzed overhead to land somewhere out of sight, its distinctive blue and red livery striking against the tomb grey sky.

After thirty minutes Calter got bored and said she would walk out of the queue and back to the station. Savage could do nothing but wait, and after another hour the traffic dissolved away and she drove the remaining couple of miles to Derriford Hospital. She struggled to find a space for the car despite the acres of parking that surrounded the ugly, brutal looking complex. Notwithstanding the hospital's primary purpose, it was no place to be born, be ill or to die. For post-mortems the ambience could not have been better.

Doctor Andrew Nesbit was perfect for PMs too. His straightforward and methodical manner gave him a detachment that at times like these Savage envied. She didn't think anybody enjoyed eviscerating the dead, but if anyone did it was Nesbit. Savage put her gown and mask on in the ante-room and went into the lab proper where the pathologist hunkered over a stainless steel gurney, his long arms working the corpse like a mantis playing with a fly.

'Ah, Charlotte, your DS left a while ago but you are welcome to stay for this one if you like.' Nesbit looked up from the cadaver he was working on, an old man with severe facial injuries, body gone a sort of yellowish-white, the veins and bones visible through the translucent skin.

'Did this man fall into the gutter in a drunken stupor or did he get waylaid and set about by a group of bored youths? Twenty years ago I'd have said the former, these days the latter explanation seems more likely. What do you think?'

'You tell me, Doc, I thought that was your job.' Savage moved closer to the dead man. Seventy or so and looking like age would have caught up with him sometime soon anyway had the tarmac not intervened first.

'Not a pleasant way to die.' Nesbit bent down again and using a pair of tweezers extracted a piece of grit from the man's discoloured cheek. 'Lying in the roadway having a cerebral haemorrhage while the good folk of Plymouth go about their business unaware you are anything other than another homeless statistic sleeping off a drunken binge. Whether an accident or foul play, either way his death was not a glorious ending.'

'I don't suppose such a thing exists for any of your patients.'

'Or for any of us. There are good ways and bad ways but only one exit.'

'If you added a line about "many paths to the Lord's feet" you'd be a passable preacher.'

'As you know, Charlotte, I'm of an entirely scientific bent. As far as I am aware the only journey this man can make is one involving the breakdown of his biological components into their constituent molecules. Of souls I know nothing.'

That was Nesbit through and through. He had once joked to Savage that the inscription on his gravestone would be 'Observation, Hypothesis, Prediction, Experiment, Results, Conclusion'. He dealt with cold bodies and cold facts with no place for emotion. Savage thought Nesbit's approach admirable because it prevented the niggling little thoughts from burgeoning into nightmares. It washed away the doubt, the fear and the uncertainty from death in the same way his assistants would hose the blood from the dissection table after an autopsy. Only sterile, gleaming, stainless steel remained, a shining truth developed from scientific reasoning rather than from a figure on the cross. It left no room for tears and perhaps that was the point. Savage didn't care much for religion either, but she knew such detachment wouldn't work for her and already the emotion was rising within.

'You've got some results on the girl?'

Nesbit sighed, paused, and with a theatrical flourish worthy of an RSC veteran he turned and dropped the piece of grit into a stainless steel kidney dish on a side bench. The bowl rang out a clear note that sounded quite haunting. Nesbit let the note ring for a second or so and touched the bowl to bring an end to the unknown man's elegy. He put the tweezers down with a further flourish and turned to Savage.

'Well?' she asked.

'Now, I found no sign of trauma causing death, externally or internally. You might be surprised to hear that, given the cut on the stomach we noticed at the scene, of which more later. I also discovered something quite fascinating, intriguing possibly.' Nesbit moved over to another body, this one covered with a green cloth.

Savage went over to join him, hoping he wouldn't need to lift the sheet, although she knew he would do so anyway.

'Now, let's see.' Nesbit pulled back the cloth and revealed the girl's naked body. He picked up a clipboard and read aloud. 'Kelly Donal, eighteen. Height one hundred and—'

Savage winced, not at the doctor's words, rather at the sight of the body. Kelly didn't look so beautiful now, not with the rough, Y-shaped scar running along her shoulders, down her chest and across her stomach. Nesbit's assistant had sewn her up well enough, but the work wasn't going to win any needlepoint prizes.

'—point three kilograms. All in all a healthy young woman with no abnormalities and no worries.' Nesbit cleared his throat. 'Apart from being dead, of course.'

'Time of death?'

'Patience, Charlotte, patience.' Nesbit scanned his clipboard again. 'First, the cut we noted on the abdomen. Remember?'

'I think you said the wound hadn't bled.'

'Yes. No blood because the incision happened post-mortem.'

'You sure?'

'Of course. The wound would have bled profusely had she been alive at the time. Even if the blood had been cleaned up externally, internally there would have been significant haemorrhaging.'

'Your guess at the weapon?'

'I deal in evidence not conjecture, as you well know, Charlotte.' Nesbit bent his head and peered over the top of his glasses at Savage; a scolding glance, but a smile forming too. 'However, I noted a small exit wound on the girl's lower back meaning the instrument was pushed all the way through the girl's body. Thus the evidence points to a thin, sharp blade approximately twenty centimetres long.'

'Kitchen knife?'

'Quite possibly, but I wouldn't call the knife a weapon since the cut was made after she died.' Nesbit flipped a page over on his clipboard and adjusted his glasses. 'Now, you asked about the time of death?'

'Yes.'

'Well, remember the core body temperature readings I took at the scene were not much use? The body was colder than the ambient air.'

'Yes, I think we thought she might have been outside in the frosty weather.'

'Right. Well I found some blowfly larvae up in the nasal cavity. I am no expert in the area, but I believe they are at the stage of development called first instars.'

'I'm guessing from my limited knowledge she hadn't been dead long then.'

'I don't know. The maggots themselves are dead.'

'You've lost me, Andrew.' Savage was struggling to understand. 'The *maggots* are dead?'

'Yes, correct. It's possible the frost killed them, but I don't think so. We will need to get some accurate weather data and I will contact a forensic entomologist to determine if my theory is possible.'

'What theory?' Savage was becoming exasperated and she wondered for a moment if Nesbit might be playing a game with her.

'My hypothesis is Kelly Donal was frozen.'

'*What?*' Savage stared at Nesbit. 'By the frosty nights?'

'No, no. Not cold enough to kill the larvae. She was *deep* frozen. That would explain why they are dead and also the reason for the odd, puffy consistency and appearance to the skin, as well as the low core temperature I observed.'

'Deep frozen? Like a pack of oven chips?'

'Wouldn't touch them myself, but yes.'

'So we can't know when she was killed?'

Nesbit seemed to ignore her and instead walked over to the lab bench at the side of the room. He pointed to a large glass jar and Savage tried to suppress a heave in her stomach at the sight of the grey lump within.

'Kelly Donal's brain,' Nesbit said. 'Before I return the brain to the skull cavity I'll take some sections for analysis. I believe the cell structure will have been altered by the freezing process although I don't think a method exists to tell us how long the body has been frozen. However, I have a couple of ideas that need a bit of work. I'll get back to you on them.'

Nesbit returned to the body and bent forward and sniffed the torso, gesturing at Savage to do the same.

'I found no other outward signs of insect infestation because the body has been washed at some point, you can smell the soap. Remember I said at the scene that the skin appeared a little puffy and there was a slight fragrance?'

Savage moved to the body and bent over. The girl's left breast was a few inches away from her face and for a moment Savage found herself looking at the body through the killer's eyes. Those curves, the flat, toned stomach leading to an enticing triangle of pubic hair, the smooth thighs and shapely calves. What man would pass up the opportunity to be close to such perfection? To kiss the body all over, to caress the skin, to wonder at the beauty and finally to penetrate it, afterwards holding the flesh close in the exhaustion of post-orgasmic bliss.

'Charlotte?'

Savage snapped back into the awkwardness of reality, aware of Nesbit's stare.

'Yes, I think you are right. Soap.'

'Now then, toxicology. I've dispatched some blood and hair to the lab to ascertain if there is any evidence of drugs or poisoning. There are some needle marks on her right and left arms, so she was a user, but my initial judgement is we won't find anything in that arena responsible for her death. I believe she died of hypothermia.'

'Exposure?'

'Not in the sense of being outside. The freezing I talked about a moment ago? That was what killed her.'

'She was *frozen* to death?'

'I can't say the manner of her death will bring any comfort to the family, but there are worse ways to go.'

'But deep frozen . . .'

'Yes, she would have been shut in a freezer. Alive. If you remember at the scene I showed you the lividity in the buttocks and thighs and concluded she had been in a sitting position.'

'Oh God.' Savage sometimes got claustrophobic in an aeroplane or if she was wedged under her sports car fixing something, but being shut in a small box and left to die was a horror of a different order of magnitude.

'I am not finished yet, I'm afraid.'

She had hoped they were nearing the end, but Nesbit looked so pleased with himself she didn't voice her feelings.

'A few more interesting points. The last of which I don't think you are going to like.'

'Go on.'

'First, I found a few black hairs, obviously not from the girl. They've gone for analysis. Second, the stomach and intestine contents are of interest. The girl liked fruit.'

'Sorry?'

'Here.' Nesbit went to the bench again. Next to the jar containing Kelly's brain was a smaller container. 'Apples, pears, bananas, apricots, grapes. The girl ate nothing else for at least a couple of days before her death.'

'What are you saying?'

'I'm not saying anything, Charlotte. Merely pointing out the facts.'

'Anything else?'

'Ah, yes,' Nesbit paused and sighed. 'This is the bit I don't think that you are going to like.'

'Go on.'

'Now look at this.' Nesbit took a fresh pair of forceps and pointed down between the girl's thighs. He teased her pubic hairs apart. 'There!'

'Where?'

'Labia majora. Can you spot the marks?' He pointed with his forceps and now Savage could see some little pinpricks in the skin, a row on each side.

'She was sewn up. Rather crudely I should say. I took some photos before I removed the thread and you will note the stitches are all different sizes, not a skilful job at all.'

'Jesus,' Savage muttered under her breath. 'That's pretty sick.'

'Disturbing, certainly. As to whether the person who did this is sick, well, psychology is not my field of expertise.'

'It's not mine either, but let's agree it is not something you or I would consider doing.'

'No, probably not.' Nesbit smiled before continuing. 'There is also evidence of sexual activity, lubricant, and a large quantity of semen.'

'More than one man?'

'We will know after the lab have done their bit. She had intercourse multiple times though.'

'Did the sex happen while she was alive or after she was dead?'

'I can't tell, although she was sewn up after she was dead.'

'Well, I'm not surprised, I mean, we—'

'Oh, there's more I am afraid, Charlotte.' Nesbit went over to a lab bench and picked up a polygrip bag. 'I discovered this rolled up and inserted vaginally into the girl, after she was unconscious I would say. It was pushed up deep in the canal, possibly by the man's penis.'

Savage moved closer to see what he had in his hand and Nesbit gave her the bag. It contained a piece of curled-up paper. The outside was plain white and on the inside was a picture, but the ink had run forming a whirl of colour similar to a toddler's drawing.

'Yes, I couldn't tell what it was at first either. Gently flatten the paper and you'll understand.'

Savage did so and a chill spread from her stomach, seeping up through her chest and then running down her arms to her fingertips. Although the ink had discoloured the paper she could now make out an image. Her fingers began to tingle and a dizzy sensation washed over her.

'Jesus Christ! It's—'

'Yes, it is.' Nesbit spoke with a soft tone and took the bag from her shaking hand. 'I've already had a few copies made so you can take one with you when you go.'

Nesbit's voice disappeared behind a rumble and her ears filled with a noise like the sound the winter storm waves made when they crashed onto the beach below her house and turned the pebbles over and over on themselves. It was a roaring, hissing, grinding sound of pure power, of chaotic elemental forces trying to tear at the foundations of the earth and destroy the fragile fabric of life. Not a one-off assault that would destroy it in a day, but an ongoing war of attrition persisting over years and decades and centuries. Slowly, but oh-so-surely it succeeded. Every person who ever breathed turned into someone else's memories, those memories into footnotes in a history book, the book itself into a crumbling artefact whose own decay told the whole story of human existence.

'Charlotte?' Nesbit handed her the autopsy papers and put a comforting hand on her shoulder. 'I know this doesn't seem to make any sense right now, but you'll get him, I'm sure you will.'

Savage nodded an acceptance to Nesbit, muttered some words of thanks and turned and walked out of the lab, up the stairs and through the maze of corridors. She wandered, lost in her thoughts, everything else a blur: figures in long, white coats, nurses in blue uniforms, patients grey with despair, colour in a black and white world. Birth and illness and death. The story started here and for most the end came here too. For some, like Kelly, it ended on a slab of cold stainless steel with your organs in a jar, bodily fluids flushed down the drain and your name in a headline in a newspaper.

And then Savage thought of Clarissa, her daughter. A picnic on Dartmoor by a roadside stream and the twins playing on their bikes. The sound of a car coming fast, the *ding-ding* of the little bell on Clarissa's bike and the nauseating crunch of the smash. Hit and run. Ambulance. Hospital. Her daughter's blank face white, framed with the vivid, contrasting red of her hair, Savage's hair. And Savage noticing Clarissa's eyes, lids taped shut. In some odd way that had hurt the most, realising Clarissa would never see her again, never have the comfort of knowing her mother was at her bedside. But the doctors said even if her eyes had been open she wouldn't have recognised anyone. She was gone, only the machines keeping her alive. Then it was decision time. The most difficult of Savage's life. Once made, electrodes had been detached, tubes pulled out, a last rasp of air escaping from Clarissa's lungs. The words from the nurse as delicate as an angel's whisper.

'We can leave you alone with her for a bit if you like?'

'Yes, of course. Thank you.'

She sat with Pete for an hour and then Savage had walked out of the hospital with the same roaring in her ears, the same numbness spreading through her. But no headlines for her daughter, mercifully. Just a news story on page seven of the local paper and a crowd of people standing in the rain on a cold and damp morning. A priest reciting empty words over an empty hole in the ground, soon to be filled with earth and mud and nine years of memories.

The corridor blurred and she swallowed hard, staggering to a wall for support. She knew emotion got the better of her sometimes, but this was feeble. She guessed the shock of seeing the picture had triggered something inside her, something to do with loss. Not only the loss of her daughter, but of her husband as well. He was several thousand miles away if you measured the distance between them on a map, but if you measured it in relationship terms then the units became light years. He had never been the same since Clarissa's death. None of them had, of course, but he was the one who had been able to escape. If only she could do likewise.

She found an exit and left the hospital buildings to walk the grounds, hoping the air would clear her head. People moved out of her way to let her pass, thinking that she was drunk or mad or both. Finding an empty bench in a quiet spot she sat down.

The roaring in her ears subsided and her heartbeat slowed. Gulping in lungfuls of air calmed her and focused her mind. The panic she had felt stopped and reality began to return. After a while she decided she might as well get it over with. She searched among the sheets of paper Nesbit had given her and found the picture from inside Kelly Donal. The picture linked the rapes and the Kelly killing and for a moment had made the whole case seem insurmountable. Life was like that sometimes, but you dealt with it the best you could and moved on. Savage looked down at the photograph. The face of a pretty girl smiled out from the copy of the stained and faded print. A dusky, cute looking Spanish girl: Rosina Salgado Olivárez.

Chapter Thirteen

Harry remembered the first time he had met the Spanish girl who looked like Carmel. He'd blinked and shaken his head, not quite believing his eyes. The girl sat on the floor of the day nursery, bouncing a baby on her knee. Her dark hair tumbled over her shoulders, and when she raised her head and smiled at Harry he'd had to turn away and chew his tongue. The likeness was uncanny. She looked just like Carmel. After he had finished his work he rushed home to scrabble in the shoebox of photos he kept in the back of a cupboard and had found the faded picture of her along with the other girls. It *was* her. Thirty years on she had come back for him and she hadn't changed one bit, hadn't decayed at all. This time he swore there would be a happy ending. This time she would stay and love him. He was sure of it.

Next time Harry saw Mitchell he told him about Carmel. How he wanted to love her. To marry her. He showed him a photograph. Mitchell grabbed the picture and laughed. Said she looked tight. Said she looked like a good fuck. Said he could help Harry with a girl like that. Harry knew then Mitchell didn't understand. Not about love. Mitchell only understood about power and destroying people. Harry wished he hadn't opened his mouth.

A few weeks later he had seen Carmel again. It had been

nine months ago, just after Christmas, when Harry had gone to Mitchell's festive get-together. She had been tied to Mitchell's big bed. Harry walked into the room and she was lying there spread-eagled with ropes binding her legs and arms. Mitchell was checking the leather gag and blindfold and RT was setting up some lines of coke on the dressing table.

'Nice, isn't she?' Mitchell said. 'Just like you told me. Happy Christmas, Harry!'

'Oh God,' Harry mumbled. He put his tongue in the corner of his mouth and chewed. Carmel. Carmel!

'She's a kitten,' RT said. 'Took a while to find her but I finally managed to pick her up at Flamingos. Lots of pretty pink in there, hah, hah!'

RT was a little shit, Harry thought. One of the people with the big words. Too clever. But then RT was the guy who got the girls and took the risks. He'd offer to buy a girl a drink and then drop a couple of tabs in on the way back from the bar. The girls were usually too drunk to notice. By the time they had finished the freebie they were too wired to care.

Harry didn't know what to do next. Couldn't figure it. He tried not to look at Carmel twisting and pulling against the restraints. She didn't seem to like it much, but they never did. Harry had learnt that by now. And he had learnt not to care as well. Tonight though he did care. Carmel should have been for him alone. Now she was going to be soiled. Used goods. He wasn't sure he could live with that.

'Get the video, Harry. You won't want to miss this.' Mitchell was naked now, moving onto the bed and beginning to use his fingers on the girl. Mitchell's expensive, broadcast quality video camera sat on a tripod to the left of the bed. Usually Harry shot the material and got to join in later, but now he just stood unmoving, and stared at Mitchell as he defiled the girl.

RT began to strip too and kicked his clothes into the corner of the room, eager to get started.

'Not joining us, Harry?' RT said. '*Campanu* not for you?'

He didn't know what RT was talking about, but he didn't want to shoot the video, didn't want to fuck the girl. Not Carmel. Not here. Carmel had cared for him like the others had. She didn't deserve this.

'I feel ill,' Harry said. 'Sorry.'

Harry did feel ill now. Sick. Too many cocktails earlier on. What a stupid word. The walls of the room began to move and RT's face became all teeth.

'For God's sake, Harry, what has got into you? If you don't want to do the videos anymore we can find someone else.'

'Richard's right.' Mitchell, from the bed, angry. 'If you are not interested then you might as well just fuck off out of here. Understand?'

An unstoppable spasm gagged in the back of Harry's throat. He was going to vomit. He rushed out of the room and down the corridor to the bathroom. First the contents of his stomach into the toilet bowl and then painful empty retching followed by bile and mucus. He was on his knees now with his face resting on the white rim, on his knees like a sinner on the edge of hell.

He clutched the toilet for support, only half-aware of the sticky residue of vomit on his hands and face. As he knelt he could hear the voices from down the corridor. Mitchell and RT. Raping Carmel.

Chapter Fourteen

Riley and Enders were trying to get to grips with North Prospect's particular brand of children. Savage had designated their next action should be to try and find out what Forester had been up to before he disappeared, and according to a report filed by one of the area's Police Community Support Officers he had often hung around one particular playground. One of the kids at the regular football nights they held had mentioned Forester, and Savage had suggested they should get over to North Prospect and see what they could find out. The PCSO said there were always a lot of kids hanging around and had figured some of them might know something.

'I think you two will have more street cred with them. I'm old enough to be their mother,' Savage said.

'Grandmother in some cases, ma'am,' Riley said.

'I'll take that as a comment on social deprivation and teenage pregnancy rates rather than anything to do with my age or appearance shall I?'

'Of course, ma'am,' Riley smiled.

They pulled into Grassendale Avenue and parked next to a small park. Out of the car and Riley was thinking that although the day felt colder, at least the rain had stopped.

'Sleet and snow,' Enders said, looking up at the sky. 'According to the guys in Wet Orifice. Rain off the Atlantic meeting cold air from the north. If the idiots are correct.'

The headquarters of the Met Office was only a few miles away in Exeter, but the scientists seemed incapable of predicting the weather for Devon and Cornwall. Riley still hadn't got used to the local practice of ignoring the forecast and as a result he'd spent many an uncomfortable day wet, cold or sweaty.

The park was bordered with large boulders, presumably intended to stop joyriders or boy-racers from wheel-spinning their way across the turf, and had a fenced-off playground for the tots, a basketball court and a larger, grassy area where four older boys in football gear were having a kick around, a coke can and a foam burger container acting as goalposts. Only one wore the dark green shirt of the Pilgrims – the local team – the other three's loyalties were divided between the deep blue of Chelsea, the claret and sky blue of West Ham and the vertical red and blue stripes of Barcelona. None appeared to be aged above nine or ten. The two detectives strolled across the muddy grass to the boys who were trying their best to stay upright as they skidded around chasing a toddler's Thomas the Tank Engine football.

'Shouldn't you lot be in school?' Riley said.

'What do you care?' The blond-haired lad in the Chelsea strip answered.

'They're the pigs and they're going to bang us up.'

'Nah, they're paedos. My mum said I had to look out 'cos they are always sniffing around.'

'They're paedo pigs, that's what they is.'

Riley and Enders stood still and the boys danced around them laughing, full of spirit and life, without a care in the whole of their limited world.

'What's your name?' Riley asked the blond-haired boy.

'Ewan,' the boy replied. 'What's yours?'

'He's a ninky nonk,' one of the others shouted out. 'I know that's what they're called 'cos my nanna told me.'

'He's not a fucking ninky nonk, Kyle, you daft cunt,' Ewan said. 'Ninky nonks are like those people in the takeaway.'

'He is too! Hey can you sell me some crack you black mothafucka?'

The other boys burst into fits of laughter and began jumping around, giving each other high-fives and mimicking a troop of bad-ass rappers. Riley took the opportunity to step forward and kick the ball, lifting it with his foot and performing a clever little flick up to Enders. Enders used his head and a knee, before dropping the ball to the ground and hoofing it high into the air for Riley to chase. Riley raced along, outpacing the kids screaming behind him. The ball bounced a couple of times and he trapped it with his foot. He stood with his hands on his hips challenging the boys to get closer.

'OK, who wants to take on Pele?'

'Who's Pele?' Ewan said.

'He was nearly as good as Ashley Cole only he wasn't a bum boy,' Kyle said.

'Ashley Cole isn't a bum boy.'

'Yes he is!'

'No he isn't.'

'Is too!'

'Isn't.' Ewan turned to Riley for some sort of adult input to settle the dispute.

'You like Chelsea, Ewan?' Riley said, pointing at the kid's shirt.

'Yeah, sort of. Better than Man U Wankered anyway.'

'Chelsea are my team too. Think they can win the league this year?'

'Dunno. Yeah. If Torres can do the business.'

'Hey, isn't there a guy who is a real Chelsea nut round here?' Riley nodded his head in the direction of North Prospect Road. 'Wears his shirt all year? Bit of a lad?'

Ewan hesitated and the boy's eyes wandered away from Riley towards the estate. Conflicting loyalties, Riley thought, and wondered if he had pushed his luck. He tried again.

'Only some of the lads at the station are thinking of organising a minibus up to the Bridge one Saturday and we've got a few spaces free. Fancy coming along?'

'Oh, you mean rabid David?' The name was pronounced so the couplet rhymed.

'That's him. Did he ever have a kick around? Like we have.'

'No. He was scary. Once he nicked our ball and booted it right out there.' The lad pointed to the Wolsey Road, a dual carriageway on the other side of the playground. 'He was a bloody nutter. Lewis almost went under a fucking bus trying to get the thing back.'

They were interrupted by a shout and Riley looked over to where a woman was getting out of a little red Toyota parked behind their car.

'Hey, can I help you?' The woman began jogging over towards them.

'DS Riley, miss,' Riley said, producing his warrant card.

'Oh, sorry.' The woman flicked a lock of dark hair away from her face and smiled. She was late twenties and wore faded jeans and a purple and black chunky knit jumper that hugged her figure, accentuating her curves. Cute, Riley thought. She continued. 'Only I got a phone call saying a couple of guys were down here talking to the kids. Can't be too careful these days.'

'And you are?'

'Julie Meadows. I run NeatStreet, a kids' charity. Minding this lot is part of the job. For my sins.' She ruffled Ewan's hair and when the boy smiled back at her Riley saw something approaching love in the lad's eyes.

'He's a real detective, Julie, 'cept he's black.'

'There are black cops as well, Ewan, only we don't get many down this part of the world.'

'Yeah, I know that. He said he was going to take some of us to watch Chelsea. Not on TV, not on Sky. For real. At the Bridge. He promised.'

'Did he now?' Julie cocked her head to one side and half-smiled at Riley. The smile hit Riley somewhere deep inside his ribcage. To hide his embarrassment he kicked the ball away towards Enders and the boys took chase.

'We are trying to find out about a man called David Forester. I understand he used to hang around down here?'

'Forester? Large guy with a football shirt? Drove a big 4x4?'

'Yes, that's him.'

'Yes, he came from here. Forever poking about with his video camera.'

'What, shooting the kids?' Riley indicated the playground.

'No, the mums. Young mums, yes, but legal. He was always promising them modelling contracts, saying he would help them get discovered. He belonged to some photo club and he said to the girls he would get them work doing glamour shoots if they would audition for him first. From what I heard an audition involved them going back to his place and taking their clothes off.'

'Anything else?'

Julie stopped. She belonged here, like Ewan, and Riley guessed she would be unlikely to want to reveal information which might make their lives any worse.

'It's important,' Riley said. 'Forester's missing, a girl is dead.'

Julie looked around, as if the whole neighbourhood was watching in judgement. She sighed.

'Forester did drugs. Used and dealt. Some of those girls ended up getting screwed by him. Metaphorically and literally. Do you understand what I mean?'

'Yes, I think so.'

'He could talk the talk, that was the problem, and round here people cling to any last hope. It is all too easy to tell them a fairy tale they want to believe. He could spin things so it seemed as if it was only one step from here to living in a mock Tudor mansion with a footballer as a husband and *Hello* magazine beating a path to your door.'

'Any idea what type of stuff he used to shoot?' asked Riley.

'Glamour, to begin with. Then he'd get them to show a bit more flesh, give them a little titbit as a reward. Next, rumour has it at least, he'd get the video camera out and start shooting full-on hardcore. I heard the material used to go up on the web on some paysite he helped run.' She shook her head. 'I'm not a prude, but to think of those girls with Forester makes my skin creep.'

'Do you recognise this girl?' Riley took out his picture of Kelly Donal.

'I've seen her on the news, yes, and once before, here actually.'

'At the playground?'

'Yes, she was draping herself over the roundabout, breasts hanging out of a halter top. Forester was using a video camera and following her around as she went on all the equipment.

Then the girl left and Forester started chatting to some of the mums.'

'Was he popular round here then?'

'I don't think popular is the right word, respected is more like it.'

'Respected?'

'Sounds stupid, doesn't it? But Forester had money and drugs as well as the gift of the gab.'

'Enemies?'

'Dozens, I'm sure. Wouldn't have bothered him though. You know, on the day when I saw him and the girl, this other guy turned up. He had a camera too. Forester seemed to be showing him the footage on the video camera when out of the blue the other guy hit Forester. Just like that. Well, Forester erupted. He chucked the camera down and laid into this other man. He was soon on the ground and Forester was kicking him over and over again. I was about to call you lot when Forester stopped. He picked up the camera, gave the guy one more kick and went off.'

'What happened then?'

'I was a bit concerned about the other guy so I went over to ask if he was alright. His face was a mess and he had blood pouring out of his nose, but I shouldn't have bothered; he told me to piss off and mind my own business!'

'Charming.'

'Anyway, I went to talk to some of the girls in the play-ground and the guy sat on the bench over there, just sat with his head in his hands. After a while he recovered and then he was scribbling things down in this little notebook. It seemed strange. I remember thinking at the time maybe he could be a reporter, but that didn't fit with him hitting Forester, nor with the way he kept staring.'

'Staring at what?'

'At me, at the girls, the mums.' Julie shuddered. 'He kept licking his lips and looking around. He was creepy and I must admit, despite what had happened, I didn't feel much sympathy for him.'

'What did he look like?'

'About your height, black hair, very pale skin, white almost, as if he didn't get out in the sun much.'

'Can you remember when this was?'

'The summer, July, August maybe?'

'And have you seen Forester or this other man since?'

'No.' Julie paused and looked over at the boys, her face saddened and reflective. 'Forester was probably no different from these kids. Then things went wrong, like they do for so many of them. I heard he used to take quite good pictures once.'

The four boys whooped and shouted and Enders was prancing round the field like he was up front for Brazil. The ball flew back and forth between them and Enders's smile was as wide and natural as the boys'. Riley wondered when the fork in the road would come for them.

'Anything else about Forester?'

'Not that I can think of. I'll ask around, ask the kids. They tell me things they wouldn't tell their parents, things you wouldn't believe.'

'Thanks. Talking of kids, shouldn't this lot be in school? I sort of think I should be reporting them to someone.'

'You do that, Detective Clever Clogs,' she laughed. 'But you'll look a bloody idiot if you do.'

'Why is that then?'

'It's the half-term holiday.'

Riley shook his head and smiled.

'Thanks for telling me,' he said, pulling out his card and handing it over. 'If you think of anything else then please let me know.'

'No problem. And thank you for offering to take the boys to a Chelsea game. I'm going to hold you to that.'

'I thought you might.' Riley stopped and, realising what he was about to say, his pulse began to quicken. 'I'll do it on one condition.'

'Which is?'

'You come too.'

Riley and Enders walked back to their car, Enders trying to brush a patch of dirt from his jacket where he had taken a tumble.

'That woman was a bit tasty, hey Darius my old Wily Riley?' Enders smiled and gave Riley a wink.

'Julie?'

'"Julie?"' Enders echoed Riley's voice. 'Don't play the innocent with me, I saw you flirting with Miss Julie fresh-as-summer Meadows. Well, I wouldn't mind going round and mowing her lawn once a week. Twice if it needs it.'

'Thanks for the fascinating insight, Constable. Your opinion of Ms Meadows is duly noted. I'll tell the boss shall I? Maybe your wife?'

'Ah, well, no need to do that.' Enders squirmed and changed the subject. 'Did you discover anything of use?'

'Forester was pushing drugs down here for sure. Supplying the young addicts and getting his leg over while doing it. And then there were the videos.'

'We knew that, didn't we? Doesn't get us any closer to finding Kelly's killer though.'

'There was another guy with a camera too. Seems like Forester and this guy had an argument over Kelly.'

'Well, she was hot and had a lot for them to argue over.' Enders grinned. 'But if the pictures the boss showed me are anything to judge by they could have had one each and there

132

would still have been enough to go round.'

'Jesus, Patrick! You're way out of order. The girl is dead, OK? I witnessed her body getting sliced open down the morgue, guts and everything on a tray. Some guy raped and killed her and all you can do is make smutty jokes.' Riley stared at Enders until he was sure he had got the message.

'What about this other guy?' Enders said after a while, sounding admonished if not contrite. 'Forester kills Kelly and does this guy too. Then he does a runner.'

'Could be, but we're missing something, I know we are.'

'Well?' Enders ruffled his hair, dislodging a piece of mud. 'What is it?'

'I reckon I'm a good detective,' Riley pointed his key fob at the car and bleeped the locks, 'but unfortunately I am not a bloody clairvoyant.'

Chapter Fifteen

'So the two killings are linked?' Hardin's hand hovered over his mouse, an almost imperceptible shake visible. A flush of red had seeped in across his nose and cheeks and Savage wondered if he was already imagining possible headlines for the local papers.

'Linked is not the right word,' Savage said. 'Related is better.'

'But the picture is not actually of the Olivárez girl?'

'The likeness is uncanny at first, although when you look closer you can tell it's not her. The photograph isn't recent for one thing. On the back is a Boots Chemist watermark so we scanned a copy and sent it off to their head office. According to them the logo is from the late seventies or early eighties.'

'Bloody hell. Are they sure about those dates?'

'Pretty much. We are sending them a sample of the photograph so they can do some further analysis. Unfortunately they can't say which of their labs did the developing. As for the content in the picture, well, you have seen for yourself.'

'The girl is standing half-facing the camera. White underwear. The bed in the background and the other furniture suggest a bedroom.'

'Yes. Appears to be a candid shot too, so not posed.'

'But where and who? And what the hell has it got to do with the *Leash* case?'

'Maybe nothing.'

'Or maybe everything.'

Savage wriggled on the chair, smoothing her skirt and flicking a piece of fluff to the floor. She didn't want to think about the possible connections because if true they had a murderer or murderers who had now killed twice. In all likelihood that meant they would do so again.

'Right, Charlotte, I can tell you *Zebo* is going to be ramped up. Garrett stays on *Leash* but will lose some bodies to you. I will be SIO, but you'll get a fair crack of the whip.'

Hardin began to run down a checklist on the screen in front of him, clicking items with his mouse as he went. He started waffling on about the PR angle, telling Savage everything had to go through the press officer. She wondered if he was more concerned with the image being projected than catching the killer.

'I don't need to tell you of the imperative to handle this one with care. We have already got massive media interest due to the discovery that Rosina Olivárez was murdered and now this.'

'They like the naked girl bit. Spices things up.'

'Creepy bastards. If I had my way I'd release nothing, keep them in the dark. It doesn't make our job any easier having them snooping around, so the less we tell them the better. OK?' Hardin looked at Savage, his head cocked on one side, his eyes expectant.

'I'd like to put a national appeal out for David Forester to come forward.'

'What? Damn!' Hardin seemed to mull the idea over for a moment and a pained expression spread across his face. A finger quivered over the mouse button as he weighed up the pros and cons. 'Do you think an appeal could work?'

'It might. He has been on the run for weeks now and must be getting pretty fed up. If he's not fed up himself then I bet the person or people who are hiding him are. From what Riley came up with it seems as if Mr Forester wasn't much liked.'

'OK, go ahead.' Hardin did some one-fingered typing and then paused. 'Can he be connected with *Leash*?'

'I don't know. We have got nothing to link him yet. Forester is involved in all of this somewhere, but I'm not sure he is Kelly Donal's killer. As one of my DCs pointed out to me it doesn't seem his style.'

'Which is?'

'GBH. In your face aggro. If he had killed Kelly, by accident or premeditated, she would have had bruises all over her. Then he'd have dumped the body in the river or the sea. Taking her over to Malstead Down doesn't fit with what we know about him.'

'What about this photography link?'

'Forester was a member of the same club Kelly's dad belonged to, the Plymouth Snappers. The club is legit, hundreds of members, everything above board. Anyway, according to Forester's mother, he had moved into video, which explains the download Riley found out about at Tamar Yacht Fitters and the information coming out of North Prospect. It seems as if he was part of a porn movie-making operation. We don't know where Kelly's murder fits in as yet.'

'Some sort of snuff film?'

'It's the stuff of fiction, respectfully, sir. There is very little evidence of real snuff movies ever having been made. Certainly not for distribution.'

Hardin was quiet again, his big frame still, an elephant acting like a snail. Then he spoke with a whisper.

'You alright about this, Charlotte? I mean Clarissa, Kelly and everything?'

The sudden interest in her personal life took her aback for a moment. She had never considered Hardin as in any way empathetic. Perhaps he had picked up something from one of the management weekends he always seemed to be attending. Or perhaps she had misjudged him and the question showed genuine concern. Either way she was grateful for the chance to put the record straight and to stifle the idea that she wasn't up to the task because of her over-emotional behaviour. Such a label was unlikely to be applied to a man.

'Fine. I am just going to do my job.'

'Ah, er . . . excellent.' Hardin shuffled some papers on the desk in front of him and made a couple of clicks with his mouse as if Savage was an item to be marked 'done'.

The meeting was done too and Savage left Hardin to his liquorice stick and bottled water lunch.

Back in the Major Crimes suite a whole bank of the overhead lights had gone on the blink, leaving the windows and the monitor screens as the only source of illumination. The weak grey daylight and the computer glare washed out all the colour in the room and left people looking pale and half-dead. An electrician stood on a stepladder and fiddled with a ceiling panel. Savage went to her desk where a Post-it note stuck on the monitor said that John Layton had called. The CSI had got some information about the tyre tracks in the field at Malstead Down. Savage called him back.

'Bridgestone,' Layton said. 'D689 size 265/70S15.'

'Don't keep me in suspense, John. Give me the make and model of car,' said Savage.

'What do you think we are, miracle workers?'

'To put it bluntly, yes.'

'The tyre is a road type, often fitted on a late model long wheel base Mitsubishi Shogun. We have checked the turning circle in the field and the other data indicate a Shogun as well.'

'Anything else?'

'The vehicle is black.'

'How the hell did you find the colour from the tyre size?'

'Didn't. That *would* be a miracle. We had help from a piece of barbed wire in the fence. A tiny speck of paint got caught on a barb as it scraped down the side of the car. We are still waiting for the analysis on the sample, but I'll bet my physics O Level the paint is from DuPont and commonly used by Mitsubishi.'

'John, if you were here I would kiss you!'

'I'm coming right over!'

Savage hung up with Layton laughing down the line and stood up to address the room. The information from Layton would go onto the system, but sometimes old-fashioned communication worked best. Her voice was instant, couldn't be overlooked, nor misinterpreted.

'Black Mitsubishi Shogun,' Savage shouted out. 'Ring bells with anyone?'

'Boss,' replied Riley. 'Belongs to Forester. At least his employer told us Forester had one. Julie Meadows in North Prospect mentioned something about a 4x4 too. Need to check with DVLC.'

Riley was already tapping away at his keyboard, accessing the car licensing database. Meanwhile Calter looked worried, pale even, as if Savage had given her some news she really, *really* didn't want to hear.

'Jane? Have you got anything for me?'

'Just checking, ma'am. Some detail I remember from yesterday.' Now Calter was busy at a terminal as well, fingers a blur as she typed, tabbed and clicked. 'Shit, I'm right! Alice Nash, the sixteen-year-old girl missing from Ashburton, we had her at number one on our misper list. Remember? She was seen accepting a lift from a man in a large black 4x4.'

'A Shogun?'

'The witness's statement mentions a Japanese marque, so possibly.'

The clatter of keyboards stopped and a hush descended. A pin-drop silence lasted until Savage choked out a 'well done everybody' before slumping down in her chair to think on the implications of it all.

Forester had Alice Nash. Right now he might be raping her and soon she could be dead. Savage picked up the phone to call Hardin and hoped that given his lack of a proper lunch she wouldn't find him in too bad a mood.

Alice tried not to breathe in too deeply because the room reeked of fermenting urine. She only had herself to blame. The glimmer of light coming from under the door had revealed a plastic bucket in one corner and she needed to go so she used it as a toilet. With nothing to act as a lid the air had become thick with the stench of piss.

A bad smell is the least of your worries, girl.

She still had no idea where she was. After she had tried the door and found it locked she crept back to the bed and pulled the duvet cover around her. Her limbs throbbed with a washed-out sort of tiredness, but the ache in her head wouldn't let her sleep so she lay in the gloom thinking about her predicament.

You have been drugged and next you are going to be raped.

Sixteen years old, and mature for her age, she reckoned she dealt with most things that came her way in life. This was something else though, something beyond her experience. She hadn't even had sex before, for God's sake. Emotion welled up inside and she rubbed her eyes to try to stop the tears. She knew the first time would be brutal, a gang of men having her for their own pleasure with no regard for her feelings. She wished she had let Luke, her boyfriend, go further, because she loved him and now she would be spoilt. Maybe afterwards he wouldn't want her anymore.

Afterwards. Would there be an afterwards?

The uncontrollable shaking returned, refusing to go away despite the warmth of the duvet.

Get a grip. Pull yourself together. If you are going to get through this you had better start thinking rationally and try to find a way out of here.

She stood up, letting the duvet fall from her, not caring about her nakedness now. The door didn't offer any hope so she needed to find another exit. She couldn't spot anything obvious, but the light from the door didn't banish the deep shadows so she decided to try and work her way around the walls. Starting at the door she explored along one wall and the next, searching from floor level up to as high as she could reach with her fingertips. Along the third wall she found a set of doors to some sort of cupboard. Running her fingers over the wooden surface she discovered a little latch and she undid the bolt and opened the doors. Strange, the cupboard had no depth; the recess was only set a few inches into the wall and at the back her hand touched something smooth and cold. Then she realised why. The recess wasn't a cupboard at all, it was a window with a pair of shutters on the inside.

No light shone through the glass. Nothing. Utter black. She ran her hands around the window. It had a metal frame but didn't seem to open. She touched the glass again and noticed a slight texture and now she understood why no light was able to get through from outside: the glass had been painted.

Using a fingernail she started scratching at the paint until a pinprick of light flared in. She worked away and the paint began to flake and soon she had made a hole big enough to peek through. She pushed her face up against the glass, blinking against the harsh daylight on the other side.

She could see a green field bordered by a grey stone wall and beyond an area of woodland, the leaves of nearby trees all autumnal: burnt sienna, rust and gold. Behind those trees a dark forest of conifers climbed a steep hill. There was no sign of any other houses, no roads, no people. Her location must be remote, deep in the countryside.

Deep in the shit more like.

She focused on the ground below the window and realised she was on the second storey. If she smashed the window she would have to jump down ten feet or more and if she hadn't sprained her ankle or worse she could run.

Where?

She scratched away at the paint again, expanding the hole until she had a better view of the back yard. A set of bean poles made a wigwam shape beside a neat row of raised beds not long dug over. A vegetable garden. In one corner a compost heap with a wheelbarrow upside down on top sat next to one of those dustbin incinerators with—

Shit!

A man stood throwing small sticks into the incinerator as flames licked out of the top. He had his back to Alice, but the black hair seemed somehow familiar. The fire roared away and the man kept feeding in sticks for a few minutes. Then he bent to pick up a cloth from a pile of rags on the ground, he held the material up to his nose and appeared to take several deep breaths before shaking his head and dropping the rag into the incinerator. Now he was stooping again and picking up something else, something bright red, an item of clothing. It looked like the blouse she had been wearing before—

Oh fuck!

It *was* the blouse she had been wearing, the one she had bought in the Debenhams' summer sale. The pile of rags wasn't rags at all, it was her clothing: her top, her cardigan, her jeans, her shoes, her *underwear*!

Alice turned from the window and collapsed on the mattress. She stifled a sob by biting her lip, but then the tears came and she let her emotions all out, just crying and crying and crying.

She must have drifted off to sleep because the next thing she was aware of was a sound at the door. A key turning in the lock. She grabbed the duvet and scampered under, like a snail retreating into its shell.

The door opened and a hand pushed a tray along the floor and into the room. The tray held a bowl of fruit – apples, bananas, grapes – and a bottle of spring water. The door swung shut.

'Wait! Who are you? Please let me go!' Alice jumped off the mattress and ran to the door.

Click. The key turned and footsteps walked off into the distance.

Chapter Sixteen

The final time he saw Carmel was three weeks after Mitchell's Christmas party. He wished he could purge the memory from his mind, but he couldn't. The images would stay with him forever.

The phone had shocked him awake sometime after two in the morning. Mitchell! Mitchell? What the hell was Mitchell doing ringing at that time? He sat up in bed, half asleep, listening to Mitchell asking for help. Mitchell wanted to meet him out at Wembury, in the car park next to the beach. As soon as possible. And no questions.

Harry got dressed and went out into the night. Got in his car and drove at a crawl through town and out east across the Plym, turning south into the country and towards the sea. At one point he passed a patrol car going the other way and he willed the police to stop and turn in the road and come after him. He'd tell them all about Mitchell and perhaps then the nightmare would end.

It didn't happen and he drove on through the dark lanes to Wembury. Down past the village and along a track to the car park that stood next to the beach. A café sat perched on the rocks right on the seafront and Harry recalled going there one summer morning years ago. He had drunk a coffee while he waited for the crowds to arrive.

He parked the car overlooking the bay and sat and waited. Drizzle misted the windscreen and he set the wipers to intermittent. Somewhere up in the clouds the moon cast a strange washed-out glow over the sea. Harry could see the tide was ebbing and more and more beach became exposed as the minutes ticked by. Harry remembered the last time. The hot sun, the drip, drip, drip of ice creams, the screaming kids. But most of all he remembered the girls. Their firm, young bodies, the colourful bikinis, the wet T-shirts, the curves, the smiles and the laughter. Click, click, click with his camera and their flesh was captured forever. Preserved. Harry chewed his tongue and swallowed spit. His eyes surveyed the cold, grey sand, the rocks and the dark clumps of seaweed. The place had transformed into something different now and so had he. Frigid. Empty. Plain absent.

Swish. Another five seconds. The dashboard clock glowed out 3:00 AM and he realised that he had now been sitting in the car for twenty-three minutes. Too long. Mitchell had told him to hurry so where was he?

As if in answer he saw headlights coming down the track. It was either Mitchell or he was busted. The car crept along, as if checking the roadside and then stopped perhaps twenty metres away. The lights were on full beam and it was hard to make out the make and model. Then the lights dimmed. Bright white to a dim yellow, fading all the time, first like a torch, then a candle, then a glowing cigarette, then off.

Mitchell's Jag.

Harry was shaking now. Mitchell scared him and as he grasped the door handle to get out he was aware of the sweat on his fingers. He wiped his hands on his trousers, clambered out of the car and walked back to the Jag.

The driver's window purred down and Mitchell sat staring ahead.

'Harry,' he whispered. 'Thank God you've come!'

'Well, you know—'

'You and me, Harry, we understand the world, we understand things don't appear as they should, plans don't transpire the way we want them to. The brave press on. The accomplished performer improvises. The fallen runner gets up and attacks with renewed vigour.'

Harry's mouth hung open. Mitchell spouted gibberish, but it went with the territory he supposed. He let Mitchell continue.

'Check the boot. Bit of a problem.' Mitchell didn't move. He just continued gazing into the distance.

Harry went round to the rear of the car and sprung the boot lid. There was a rubber dinghy folded up and crammed in there, not the sort you could buy on the seafront, but a heavy inflatable from a chandlery store. He didn't say anything, just stared and wondered what the hell was going on in Mitchell's head.

'Get the fucking dinghy out and see what is underneath.' Mitchell's voice floated out from the window.

Harry tried to pull the dinghy out but it took all his effort to get even part of it over the lip of the boot. Then he saw the hand poking out from underneath the rubber. Pink nail varnish. The odour of perfume mixing with the PVC smell of the new dinghy.

Clunk.

Mitchell got out of the car and stood beside Harry.

'Bit of a problem,' he repeated, as if Harry hadn't heard him the first time.

Harry groaned, but Mitchell didn't seem to notice. He slapped Harry on the back and reached into the boot.

'Let's get this pumped up and down to the beach.' Mitchell grabbed the dinghy, his voice calm and ordered as if they were on a day out at the seaside. The dinghy rolled over the lip of the boot and flopped onto the floor, lifeless. Harry peered in the boot. Hand connected to arm, to body, to some hessian material. The girl was hooded with a sack tied tight around her neck. He looked down at her body. Light brown skin wrapped in a baby-doll nightdress, a silver cross on a chain nestling in ample cleavage, toned muscles, a little tattoo of a dolphin high on her left inner thigh.

'The Spanish girl?' Harry said, feeling quite unwell and putting a hand out to steady himself against the car.

'Precisely,' Mitchell said. 'The pretty Spanish girl who knows a bit too much about the English. I've given her a little something to help her forget.' He reached into the boot and took a bellows-type foot pump out. 'Possibly a bit too much of a little something. Couldn't call an ambulance, could I? Too many questions. Too many silly little questions.'

'I thought she had gone back to Spain?' Harry struggled to get the words out, aware of the quiver in his voice.

'She had.'

'And?'

'She came back again. Unwillingly, of course. I drove through Customs with her on the back seat covered with a blanket.'

Harry could imagine Mitchell doing that. Crazy.

Mitchell began to pump the dinghy. The air made short hissing noises as it forced its way past the valve. Like sharp intakes of breath. Like the sound the girl had made as Mitchell and RT had fucked her as she lay tied to the bed.

'But why?' Harry asked. 'Wasn't it better with her over there? Out of the way?'

'Out of the way. Exactly,' Mitchell said. But he shook his head. 'RT's fault. The blindfold came off. Afterwards he realised that he knew the girl.'

'Richard? Afterwards?'

'That's what I said to him. A bit bloody late in the day. Fucking idiot. Anyway, couldn't risk her blabbing once she was safely home so I brought her back to the UK to try and reason with her, persuade her to keep quiet. She wasn't having it, went mental, so I decided to keep her round my place for a bit. Have a bit of fun. Seemed a shame not to!'

Harry said nothing. He didn't know what to think. Mitchell was grade one rocket fuel. Unstable. One little spark and he would blow and take Harry with him into oblivion.

'Help me!' Mitchell lifted one end of the dinghy and nodded at Harry to grab the other end. He did so and they stumbled across the car park and down the steep path to the beach. They manhandled the little boat across the wet sand and rock to the sea and Harry felt icy cold water surge around his ankles as they staggered into the surf. Mitchell left him holding the painter as the boat bobbed around on the swell and he ran back to the car park. A couple of minutes later he stumbled into view again, the girl thrown over his right shoulder in a fireman's lift and a grab bag with something heavy in it in his other hand.

Mitchell dumped the girl down and she slumped onto the edge of the dinghy now, a pretty marionette with all the life gone out of her.

'Get her out there,' he said, gesturing with his arm somewhere in the general direction of France. 'Chuck her overboard with something to weigh her down.' He pulled a length of heavy chain from the bag, bent down near the girl's ankles and grinned. 'This should do!'

Harry wondered if Mitchell was quite right in the head. But of course he wasn't. The two of them were here on a beach in the middle of the night with a corpse and Mitchell was smiling.

'Harry! What has happened to you? We are living man! That was why I told you to stop taking the pills. Experience things as they really are. Live on the edge. Did you think that was only talk?'

Harry gazed down into the inky water, feeling the sand shift beneath his feet as another wave frothed by. The dinghy bounced against his legs, spinning, alive. The girl lay still, the only noise the surf and a small hiss as if air was escaping from a leak somewhere. Harry prayed the police would be along soon and they would be caught, but at least he would be safe. Pulled back from the brink before he went one step too far. He was aware of Mitchell staring at him, but he didn't say anything. Couldn't. He was too scared.

Suddenly the girl twitched and a leg shot out catching Mitchell on the left knee. He staggered backwards and fell into the surf, cracking his head on a rock. Blind from the sack the girl flailed her arms at nothing, jumped up, stumbled and tripped on the painter line on the dinghy. For a second she thrashed in the surf, but then she was on her feet, running away across the beach, her hands clawing at the sacking, a nightmarish figure disappearing into the gloom.

Mitchell was up now, grabbing the bag in his right hand and roaring at Harry.

'Bloody bitch! Come on!'

Harry jumped up and followed him, the sand already sapping his energy with every stride. Mitchell loomed somewhere ahead, thump, thump, thump, thump. He looked back and gestured for Harry to hurry up. The girl had run along the beach, but she was running west, away from the car park, where there was only a rocky foreshore with steep cliffs blocking the way to the coastal path. A vast plateau of rock stretched out to the sea and the girl was stumbling across it. Harry could see her ahead now and it was plain that they

149

were going to catch her. All of a sudden she disappeared from view, she had gone down a fissure in the rock, a sandy finger that led to the sea. Mitchell gestured again and Harry understood his plan. He wanted him to go to the next crack farther on so he could cut off any chance she had of escape, for that was the only other way out from the plateau.

With renewed vigour Harry sprinted the remaining distance and reached the second fissure. He stopped with hands on hips for a moment, panting.

'Harry!' Mitchell's voice rang out, echoing off the rocky cliffs. 'Down here!'

Harry took a deep breath and jumped down onto the sand and headed seawards.

'Quickly!'

Harry raced along the sand, half-groping in the dark, afraid he might trip and smash his head on a rock. Then a bright light in his eyes blinded him for a moment as Mitchell pointed a beam from a torch at him. Right in his face. The girl cowered against a boulder, knees drawn up to her chin, and Mitchell stood over her, one hand clamped on her shoulder.

'The trouble is she knows Richard, Harry. And now she knows you too, doesn't she? Recognises you from when you first met her.' Mitchell shook his head. 'Hold her down.'

The words froze Harry, grabbed hold of his heart and squeezed hard. He stood motionless as Mitchell seized the girl and threw her to the sand.

'What are you going to do, Harry? Phone the police? You get too pushy with some real cute pussy and this is the result. What do you think the police will say when they find out about all those girls you have been following around town? And all those pictures? Tut, tut, tut. I think they will call the doctors, don't you?'

'Can't we just—'

'What? Ask her if she will forgive us?'

The torch beam left Harry and shone down on the girl. Her face was poking out from behind her knees, the sack hood missing, her nightdress torn. With her long, dark hair and light brown skin the likeness to Carmel was frightening and Carmel had been special to him. Very special.

'Can't we take her somewhere? Talk about this. Work something out.' Harry couldn't find the right words, but he knew he wanted to help Carmel, to try and save her from Mitchell. Perhaps she would be grateful. Perhaps they could even be together.

'OK, Harry, you win.' Mitchell looked resigned. 'Hold her, will you, while I find my phone to call an ambulance.'

Harry took Mitchell's place, holding the girl's left arm and thinking this was the first time he had touched her. Mitchell took something from the grab bag, some sort of medical device, metallic, cylindrical. Not like a phone at all.

'What the hell is that?'

'Just something to put her to sleep so we can deal with her.'

At the word 'sleep' the girl struggled once more and Mitchell screamed at Harry to hold her.

Then Mitchell had the thing against the girl's head and there was a loud bang. The head jerked back and blood sprayed out, bubbling over Harry's hands and arms, warm and sticky. There was a burnt smell like a kid's cap gun, only a kid's cap gun never busted someone's head like that.

'Fucking hell!' Harry was up on his feet, stumbling backwards, unable to take his eyes from the horror.

Blood was still spurting out, cascading over Mitchell, over the stones, the girl's body was shaking and quivering and then all of a sudden she was silent and still, only the distant sound of the waves washing over the rocks in the gloom.

'Shit,' Mitchell smiled and got up and wiped his hands on his jacket. 'Didn't think it was going to be quite as much fun as that!'

Harry turned from Mitchell and ran into the blackness.

Chapter Seventeen

Crownhill Police Station, Plymouth. Thursday 28th October.
2.38 pm

Hardin must have got indigestion from too much liquorice because he had been in a foul mood when Savage told him about Alice Nash, threatening to skin the officers who failed to follow up on the Donal case. Thank goodness those responsible weren't on her team because those picked out for the Hardin treatment would get pissed on and the splashback would hit anybody within range. With the metaphor stuck in her mind she went for lunch, unsurprised when she found she didn't fancy much apart from a pastry and coffee. She finished off the pastry in record time and took the coffee back to the incident room. The heating had been turned up and a distinct fug hung in the warm, bright air. Officers bustled to and fro in shirtsleeves, oblivious to the weather worsening outside the windows, and the place felt like a haven from the brewing storm. DS Collier sat in front of a terminal showing Calter some reports of various sightings of Forester. The two of them looked an unlikely pair with the sergeant's greying military-style hair and shirt and tie contrasting with Calter's bouncy shoulder-length bob and casual outfit of distressed jeans and tight top. Collier had collated all the statements and they pointed to Forester disappearing sometime in early August. He had started to tell Savage about cross-referencing the dates with the bank and mobile records when DC Enders called across from his desk with a flush of excitement on his face.

'Ma'am, phone call for you. A guy with some information. Won't give his name and won't speak to anyone but you.' Enders indicated a phone near where she was standing. 'Line one.'

The whole room fell silent as Savage moved to the desk, plucked up the handset and punched a key.

'Detective Inspector Charlotte Savage speaking, who is this please?'

A pause before a voice came on the line. A man's voice, but muffled and quiet, a whisper almost. Maybe he was holding something over the mouthpiece?

'It's about Forester. I have some information. He murdered the girl. Poisoned her. You wouldn't know from looking, but he killed her. From the inside out.'

'Could I have your name please?'

'No. I'm not telling you that.'

'Anything you say will be treated in the strictest confidence, but if you do not want to give your name that is fine.'

'Good. Because I'm not going to.' Another pause. 'You sail boats don't you?'

'Pardon?' Despite the warmth of the room a cold chill slid over her for a second. Then she remembered the newspaper story about her and Pete again, the one Nesbit had mentioned. She continued. 'Yes, when I get the chance.'

Silence. Savage sensed the man was waiting for something more, some elaboration and if she didn't oblige the call would be over.

'I sail a Westerly out of Plymouth, a little family boat, mostly coastal pottering, but we go down to the Isles of Scilly occasionally, across to the Channel Islands and Brittany if we have the time.' Savage waited a moment. 'You said you had some information about David Forester?'

'Zero five zero point six three zero one degrees north. Zero zero three point nine nine eight six degrees west.'

Savage motioned to Calter, waving her towards the terminal on the desk as she scratched the numbers down on a pad.

'Can you repeat that please?'

Then nothing but dead air and the sound of the caller hanging up leaving Savage repeating the numbers aloud and cross-checking with what she had written.

'Google this,' Savage said, handing Calter the piece of paper. 'Lat long.'

'Sorry, ma'am?' Calter crooked her head on one side and squinted at Savage's writing.

'The caller gave me those, a latitude longitude plot supposedly pointing to where Forester is hiding. Put it into Google Maps and we might just have a result.'

'The position is on Dartmoor, ma'am.' Enders, beaming and pleased with himself.

'How do you know that?'

'Well, it's a bit, um, embarrassing. A little like train-spotting.' The pleased look had turned sheepish, Enders staring at the desk.

'What is?'

'Me and the wife, we are into a bit of letterboxing.'

'I am assuming this letterboxing is not some sex game involving post office uniforms and boxing gloves?'

'No,' Enders laughed. 'All over Dartmoor are little boxes hidden in out of the way places and the idea is to visit them all. A bit like Munro bagging.'

Savage had heard of Munro bagging. It was something to do with trying to climb as many Scottish mountains as possible.

'We do the modern version of letterboxing, called geocaching. The kids love the adventure and anticipation. We use a GPS to navigate our way to a spot where something has been hidden. Doesn't take long before those numbers, the lat long coordinates, become real in your mind. I couldn't tell you exactly where they point to, but the location is somewhere on the northern part of the moor, well away from civilisation.' Enders stopped, as if aware of the implications of what he was saying.

'He's right, ma'am!' Calter was at the computer. She had brought up a satellite image of Dartmoor and a little icon marked the position she had plotted into the search box.

Savage checked the coordinates Calter had entered with the ones she had written down. They matched.

'It's in the middle of nowhere,' she said.

'Not only in the middle of nowhere, ma'am,' Enders said, 'there is *nothing* there.'

Calter clicked the mouse and the image zoomed in. Now they could see open moor. A couple of rock outcrops, some bog, a leat weaving along the contours, clumps of heather, patterns in the ground caused by winter runoff; nothing else. No roads, no buildings, no trees, just empty and desolate moorland.

No one said anything and Savage shivered again, aware of the rain and hail that had begun to spatter on the windows. Calter broke the silence in her own inimitable way.

'What the fuck would anybody in their right mind be doing out there?'

*   *   *

156

The street lamps burned orange against a sky darker than it should have been at four o'clock in the afternoon and heavy rain slashed from the clouds. Their vehicle ripped through the floods and even before leaving the outskirts of the city Savage had decided that commandeering one of Traffic's Landrover Discoverys, complete with an experienced driver, had been a good move. Rivers of water poured across the roads creating huge puddles everywhere and daylight seemed almost a memory. Cars ahead of them moved into the gutters, diving out of the way of the strobing lights and siren. Savage gripped the armrests, eyes front watching the road. Calter and Enders larked around in the back, the two of them behaving like children on a day out.

'Be falling as sleet up on the moor,' Enders said, sounding excited. 'If not snow.'

'Like this sort of weather, do you?' Savage asked.

'There's no such thing as bad weather, ma'am, only the wrong sort of clothing. Something like that.'

It took twenty minutes to get out of Plymouth, along the A386 and onto the B3212 that led across the moor towards Princetown. Sleet was falling now, reducing visibility to a few car lengths and slowing their speed to little more than a crawl. The sleet swirled around in the wind and every now and then the Landrover would be bludgeoned by an extra-strong gust that threatened to overturn them. The driver peered forward, concentrating hard and fighting to keep the vehicle on the road.

At Princetown their headlights reflected on the fluorescent strip on an otherwise invisible white Defender parked by the side of the road. The vehicle's siren blooped out a greeting and Savage spotted the Dartmoor Rescue Group logo on the side. She had phoned ahead and requested their services to guide them onto the remote part of the moor. Enders seemed offended, insisting he knew about search and rescue, but Savage pointed out he wasn't leading a summer letterboxing expedition with the family and they needed all the help they could get. Besides which the team had search dogs that might prove extremely useful.

'Are we looking for a body, ma'am?' Enders had gone serious and stopped larking about.

'No idea. But who in their right minds would be up on the moor in this kind of weather?'

'Unless they had a death wish.' Calter, the fun gone out of her too.

'That's what I'm worried about.'

They pulled up and Savage got out, battling to open the door against the gale. She struggled into her waterproof jacket, cursing as a hank of hair blew across her face and got caught in the zip. A big man, the sort you would want on your side in a drugs bust, climbed down from the rescue team's Landrover and strode over to Savage. The wind flattened his waterproof gear against his body, but he seemed unaffected by the weather. He offered his hand.

'Callum Campbell,' he said in a Scottish accent, his clear blue eyes holding her gaze a split second longer than was comfortable.

'Thanks for meeting us.' Savage handed him the GPS coordinates. 'We are looking for someone at this location.'

Campbell returned to his vehicle and retrieved a handheld GPS. The unit had a little screen with a map, and once he had entered the coordinates he tapped the display and shook his head.

'Nothing out there but lousy weather and a few stupid sheep.'

'We know. Why do you think we called you?'

'Aye. Best get moving before this lot turns to snow.' He

gestured at the sleet, turned to walk back to his vehicle, but then stopped and shouted over his shoulder.

'Are we looking for a live one?'

Savage hesitated, the informant hadn't specified anything, only that the information concerned Forester. The whole thing could turn out to be a wild goose chase.

'We are not even sure what we are looking for.'

'No problem, I'll alert the guys and gals. No sense in busting our guts or risking our limbs if there isn't someone alive out there.'

They left Princetown in convoy with the rescue team leading the way. Sunset had long gone and the weather showed no sign of letting up. Warm air blew from the car's heater ducts and Savage stared through the side window and wondered what it would be like to be lost out on the moor in the blackness.

Five miles northeast of Princetown Campbell's Landrover turned off the road and onto a rough track. Savage's driver muttered a 'bloody hell' and followed. The vehicles lurched along, bouncing over exposed rock and crashing into potholes, progress slowed to not much more than walking pace, limited now by the terrain rather than the visibility. Through the windscreen in the headlights Savage caught a glimpse of a few clumps of heather and scrub and beyond the nothingness of the whiteout.

She estimated that they were averaging only about ten miles an hour and after some thirty minutes the rescue vehicle stopped. Campbell got out and came back to speak to them. Savage sat on the sheltered side of the Landrover so she rolled her window down. Campbell poked his head into the fug.

'Nice in here, isn't it?' He grinned. 'Did you bring a picnic?'

Savage could see the funny side, but didn't feel much like laughing.

'Are we there?'

'The waypoint is about a thousand metres due north.' Campbell pointed off into the dark. 'No chance of using the vehicles so get yourselves kitted up.'

Enders had retrieved his mountain gear from his car back at the station and he looked the business in a matching Karimor jacket and trousers and solid looking climbing boots, like he was about to try for the final push for the summit of Everest. His round face beamed out from under the peak of his hood, eager to get started. The rest of them pulled on the high-vis waterproofs they'd snatched from Traffic. Looking at the sleet whipping through the beams of the headlights Savage was beginning to think they would be useless.

Three more of the rescue team clambered out of the back of the Landrover. Two guys and a girl, all decked out in waterproofs and equipped with head torches and a big hand-held searchlight. A couple of border collies jumped down as well and the dogs began scampering around, snapping at the sleet and spinning in circles with excitement, their eyes bright and missing nothing. Like Campbell they seemed oblivious to the weather.

'OK, listen up!' Campbell sounded serious now, balling his orders out against the howling gale. 'We are only going about one kilometre from the vehicles but in these conditions you can lose sight of someone in ten metres, so everyone stay close. Slip over and sprain your ankle and get left behind and you are in trouble. The wind will carry your cry for help away and the same wind will be sapping your core temperature. The dogs might find you but then again they might not. By first light you will be dead.'

The wind seemed to be slicing through Savage's waterproofs and Campbell's remarks didn't make her feel any warmer.

'Jeff will stay in our vehicle and your traffic officer will stay here too. I'll lead the way with Carole and her dog. Next you guys,' Campbell indicated Savage and her two DCs. 'Then Adrian will bring up the rear with his dog. Adrian and I have radios as does Jeff so we have contact with each other and with our base. If we need to cas evac there is no chance of a helicopter in this weather so Adrian has got the stretcher packed up. If we find a body I suggest we wait until daylight. OK, any questions?'

No one said anything so he muttered a 'let's go' and with a deliberate, methodical stride began to pick his way out across the open moor.

Savage and the others followed, not moving much beyond a slow walk. Within a couple of minutes they lost all sight of the two Landrovers and the track. Savage became disorientated to such a degree that she had no idea in which direction they were heading. Picked out in the torchlight Campbell was just a lumbering shadow up ahead, beyond him the sleet reflected the light for a few metres and beyond that was total blackness. Campbell had been right, step away from the group and you were a goner.

There was no path, only the occasional sheep track criss-crossing their route, and the terrain was typical Dartmoor: one minute the ground would be firm underfoot, rock peeking between the grass and heather, the next you would be squelching through mud and bog.

Every so often Campbell stopped and a pale light flashed on his face as he peered at the GPS screen and used a tiny penlight to cross-check with a compass and a map encased in a plastic holdall. Check complete he would stride forward, his steady gait eating up the ground with ease. He might have been a volunteer, but he practised his art like a professional.

After about twenty minutes the shape of a rocky outcrop

161

loomed ahead in the torchlight. The craggy granite, cold and rough, was incongruous after the softness of the boggy moorland.

'Fur Tor,' Campbell shouted against the roaring wind. 'This is it!'

They moved closer and stopped in the lee of the towering rock where the wind was somewhat lessened. Savage stood with her hands on her hips taking deep breaths. Campbell breathed easy though, not fazed by the weather or the terrain.

'The exact coordinates are over on the west side, but sometimes the GPS can be out by quite a bit compared to the map and we have got no idea if the position given is accurate anyway. I suggest we split and skirt the tor in two teams, each with a dog. Keep close to the rock, and if you lose sight of each other for God's sake stay put.'

The sleet had turned to snow now and even with the powerful torches visibility was down to no more than a few metres. Savage followed the dog handler and Campbell as they skirted the rocks anti-clockwise. A strange howling whistle filled the air as the wind lashed round the rocks, driving the sleet and snow with a force that stung her exposed skin. Savage was glad she was with Campbell.

Up ahead the dog zipped back and forth, disappearing into each rock cleft and running out again to scamper about. Every now and then it would stop and raise a wet nose into the air and whine and race off again. Then a startled sheep shot out from one fissure, the creature's eyes flashing green in the torchlight. The collie spun around and around and barked for all it was worth, the excitement in the dog's eyes a counterpoint to the fear in the ewe's.

'Was it the sheep?' Savage asked the handler.

'No. She's trained to ignore them. It's something else.' The handler bent down, grabbed the dog by the scruff and shouted an order. The dog yapped once and looked up at the tor where a sheer rock face rose into the darkness. The dog gave a whine and shot across to a crack in the face, bounding upwards in a huge leap until it was a couple of metres from the ground atop a small ledge. Short, sharp barks echoed for a moment before being snatched away by the wind.

'We'll not get up there,' Campbell said. 'Let's walk round to the side of this little crag and we might be able to find an easier route.'

Sure enough Campbell was right. Twenty metres farther on a grassy slope led up the side, and they scrambled up and round until they stood atop of the rock. A metre or so below them the dog perched on the ledge. She had found Forester. He wasn't alive. In fact, as Savage would recall later, he didn't even look human.

Chapter Eighteen

St Ives, Cornwall. Saturday 30th October. 10.51 am

It took Tatershall a few days to get round to returning to St Ives. The missing couple didn't figure high on the list of priorities and if DI Peters hadn't badgered him he might not have bothered. However, a break in the weather at last brought a beautiful clear day and the prospect of a nice drive, a spot of lunch and the sun falling on Kate Simbeck's perfect face was too much to resist.

Now he and Simbeck were leafing through the couple's papers, trying to sort them in some meaningful fashion, Tatershall wearing his new glasses and trying not to feel self-conscious with them on. A few weeks back his wife had noticed him squinting at the evening paper and insisted he went for an eye test. The result had been a pair of the least biddyish looking reading glasses he could find and a feeling of age catching up with him. Simbeck had said the grey of the wire-framed glasses matched his hair and made him look distinguished, which hadn't helped a whole lot.

Finding the big cardboard box in the back of a cupboard in the flat's utility room had been a bonus because it seemed to contain the only solid evidence that the couple existed at all. The rest of the flat had been devoid of anything much personal. As if they didn't want to be reminded of who they were or where they had come from. The box contained a number of manila folders, each stuffed with documents. From share certificates to a car registration, from a manual for the microwave to old utility bills.

'It's like everything else in the flat, sir,' Simbeck said. 'All practical stuff. Nothing emotional. No letters, no postcards, no birthday cards, no memories. A couple who didn't want to remember anything from their past.'

'Very poetic, but I am not sure it's the basis for a case against them.'

'I wasn't trying to say that. I just don't understand how anyone's life can be so sterile.'

'Like the woman's paintings?' The gallery below the flat displayed several examples of her work, hyperrealistic watercolours of the harbour at St Ives with every detail painstakingly copied. You may as well have used a camera, Tatershall thought, though even a photograph would have had more warmth.

'Exactly.'

They carried on the work, ploughing deeper into the box, making a note or two, but finding nothing to give them a handle on the couple's life.

'Remember, we are trying to find something to connect them with Devon, with Dartmouth maybe,' Tatershall said.

They didn't find anything. Tatershall even tried ringing Dartmouth police to see if they knew of the couple, but they didn't. In fact the officer on the end of the line seemed to think he was a bit of a joker for even suggesting they might have. She asked if Tatershall realised how many hundreds of thousands of tourists visited Dartmouth each year. Tatershall didn't know and didn't want to know either, but the woman on the end of the phone proceeded to tell him anyway. The place sounded like St Ives, only with more boats. Feeling admonished Tatershall hung up.

'Fucking idiots!'

'Dartmouth?'

'FootInMouth. No help at all. Bloody English tossers.'

'Never mind.' Simbeck stood smiling, mischief on her face. 'Why don't you come down and peruse my etchings instead, sir?'

She led him down the stairs and into the gallery where halogen light blazed from overhead. While he had been on the phone she had been having a nose around and from her expression she had discovered something.

'There.' She pointed at a picture on the wall. A little notice beneath said the painting was not for sale. Tatershall had to look twice to tell the image wasn't a photograph.

'And?'

'The inscription.'

Tatershall looked again. The artist had signed her name and just above the signature were some tiny printed words: *Netherston Cottage, South Hams, Devon, 1983.*

'An address, sir. No idea where, but I bet your new friends at Dartmouth nick could find out for you.'

Saturday morning and Savage had woken to the bed in motion; Jamie bouncing up and down and imploring her to get up.

'Daddy is calling today.'

Jamie was right, Pete would call later. She had looked at the clock and noted the darkness behind the curtains. 6:30 am. Something like Christmas morning behaviour for Jamie. Nothing wrong with his enthusiasm, but considering her moorland excursion Thursday evening she could have done with a lie in.

Now it was mid-afternoon and Jamie and Samantha jostled in front of Savage's laptop, Pete's voice gurgling through the speakers, the kids' own words tumbling forth in a stream of questions while at the same time Samantha Googled 'Panama Canal' and found a live webcam situated at the Gatun Locks. Pete told them about the passage up the coast of Chile and the journey through the canal and sent through some pictures of the frigate navigating one of the locks.

Savage had spoken to him before calling the kids down and the only thing she could think of now were his opening words to her: 'I'm coming home.' Of course she had known already since the ship's itinerary, barring unforeseen events, had been planned for months, but hearing the words had lifted her spirit and now she couldn't stop smiling.

The children burbled on, Savage managing a word here and there, and then it was over, Pete's 'I love you' echoing in the silence for a moment before Jamie asked for a biscuit and Samantha ran upstairs to text a friend.

For the kids Pete being away was nothing unusual. They missed him, sure, but they had grown up with his prolonged absences and a snatched call and a few emails each week was normality. Savage thought it stank and not for the first time she hoped he would settle for a desk job on his return. Improbable though and a little like her working fewer hours or not spending the coming night on Hardin's undercover operation.

She went to the phone and dialled through to Stefan in the annexe to remind him he was babysitting and then went upstairs to find something suitable to wear.

Savage entered the briefing room at the station at Charles Cross in the centre of town to a very strange sight. DC Carl

Denton whirled around in the centre, dancing and singing, his mobile held to his lips like a microphone as he sang the first few lines from 'Saturday Night' by Whigfield. He ended with a fancy pirouette and sat down on Enders's lap.

'Anytime babe, anytime,' Enders said, stroking Denton's hair. 'Only do you think you could lose the aftershave? I prefer my girls not to smell of old jockstraps.'

The station had never seen anything to match it. The room heaved with an assortment of colourful looking characters, some smart and suited and booted like Riley and some casual like Enders. Being as Sunday would be Halloween a few had even come in costume and Savage spotted two devils and a witch. As for Calter, she leant against a desk chewing gum, a right sight in a miniskirt Savage thought more suited for use as a belt.

'Nano, ma'am,' Calter said. 'It's the new micro.'

'Well I hope you've had your flu jab or you'll catch your death in that.'

'A rabies jab would be more appropriate,' Enders said, 'with the type of animal that's going to be coming after her dressed like that.'

Calter proceeded to give Enders the once over, starting at his shoes and moving upward, nodding with approval at each item.

'I've seen better looking jackets on a potato, but I'm glad you've found a use for those Oxfam vouchers at last.'

Savage gazed around at the rest of the people in the room. They numbered around thirty-five in total, the younger members dressed for a night out clubbing, the older detectives wearing clothing more appropriate for dinner in a restaurant.

Hardin bounced about at the far side of the room greeting people, face red from the heat, the handkerchief in his hand in constant use wiping the sweat from his brow. She reckoned it had been a long time since he had walked the streets of Plymouth late at night because he wore a blazer and tie and looked like something from a yacht club do. At least nobody would mistake him for a policeman, just a right prick.

Hardin rapped on a table top and brought the meeting to order.

'OK boys and girls, operation Big Night Out is ready to go.'

A big cheer and a couple of whoops rang out and Hardin continued. He outlined how the operation would work. The bright young things would be inside the pubs and clubs, working in pairs, trying to spot anything suspicious. Some of the older detectives would be walking the streets as if they were going to or coming from the theatre or restaurants, and to back them up there would be four unmarked cars patrolling. Finally Davies and a couple of others would monitor events from the city-centre CCTV control room.

Savage heard Enders mutter something about it being 'nice and warm in there' but Hardin didn't hear.

'I would really like to end this night with these bastards banged up so let's be especially vigilant.'

With that Hardin let them go and they trickled from the station in pairs heading out into the damp night air.

Savage found DCI Garrett and confirmed they would be walking a route that would take them down to the Barbican, across to the Theatre Royal and up to the university. From the uni they would return to the station and head out on a new beat.

'This will be a long night,' Garrett said.

'Tell me about it. My feet are killing me already.'

Calter came off the dance floor to find a grumpy looking Enders leaning against a mirrored pillar waiting for her.

Behind her a medley of songs was reaching a climax and hands rose into the air, fingertips disrupting a plateau of pale blue laser light that painted a horizontal curtain just above head height. Around the bar a crush of bodies jostled for the attention of the overworked bar staff and the air smelt of perfume, sweat and beer. Calter grabbed her pint of bitter from Enders, took a gulp and held the glass against her forehead.

'Hot work,' she shouted across at Enders.

'You're not supposed to be enjoying yourself, Jane, we're on duty,' replied Enders.

'Just trying to blend in,' Calter said, catching Enders take yet another glance down at her legs.

'Fat chance of that, you've got half the guys in here gawping after your every move.'

'Only half?' She smiled.

'Well the rest must be blind or gay.'

'Or both,' Calter quipped.

She scanned around the club. It was on several levels with the dance floor up one end, a long bar down one wall and a couple of raised galleries with little cubby holes where all manner of things could go on unseen. If their target chose to do his business up there they would have no chance of spotting him. They had already been here for over an hour and a half and the time was now after one in the morning. So far nothing of interest.

'Come on, let's go for another mooch about.'

She took Enders's hand. His palm felt hot and sticky and she wondered why on earth he hadn't left his jumper in the cloakroom. In the current situation he looked ridiculous.

A big, muscled guy with the kind of body Calter would have liked to explore in more detail moved across in front of her.

'Can I buy you a drink, luv?'

'Thanks, but no thanks.'

'He with you?' The guy turned and with an expression of puzzlement he pointed at Enders.

'Yes, he's my brother,' she nodded. 'Got learning difficulties.'

'Maybe later then.'

Calter nodded again and the guy backed off. She led Enders along to the steps that went up to the galleries.

'Learning difficulties?' Enders said. 'Thanks a bunch!'

'I needed a rational explanation as to why your appearance resembles a Ryder Cup entrant. That was the first one I thought of.'

Up top they stood against the railings and Calter made Enders remove his jumper. The shirt underneath didn't shout style, but at least he might cool down a bit.

The galleries gave a good view of the dance floor and she would also be able to sneak a glance into the cubby holes without appearing too inquisitive.

'Here,' Calter pulled Enders towards her and placed his hands on her bottom. 'Hold me like this and I can take a peek into the booths and you can look down onto the bar and dance floor.'

Enders didn't seem to be complaining much although he was holding himself away from her body in an odd way. She suspected he had a hard-on. Calter hugged Enders, pulling him close and half-burying her face in his neck, and now she felt his erection pressing against her.

'Jesus!'

'Sorry, only natural, like my mother used to say.'

'Not that, although I have known bigger. No, there's a guy in the booth who has just dropped something into a vodka and orange.'

'You are joking!'

'No. He's on his own, but there is a phone on the table next to the drink.'

'So?'

'It's a pink phone with glittery bits stuck all over.'

'Oh, I see.'

Calter risked a glance, but she couldn't spot any obvious partner for the man. Perhaps the woman had gone to the loo. Last time Calter had been the queue snaked out into the corridor so she might be some time returning. The man appeared to be quite old for the venue, mid-thirties and dressed not unlike Enders. He gazed around, for a moment meeting Calter's eyes.

'Hold me tighter, grope me.'

Enders didn't need much encouragement and one hand went down between her thighs, the other to her left breast. The performance may have convinced the man, but in real life Enders would be going home empty handed. His hands moved over her body more like a potter fashioning a vase from clay than a lover trying to turn her on, but then having three young kids Enders probably didn't get much practice at home. After five minutes of the sculpting treatment Calter got bored of the petting and was about to suggest they stopped when she noticed a girl coming towards them.

Girl? The thick make-up couldn't disguise the lines on a face a bit too old for their usual victim profile. Calter guessed early thirties at the very youngest, but she was dressed to impress with a skirt as short as Calter's and a top that left nothing whatsoever to the imagination.

The woman staggered to her seat and fumbled with the pink phone, knocking it to the floor. The man retrieved it from under the table and moved over next to her and helped her with her glass, encouraging her to drink up, which she did. Then the man said something and the woman squinted at her phone, maybe reading the time. The two of them got up and walked past Calter and Enders, heading for the exit.

Calter untangled herself.

'Put your stiffy away, lover boy, and call for the cavalry. It's him.'

Savage and Garrett did the Barbican circuit once and went straight out again on a run that took in the railway station. Afterwards they'd had a short break and grabbed a coffee in the canteen before doing the first route all over.

A dust rain began to fall, the tiny drops swirling in the glare around the street lamps, and by the time they reached the Barbican the long cobbled street gleamed in the light. A throng of people walked and stumbled along the road and the air reeked of fish and chips and fast food. An underlying tension threaded amongst the crowd and hinted at sex and violence.

A pink stretch limo cruised by, filled with a gaggle of girls on a hen night, bare arms waving out of the windows, one sticking her bottom out and flashing her knickers at a group of appreciative lads.

'Gerrum orf you fat slag!'

'Show us your tits!'

'Fancy a good knobbing, do you?'

The car pulled away and Savage wondered at the height of Plymouth's Saturday night sophistication.

'Is that the best the youth of this town can manage?' she asked Garrett.

'You'll find the same everywhere, take away the street names and this might be any town in the country. Broken Britain they call it, don't they? Although I suspect the country has always been broken. Rose-tinted spectacles and all that.'

173

'I certainly don't remember shoving my bum out of a car window, but maybe I got too drunk to notice.'

'That's the point. Those girls get too drunk to notice. They lose their friends, someone gives them a spiked drink and the next minute they are tied to a bed being gang raped.'

They wandered through the Barbican area and up Madeira Road, across the Hoe and down towards the theatre. They were turning off Amada Way onto Notte Street when Savage got the call on her mobile.

'Are you near the theatre yet?'

'Five minutes.'

'We've got an IC1 male and female walking along Princess Street, possibly heading for the Theatre Royal car park. Male dark hair, brown jacket, brown trousers. Female blonde, white coat, bare legs. Observe, do not apprehend as of yet.'

Savage told Garrett and they ran along Notte Street and down Lockyer to join Princess Street, slowing to a walk when they saw the couple walking towards them. The woman wandered all over the pavement and the man struggled to keep her upright. Savage took Garrett's hand and faced him.

'Call you next week sometime?'

'Er, yes, that would be great.'

'I've really enjoyed this evening, honestly. I can't remember a time when I have had as much fun.' Savage couldn't help smiling which she thought must have added some realism to the act.

The dialogue was wasted on the couple who seemed oblivious to anything as they weaved back and forth. They reached the car park and went down the side to the stairwell. Savage spotted Calter and Enders coming along Princess Street and she made a sign to suggest that they should go to the front of the car park and wait near the barriers while she and Garrett followed the couple. The car park was one of the pay-on-foot types where you had to put a ticket into the machine and pay the amount due before you went to your car. It seemed as if the man had lost his ticket because the couple were hanging around the machine for ages. Eventually he produced a piece of scrumpled cardboard and with some difficulty got the machine to accept it.

Savage and Garrett trailed the couple as they went up two flights of stairs, stumbled out onto the third level and made their way over to a green Audi, where the man opened the rear door for the woman. She clambered in and sat back in the seat, leaving the door open. The man didn't go to the driver's side, rather he opened the front passenger door and, taking something from the glove compartment, he returned to the woman. He blocked Savage's view for a moment and the door slammed shut. The woman leant forward now, hands on the front headrest. The man got in and the car started, reversed out of the space and moved forward.

'Bloody hell!' Garrett had spotted something. 'Handcuffs!'

The car moved out of the shadows and a glint of silver shone out from within. Savage saw Garrett was right. The woman had been handcuffed to the front headrest.

'Shit!' Savage raced forward to block the ramp to the next level. The driver floored the accelerator, the tyres screeching as the rear end spun out.

'Stop police!' Savage shouted.

The car was coming right at her, the man's black eyes wide, white knuckles grasping the steering wheel.

'Charlotte!' Garrett shouted.

She didn't need the warning and she jumped clear as the car careened across the ramp and glanced the side barrier. It slid sideways, straightened up and then lurched into a pillar, stopping dead. A loud bang echoed through the whole level as the front airbags exploded and a huge piece of concrete broke away from the pillar, bounced on the bonnet and smashed into the windscreen.

An empty car parked nearby started up with the rhythmic beep, beep, beep of an alarm and Savage heard the sound of running footsteps from the floor below. A moment later and Calter and Enders came up the ramp, breathless.

'We got him, ma'am. Bloody hell!'

The four of them gathered round the car. The man slumped against the side window, face half-buried in the airbag and a trickle of blood running from his nose. The woman had just been sick on the back seat.

Savage opened the rear door. She clicked the catch on the headrest and pulled it upwards and away, freeing the woman. The woman rubbed her hands and Savage could see red marks where the cuffs had cut into the skin when the car crashed. She scowled as Savage fumbled with the seatbelt.

'Don't worry, we will have you out of there in a moment, you're OK now.'

'Of course I'm fucking OK!'

'Did he touch you?'

The woman laughed.

'Chance would be a fine thing.'

'Sorry?'

'You've made a big mistake.' The woman paused and smiled. 'You know who Sleeping Beauty up front is?'

'No.'

'He's my husband.'

Chapter Nineteen

Harry risked a journey to the big Sainsbury's supermarket at Marsh Mills in Plymouth because he needed a load of fruit and a set of bra and panties for Emma. Plain white, like all the girls from his childhood had worn. He suspected his mother had insisted on it. She wouldn't have wanted all the frilly stuff because it would have made his father get a little bit too excited.

Harry found a space to park and sat in the car remembering the first time he had seen the white cotton offset against smooth, young skin. He had found a hole in the back of a built-in cupboard in an adjoining room. Through it he spied Carmel sitting on the bed in her bra and panties. Removing the bra and exposing her breasts and then standing up and peeling her knickers down to reveal a dark triangle of mystery, black alongside the pure white, Harry's heart thumping even though he was still so young.

After that Harry sneaked into the spare room whenever he could and secreted himself in the cupboard with the little pinhole. He would watch Carmel for hours and sometimes she did little, just reading or watching the tiny black and white TV his parents had provided. At other times she would be getting ready to go out and Harry loved to watch her choosing her outfit and applying her make-up. Late at night, when she returned, he would creep from his bed and sneak a look at her undressing, watching as she cast her knickers into the linen bin for him to retrieve the next day and hold to his face, the material suffused with a strange, musty smell which was both frightening and intoxicating. Back then he felt nothing sexual; instead a wonderful warmth blossomed right in the centre of his chest, causing butterflies in his stomach and a lightness so beautiful it brought tears to his eyes.

When Carmel had gone he thought nothing could replace her, but soon a new girl arrived for him to spy on. The same white underwear, the same purity on one side of the wall and Harry on the other.

He was brought back to the present by a woman getting into the car parked next to his. She hurried to get in and as he met her eyes she pulled the door shut and flipped the lock down. He turned the radio on and pretended to fiddle with the controls. The station blared out the news. They were talking about him again. That made him feel special. Of course they didn't mention him by name, they simply talked about a body which had been found on Dartmoor. The newsreader reported the police saying it could be a walker who had got lost, but Harry knew the police didn't really think that. Not when they were keeping quiet about the tipoff which had led them right to the little shit's body. Harry smiled at the thought of the man dying up there on the moor. The bastard as good as killed Trinny and Harry hadn't been willing to let him get away with that. Not after he had seen the movie on the scrote's video camera.

On the journey back the sun played hide and seek behind heavy clouds, but by the time Harry arrived at the cottage the weather had turned damp and miserable. Like his mood. In the past couple of days thoughts had spun through his mind the way clothes tumbled in a hot, soapy wash, the colours running into one another, bleeding from each garment, mixing with the dirt and the grime. Now at last the stream of consciousness had reduced to a trickle, a grey discharge, and a flatness descended which deadened everything from before. At least inside he knew a hint of magic waited for him, someone to raise his spirits again.

Do you mean Easy Emma, Harry?

Trinny. Still butting in with the occasional comment. He had heard her less and less though and soon, he thought, she would be gone for good.

Don't know about that, Harry. Anyway, there will always be one of us to keep you company.

Trinny's words disturbed him. He didn't want voices. He would need to think of a way of keeping the next one he had to deal with quiet.

You mean Legs Apart Lucy? Did she turn out as slutty as me then? Don't say I didn't warn you!

Harry grunted. Trinny was only jealous. She had no interest in his project now she was not to be the one.

And neither does Lucy. I feel sorry for her so I think I will help her to stay around too. With both of us here I think we can stop you getting into so much mischief.

That was not good news. If Emma turned out not to be the one either there could be three voices in his head. And who knows how many more to come?

There are only six of us, Harry.

Yes. Six. Trinny was right about that if nothing else.

Harry got out of the car and went into the cottage leaving Trinny muttering to herself outside in the drizzle. He remembered she had been the last girl his parents employed, the one who had caused all the trouble, so maybe that had something to do with her attitude. Some months after she arrived she had an argument with his mother and later the same evening the police came calling. That night Harry watched his mother and father being led out of the house in handcuffs, a crowd jeering and throwing stones as they were driven away. He went up to his bedroom to wait and shiver in the darkness and before long the light came on and a policewoman arrived to take him away to a new home.

Ah didums. Poor Harry.

Trinny had come inside to tease him. He would ignore her.

Temper, temper.

He wished she would go away. He didn't want to remember.

But remember you must. Remember the children's home.

There he hoped to find some relief from the terrors inflicted by his father.

Wrong.

He remembered the shock at the end of his first day when three boys he thought of as new friends had beaten him half-senseless and proceeded to shove his head down a toilet. And then there was Mr Grimes, the Principal. His name was only the sub-plot, his after-dark activities the main story. How could Harry have been so mistaken? But then hadn't he also been badly misled by the girls who looked after him as well? Each seemed to be the one who would give him love, but in the end each left to find it somewhere else.

I had to leave.

Now he had guessed why Trinny had left, dirty girl.

I was assaulted by your father. Raped. I was a young woman, a girl.

Exactly. Dirty.

So why are you still chasing after us?

He wanted what he had back then. He wanted the closeness of the flesh without the perversion of desire.

You've got a funny way of showing it.

180

That was because they were all sluts. He couldn't help himself.

Looney tunes, Harry.

Harry ignored her as he busied himself laying a fire in the front room. He wanted it warm for later. For Lucy. Then he thought about Emma. Up there in the room all alone. He hoped she was OK. And, because he was thinking of what was upstairs, he thought of THEM. They lived upstairs too. In the attic. How appropriate. He gave them water and some stale bread a few times a week, but they didn't have much of a life. They must be cold and frightened and in the deepest despair imaginable.

The thought lifted his mood. He felt happy and quite content. He struck a match and the fire burst into life, darting yellow and orange, little popping sounds coming from the kindling. The room began to warm and his mind turned to Emma once again. He hoped she was the one.

She isn't, Harry. You know that.

It wouldn't matter. There were plenty more out there.

Chapter Twenty

*Derriford Hospital, Plymouth. Monday 1st November.
9.00 am*

Forester's post-mortem was scheduled for first thing Monday morning but Savage lost no sleep over it. The jaunt on the moor on Thursday combined with Saturday night's late shift had left her shattered. Not to mention that she had spent the whole of Sunday trying to keep Samantha and Jamie entertained. The day had been fun, but she hadn't had any time to relax.

Doctor Nesbit emerged from his office in his green robes, bright eyes glinting as if he couldn't wait to get started. He spotted Savage leaning against a wall and sent her and Enders away to fuel up on coffee and buns while he and his assistant prepared for the PM. The coffee came strong, black and acrid, but the iced buns tasted lovely and when she returned the combined caffeine and sugar rush had heightened her senses to beyond the point she had wished for. The stench from the morgue lingered in the air, despite the whirr of the extractors, and not for the first time in her life Savage remembered the fact that all odour was particulate based.

Nesbit greeted them in a contemplative mood.

'I have hypothesised a direct correlation between the number of times I encounter you chaps each month and the state of British society. Recently I find myself wondering if things aren't getting a little bit worse.'

Nesbit moved over to the body of David Forester, or rather the remains of Forester, for the heap of skin and bones didn't resemble a man in any meaningful way. The body had been up on the rock for weeks and the sun, wind and rain had been hard at work. Not to mention the crows and other scavengers. Bits of flesh hung on bleached white bones and the grin on the face and the staring empty eye sockets looked like something from a zombie movie. Under the glare of the lights and before a small, select audience, Forester prepared to make his final performance.

After the discovery on Fur Tor they'd had no time to contemplate the scene. The wind had picked up even more and the snow fell in large flakes. Campbell said they should head back before the weather got even worse. Savage had noted the state of the body and little else. Not until the next day, when John Layton called, had the full horror of what Forester had been through become apparent.

'Chained round the neck to the rock. Handcuffs behind the back. Not a scrap of clothing on him. I'm not doing the pathologist's job but I'd stake my pension on him having been alive up there at some point.'

Layton said they had found faeces on the rock beneath the body and what appeared to be urine stains too.

'So you think he starved to death? Or died of thirst?' Savage had asked.

'Luckily for him I reckon the exposure got him before he reached that point. Hypothermia, I'd say. Death would have been a relief.'

The body lay half-curled on the post-mortem table, hands

still cuffed behind the back. Savage wondered if Forester had died in the same position. Alive a thug, but dying like a baby in the womb, she thought the tableau in front of her showed a sort of poetic justice, but she couldn't quite figure how.

Nesbit peered into the chest cavity and prodded about between the ribs with a long pair of forceps.

'Not much of interest for us, Charlotte. All the internal organs are gone or virtually so. My job here is more like archaeology than pathology.'

'No chance of testing if he had been drugged then?'

'Not today, no. We'll open up his skull in a moment and get a peek at what's left. Not that there will be much I would think.'

Nesbit poked his forceps into the left eye socket and bent over to look right inside.

'Hah! Something the crows didn't get at least.' He uttered a cry of delight and withdrew the forceps. Clasped in the end was a small, clear and shrivelled piece of plastic. 'Contact lens.'

The lab assistant held out a dish and Nesbit dropped the lens in.

'Not that it tells us anything, I'm afraid.'

'Except he was short-sighted,' Enders said.

'Does that help?'

'In fact I suppose it could be helpful,' Savage said. 'The lens tells us he may have been out and about when he was kidnapped. He wouldn't wear contacts while asleep and depending on his prescription he might not have worn them at home.'

'Now then.' Nesbit was making a second pass over the body. 'What is this?' He pointed down at the left leg where the flesh and muscle had rotted away to leave nothing but bone.

Savage moved closer than she wanted to and saw a line where the bone was broken.

'Observe.' Nesbit tapped his forceps on both sides of the leg. 'Both tibia and fibula are fractured.'

'RTC?'

'Common when a pedestrian is hit by a vehicle, yes. As to whether the break is a result of a road traffic *accident* . . .'

Nesbit was now working his way up the body, examining the other bones one by one.

'Ah, look at the shoulder.' He used the forceps to peel back a piece of stringy muscle. 'The left clavicle is badly broken, smashed even. I can't see this amount of damage having come from a collision with a car though. If the pedestrian was walking across the road and was hit on the left hand side he would be thrown on the bonnet, or against the front of the car. This injury appears as if inflicted from above.' Nesbit made a chopping movement down on his own shoulder to illustrate.

'Something like a baseball bat or a sledgehammer handle?' Savage asked.

'Not out of the question. With this little flesh to examine I can't say much, but he was probably hit from behind. If this had been a high-speed collision with a car I think we would be looking at other fractures too.'

'That wouldn't be the cause of death?'

'No. He'd be in a lot of pain though. An awful lot. From the leg too. Plus any other injuries we can no longer ascertain.'

Savage grimaced, imagining Forester chained in the cold and dark and shitting himself, literally, as he was dying.

'So Forester crosses a road and is hit by a car. As he lies on the ground or as he rises someone attacks him with a baseball bat. They put him in the car and drive him up to

Dartmoor where they chain him and leave him to die. Anything wrong with my hypothesis?'

'Nothing at all, Charlotte.'

'And if they had wanted to kill Forester they only needed to run him over with the car or batter him further while he lay on the road.'

'Hitting him over the head would have finished him then and there and saved the attacker a lot of trouble.'

'So the manner of Forester's death was premeditated?'

'That's your job to determine, Charlotte, not mine.'

Savage considered the sad heap of bones, once a man, now an exhibit. Forester didn't deserve much sympathy, but nobody should have to die like this she thought. Enders seemed to be reading her mind.

'Couldn't have happened to a nicer guy, ma'am,' he said, as if his words provided some comfort.

Savage ignored him.

'What about when he died?' she asked.

'Time of death is going to be difficult. We won't find any entomological clues to help us after this period has elapsed. The body has been exposed and partially disturbed by animals; the wind, sun and rain have done their worst as well. My best guess is somewhere between two and four months. Possibly the faecal deposits might yield a more accurate span.'

'The date is essential, ma'am, isn't it?' Enders asked.

'Yes. If Forester died after Kelly Donal we can posit Forester killed Donal and was himself killed as an act of revenge.'

'If he died at the same time then we are looking for just the one killer?'

'And a very dangerous one at that.'

*   *   *

186

Back at Crownhill and Nesbit was on the phone barely a minute after Savage had sat down at her desk.

'Something else about Forester you forgot to tell me?' she asked.

'No. I've got some toxicology results on Kelly Donal. Told the lab to fast-track them for you. Looks like they worked over the weekend.'

Savage groaned. Fast-tracking would add hundreds of pounds to the invoice, an amount she would have to justify to Hardin.

'Sorry, Charlotte, I should have asked first, but I think you'll agree it was worth it.'

'OK, Doc, spill the beans.'

'I asked for a detailed segmentation test on the hair sample. That means the hair is cut into lengths and each section tested. The result is a historical map, if you like, of any drug use. An analogy would be the rings you see in a cross-section of a tree trunk.'

'Go on.'

'She was a heroin user and had been for several months. I had already hypothesised that from the injection marks on her arms. However, she had also taken gamma-hydroxybutyrate some time between seven and fourteen days before her death. It takes around seven days for the drug to show in the hair sample, so that is the minimum period. Longer than fourteen days and it would have been in the next segment of hair. Can you see where I'm going with this?'

'That the GHB was used in her kidnapping?'

'Yes. But more than that. Remember I couldn't tell you how long she had been frozen for? Well, if the drug was given to her when she was abducted then we can posit that she only remained alive for a maximum of fourteen days before she was killed and frozen.'

'You mean—'

'I understand there is another girl missing . . .'

She thanked Nesbit and hung up. Then she worked through the dates in her head. Alice Nash had been missing for seven days. It was possible that she only had another seven to live.

Pondering that awful thought, Savage went to the canteen for a late lunch and found the room buzzing with the aftermath of Saturday night's little debacle. The worst of it was that two Special Constables had spotted a man trying to drag a girl into the back of a car across town near the railway station. The Specials shouted a warning and the man drove off leaving the distressed student lying in the road. One of the officers managed to note the registration and got a good look at the car, a blue-coloured BMW. Volunteers one, professionals nil. CID was a laughing stock.

'Clubbing Idiot Dickheads is the one currently doing the rounds,' grunted Davies as he, Savage and Garrett gathered later in Hardin's office for a meeting. On the wall the calendar of Greek Islands was still stuck on December last year: Santorini, the white buildings cascading down the side of the island's caldera like Christmas snow. Four weeks' time and at least it would show the right month, Savage thought.

Davies appeared rougher than usual, which meant he'd probably done a bottle of whisky after his stint in the CCTV room on Saturday night and slept in the clothes he was now wearing. Garrett looked like he'd spent Sunday at a health spa and then returned home to iron shirts and press trousers. Some of the worry lines had faded too. Other people's arses were on the line now.

The initial PNC check on the vehicle registration on Saturday night had found nothing. The plates turned out to be false. However, the next morning a *Leash* team member fired up the Vehicle Online Descriptive Search application to pull out a bunch of results.

'Two hundred and sixty-two matches registered within twenty-five miles of Plymouth according to VODS,' Hardin said, looking up from his laptop and beaming as if he had tracked down the Holy Grail.

Needles in haystacks more like, Savage thought. The amount of work to visit, interview and collate all those leads would mean the *Leash* team were going to be doing nothing else for the next week.

Hardin focused on the positives and the fiasco of Saturday night didn't seem to be affecting his mood at all.

'Doesn't matter how much footwork we need to do now,' Hardin said. 'We are close, I can sense it. Big Night Out was a bloody disaster, but some good old-fashioned policing produced the goods. Now, what about Mr and Mrs Kinky, any word from the lab yet, Mike?'

'Colin and Jessica Abbott are their names,' Garrett said, turning a page in his notebook, 'and I'm still waiting for the results. Using one of our own testing kits we got a negative, but we will have to wait for the full analysis to come back.'

'So we think the drink contained what?'

'Sugar. Mr Abbott said he poured a sachet into the drink. When his wife returned from the toilet she tasted the drink had been spiked with something and role-played as if she had been drugged.'

Hardin bit his top lip and grabbed one of his liquorice sticks.

'And they maintained the whole thing was a mock kidnapping scenario, a game?'

'Consensual, yes. If we hadn't intervened they would have woken up Sunday morning with the papers as usual.'

Hardin ruffled his notes, scanned his monitor screen for

inspiration and shook his head. No wonder, Savage thought, he would be having a hard time understanding this one. Especially since the couple hadn't been charged.

'Resisting arrest and trying to run Charlotte down?' Hardin said, turning to Savage and sounding hopeful.

'He thought Mike and I were carjackers,' she answered. 'That's what the solicitor is going with. Mr Abbott wasn't even over the limit. To be honest we will be lucky to get away with just a car repair bill.'

'Bugger.'

Hardin made a hissing noise between clenched teeth, the big man diminishing in front of her eyes like a balloon with a leak, before perking for a second.

'Never mind. Let's hope the VODS data gets us somewhere.'

Hardin paused and any remaining signs of the euphoric mood from earlier slid away as he read the agenda on his screen.

'Now to something as pressing, if not more so. Alice Nash and *Zebo*. We located Forester, but he's dead so there is no chance he's our man. That would have made things easier all round, hey Charlotte?'

'Not really, sir,' Savage said. 'I mean, Forester was killed by someone. He didn't volunteer to go for a jaunt on the moor. Whichever way you view it a brutal murderer is on the loose.'

'Ah, yes, I suppose you are right.' Hardin hissed again. 'Where are we at then? Any news on the girl?'

'Last week she was seen getting into Forester's 4x4, but Forester has been dead for weeks so we are mystified as to who was driving. You probably watched the appeal her father made on TV over the weekend. So far that has produced nothing but crank calls. No reliable sightings of her or the Shogun.'

'She's only sixteen?'

'Yes.'

'And the forensics from over at Malstead put Forester's car at the scene?'

'I'm afraid so. Tyre tracks and paint match. Whoever dumped Kelly's body in the field picked up Alice a day later. Nesbit has a theory and if it's correct then things don't look too good for Alice.'

'Theory?'

'He reckons Kelly was kept alive for anything up to fourteen days before she was killed. So far Alice has been missing for seven days.'

'Jesus. This really can't get any worse.' Hardin pinched his top lip between his thumb and forefinger and made a sucking sound as he let it smack back against his teeth.

'Let's hope not, sir.'

'What about Forester? You attended the PM this morning?'

'Yes. The PM suggests Forester was run down and then beaten. There was little other forensic evidence and Nesbit isn't hopeful of getting anything from the lab reports because the body had been out on the moor for some time and the foxes and rats have got at it.'

'Lovely!' Davies let out a little snort and grinned. 'Wonder what the press will make of that when they find out?'

'Quite,' Hardin sighed. 'If we hadn't put out the appeal then they wouldn't be able to make a connection between the Donal girl and Forester. They may have assumed his murder was some type of lowlife punishment killing.'

'Still possible it is, sir,' Garrett said. 'The actual murders may not be linked at all. We've been picking up intelligence in recent months about some Bristol lads planning to make a move down here. They think the city is easy pickings; bit of a pushover is the word on the street.'

'What, us?' Hardin's face creased, thinking about the headlines again no doubt.

'No, sir,' Garrett laughed. 'The No Prospect lot. A complete bunch of smack heads. We can't even produce any decent crimos round here.'

'You could be right.' Hardin looked hopeful for a moment. 'Let's keep our fingers crossed Doctor Nesbit can get some meaningful toxicology to give us something else to go on.'

It seemed to Savage that Hardin wanted to cling to anything that would steer them back to charted waters. He wanted something he understood, something he could deal with by piling in resources. A lone nutter was unfathomable and even a gang selling smack to twelve year olds was better.

'We wondered whether Forester was mixed up in a porn or prostitution ring,' Savage started to explain. 'We've dispatched his computer to Hi-Tech Crimes and are awaiting results, but for now we know both he and Kelly were into glamour photography and he had managed to persuade her to do some hardcore videos. He's done that before with other girls so what the difference is with Kelly we don't know.'

'Did the shoot go wrong somehow?' Garrett said. 'Could she have been killed by accident? Or deliberately, some sort of snuff film?'

'I don't buy the snuff angle, as I've said before, sir,' Savage said, 'but an accident is possible. However, whatever the reason for Kelly's death Forester couldn't have dumped her body. He's been dead for weeks. A couple of my people are working up something around Mr Donal. Perhaps he killed Forester in revenge for Forester killing Kelly. How the theory fits in with Malstead Down, Kelly's body being frozen and the picture that resembled Rosina Olivárez though . . .'

Hardin shook his head and made a final hiss, all the air gone out of him now. He didn't move for a minute or so and

Savage and the others sat waiting. Then he opened a drawer and fumbled in his desk for a moment. Savage half-expected him to pull out a bottle and offer it around. Instead he brought out a newspaper.

'I am aware you guys laugh about my obsession with the media, but in this case it's no joke. Did anyone see this morning's *Sun*?'

Hardin held up the paper in front of them. The headline wasn't one of the clever ones, it was just three words, but they took up the whole of the front page and the effect was chilling. The words had been superimposed over an outline map of Devon and Cornwall and said: 'West Country Ripper?'

Chapter Twenty-One

Hardin had said thank God for the question mark, and when Savage returned to the incident room and told Riley, Calter and Enders they burst out laughing.

'What does he think they are questioning,' Riley said, 'the fact it's in the West Country or the fact there is a ripper?'

'He's going to doctor the page using Photoshop,' Calter chipped in. 'He'll put a "T" in front of "Ripper" and tell the CC we might be expecting a good tourist season next year.'

That had them in stitches, apart from Enders who scrunched up his face in bemusement.

'Huh?'

'Keep taking the pills, Patrick,' Calter said.

The banter was still going on five minutes later when a couriered package arrived for Calter.

'The dump from Forester's hard drive, ma'am.' Calter opened the package and read the accompanying letter. 'Seems Hi-Tech had an easy job. Forester didn't take any special measures like encrypting his files or anything. They've written all the stuff to DVD, documents, emails, images and a bunch of movies. We've got a load of disks here, must be a couple of hundred gigabytes of material in total.'

'Sounds like an interesting afternoon ahead of us,' Enders said.

Calter turned up her nose. 'If you enjoy filth.'

'Depends if you are the main feature, babe.' Enders put on a camp American voice and held his hands up, making a rectangle shape with his fingers and thumbs and peering through, like a film director working up shot angles.

'Now, now folks,' Savage said, 'let's get started on this then. And I don't want to come over all politically correct, but remember we are dealing with rape and murder here so save the banter for the piss-up we are going to have after we have caught this guy, OK?'

Savage grabbed every spare body and managed to get eight of them working on the material, two to a monitor. Text began to scroll across screens and images flashed by, movies played in little windows and the sound of sex filled the room. At first everyone concentrated, focusing on the task with an intensity Savage admired, but as the hours dragged, chairs tipped back and feet went up on desks. This much porn was just plain boring.

DC Carl Denton made the breakthrough. Denton had popped along from the *Leash* incident room and became ensconced at one of the screens with Calter and Enders. They had found a set of videos showing some very graphic imagery with girls blindfolded and tied to a bed in what appeared to be a mock rape scenario.

'Fuck!' Denton exclaimed.

'I think the language you should be using in your report is sexual intercourse,' Enders said, causing Savage to cast him a warning glance.

'No, I mean she's one of them. I'm sure she is.'

'One of who?'

'Wait a moment.' Denton jumped up and dashed from the room.

'Did I say something?' Enders held out his arms, palms up.

A few minutes later Denton returned, brandishing a piece of paper, a victim sheet with a little picture of a pretty girl stuck in the top right corner.

'Georgina Wilkinson. It's bloody well her!'

Denton appeared stunned as well as pleased with himself, but nobody else seemed to know what the hell he was going on about.

'Who the heck is Georgina Wilkinson?' Enders said.

Savage sussed it.

'Carl is from operation *Leash*, work it out!'

'Georgina Wilkinson is one of the *Leash* victims? Bloody hell!' Enders understood now and soon everyone else in the room did too.

Once the implications of the discovery sank in all hell broke loose. Some officers began crowding round the screen, others ran up and down the corridor and started to brag they had solved the *Leash* case. The atmosphere was one of fevered chaos and Savage tried to bring some order to the situation. She dispatched Denton back to the *Leash* incident room to obtain pictures and info on all the girls involved. Then she called Garrett, telling him they now had hard evidence that the rapes the *Leash* team were investigating were in some way connected with the murder of Kelly Donal. The next thing was to get everyone back at their screens and concentrate the team's effort on looking at video files only, searching out those that depicted rape scenes. Finally, she decided Hardin needed to hear the good news.

By mid-afternoon they had reviewed seventy of Forester's video files. Sixty-four of those were sex scenes which, although graphic, did not seem to involve any coercion. The remaining six files involved rape and it didn't appear to be simulated. In four of those they were able to identify victims already known to the *Leash* team.

Hardin came down to the incident room to congratulate the troops on their work and he was gushing in his praise.

'Christmas has come early this year. First the success on Saturday night and now this. It's good policing. Bloody good. Well done everybody.'

'There's more, sir,' Savage said. 'I saved the best until last.'

She motioned for Hardin to take a seat next to Enders and called for quiet.

'Patrick?'

'Right, ma'am.' With a couple of clicks of the mouse Enders had cued up a movie. 'This isn't pleasant, sir, but don't watch if you would rather not. Just listen to the audio track.'

The video started to play and Hardin flinched at the sight of a girl tied in the centre of a double bed. A black sash cut across her face covering her eyes and as she struggled her image was reflected in full-length mirrored wardrobes on one side of the room. A couple of masked figures passed in front of the camera, both men, both naked. One of the men moved to kneel on the bed near the girl's head and said something to the girl, but the words were muffled and indistinct, however the look on her face changed and she fought against the ropes again. Then a strange rumbling came from the speakers followed by a sound like the wind on a stormy night and Enders paused the video, the naked images frozen in time.

Hardin crinkled his brow and puffed out his cheeks, mystified.

'I didn't hear what he said to her.'

'No, sir,' Savage said, 'neither could we. But that doesn't matter, we are not interested in their speech.'

'I don't understand.'

'The date stamp, sir. Note the date stamp on the bottom right of the screen.'

'Twenty-fifth September, four twenty-seven pm.'

'Yes, the girl is Mandy Stilson. If you remember she was the odd one out because she was picked up on a Sunday lunch time.'

'I'm sorry, Charlotte, you have completely lost me,' Hardin said, shaking his head and smiling. 'Too many years away from the sharp end I expect.'

'It's the noise at the end we are interested in. Play the segment again please, Patrick.'

Enders clicked the mouse and played the last few seconds of the clip again. Hardin's expression changed from one of puzzlement to a look of revelation.

'A train!'

'Yes, but not just any train. We are guessing it is the Sunday four sixteen departure from Plymouth to London Paddington. The house must be close to the railway.'

'I don't understand how you know which train it is, and even if you did there must be hundreds, if not thousands, of houses backing onto the line.'

'You are right, sir. But we took a list of all train departures on the date from all stations within a twenty-five-mile radius. We then worked out roughly where each train would be at four twenty-seven – the time on the date stamp. Also, according to several of the victims, we are looking for a large, luxury house with a gravel driveway.'

'I don't see how that helps us. There still must be hundreds of houses, we need something to narrow . . .' Hardin paused and then looked astonished. 'Bloody hell, the VODS data! You haven't?'

'We have, sir,' Savage said, smiling. 'I realised we could use the VODS data for the car spotted by the specials cross-referenced over the geographical areas we came up with for the train times. The database gives us only two results. One of them is a terraced cottage on the outskirts of Saltash. We don't think the property fits because two of the victims talked of a big house and garden. The other location is number nine Moor Vale, a large house on a select development surrounded by woodland and situated just outside Plympton. The development backs onto the main railway line.'

It was late Monday afternoon when three squad cars full of bodies raced across town to Moor Vale, screaming their way through the rush hour traffic. Savage sat in the rear of a vehicle, merely along for the ride as this was to be Garrett and Davies's shout. That suited Savage fine. She'd already got her fair share of kudos for using the VODS data to find the address of the owner of the BMW, one Mr Richard Trent, a lecturer at the University of Plymouth.

Off the A38, skirting the eastern end of Plympton and onto an industrial estate. It seemed like they had taken a wrong turn as they drove between the bleak monoliths, but soon they were leaving the estate and on a country road which dived down the side of a wooded hillside. Their sirens sent a startled dog walker leaping for the verge and then the trees ended and they entered a parkland setting with perhaps a dozen large houses scattered around. Big gardens, double garages, the glimpse of a swimming pool behind one of the properties. The epitome of middle-class desire.

Moor Vale was a misnomer. Woods and a hill blocked any

glimpse of Dartmoor proper, which lay several miles away. Like the rest of the development number nine appeared to be only a few years old and was all glass, steel, wood and concrete; what one would call 'architect designed' as if normal houses came off a production line, which perhaps they did. The style did nothing for Savage but the place looked nice enough. A powder blue BMW was parked in front of the garage.

The cars halted at the driveway, one taking up a position to block the road. Davies and DC Denton jumped from their car and walked to the front door. Garrett and two officers from one of the other cars skirted round the back of the property. Savage and the others got out and stood waiting by the cars.

A pheasant called out a warning from somewhere in the woodland and then silence for a moment before Davies rapped on the door, the sound echoing around the estate.

There was a pause and Savage was aware of her heart beating fast. The door opened and a woman stood in the porch. She was short with dark hair. Her features were plain and her face was etched with a sadness and a faraway expression.

Motion. Davies pulling the woman out of the way so that she stumbled and fell down the step and then he was dashing into the house with Denton following.

'Go! Go! Go!' A crashing sound came from the rear of the property as the back door was smashed in. Savage and the other officers ran from the cars to the front door and into the house.

Large entrance hall, wide stairs twisting upwards to a sort of galleried landing where Davies stood shouting.

'Bastard's in the bathroom trying to top himself!'

There was another crash and a scuffle and a shout.

'Jesus Christ!' Davies disappeared from view and Savage directed two of the officers up the stairs.

'Man down! Man down!' Davies shouting again, hysterical this time.

Savage followed the officers up the stairs. A man lay in one corner of the landing, trying to protect himself by wrapping his arms around his head. Davies was kicking the shit out of him.

'You fucking wanker. I'm going to throw you over the banisters when I have finished and no one here is going to say you didn't jump.'

In the bathroom Denton sat on the floor slumped against the bath. A cutthroat razor lay beside him and he was using one hand to try and stem the flow of blood from a gruesome looking gash on his left cheek. A huge flap of skin hung loose and Savage could see the white of bone in amongst the red. Denton smiled up at her from a pale grey face and spat blood into his free hand.

'Ambulance!' she shouted behind her and rushed to the bathroom. A mirrored cabinet reflected the horror in the room and she ran over and threw the door open.

Aftershave, deodorant, packets of soap, bath scents, sanitary towels, everything came tumbling out as she ransacked the cupboard. Fuck! No first aid!

She grabbed the box of sanitary towels from where it had fallen into the sink and ripped the packet open. Out came a towel and she tore the packet apart.

Denton grinned from behind a mass of flesh and blood.

'I've always liked kinky, ma'am, but I don't want to die with a Simon Cowell on my face.'

'You aren't going to die you daft bugger, I just don't want you looking like the elephant man when you come back to work. Now shut up and keep still.'

She moved Denton's hand away from his face and pressed the flap of skin back in place. Denton flinched but didn't cry out. Then she took the sanitary towel and placed it over the wound.

One of the other officers had come into the bathroom and Savage told him to open some more packets. She pressed a couple more towels on the wound and that seemed to staunch the blood. Denton was losing consciousness now though, eyes closing, head lolling.

'Carl, stay with me, stay with me!'

Denton's eyes flickered open and his head moved in acknowledgement. Then his eyes closed again.

It seemed like ages before she heard the wail of the ambulance, although it could only have been a couple of minutes. There was a commotion from the hallway down below, a clattering on the stairs and the paramedics arrived on the landing with a stretcher. One came in and knelt beside her and assessed the situation. He put his hand on Denton's head, used his thumb to lift an eyelid and shone a penlight in Denton's eyes.

'Keep holding that, love,' the man said to her. 'He's lost a lot of blood, suffering shock too, but I think he's going to be alright.'

Chapter Twenty-Two

Back in early summer it had been cold, the promise of a scorcher that a few warm spring weeks had hinted at long gone. Day after day of rain kept him cooped up inside the cottage, wallowing round the place, the gloom more to do with his mood than the fact he had the curtains drawn.

There had been a knock, knock, knock on the door. Rap, rap, rap at the entrance to his very soul.

'Hello, Matthew. It has been a long time.' Two figures stood outside in the drizzle sheltering beneath a large umbrella, each wearing cheap tourist-type translucent yellow waterproofs and thin smiles.

Harry stumbled back from the door, shocked at the apparitions. Ghosts weren't supposed to appear in broad daylight.

'You bastards!'

'We need to talk.'

'Too right we do. Get the fuck inside.'

Once inside they talked and Harry listened. Like always. They explained, reasoned, apologised, pleaded. Finally they grovelled and begged for the absolution which Harry knew they had come for. Selfish as ever.

Their words and moans and sobs blended into a cacophony that drilled down through his skull and into his brain. An egg whisk went to work in there, mixing and blending and churning until the only thing remaining was a uniform mush that meant nothing. Harry couldn't take it anymore so he left them in the house and went outside. The earlier rain had stopped and now the air was still, the smoke from the chimney rising in a vertical column. Up in the heavens a formless grey mess hung like a suffocating blanket; no cloud shapes, no sun, only bleak sky.

And that was how he felt. Empty and cold. But he also knew he could be full again. Like Mitchell said, you had to grasp the moment and then you could be free. Problems, problems, problems, he thought to himself.

He trudged round to the barn at the side of the cottage, went inside and knelt in the dirt. With his eyes screwed shut he prayed to God to do something, to show a sign, but he knew God would remain silent. God wasn't merciful and the meek did not inherit the earth: they got fucked while tied to a little wooden bed in a cold attic room.

Harry opened his eyes and stood up, soggy knees the only sign God had sought fit to give him. Then he noticed a beam of light coming through a hole in the rear wall. The light danced across the space like some sort of primitive laser, illuminating motes of dust in the air on its way. Where the beam hit the far wall it shone on a rusty six-inch nail struck in there at a weird angle. Hanging on the nail was a long piece of chain and a couple of padlocks.

Chapter Twenty-Three

Tuesday morning at the station and a feeling of anti-climax hung in the air. Richard Trent's brief had made an allegation of police brutality and although Trent hadn't been sprung from his cell, Savage reckoned it was only a matter of time. 'He was resisting arrest,' Davies had told Hardin. Savage played back the incident in her mind and decided Davies's account lacked one or two small details. If Trent's guilt proved short-lived then maybe she would have to have words with Hardin about those missing details. For now she was content to keep quiet.

DC Carl Denton's bed for the next few nights would be up at Derriford Hospital, but he was doing OK. The surgeons had sorted out his face, although they spoke of a nasty scar being forever on show for his efforts. At the morning meeting Hardin was talking about recommending Denton for a bravery commendation.

'Saved a man's life and that's no small thing.'

'Saved a piece of shit if you don't mind me saying, sir,' Davies said. 'World would be better off without the likes of Richard Trent.'

205

'Ah, but if Mr Trent had succeeded in topping himself we'd be in a spot of bother, wouldn't we?'

'We are in a spot of bother, sir,' Savage said. 'The VODS data was useful intelligence, but the information has zero evidential value. None of the rooms at Trent's place match the decor or layout of the rooms in the videos and the initial search didn't find any ropes or bondage equipment. The team are going through the house room-by-room, but so far nothing. And according to a neighbour the BMW gets cleaned once a week, every week. On a Monday. When he heard that Layton headed down to the car valeting place and impounded every vacuum cleaner they own. But if he can't get something from them or the car we are stuffed.'

'And do you think he can?'

'He reckons if any of the girls so much as glanced at the car he'll find something.'

'Good, I'll keep my fingers crossed. Can we identify Trent in the videos?'

'We are pretty sure in several cases, but the perpetrators are either wearing masks or facing away from the camera. In a couple of the scenes some special software has been used to pixellate the faces and anyway the lighting is not great. To ask a jury to convict without supporting evidence is going to be a no-no.'

'And last night's session produced nothing?'

Davies shook his head. 'DC Jackson and me did a two-hour stint and to be honest I expected him to come crying home to mummy, what with the weight of evidence I thought we had.'

'So what happened?'

'As soon as we got word the house was wrong I knew that we were in danger of losing the plot. And Mr clever clogs

Ph bloody D knew as well. There was something else though: I reckon he was scared.'

'As well he might be after the kicking you gave him. Mr Trent has some pretty impressive bruises.'

'Yeah, well, Denton and all. Anyway I don't mean he was scared of me. Every time I asked him a question his tactic was to say nothing, but I got the feeling he wasn't only worried about implicating himself.'

'Well, the others are still at large, aren't they?' Savage said. 'Possibly a network, perhaps organised crime. He wouldn't want to be the sneak in the latter case.'

'Figures,' Davies said. 'Either way, Trent said zilch because his brief had told him to keep stum. The bitch realises that if the house and car search come up empty then we don't have anything else.'

'The assault on DC Denton?' Hardin said.

'He's claiming self-defence, sir,' Savage said. 'Nice middle-class lecturer is at home having a shave in his bathroom when two men burst in and attack him. He has no idea what is going on and one of the men gets hurt in the struggle.'

'But he was trying to kill himself. What does he say about that?'

'Denies it, sir,' Davies said. 'Claims he was shaving and then seeing us he used the razor in self-defence. Doesn't wash with me, if you'll excuse the pun. It was late in the afternoon, a funny time for a dig in the grave.'

'This is getting to be like groundhog day,' Hardin said. 'First the kinky husband in the car park and now Mr Trent. It would be good for my health if the next arrest you lot make was a bit more clear-cut.'

'I was thinking about Forester,' Savage said to Davies. 'Did you mention him? The only information we released is that a body has been found on Dartmoor, no name, no cause of death, no details. The media went with the idea the corpse belonged to a walker who sprained his ankle, so it's possible Trent doesn't even realise Forester is dead. We might be able to use that.'

'Good idea, Charlotte,' Hardin said. Then he got to his feet, went over to the window and stared out.

'I've just had a call from somebody in the custody centre at Charles Cross. Apparently they have had to place a couple of uniforms down at the front door to prevent anyone getting to Trent. A shocking waste of resources. There are the usual castrators and hang 'em high brigade, plus a lot of students. A lot of *angry* students. Either group would be only too pleased to get their hands on Mr Trent, although I doubt there'd be much of him left for us if they did.'

'Yes, sir,' Davies said. 'Not much peace and love by the sound of it.'

'I want you to get over there and try again. Charlotte and DC Jackson this time. The beauty and the beast act, please.' Hardin continued to look out of the window as if he could see all the way across the city to the station in the centre of town. 'If that doesn't work we release him, do you get my drift?'

Interview room three stank of vomit, the grey carpet tiles in one corner turned a lighter shade by the contents of some drunk's stomach. A whiff of stale cigarette smoke suggested that somebody had ignored the big red 'No Smoking' sign on the wall as well. They had been scheduled to start at eleven but the interview didn't begin until nearer twelve since Amanda Bradley, Trent's brief, had turned up late. Bradley sat down next to Trent, her short skirt riding up to expose chunky thighs wrapped in sheer black tights.

The outline of a black bra showed through her flimsy shirt as she removed her jacket and hung it on the back of the chair. Jackson's eyes widened as Bradley apologised for her tardiness.

'Had to come in from a previous appointment out of town,' she beamed through white teeth, glossy red lips and a mouth that was a bit too big. 'Traffic was horrendous.'

Savage didn't believe her excuse. Bitch Bradley had the handle on them. She knew the PACE clock was running and, even allowing for a twelve-hour extension, come five thirty the next morning Trent would be out. They might be able to get a further extension following a court application, but if the searches turned up nothing at all it was unlikely.

Jackson put fresh tapes in the machines and got the formalities out of the way, introducing those present and cautioning Trent. He explained to Trent why they were continuing the interview and went through the rapes one by one asking Trent where he had been on the dates they had taken place.

Trent sat fidgeting, first with his hair, winding the strands around his fingers like a teenage girl, and then with the zip on the over-sized shell suit he was wearing. Some kind soul had rooted the purple and lilac monstrosity out of the lost property box to replace Trent's own clothes which were covered in DC Denton's blood and had now become evidence. In contrast to his body language Trent's voice came out in a flat monotone and he answered each allegation the same way. The final date brought the same reply.

'Like I told you yesterday, I was at home that night.'

'Mr Trent, we know you were at home,' Jackson said, bristling with anger. 'The question is whose home and what you were bloody doing there!'

'My home. Watching TV.'

'What did you watch?'

'Can't remember. Some reality show, maybe later the news?'

'The news? How convenient. The news is on every fucking night so the fact you watched the programme isn't exactly an alibi, is it? Next you will be telling me that you went to bed with the bloody *Guardian*.' Jackson thumped the table with his fist. Savage could only imagine what the interview had been like the previous night with Davies joining in as well. Time for beauty to step in.

'Richard,' she said, trying to bring an air of calm to the proceedings. 'Has anybody told you David Forester is dead?'

'No!' Trent put his hands together in front of his opened mouth, as if in prayer. 'Dead?'

'Yes. Murdered.'

Trent swallowed and glanced at his brief. Bradley turned to Trent for a moment, her eyes wide, before she returned her attention to Savage.

'I don't believe I have been informed who David Forester is. Do you mind if I consult with my client?'

The two heads bent towards each other and a few murmured words passed between them.

'My client doesn't know who David Forester is,' Bradley said, her composure restored.

'Bollocks!' Jackson said, ignoring the solicitor and addressing Trent. 'You do know, and you killed him!'

'Wait a moment,' Bradley said, putting her arm out in front of Trent as if shielding him from the accusation. 'Is this a fresh allegation?'

'Did you know David Forester, Richard?' Savage said. 'It seemed as if you did a moment ago.'

'I . . . no. I never met him. Don't know who he is. I must have seen his name in the papers or on TV.'

'Wrong answer Mr Know-it-all lecturer,' Jackson said. 'The papers never reported his death. You just flunked your finals.'

'I don't know who he is.' Trent seemed more confident, as if he had weathered the storm. He repeated the denial several times and neither Savage nor Jackson could persuade him to say anything else on the matter.

Bradley had a half-smile on her face now, the glee evident. On the desk in front of her a latest model iPhone flashed a little icon on the screen as it recorded Bradley's own copy of the interview. Savage fancied shoving the phone right in between those big teeth, ramming the hideous pink contraption down her throat until she choked on Trent's weasel-like words. Instead she decided it was time to move to the back-up plan Hardin had proposed.

'OK, Mr Trent, I think we are finished for now. You are free to leave.'

'Interview suspended at twelve thirteen pm,' Jackson said and proceeded to stop the tapes and remove and seal them up.

'There's a bit of a crowd outside, but you should be able to get through.' Savage smiled at Trent and pushed back her chair to get up.

Trent's face cracked like an egg hit with a spoon and he turned to plead with his brief. Bradley put a hand on his arm to stop him.

'My client will require an escort away from here.'

'Oh I don't think that will be necessary. There are only a few photographers and a couple of hundred students. I have no idea what they are doing to be honest. Something about a paedophile.'

'Paedophile?' Trent said. 'But they . . .'

'They?' Savage said. 'The girls you mean? Tracy Williams was I believe fourteen. Granted she appeared a whole lot

211

older covered in make-up and wearing a cutesy little skirt. The push-up bra helped too, amazing what those things can do. Obviously the press don't know any of that because we have to shield her identity.'

'You have to protect my client. You have a duty of care.' Bradley had picked up the phone, but Savage noticed she hadn't stopped recording.

'Calm down, Ms Bradley, of course we do. We will put Mr Trent in a car and take him home. I believe a few people are hanging around Moor Vale as well, but we can put a uniform on the door. For tonight, at least.'

Bradley nodded, but did not comment. Trent stared at his hands on the table, almost as if they did not belong to him. The right hand jerked up and down with little shaking movements until he put the left hand on top.

Savage continued. 'To be on the safe side we will put out a statement saying Mr Trent cooperated fully with us and has provided some very valuable leads. We will explain that we expect to be making a number of arrests in the next few hours.'

'No!' Trent said. 'I mean I don't want to go home. I want to go somewhere else. Away from here, away from Plymouth. I need a new identity, I need protection.'

'This isn't a movie, Mr Trent, this is real life, and the last time I enquired Devon and Cornwall Police weren't running a travel agency. Pity really, I could do with a break.'

'But it's not safe, they will get me and kill me.'

'Who exactly, Mr Trent? The mob outside or someone else? We can't do much about either, I'm afraid.'

'Jesus!' Trent leant forward and put his head in his hands. He started to hyperventilate and talk to himself. Then he began to sob. Bradley wriggled on her seat and Savage noted she didn't make any attempt to comfort him. Cold bitch.

After a couple of minutes Trent looked up, his eyes glassy and his face white like a blank sheet of paper awaiting a story. Jackson unwrapped a fresh set of tapes and stuck them in the machine.

Alice had been in danger of losing track of the days until she hit on the idea of the pips. Every morning she woke to find a tray with fresh fruit and a bottle of water at the door and from the third day she started to secrete apple pips under a corner of the mattress – one for every day. Now she held the little brown seeds in her hand and counted off the days until she arrived at Tuesday. Or Wednesday. She couldn't quite figure the precise day because she didn't know how long she had slept at the beginning of the ordeal, but as she put the pips back under the bed she reckoned it was a pretty good guess.

She lay back down on the mattress and for the umpteenth time tried to work out what the hell was going on. As each day had come and gone she began to think maybe she wasn't in the hands of some nutter after all. Perhaps she had been kidnapped and was being held to ransom. If so, then the kidnapper had made a big mistake. Since her mum had died Dad had given up his job in Exeter and now taught part-time at the local college. They hadn't been well off before then, but now they had no money. That was why she had the job at the nursery.

Thinking about her mum made Alice cry again, but it also gave her some resolve. Mum had said Alice had to be brave and look after Dad and Alfie, her younger brother, and Alice promised she would. She wasn't going to let some guy make her go back on her word.

She got off the bed and for the umpteenth time took a tour of the room. She touched the wooden shutters and moved on. At first the window had seemed like the obvious way out, but no longer. She had scratched a larger hole in the paint and discovered iron bars set into the stonework on the outside. No way out there. That only left the door. She went over and tried the handle but it was locked, as always. She bent to look through the keyhole expecting to see the opposite wall of the dark corridor she had seen many times before. Nothing. The hole had been blocked up or . . . the key was still in the lock!

She remembered a trick her dad had shown her where you slid a piece of paper under the door and pushed the key out from the inside, retrieving the paper with the key on it. She didn't have any paper, but she did have the tray from her morning delivery. The tray was a single piece of preformed plastic, the sort you got in a cafeteria, and the gap beneath the door measured about two fingers, just enough to allow it to be pushed under. Now she needed something to poke the key with. She racked her brains, listing things in the room she might use. She had gone through everything and was beginning to despair when . . . fruit to the rescue again: a banana. She grabbed the peel and felt the woody stalk, perfect! The stalk didn't fit into the keyhole so she whittled away at it with her fingernails until she had trimmed the excess and then pushed it in. The key wasn't straight in the lock so it didn't drop out, but after a bit of wiggling and twisting she heard it fall down and clatter onto the tray.

Silence. The only noise the beating of her heart. Thump, thump, thump, thump. No footsteps in the hallway, no sound of anybody coming to investigate. She pulled the tray in, picked up the key and tried it in the lock. Click. She pushed the handle down and opened the door.

The door swung open to reveal a hallway lit by a bare

bulb glowing white and hanging from an old, twisted wire. A carpet ran down the centre exposing stained wooden floorboards either side. The carpet was ancient and in an old-fashioned style, coloured deep red with gold swirls in amongst the dirt somewhere, the pile worn and threadbare. A short way along the corridor to the left a door stood half-open. Inside the room a huge roll-top bath sat beneath a window. There was no blind or curtain, just glass with condensation streaming down in rivulets. The bath and a cracked washbasin had antique fittings, the tap on the basin dripping dirty water onto brown stained enamel.

To her right she could see another door, closed this time, and beyond the corridor turned a corner. In front of her stairs led down to either a hallway or a room below. The stairs were steep with the carpet held in place with brass rods and had a wooden banister to the right.

Alice retrieved the duvet from the bed and wrapped it around her. Then she padded out of the room and across to the stairs and began to descend, stopping on each step to listen.

For what?

Nothing but the distant drip, drip, drip of the tap echoing the cadence of her heart thumping.

A board creaked under her foot and she froze. She lifted her foot and eased it away and down onto the next step. An old song, one of her mum's favourites, began to play in her head. Kris Kristofferson was it? And how did it go?

One step at a time, sweet Jesus, only that didn't sound quite right. *Fuck knows, who cares anyway?*

She carried on down, mouthing the words of her new song until she reached the bottom step.

Another corridor, a closed door next to her and the hallway turning back in the opposite direction from the stairs.

Halfway along another bare bulb hung down, the light so weak she could see the coil of red glowing wire inside the glass. At the end of the hall was a big, old door, thick with years of paint. Black iron bolts top and bottom and a burglar bar dropped into U-shaped brackets fastened to the frame. A rough, bristled mat lay on the floor.

Front door. The way out!

She eased herself along the corridor, half-sliding, half-shuffling. Down on the left an opening revealed a large room, dim with no light. In the gloom she could see a long table with high-backed chairs. She inched past the room and moved towards the front door. To the right yet another door stood open, a flickering light dancing within. She crept nearer. There seemed to be a rhythmical sound, a slight rubbing noise, coming from somewhere close.

Shuffle, slide, shuffle, slide. Her own rhythm this time, the Alice Nashville two-step.

She was at the door now and when she peered in she had to bite her lip to prevent herself letting out a cry.

In the centre of the room a man knelt on the floor. Short dark hair, late thirties and naked. And she recognised him. The nakedness shocked her, but the recognition chilled her.

Always best to go with your first opinion of someone, girl. Best not to go for a drink with them. Asking for trouble that.

She remembered now. It had all been Cath's fault. She said it would be a giggle so when he asked them to go to the bar with him they accepted.

Who is giggling now, Cath?

She didn't think he had taken her for the money. He as good as had weirdo tattooed on his forehead. She had felt uncomfortable when she first met him, the way his eyes drank her in and his tongue flicked in and out like a snake or a lizard tasting the air.

216

The man was sideways on to her and she had a clear view of his right hand moving up and down in the age-old manner. The man's face contorted, creasing and flattening in time with his hand's rhythm, although whether the expressions showed pleasure, pain or grief Alice found impossible to tell.

To each side of the man a candle burnt in a tall, silver candlestick. The candles guttered every now and then sending shadows feathering across the floor, the fluttering light picking out a bare room with heavy velvet curtains at the window and an open fire crackling in a grate.

The man was staring forward, a grey tongue lolling in the corner of his open mouth as he gazed at something in front of him. Alice couldn't see what it was. She knew she should turn and run, but she didn't. Instead she edged closer to the door, craning her head to see.

Oh no. Fucking hell!

Her mouth dropped open and the shakes returned. Now she knew she should move and she tried to inch backwards. One step. Two steps.

A creak from a floorboard.

The man's hand stopped moving for a moment, but then started again, his breaths now coming in short gasps, a strange guttural sound arriving with each one.

Alice stepped back again and turned, brushing into the bar on the front door. The bar clinked against the brackets and she froze.

The sounds from the room continued. Rub, breath, gasp. Rub, breath, gasp. She reached out for the bar, hands shaking until she clasped them tight around the cold metal. She lifted the bar up and out of the brackets, lowered it to the floor and rested it on the mat. Now for the bolts.

The lower one was easy and she slid it across, careful not to make a sound. The top one was high enough to mean she had to reach up on tiptoe and as she did the duvet slipped off her shoulders and fell to the floor. Now naked, she shivered as she used the fingers of both hands to try and work the bolt free. Layers of paint encrusted the runner it sat in and she had to wiggle the bolt back and forth to move it. Little by little it started to slide free. Then all at once it came, shunting across with a clatter.

Alice brought her hands down and grabbed the doorknob, aware of a scream from off to her right. She turned the knob, wrenched it, but the door wouldn't budge.

A shadow appeared on the wall, the shape elongated and then distorted as the candles flickered. The shadow morphed once more and then the man was standing in the doorway.

'Going somewhere, Emma?' He cocked his head on one side, a smile broadening on his face before changing to a manic grin below staring eyes of pure madness.

Chapter Twenty-Four

*Crownhill Police Station, Plymouth. Wednesday 3rd
November. 10.15 am*

Back at her desk Wednesday morning and Savage was trying
to make sense of it all. As she scribbled a couple of Post-its
and clicked through some documents on her screen she
began to realise how much the scope of the investigation
had widened. As the boundary between *Leash* and *Zebo*
became indistinct the clear picture the team had been
working with blurred. Focus shift. She had seen it before
and knew the danger. They now had a tangle of threads to
tease apart: Rosina, Kelly, Forester, Trent, *Leash*, *Zebo*. Kelly
had got involved with Forester through the modelling and
the drugs and they had linked Forester with the rapes thanks
to the videos and the GHB the CSI team had found at
Forester's flat. But what did the videos have to do with Kelly's
murder?

The answer came with Riley. He breezed in with a cup of
coffee for Savage and some good news too. He had been
given a heads up by DC Susan Bridge, the statement reader
on *Leash*.

'Photography, ma'am. That's got to be the answer.'
Riley showed her the printout DC Bridge had given him.

'Door-to-door has come up with the goods. Old-fashioned policing as Hardin would say.'

Savage read the statement. The account came from a neighbour who had seen something odd going on at the house opposite Trent's late one night.

'Flashes, ma'am. Up at a first-floor window. Like someone taking pictures. And the neighbour claims to have spotted a woman at the curtains. Naked.'

'Interesting viewing for the neighbour, but taking pictures of your missus in your own house is not illegal, is it?'

'Not at all. Not had the chance myself mind you.'

'So? I get the impression you've got something else,' said Savage.

'Plymouth Snappers.'

'The photography club Donal and Forester were members of?'

'We obtained a list from the club secretary comprising some two hundred names of current and recent members. Trent is not on the list of course, we checked already, but I went back and had another scan through. The house where the neighbour saw the flashes is owned by a man called Everett Mitchell. Just happens he's a former member of the Snappers too. That gives us a link to Forester, but there is something else too.'

'Go on.'

'Mr Mitchell is self-employed and I took a little look into his business affairs. Now what type of business do you think he is involved in?'

'I have no idea, but I expect you are going to tell me.'

'His registered business name gives a clue: Devon Cream Film Distribution.'

'I don't need to ask, do I?'

'No. It's a porn company. He sells DVDs and downloads

220

from a number of websites. The business is legit, above board and everything, but bearing in mind we know Forester was involved in some dodgy videos I'd call the fact one hell of a coincidence, wouldn't you?'

An hour later Riley and Enders coasted into Moor Vale in an unmarked pool car. Savage had said Mr Mitchell would need to answer some questions, especially because in his statement given to the officers on the door-to-door enquiries he claimed not to know David Forester.

Mature trees of oak, ash and beech half-hid the houses and though the autumn leaf fall had long since started the lawns were clean and well-manicured.

'Fantastic place this,' Enders said as they cruised by the first couple of properties. 'I'd get a pad here if I won the lottery.'

There was a certain air of refinement about the place, but Riley didn't think much of the development. It seemed a little too sterile, a little too footballers' wives.

'Where is the atmosphere? The concept is a bit artificial for my liking.'

'What are you talking about? Look at all that lovely grass. And this road goes nowhere. My kids could have a whale of a time here.'

'Are you joking? What do you think Mr and Mrs We-Paid-Good-Money-For-This would say when your Connor goes whizzing around on his scooter? Or when the two little ones start playing Aliens versus Predator in the neighbour's rhododendron bushes?'

'Ah well, if my numbers came up I could send them to boarding school!' Enders grinned. 'I tell you what, I would think somewhere like this would suit the lovely Ms Meadows very—'

'Shut up. Anyway, we're here.'

Everett Mitchell's house was number seven. White plaster, black wood and shiny steel intermingled with diagonal lines running in all directions. Little windows sat juxtaposed with big windows, huge windows trumped the lot. A hotchpotch of styles and materials vied for attention in a physical manifestation of an architect's wet dream. They drove up the curving S-shaped drive across gravel that crunched with the sound of money and stopped in a turning circle in front of a double garage attached to the left hand side of the house. Riley wondered if an internal door in the garage led to the inside. If so it would be easy to bundle a girl from the car and into the house without any risk of being seen.

As they got out of the car the front door opened and a man came striding out. He was in his forties or early fifties with dark hair and a jet black goatee beard and had the air of a country landowner about him. He dismissed them with a wave of a hand as if to shoo them away.

'No thank you. Whatever you are selling I'm not buying, I don't want any hassle and nobody else on the estate does either. We don't need you lot round here. Back in the car now. Go on, or I'll call the police.'

The voice rang with a confidence belonging to someone used to getting their own way, the type of voice Riley despised. He had heard the tone often enough in certain parts of London and the man's manner gave the lie to the myth of a classless society. Some people assumed the world moved for them and them alone. In this case Riley would enjoy showing the idiot how wrong he was.

'Shocked as you may be to hear, sir, we *are* the police. Detective Sergeant Riley and Detective Constable Enders. If you could step back into the house we'd like a word. Assuming you are Mr Everett Mitchell, that is?'

'Yes, I am but I don't have the time for—'

'I will rephrase what I said, sir. Step back in the fucking house before I change my mind and decide to take you down the station.'

For a moment Mitchell appeared taken aback, but then he smiled and a new persona slipped into place. 'Well, why didn't you say so to start with? Your scruffy little car doesn't exactly say "police" to me. It says "trouble". Come on in.'

Mitchell turned and walked back to the house and Riley clenched his fists, digging his fingernails into his palms to stop himself from boiling over.

'Let's face up to reality, Darius,' Enders said, giving Riley a wink. 'I'm a paddy and you are black. We are not worthy to lick the shit from the man's shoes, let alone his arse. However, what has really upset me is what he said about our poor car. She'll never get over such blatant prejudice.'

Mitchell disappeared inside the house and the two detectives followed him across the threshold and went into a hall with snow-white carpets and dominated by a sweeping staircase. A shout came from a room off to the right. They walked down the hall and into a spacious lounge where Mitchell was reclining on a huge sofa.

'I've told the wife to make some coffee. Should be here in a minute,' Mitchell said, waving at them to sit down. 'Now what can I do for you? I assume you are investigating the awful business with Mr Trent.'

Riley sat in an armchair and began by asking Mitchell the same questions that had been put by the door-to-door team. Had he noticed anything suspicious? Had he any inkling of what Trent was up to? How well did he know Mr Trent? When Mitchell answered he seemed relaxed, not an ounce of tension in his voice.

'I know him of course. Lent him my lawnmower once

223

and I chatted to him in the road occasionally. We went to a barbecue a year or so ago but the do wasn't my type of thing at all. Full of academics. Load of bollocks. Hot air and canapés. Fizzy wine. Environmentalists with big people carriers and tales of holidays in Peru. Labour voters and hypocrites. Poor show indeed, I thought. Those kinds of people don't know how to have any fun.'

'What is your impression of Mr Trent himself?'

'Weasely, isn't he? No confidence. Of course the news came like a bolt out of the blue when he was arrested, but on reflection it figures. Sneaky kind of guy like him. Unattractive. Wife probably keeps her legs shut and I wouldn't blame her.'

'So you had suspicions?'

'No, of course not. I'm just saying now you have got him I'm not entirely surprised.'

At that point a woman entered the room with a jug of coffee and cups on a tray. Long blonde hair framed a model-like face and a white towelling dressing gown hugged her full figure. As she walked across the room Riley glimpsed a flash of golden thigh.

'Ah, Catherine. Meet Chief Inspector Morse and Sergeant Lewis. There has been a murder. Ha, ha, ha!'

Riley introduced himself and Enders and explained the reason for the visit. Mrs Mitchell nodded and poured the coffees. Then she went to sit on the sofa next to Mitchell. The top of her dressing gown fell open and her left breast slipped into view. She made no attempt to cover herself and Riley averted his gaze.

'Oh come now, Mr Riley. Don't be shy. My wife isn't.'

Riley wondered how much longer he would be able to refrain from hitting Mitchell. He was turning out to be an annoying little shit. But then there were a lot of them about these days. Riley turned to Enders, the cue for him to take over the questioning.

'Mr Mitchell. Do you know a man by the name of David Forester?'

'David. Forester.' Mitchell's face crinkled in puzzlement for a moment. 'Ah, David Forester. Yes, of course. Nasty guy. Met him at the Snappers. Photography club in Plymouth. Didn't take to him. He likes young models. Girls. If you get my drift.' Mitchell patted his wife's leg. 'I prefer something a little more mature myself. Ha, ha!'

'Did he ever come here?'

'Forester? Good God no. I wouldn't let scum like him in my house. As I said, I only met him the once.'

'Mr Mitchell. Your business interests.' Riley took over again.

'Ah, I thought it wouldn't be long before you got onto that.'

'What do you mean?'

'Everybody buys it, everybody uses it, but those of us providing the stuff are viewed as little more than pariahs.'

'I don't care what you get up to as long as it's legal. What I want to know is have you ever got involved in harder material? Mock rapes, that sort of thing.'

'You don't get it do you? I sell porn, yes. Explicit, yes. But the sex is clean, above board. Your assumption is because I am in the industry I must be a paedophile rapist animal buggerer. It's like me labelling you and your colleague sadistic thugs because of the violent behaviour of a tiny percentage of police officers.'

'And Forester? Your business had nothing to do with him?'

'Forester!' Mitchell shook his head. 'So if you can't get me on the dodgy porn you'll try and link me to some scrote drug dealer? Give me a fucking break.'

'Mr Mitchell,' Riley decided to try a change of tack. 'We had a report of some bright flashes of light from one of your upstairs windows. As if someone was taking photographs in the middle of the night. Can you explain that?'

'Of course.' Mitchell seemed unperturbed, got up from the sofa and went to a bureau where he opened a drawer and took out a small camera. 'I used to make the films, years ago, but now it is cheaper to buy them in. Still, me and the wife, we like to take a few pictures for old times' sake, don't we love?'

Mitchell strode across to Riley and showed him the screen on the back of the camera. Riley's heart beat a little quicker when he saw the screen showed a naked woman tied to a bed, but the bed and the room did not look anything like the scene in Forester's videos. And the woman was Catherine Mitchell.

Mitchell pressed a button on the camera and another picture appeared. This time Catherine sat topless on the bed. Click. Mitchell himself, naked and tied to the bed. Click, click, click. The pictures streamed by, each one either of Mitchell or his wife. There were ropes, handcuffs, dildos, whips, candles and other paraphernalia, but Riley's overriding impression was of flesh.

Mitchell was chuckling now and a giggle came from Mrs Mitchell too. When Riley looked across at her she smiled and opened the lower half of her dressing gown; she was wearing nothing down there either. Enders was gawping and Riley began to wonder if they were losing control of the situation. He pushed the camera away and stood up.

'Mr Mitchell, we'd like to take a look upstairs, if you don't mind.'

'Because I took a few photographs for my personal use and some peeping tom wanker reported it? Do me a favour.'

'It's a request, that is all. We can go and get a warrant.'

'Sorry I do mind.' Mitchell raised a hand to his forehead, wiping an almost imperceptible bead of sweat away before he continued. 'Our daughter is upstairs. She has not been feeling well so she slept in our bedroom last night. I would hate for her to be disturbed.'

'We will be back, Mr Mitchell.' Riley beckoned to Enders and they left the house to the sound of Mitchell's raucous laughter.

As they walked to the car Enders was laughing too. Riley gave him a look of disapproval.

'No, no, boss, this is serious. I need some professional advice. What the hell do I tell the wife when she asks how my day was?'

Riley shook his head. He was more concerned with what he would tell DI Savage. Maybe it might be better to skip over the part with Mrs Mitchell and her dressing gown and only mention the pictures and the fact Mitchell wouldn't let them upstairs because of his daughter. Then something came to him.

'Patrick, we need to get back to the station pronto, there is a hunch I want to check. If I'm right then I think we might have the bastard.'

Chapter Twenty-Five

Harry woke late and took a shower. Truth be told the shower in the cottage was pretty ineffectual. The water dribbled out like pus from a sore and could hardly clean the dirt away, let alone the shame.

Last night. Again.

Never mind. He hoped Emma would be OK, but she would need to learn not to be naughty like that. Guests shouldn't go nosing about in other people's houses as if they owned the place. And her seeing him with Lucy, he didn't like that at all.

She had tried to run, but didn't get far. At the top of the stairs he managed to grab her foot and she fell face down on the landing. He forced his body on top of hers. Shameful, disgusting, but of course Emma was to blame. He hoped she wouldn't prove too troublesome, but either way there were only a few more days and then the process would be done. God had only needed seven days to create the world, true, but Harry reckoned he needed fourteen to clean the girls and get all the badness out of their systems. Two weeks of fruit and water would purify their bodies and then he could test them.

After the business with Emma he couldn't bring himself to go back down to Lucy for quite a while, worried about what she would say. He knew she would have guessed what had happened, for naked girls did not turn up in the living room unannounced as a general rule.

When he got back to her she sat still and said nothing. Harry decided not to try and explain. He simply kissed her, gave her a quick cuddle and said goodnight.

Goodnight, Harry.

Was the voice in his head Lucy or Trinny?

Lucy, Harry.

Strange. Where had Trinny gone?

She's gone for good. She left me to deal with you now.

Thank goodness, Harry thought. Then he went to bed, leaving Lucy alone in the living room for the night.

After the shower he dried himself and thought about getting Lucy up to the bathroom so he could prepare her for her leaving. He had showered in order to save the hot water for her. She was heavy and uncooperative when he carried her up, but she seemed to brighten up a little when he plopped her in the bath.

Nice smell.

The bath overflowed with bubbles. Harry had tipped in half a bottle of Lucy's favourite peach infusion.

How sweet of you.

He had wanted to make the occasion special since this was their last day together.

Is it?

Yes. He was sorry it hadn't worked out.

I am sorry too, Harry. I saw the new girl.

Shit.

Harry felt guilty now and the anger returned. Emma had spoilt things between Lucy and him. He tried to explain to Lucy, but she went all silent and moody. Still, he thought she was listening when he told her he still loved her and that he would never forget her.

Thank you, Harry. I won't forget you either.

Good. He started to wash Lucy, rubbing the foam all over her and trying to ignore the patches of blue and purple skin.

Harry. The little whore Emma isn't the one you know?

He hoped Lucy was wrong about that, but he knew he would have to wait and see.

Harry washed her all over and then removed her from the bath. He dried her thoroughly, and because she had been a bit naughty in mentioning Emma he decided to fuck her once more. He moved inside her, trying to be gentle and came with a gasp after only a few seconds. His eyes brimmed with tears as he looked down on Lucy's face, knowing he would not have her again. He rolled off and then took his sewing kit and did his work, making sure nobody else could have her either.

All this time Harry had had the radio playing a local music station to try and take his mind off things. But just after he finished dressing Lucy, the bitch newsreader went and ruined the whole day.

Mitchell.

The police were closing in on him. The bulletin said Richard Trent had been arrested and the police had questioned his neighbours. If the police got Mitchell they would break him and then Harry knew he would lead them to him. Mitchell would be able to talk his way out of their hands, feed them some candy and fuck them over.

He looked at Lucy and saw she was smiling, a great big grin on her face as if she had thought of something ingenious. He asked her what it was.

I've got an idea, she said. Then she told him what to do.

Chapter Twenty-Six

Savage moved the phone another six inches away from her ear in an effort to reduce the volume of the tirade coming from the earpiece. Hardin had phoned ten minutes ago and the bellowing hadn't stopped long enough for her to get a word in.

'Results, Charlotte. Yesterday would have been fantastic. Today would be good. By the weekend fucking mandatory. Understand?'

She did and she knew the reason for the anger too. A couple of the Sunday papers had sent reporters down from London looking for titbits and they had been trawling round the city. They had even contacted one of the victims. If any of the papers went front-page with the murders and rapes on Sunday, the Monday morning briefing would be hell. Might be better to call in sick.

Hardin's rant continued but he began to veer into a more general moan about budget cuts and pressure from above to deliver, and Savage put her mouth on a 'yes, sir, no, sir,' autopilot setting, kicked off her shoes and put her feet up on the desk. When Hardin went off on one of his political

231

diatribes the one-sided conversation could continue for a good half an hour.

The return of Riley and Enders to the Major Crimes suite interrupted the rhetoric and Savage cut Hardin short, mentioning a possible new piece of evidence coming to light. Riley stuck his thumbs up and Enders nodded, a big smile painted across his face. Hardin told her to get back in touch. Soonest. Savage hung up and asked Riley what was up.

'Mr Everett Mitchell is up,' Riley said.

'Aye,' Enders said, 'and from what we have just seen up is how he likes it. Priapic. A permanent condition.'

'There's the wife as well. She is, ah, well you might say she's not shy about coming forward.'

'Darius is right, ma'am. Mrs Mitchell is a bit of a stunner. No. I meant to say she's quite a lady. Well, maybe lady isn't the right—'

'I don't do cryptic, Sergeant Riley and Constable Enders,' Savage said. 'Could you please tell me in plain English what the hell you two are talking about?'

Riley explained about what happened with the camera and Mitchell's refusal to allow them upstairs.

'Well, I don't think I would want a couple of strange men snooping around my house if Samantha was tucked up in bed. Maybe his daughter really *is* ill.'

'I somehow doubt it, ma'am.'

'Why is that?'

'I did some checking and Mr and Mrs Mitchell don't have any children.'

'Well, well, looks like Mr Mitchell just perjured himself. The only thing worrying me is his eagerness to show you those pictures.'

'I can tell you, ma'am, it worried me too!'

'No. What I mean is you said the room in the pictures did not match the room in Forester's videos.'

'Those houses are four beds, ma'am.' Enders this time. 'They might have a special room for that kind of stuff. Lots of couples do.'

'Do they?'

'Well, no, I mean not me and the wife. We haven't got the space, not with—'

Savage waved at Enders to stop and reached for the phone and called Hardin. He sounded sceptical but agreed that as a line of enquiry anything was worth a punt. If even one of the girls had been in the house then there would be some trace of them, and the video option and connection with Forester and *Zebo* would be a bonus.

'So we need a warrant, and urgently, I'll bet?'

'Please, sir.'

'OK, but Garrett and Davies will be doing the knocking. This sounds like it has more to do with operation *Leash*.'

'Yes, sir.'

'And Charlotte, you had better be right on this one. The spotlight is shining on us. Any cock-ups will be all too noticeable. Understand?'

'Yes, sir.'

As she hung up Savage couldn't help thinking of Riley's description of the pictures on Mitchell's camera. Noticeable cock-ups seemed to be everywhere.

She was starting to explain to Riley that it was jobs-on-the-line time if his hunch didn't pay off when the phone rang again. Hardin back on the line. He didn't know what the fuck was going on, but Davies was already on his way to Moor Vale. Along with an Armed Response Vehicle.

* * *

233

Enders did the driving while Savage got Riley to get on the radio and find out the full story.

'Triple nine, ma'am. From one of the neighbours. A man has driven into Mitchell's front door ram-raid style. The neighbour saw the man get out and rush inside with some sort of weapon. Sounds as if someone has beaten us to it. But they can't have known we were coming back, can they?'

'No, but one good thing is this gets us in with no waiting around for the warrant.'

As they raced into the estate it was obvious which house had been targeted. A blue Ford Galaxy had smashed into the front colonnades of number seven and the porch had collapsed on top, smashing the windscreen. After mounting the three little steps the car had flattened the door and torn away the frame and a substantial section of the supporting wall. Enders brought them to a halt next to a patrol car and even from fifty metres Savage spotted the Plymouth Snappers sticker on the rear window of the Galaxy.

'It's Donal's car.'

'Kelly's dad?' Enders said.

'Yes. How the hell he has connected Mitchell with Kelly I have no idea.'

Nearer the house another two patrol cars and an unmarked vehicle lay scattered across the road with several armed response officers crouching on the ground, keeping a good chunk of metal between themselves and the house. Standing behind one of the vehicles two armed officers covered the front door with their weapons.

DI Davies sat up against the unmarked car and seemed to be in overall charge, barking out orders to everyone around him, a cigarette jammed in the corner of his mouth. He'll be loving this, Savage thought, as she jumped out. She took a glance at the house, sprinted across to him and dived behind the car.

'Inside with a crossbow. He appeared at the upstairs window a few minutes ago. Next time there's a clear shot they'll get him.' Davies nodded at the armed officers.

'No they won't, I'm going in.' Savage stood up, catching the attention of the two men covering the door. Davies went apoplectic.

'Get down you stupid bitch. I'm in command here and I say the situation is too dangerous.'

'Fuck off. I know the man. Donal has lost one child, I don't want his other two to lose their dad.'

Savage moved out from behind the car and edged across to the driveway. The damage to the front of the house and the rubble lying on the ground made the place resemble a war zone and, like a derelict property, it appeared deserted. She held her arms out to the sides, palms forwards.

'Mr Donal,' she shouted. 'This is DI Charlotte Savage. I am unarmed and I'm coming in.'

Nothing. No sound, nobody moving.

She stepped onto the driveway, her feet crunching on the gravel.

Gravel?

Trent's drive was brick; the *Leash* girls had talked of gravel. Riley and Enders hadn't mentioned anything to her in their report, but this was not the time to ponder on the significance of the driveway and she continued walking towards the front door. She scrambled over the debris, squeezed past the car and then ducked down and crawled under part of the doorframe, all too aware of her vulnerable position.

Inside she stood up and surveyed the damage. The white carpet glistened with the remains of a chandelier, the little crystals scattered everywhere and reflecting the light like a lawn on a spring morning. Bits of plaster and wood lay strewn around and a large RSJ had come out of the wall above the door and crushed a small table. She picked her way across the floor and stood in the centre of the hall. The morning sun streamed in through the doorway and dust motes floated in the draught. To one side of the hall was the living room, to the other the diner and kitchen. Stairs swept upwards in a grand fashion to a landing above.

'They're upstairs.'

Savage whirled round to see a woman standing in the kitchen doorway, a wine glass in one hand, the bubbles in the glass fizzing in the sunlight. She was tall with a curvy figure and wore jeans and a fisherman's smock, but still managed to appear glamorous, like a catwalk model. Savage noticed the other hand was holding a bottle of champagne.

The woman followed Savage's gaze.

'Like one?'

'No thank you, Mrs . . .?'

'Catherine Mitchell. But not for much longer. That's why I'm celebrating. The end of all this crap.' The woman swung the bottle around in a sweeping gesture.

'Mrs Mitchell, where is your husband?'

'Everett is upstairs with some lout.'

'What are they doing up there?'

'No idea. Everett was in the bathroom when this idiot comes crashing through the door. We've got a doorbell but he didn't seem to know how to operate the thing. So he says to me, "where is he?", so I says "upstairs," and then he rushes up without a word. He didn't even apologise for that.' She indicated the mess Savage had scrambled over.

Catherine Mitchell was swaying now and Savage feared she might fall over.

'Could you please go out the front door. Put the glass and bottle down first and leave with your hands in the air. It's not safe here.'

'Really? Can't say I had noticed.'

She turned and retreated into the kitchen and Savage was about to go after her when she heard a shout from upstairs. She recognised Donal's voice, the distinctive brusque tone echoing through the house.

Savage left the woman in the kitchen and went up the stairs. Voices were coming from off to the right of the landing, and as Savage edged upward she could make out Donal's words and those of another man, the latter almost a whisper.

'I didn't do it, Mr Donal. You've got the wrong man. A rather unfortunate case of mistaken identity, I am afraid.'

'Oh but you did and now you are going to pay.'

Savage crossed the landing and now she could see through the door where the voices were coming from. A large bedroom, probably the master. Donal stood in the middle holding a loaded crossbow, the weapon incongruous against his jacket and tie. His bulky frame filled the clothing, red neck and face poking through the tight collar, and patches of damp showed at the armpits. He noticed Savage, met her eyes and then peered down the crossbow's sights again.

'He did it, Inspector Savage. He killed my Kelly.' The crossbow moved a little as Donal's hands shook.

Savage stepped forward to see more of the room. A man was standing over against a set of built-in mirrored wardrobes. He was wearing a blue towelling dressing gown and had damp hair, either from a recent shower or maybe sweat. The man was slumped over, his knees buckled, as if about to fall. He hadn't done so because he had been impaled through his right shoulder by a crossbow bolt, the mirrored glass behind him cracked in a crazy cobweb pattern. There didn't seem to be much blood until Savage looked down at the floor. A pool of red liquid was gathering on the snow white carpet at the man's feet, oozing over and through the deep pile. Vivid colour, somehow both chilling and beautiful at the same time. The man raised his head at Savage.

'Everett Mitchell. Your men were here this morning. I didn't like their attitude but it was preferable to this. Perhaps you might . . .' He made an almost imperceptible movement of his head in the general direction of Donal and let out an awful rasping sound.

'Mr Donal,' Savage began, 'we need to question Mr Mitchell about some offences, but at the moment I have no evidence he is Kelly's killer.'

'Well I do. I got a package.'

'What sort of package? Who from?'

'Didn't say. Came by courier this morning. Contained a DVD and a letter. Told me about Mitchell here who I now find out you had been questioning earlier. Told me to check out the DVD. I did. The material was shot by Forester. In this room. Everything makes sense now. The rapes, Kelly, the whole story. Just like the newspapers said.'

'Don't believe everything you read,' Mitchell said. He laughed, but the noise turned into a sort of snort and he coughed, blood trickling from his mouth. Savage moved forward, sliding one foot across the carpet.

'Mr Donal, think of your children and your wife, don't throw your life away.'

'I am thinking of my children. Not only *my* children. Yours as well. Everybody's children. These people can't be allowed to get away with their crimes. The judge says a dozen years and they are out in six. The rest of us get life with no parole.'

'If Mr Mitchell is guilty you have my word he won't be

getting out in six years, but we need proof. Do you want him to die if he's the wrong man?'

'OK. Tell me about it then.' Donal turned to Mitchell. 'FUCKING TELL ME!'

Donal clasped the crossbow and stared down the sights again. Savage risked another small step forward. She was now getting near to being in the line of fire and perhaps she had a chance to make Donal think twice about shooting. Mitchell groaned and muttered something about not knowing anything about Kelly's killer.

'Someone connected with a Spanish girl called Rosina Salgado,' Savage said, thinking about the photograph Nesbit had found inside Kelly.

Mitchell sniggered, a nasty bubbling sound came from his nose and a drop of blood rolled out.

'Oh, Mr Weirdo. We had a lot of fun with him. You think I am bad? Well Harry is mad, crazy like nutcase crazy. Blame the parents, that's what I say. Apparently mummy and daddy weren't very nice to him when he was a kid. Poor Harry. Now he likes girls. Oh we all do, of course, but Harry likes the caring sort. Reminds him of when he was little, he told me. Never understood it myself, but each to his own.'

Mitchell was weaker now, his face pale, white like the carpet. Savage reckoned he didn't have long unless she could end this quickly.

'Harry who?'

'Harry Houdini. Now you see him now you don't. International man of mystery, our Harry. Except there is nothing mysterious about him. He is just a sad little pervert wanking over his pictures.'

'SHE SAID HARRY FUCKING WHO?' Donal shouted, enraged now and swinging the crossbow back and forth with a violent motion.

Savage moved again. Mitchell's face was ashen, his eyelids flickering. She sensed he realised he was dying, either way.

'You'll never know,' Mitchell said. 'Never know who stripped and fucked your Kelly.'

'BASTARD!'

Donal fired the crossbow and the bolt passed through Mitchell's chest and embedded itself in the wardrobe behind with a thud, cracking the mirrored glass a second time. Blood spurted out splattering the mirrors and showering over the floor. Mitchell's eyes rolled down, as if noticing the mess on the ground for the first time.

'Didn't like this room, Harry. Bad lighting. In the end I guess he was probably right about that.'

Mitchell's eyes closed and he let out a horrible wheezing sound as a final breath of air was expelled from his lungs. Then his body went limp and slumped down. Donal dropped the crossbow to the floor, went over and sat on the bed and put his head in his hands. Savage walked over to where Mitchell hung like an inanimate puppet and placed two fingers on his neck. There was no pulse and, judging by the amount of blood on the floor, no chance of resuscitation. She went over to Donal and put a hand on his shoulder.

'I wish you hadn't done that, Mr Donal. I really wish you hadn't done that.'

'I had to, Inspector, I just had to.'

Savage thought of Kelly. The beautiful girl lying on the cold earth. Then she thought of the students Mitchell had raped. Finally she thought of her own children, Samantha and Jamie and poor little Clarissa.

'I know,' she said.

* * *

When Savage got outside Hardin was waiting for her.

'I expect you think you deserve a bloody medal, hey, Charlotte?' Hardin shook his head. 'Well, I have to tell you a suspension is the more likely outcome. Davies told me he ordered you not to enter the building.'

'Sir, I knew he wasn't going to hurt anybody but Mitchell.'

'And suppose Mr Mitchell is innocent?'

'The pictures he showed Riley and Enders were taken in the spare room, I checked. Take a look at the master bedroom. Mirrored wardrobes, like in the video footage we got from Forester's computer. The bed is the same too.'

As if to back up her words the air filled with the noise of an approaching train. Through the trees to the back of the property a long streak of colour flashed by, the sound increasing in intensity for a moment before leaving a diminishing whoosh. Hardin stared into the wood where a blizzard of leaves spiralled in the train's wake.

'So what if Mitchell was guilty of rape and maybe murder? Last time I read up on sentencing policy we didn't have the death penalty for homicide, for anything for that matter. He didn't deserve to die.'

'Nine girls we are aware of, probably countless others who have never come forward. I'd say Donal did us a favour.'

'Charlotte, I'll pretend I didn't hear you.'

Donal was being led out of the house now and put in a car. He appeared calm, his face having an almost serene appearance. He thought he had achieved closure, but Savage wasn't so sure. Closure didn't come so easy. It took years, if it came at all.

The car drove away, Donal in the back with Davies, the detective grinning and patting Donal on the shoulder. Meanwhile Hardin was mulling things over. Maybe Mitchell *had* killed Kelly. It would solve a lot of problems, he

241

explained. His reasoning was that in the ring of depravity comprising Mitchell's group of rapists, Mitchell had gone one step further.

'Anyone capable of carrying out so many attacks is surely capable of carrying out murder as well. He probably killed the Olivárez girl. Why not Kelly too?'

'I'll see what we can find to eliminate him, sir.'

'No! I want you to see what you can find to evidence him.'

'He didn't kill Kelly, sir.'

'Fuck it, Charlotte! He didn't do it or you want to believe he didn't do it? What's got into you?'

Hardin began a rant about Savage's obsession with the *Zebo* case, how she was wallowing in her own self-pity, wanting the agony to be prolonged, enjoying the masochism. He wanted her to face the truth. Fact, Mitchell was linked to Forester. Fact, Mitchell was a serial rapist. Fact, he was sadistic. Fact, he had the opportunity and ability.

The words washed over Savage although she realised Hardin was right about the self-pity. The loss of her daughter and the loneliness she felt with Pete being away should have had no bearing on her police work, but emotionally the whole lot were bundled up together, threads of feeling intertwined and looping back and forth until they created one huge tangle. That didn't change the evidence though. If Mitchell was the killer then where was Forester's Shogun, and where was Alice Nash?

'Harry,' she said. 'We are looking for a man named Harry.'

Chapter Twenty-Seven

Crownhill Police Station, Plymouth. Thursday 4th November. 1.40 pm

Sorting out the chaos created by Donal killing Mitchell had taken up most of the rest of the day and a good part of the next so it was Thursday afternoon before Savage was able to return her attention to *Zebo*. Because Savage had been present at Mitchell's murder an inquiry had been initiated and the PIP, or Post Incident Procedure, was in full swing. Whether the matter would be dealt with internally – by Standards – or whether the IPCC would need to get involved, Savage had no idea, nor did she really care. She had done her best in the circumstances and had slept easy, knowing Donal, at least, was alive. Thank God she had persuaded Hardin that immediate suspension would be an overreaction. He had agreed she should carry on working.

Hardin was now ensconced upstairs somewhere, getting all friendly with the incident manager no doubt and trying to charm away any trouble. Sometimes Hardin was a right pain but Savage knew he would support her all the way.

Back on *Zebo* and Savage was getting the team to focus on finding someone called Harry.

'Nothing in our records, ma'am,' Enders said. 'Nothing in

the statements, no witnesses with the name. Checked the Henrys as well. Nowt.'

'Everett Mitchell also said something about this Harry liking the caring sort, whatever the caring sort means.'

'Alice Nash,' Calter said. 'She is the caring sort, I mean. She works part-time at Cotton Socks Nursery in Ivybridge.'

'What?' The realisation hit Savage like a psychological battering ram. 'Kelly Donal was doing an Early Childhood Studies course at the uni and she had a work placement at Little Angels nursery. How did we manage to miss the connection?'

'Alice worked as a checkout girl as well as at the nursery. The supermarket job is down as her main employment. I only remembered now because the photograph her father provided for the appeal was of her in her nursery uniform.'

'Ma'am?' Enders said. 'This gets worse. I've just run the misper search again. Remember the results included a number of girls who did not match Kelly's description?'

'Don't tell me . . .' Savage groaned.

'Yes. Simone Ashton. Full-time job at Robins in Plympton.'

'Ma'am?' Calter, sounding even more tentative than Enders had. 'Rosina Olivárez.'

'So?'

'Just a hunch, ma'am. Bring her up, Patrick.'

Enders switched programs and brought up the *Leash* files. Click, click and Rosina's details flashed up on the screen. Occupation: Student. Occupation Notes: Degree in Aquaculture. Part-time job at Tina's Teds Playgroup in Mannamead.

'Bloody hell,' Savage said. 'There needs to be a major review of how the data is entered and analysed. The connection was right in front of us, but the system hid the link away. Whatever, this isn't looking good.'

'Coincidence?' asked Enders.

'Possibly. If not then I sure don't know what to think. I mean, are these girls being targeted because they are child minders?'

'Isn't there a fetish where men dress up as babies, complete with nappies and dummies and stuff?' Enders said, a look of disgust on his face.

Riley came into the room carrying a pile of documents. He dumped them on a desk and nodded at Enders.

'Paraphilic infantilism is the correct term: the desire to be treated like a toddler again. But last time I looked your average toddler wasn't killing teenage girls, or stripping them and having sex with them.'

'Alright Mr Fast-Track, what's your suggestion then?' Enders said.

'As you guys are always telling me, I'm the ebony boy from the ivory tower. What do I know about the real world?'

Touché, thought Savage.

Calter moved over from her desk to join the boys and soon the three of them were talking about fetishes, Enders arguing that if sex wasn't in bed and the light wasn't out then it was not for him, Riley insisting that having some kind of fetish didn't make you mad, Calter saying she would try anything once with the right person. The conversation wasn't leading anywhere useful so Savage grabbed her cup of coffee, got up and moved away.

The main whiteboard had one victim photograph taped slap in the middle: Kelly Donal. How many more would they need to add? How many girls who never knew each other linked forever by death? How many more families destroyed?

DS Collier joined her.

'Problems, ma'am?' He nodded at the board.

'I think we may have some more,' Savage indicated the screen which Enders was sitting at, with the thumbnail pictures

245

of the girls smiling out. 'We need action points on those three. Their workplaces, Rosina Olivárez, Simone Ashton and Alice Nash. I want their pictures up here on the board as victims.'

'Sorry, ma'am, you've lost me.'

Savage realised she was rambling, but she did her best to explain the nursery angle, how the victims had something to do with caring for young children. Collier said he didn't like it. He didn't want to generate a load of new actions around hunches.

'We don't know these new mispers are victims yet,' he said. 'We are stretched enough as it is and this will simply generate more and more threads to follow. We will be wasting precious resources on girls who might turn up tomorrow. We will have officers out on wild goose—'

'Shut it, Collier,' Savage said, angry with Collier's focus on silly administrative details. 'If the girls turn up alive and well then that is a result in my book. If, God forbid, they turn up dead then we will have done some useful ground-work. And anyway, I might remind you the Olivárez girl is very much dead.'

Collier shrugged. He didn't dare argue with his superior, but Savage saw he was riled. His office system was in danger of being overloaded now he was going to have to insert material from *Leash* into operation *Zebo*. All his careful planning was being blown out of the water. That couldn't be helped though. Every piece of data would need to be re-evaluated in the light of the new evidence. It was going to be a mammoth task. Savage attempted to placate him by placing an arm around his shoulders.

'Come on, I'll get some fresh coffees and we will see how we are going to handle the new data. And then I'll go and see Hardin and persuade him to get me some extra bodies in here.'

* * *

Savage had got the coffees and Collier began to explain about the problems of not letting *Zebo* get overloaded by the sheer quantity of data that had been gathered during the *Leash* inquiry.

'*Leash* has been going on for twelve months flat out,' he said. '*Zebo* has been going a week. There must be a hundred times more material in the *Leash* case.'

Savage didn't have time to address his concerns because DI Davies and DC Jackson had come in. Their faces wore glum expressions, like little kids who had opened all their Christmas presents at once and didn't have anything else to look forward to.

'It's that little prick, Dickie boy Trent,' Davies scowled. 'He retracted his confession. He is now saying Mitchell carried out all the rapes and he just drove the car. He fingered Forester too. Told us Forester supplied the GHB and took the videos.'

'He knows Mitchell and Forester are dead?'

'We had to tell the bitch Bradley, yes.' Davies looked downcast. 'Disclosure of evidence and all that fucking crap.'

'Very convenient.'

'Yeah. With those two out of the way, him and the bloody lawyer can concoct whatever story they like.'

'So you are here about Forester?'

'Clever girl!' Davies beamed, a smile spreading like the Cheshire cat just got the cream. 'We need to get into his network and find out what connections he had.'

'Have you threatened Trent?'

'What with? Having charged him with the nine rapes he's going down for life even if he tells us where Elvis is living.'

Savage could imagine Trent had worked everything out. Once he had admitted the rapes he would have known his situation couldn't get any worse if he kept his mouth shut.

He had been right because the other two suspects were dead and by changing his story he now had a way out.

'We've got Forester's mobile phone logs, they might be some help.' She nodded at Collier and he went off to get a printout.

'Great. We think Trent had a Pay As You Go contract, because we can't find anything in his bank statements and we can't locate the bloody phone. If we can get Trent's number from Forester's phone we can go to the mobile operator to get the complete record set.'

'So where did the phone go?'

'Little wifey,' Jackson said. 'She seemed so sweet and put upon, but we reckon she grabbed the phone while we were running around securing the house. If you remember she refused the offer of an FLO and went off to a friend's for the night. Must have ditched the thing because she's denying all knowledge.'

'Wait a minute, if . . .' Savage paused. 'If Trent says the rapes took place at Moor Vale then can't you put it to him the wife must have known?'

'And she goes down as well? We tried, he just shrugged and said "prove it".' Davies tapped his head with his forefinger. 'Mr Know-All. He's got an Excel bloody spreadsheet up here filled in with all the possibilities. His wife going down for any more than being a pain-in-the-butt isn't one of them.'

'Here you are, sir.' Collier had returned and he handed a printout to Davies. 'All the numbers Forester called in the month before he went missing, ordered by frequency.'

'You gone through these yet?' Davies asked.

Savage sighed and was aware of Collier looking at her with a little smirk on his face.

'No, it's on the to do list.'

'That's Trent's direct line at the uni.' Davies pointed to a

248

number in the middle of the sheet. 'We will need to get a reverse look up on the other landlines.'

'Do that. If you could get the results back to us that would save another job. And if you find any numbers on the list to do with nurseries then let me know as a matter of urgency.'

Davies looked puzzled, his head tilted on one side like a squirrel with a nut it couldn't crack.

'Nurseries? What, you mean geraniums and stuff?'

'No, babies. Childminders, nannies, day-care staff. There's a bit of a shortage of them around here at the moment.'

Thursday afternoon at Cotton Socks nursery and DS Darius Riley was bricking himself. A little girl had toddled over to him and introduced herself as, 'Lisa and I've got a big poo in my nappy.' Riley hadn't had much experience with children; as an only child and thus with no nieces or nephews he didn't have a clue what to say or do. A druggie rushing at him full of ketamine and armed with a knife he could deal with, but an infant in possession of a hazardous substance? Way too scary.

Thank goodness Enders was covering him and, being a family man with three of the little brats under seven, he knew how to handle the incident. He bent down, held the girl's hand and took her across to one of the nursery staff. Simple when you had done the training.

'Thanks mate,' Riley said. 'Thought I was a goner for a moment.'

The nursery in Ivybridge was the third they had visited so far that morning, but Riley still hadn't got used to the stench of urine in the baby and toddler rooms.

'Don't know how you manage at home, the smell of the shit and piss makes me gag.'

'Oh, once you've got past the thousand-nappy milestone

249

you get used to it. The first poo they do is the worst. Long, black, sticky and stinks like you wouldn't believe.'

'One would be bad enough, but a thousand! Never going to happen to me for sure.'

'I can see Ms Meadows looking lovely with a couple of kids in her arms.' Enders winked. 'And I hear she was in town last night at that new tapas bar. With a handsome black guy. Now I wonder—'

'How did you . . .?'

Enders dropped out of Riley's line of sight onto his haunches to talk to a little boy hugging a big pink teddy bear. Riley smiled to himself. Enders was right, and not just about the fact he had been on a date last night. Julie Meadows would look beautiful holding a baby, *his* baby. Then he shook his head. Broody, him? Mr notch-em-up-on-the-bed-post-new-girl-each-month Riley? Yes, quite possibly. Still, he reckoned he could do without the smells.

Alice Nash worked at Cotton Socks so the nursery had been visited before, but not by members of the *Zebo* team. Savage had insisted the work places relating to the four dead and missing girls should be visited or revisited. This time by the same people.

'I want the same pairs of eyes at all the locations to see if we can find something missing from the stuff we are putting on the system.'

'What is this, ma'am, Kindergarten Cop?' Riley had asked.

'Without the muscles, yes,' Savage said, smiling. 'Now get along the both of you.'

The task had turned out to be a tedious one as there seemed to be nothing of much interest at any of the places they visited, but Riley was pleased Savage had picked on him. It showed she had the confidence in him to come up trumps when everything else appeared to be failing.

Riley looked around the nursery and shook his head. Maybe DI Savage had misplaced her faith in him. The place seemed pretty much the same as the others they had been to and nothing stuck out to him as an obvious clue. In the entrance hall the same pictures of the smiling staff and a group picture of all the babies and children, notices about the dates for the nativity, something about a case of hand, foot and mouth disease – which Riley thought sounded serious – a 'thank you' for the money raised for this year's Children in Need appeal, a copy of a recent OfSTED report . . .

The layouts were similar too. Some elements might be transposed, an item or room added or missing, but the basic theme remained the same. Which was part of the problem. Usually he would look for something distinctive, something out of the ordinary, something out of place. That was what clues were after all: a footprint in a flowerbed, a car parked in an odd location, a fingerprint they couldn't eliminate. Here they were searching for something or someone common to all the nurseries.

Enders sprang back to his feet again, reading Riley's mind like he often seemed able to.

'Play equipment suppliers?'

'On the list and being checked.'

'Then I reckon we are soon on to the parents.'

'That will be a hell of a job.'

'A hell of a fuss too. Especially if the brass decide to go with a DNA sweep.'

Didn't bear thinking about, Riley thought. The problem of coordinating that kind of action across the city, possibly farther afield too, would be huge. The DNA trawl would involve hundreds of parents, perhaps thousands, and the outcry about civil liberties would be deafening. Many people would refuse to be tested and those would have to be interviewed and eliminated in other ways. Then there was the issue of missing someone or eliminating the killer by mistake or through fraud.

At each nursery they had talked to the owners and workers, but so far there had been nothing much of note. One thing Riley had picked up on was the high turnover of staff. Five of the girls Rosina had worked with at Tina's Teds had left, along with a couple from Little Angels, Kelly Donal's place. Even Robins, the establishment where Simone Ashton had worked, had lost a member of staff in the six weeks since she had gone missing. Riley didn't know if the high turnover was relevant or not, but it meant there would always be fresh faces around. He mentioned the fact to Enders.

'If you returned to a nursery after a few months you would be sure to find some new girls.'

'You mean staff turnover in these places is a factor?'

'Yes, but I still can't fathom why a nursery? Last time I took a gander out of the window at the station I spotted some new girls. Every hour hundreds of them pass by that I have never seen before.'

'Yeah, I play the same game. Especially in the summer when you can see down their tops. Don't make a habit of it mind.'

'Better not, Patrick. You know the boss. If she catches you she'll cut your bollocks off and feed them to the tourists in a pasty.'

'Ouch.' Enders squirmed, as if he possessed rather too vivid an imagination. 'Anyway I don't buy that, Darius. It's something to do with this fetish business. Polaroid infants or whatever you called it.'

Riley started to correct Enders's terminology when he realised it was a wind up.

252

'Very funny. But you might just be onto something with your little joke. Polaroid infant. What about the picture found inside the Donal girl? The photograph turned out to be ancient, didn't it?'

'Thirty years old.'

'Looked like Rosina Olivárez?'

'You are saying the girl in the picture was a nanny?'

'Not saying, speculating. The girl in the picture meant something to the killer because she looked like Rosina. Rosina was a child care worker so maybe the girl in the picture was too.'

'Darius my boy,' Enders shook his head. 'I have finally worked out why my career is stuck on some dead-end branch line while you are fast-tracked to stardom. It's because you're on L S bloody D.'

Chapter Twenty-Eight

He watched the rockets climb skyward and burst in crimson blooms, the bangs coming seconds later. For a moment or two he continued to stare up at where they had exploded, looking at the empty patch of sky now filled with nothing but a background of twinkling stars. A short life, he thought, but a spectacular end.

Harry stood on Plymouth Hoe, the place where he had done so much watching, not quite believing he was taking such a risk. Now though, the time for watching was over. Now it was time for action.

Action, Harry?

Lucy still buzzed in his head even though he had dumped her. This time he had managed to carry out his plan and leave her exactly where he had wanted to leave Trinny. She would give the God bods something to think about, for sure. Fearing that, like Trinny, Lucy wouldn't stop speaking simply because they were apart, he decided to shut her up for good. After he had pushed the big knife down into her stomach, pressing hard so it went right in where babies grew, he used the blade on her mouth. It seemed to have made no difference. He couldn't quite understand why she still pestered him since she knew she was not the chosen one.

But neither is Emma.

No, Emma was proving to be a disappointment.

I told you so.

Lucy would know, being a little slut herself.

Slut is a very strong word.

True, but Lucy was a very naughty girl.

And you, Harry, what are you?

Harry thought for a moment. He was just Harry. Like Mitchell once said, being yourself is all you can ever be, so don't try to fight it. And Mitchell had done being anything now. But that really was for the best. As for himself, he hadn't even started yet.

On the Hoe throngs of people were watching the fireworks. Harry stood on his own next to the lighthouse, peered round the curved wall and tried to spot his target.

My boyfriend!

Shush, Lucy! Harry thought, even though he knew nobody could hear her annoying wittering.

Sorry, I should have said my ex-boyfriend. I'm yours now, Harry. Forever.

He looked round the side of the lighthouse again and he could see a figure standing all alone over by the sea wall. The boy lived in one of the student blocks in town and Harry had followed him from there to the Hoe. On the way the boy stopped for a drink at a trendy little bar on Derry's Cross. All on his own in the bar he had looked so sad. But he would be, losing Lucy like that. Now he gazed out across the inky black water and of what he was thinking Harry had no idea.

Plenty more fish? Hey, Harry?

Harry walked from the lighthouse across the grass and trotted down the steps to the road, pausing for a car. Down here, below the plateau of the Hoe, it was quieter, just one or two people hurrying up the road to see the display. He crossed over to the wall and walked along the pavement, just another patron heading down to the puke-filled streets of the Barbican. Nearer now and he realised the lad stood right next to one of the openings in the wall, which led to the maze of terraces below. There was a café to the right – closed – and to the left little paths weaved along the top of the steep cliffs and amongst low scrub. No one would be down there at this time of day. Harry looked back at the Hoe where the firework display was reaching a crescendo. A myriad of rockets streamed into the air and all heads craned skywards, eyes fixated on the colourful patterns being painted onto the black canvas. Harry turned to the boy and moved closer.

'Excuse me? Could you tell me the—' The figure turned to face him and Harry brought what he was holding in his left hand up level with the boy's eyes. Flash!

'What the fuck?'

The boy's arms went up to shield himself and he knocked the camera from Harry's hand. It didn't make any difference because with the other hand low down Harry thrust the kitchen knife forward. Sheffield steel glided through Far Eastern cotton and into Devon flesh. A strange gurgle came as the boy opened his mouth, but he didn't scream. Harry was disappointed the boy's face showed no sign of surprise. Never mind, there would be plenty of time for surprises later. Like there had been with Forester.

Harry wheeled the boy around and pushed him through the gap in the wall, bustling him to the ground in the darkness on the other side. He flung the knife seaward and brought out a couple of cable ties from his pocket. He pulled the boy's arms behind him and secured the wrists with a satisfying zip sound. Then he secured one around the boy's ankles. Finally he took the leather gag out and fastened it, pulling the fastening tight with his knee on the back of the boy's skull. It was all over in a few seconds and Harry dragged the groaning lump ten metres along the path and left him concealed under a small bush.

Nice work, Harry! I never liked him much anyway.

'Thank you, Luce.' He realised he had said the words aloud and wondered if he wasn't going a little bit mad.

Harry went back to where he had attacked the boy and scrabbled around on the ground looking for his camera, but it had bounced away off the path and down the cliff to the sea below. Never mind, the thing was only a point-and-shoot. Now for the car. He walked back towards where he had parked it thinking all the time how easy the job had been.

But why, Harry? He was so ordinary, he hadn't done anything, he wasn't doing any harm.

He touched Lucy, that was why. The same way Forester soiled Trinny and Mitchell ruined Carmel. People couldn't be allowed to get away with doing things like that. Not when they involved his girls.

Do you mean he fucked me?

Yes. He spoilt her. Lucy had been Harry's girl. He sat on her lap when he was little and she had been supposed to be pure for him to love. He had given her a chance, but sadly it had turned out she was dirty. Like the rest of them.

You knew I had a boyfriend. Did you think that meant just holding hands?

He knew boyfriends did more than just hold hands but he had been appalled at what it had turned Lucy into.

Harry took fifteen minutes to walk back to his car, all the time with Lucy still whispering in his head about a world populated only with sluts. Ignoring her he got in the car and drove round to get the body. The road up along the seafront was a one-way street so to get to the gap in the wall he had to first drive round through the Barbican and that's when he saw the flashing lights.

Not red or green or white like the ones out in the Sound, but blue.

That's OK, he thought, probably sorting out some ruck outside a bar.

No Harry, look where they are heading.

Lucy was right and he followed the police car through the Barbican and up round the curve of Madeira Road towards the Hoe. There were more blue lights and Harry spotted another police car and an ambulance. He swung past at a crawl and could see paramedics attending to someone on a stretcher.

God moves in mysterious ways, Harry thought, but sometimes the bastard didn't get it.

He headed back up past the Hoe and then down into town again and along Bretonside, intending to return to the cottage. At one point he nearly knocked down a group of girls. Bare legs and heels, push-up bras and quivering hemispheres of white temptation.

Sluts, Harry. A world full of sluts.

Maybe Lucy was right, but where could he go to find someone pure enough? Emma was sixteen and yet she had turned out to be a little tart.

Younger, Harry, younger.

Younger? Younger than Emma? He didn't like that, it was disgusting, illegal.

Lucy was beginning to sound like Mitchell, Harry thought, as the car sped along Embankment Road and out across Laira Bridge. The Plym glided by beneath, black, glossy and shimmering in the starlight like the PVC skirt on one of the girls he had just seen.

We can find her, Harry. But not in this town. There is nothing pure here. But don't worry, if all else fails I know where she might be.

Chapter Twenty-Nine

St Michael's Church, Malstead Down. Saturday 6th
November. 9.12 am

Jean Sotherwell was quite aware of the kerfuffle surrounding
her monopoly of the flower arranging at St Michael's, but
to let on would be to stoop to the level of her detractors
which would never do. After all, only one woman in the
village had the required skills and artistic flair to please the
Rector, not to mention the dear Lord of course, and if Hilary
Osbourne, the old crone, couldn't accept the fact then tough.
She should stick to her simple ArrowWord magazines and
those mindless reality TV programmes she wittered on about.
But then, Jean thought in a moment of contrition, the good
Lord did insist on loving one's enemy as thine own brother.
But she found it so especially hard when they were ignorant
and stupid.

It had been the same in her career as a nurse. She enjoyed
caring for the injured, ill and dying when those people were
clever, witty and imaginative. The ignorant, simple-minded
majority had been more of a challenge. Their rude manners,
boorish behaviour and incessant demands often got to her,
and she had questioned her vocation and at times her faith.
Still, her working days were over now and at the final tally

she thought the real good she had done would outweigh the bad thoughts. And her good deeds hadn't finished yet, she reminded herself.

A year or two ago she had been involved in a campaign to clear up the dog mess that these days seemed to be everywhere. The campaign went national and she had featured not only on *Spotlight* – the local news show – but also on the BBC *News At Ten*. Huw Edwards had interviewed her and for weeks afterwards she was entertaining friends with descriptions of what it was like to be a media celebrity. Of course the campaign might never have amounted to much if it hadn't been that her son-in-law was the Chief Constable of Devon and Cornwall Police, but then he was *her* son-in-law, wasn't he?

Once the dust settled she had handed over the running of the campaign to other people, partly because it had taken up too much of her precious time. That was how Hilary Osbourne had managed to muscle in on the flower rota and that could not be allowed to happen again.

Today's arranging was to be extra special and it took several trips to get all the materials into the church what with the flowers, the branches and bark and the sack of fallen leaves. After the ferrying she spent a good hour getting the trestles and table tops from the vestry and she assembled them all at the top of the aisle. She looked at her watch. Her friend and helper Marjorie would be here in a few minutes and they could get to work on the display.

Catching her breath Jean thought she would walk up the aisle to the chancel and stand before the altar. From the top of the church she could see if she had placed the tables in the correct position. It wouldn't do for the Rector to turn from the cross to be presented with the effrontery of the best display he had ever seen being off-centre.

Halfway up the nave an uneasy feeling came over her. A strange odour wafted through the air. Not incense or a candle burning, but something sweeter, a fragrance she had not been able to smell before because of all the flowers. She turned around to see if Marjorie or somebody else had entered unannounced, but the church was empty. She resumed her journey up the nave and now noticed the altar arrangement looked wrong. The candlesticks and the cross stood on the floor and the white cloth that covered the altar between services had been folded back on itself in a heap. Moving closer she could see the cloth covered something on top of the altar itself. She moved forward. This would all have to be tidied before she could get on with the flower arranging. She supposed she ought to telephone the Rector too, but she would put the altar right first so as to avoid anyone else becoming distressed.

She walked forward, took hold of the cloth and tugged at the fabric, but the bundle didn't move. She pulled again, angry now. She braced her feet against the altar foot, reached over the mass of cloth and heaved with all her strength. The cloth slid towards her, bringing whatever was wrapped up in it along too. The whole bundle slipped off the altar and knocked her backward. She crashed down on the floor and the mass of cloth tumbled on top of her. She let out a cry of pain as her back and then her head slammed onto the hard stone floor.

The roof of the church was now spinning above her and a grey milkiness blurred her vision. A heavy weight pressed down on her chest and she felt nauseous. She closed her eyes and took several deep breaths, trying to calm herself and at the same time cursing her stupidity. If only she had waited until Marjorie had arrived they could have sorted this together.

Sighing, she tried to move but found she was pinned to the floor, the bundle of cloth lying across her chest, something inside heavy but yielding. She extracted her right arm and moved her hand up to touch one side of her head where it throbbed like crazy. Her temple felt sticky and warm and she knew if she opened her eyes she would see blood on her fingers. Better to lie here rather than risk causing any more damage to herself. Marjorie would be along shortly and she would get help.

To pass the time she started thinking about the flowers she had brought with her and how their colours would have complemented the carpet of autumn leaves in her design. What a pity. The display really would have been one of her finest works. Now Hilary Osbourne would be receiving the Rector's thanks on Sunday and not her. She breathed deeply again. Strange how she could smell the fragrance of the flowers from so far away. A musky smell, sweet and sickly with a hint of peach. It was resonant of . . . well . . . sex. Those nights, so long ago now, when her late husband Albert had made love to her, when he had—

A creak echoed through the church. Marjorie! Thank goodness for that! Footsteps tapped out as someone walked up the nave.

'Jean? Where are you? What . . .'

The footsteps stopped for a moment before continuing, climbing the three steps to the chancel.

'Oh Jean, you poor love, whatever has happened here?'

'Marjorie, thank God you have come.'

'Hush, lie still, let me help you,' Marjorie said.

Jean stared up at Marjorie as she bent down to remove the altar cloth. Jean closed her eyes again, relieved she was going to be alright.

The next sound she heard was something she would never

forget as long as she lived. It was Marjorie screaming. One of those long drawn out screams that would not have been out of place in the old black and white Hitchcock films Jean had watched when she was young.

'Oh my God! Jean! Jean! Jean! Help someone, please help!'

Jean opened her eyes and glimpsed what was lying on top of her. What had caused Marjorie to scream. It was a body. Naked, dead, female from the look of the long blonde hair cascading out from the altar cloth. Thoughts flashed through Jean's mind: The body was naked because you went to meet God in the same state as when you were born. Dead because the mess of flesh around where the girl's mouth should have been could not possibly be part of a living thing. Jean wanted to scream, scream like Marjorie had, but nothing would come out. A pressure began to build in her chest, a sharp pain spreading to her neck and shoulders. At the same time the church roof began to spin once more and the feeling of nausea returned.

As a former nurse she recognised the symptoms only too well.

Heart attack!

Jean Sotherwell closed her eyes again and began to pray.

When Enders shouted the report across the room Savage couldn't believe what she was hearing.

'Malstead Down? You're sure about the information?'

'Yes, ma'am. A DC Newlyn. He says they have found the body of a blonde girl. And he sends his regards, ironically I think.'

Savage remembered the fresh-faced, eager young detective and wondered what he must be thinking, only a month on the job and already two murders on his patch. As a DC Savage had waited years for her first, and the case had been a domestic with the husband holding his hands up as they smashed down the front door.

'This is bad, ma'am, isn't it?' Calter said, her chirpy manner absent. 'I mean, I have done my serial killer 101 course and this sounds like escalation.'

The last word hung for a moment, the room's usual buzz stilled apart from a trilling phone. A knocking sound made everyone turn to where Riley stood at the big whiteboard tapping his fingers on the picture of Simone Ashton.

'The question is who is the unlucky one this time?'

Savage shivered at Riley's words. The pretty face in the photograph smiled out, the expression unaltered from a minute ago. And yet now it was possible the girl might be dead.

'Answer that, someone!' Savage broke the spell, pointing at the ringing phone. 'Darius, inform Hardin and wait here until I call. If I can get an ID, and the body belongs to one of the misper girls, then I want you at her place of work pronto. Jane, you are with me, come on!'

Everyone became animated again, the phone answered, a babble of conversation starting up, people moving with renewed vigour. Savage looked on for a few seconds and then she was sprinting from the room with her trusty DC in tow.

The blustery weather that had brought sunshine and showers for their last visit to Malstead Down was gone and now rain fell vertically from a blackened sky. Without a breath of wind to shift the clouds it seemed to Savage as if the rain might continue forever. She parked the car on the edge of the green, well away from the church. With the engine off the only noise was the drumming of water on the car roof. They sat for a couple of minutes, almost as if not moving would freeze the passing of time and maybe prevent anything bad from ever happening again. It was Calter who brought some lightness to the occasion.

'Grim, ma'am,' she said, peering out of the windscreen. 'But if that is your DC Newlyn then I might just move to Totnes.'

Newlyn was walking over the green towards the church. Well wrapped in waterproofs, his handsome, boyish face poked out from the hood. He spotted their car, waved at them and jogged across. Savage lowered the window.

'Morning, Constable. This is becoming a habit. Who discovered the body?' Savage asked.

'Morning, ma'am,' Newlyn nodded at Savage and beamed in at Calter. 'Jean Sotherwell.'

'Oh no, please tell me you are joking?'

'No, I'm afraid not. She was doing the flowers for the Sunday service. She went to the church first thing this morning. When she found the body she had a heart attack.'

'Bloody hell. That's not good.'

'Not for us or her. Thankfully she was conscious when the ambulance arrived and the paramedics seemed hopeful.'

'Well, that's something. I bet it won't be long before old Foxy starts poking his nose in.'

'Apparently he's at a Chief Constables' conference in Birmingham. On his way back this afternoon.'

'We had better get a move on then.' Savage looked around at the mixture of cottages and larger dwellings dotted about the green. They had a good view of the church. 'All these houses will need to be door-stepped again.'

'Yes, ma'am.'

Savage got out of the car and put waterproofs on, leaving Calter flirting with Newlyn. She walked over to where a SOC van stood near the church. Next to it a stepladder was leaning against the churchyard wall. Savage spotted another familiar face as John Layton got out of the van, pulling on his raincoat and plonking his Tilley hat on his head.

'We must stop meeting like this,' Savage said. Then she pointed at the ladder and the tape running to the church. 'You like your ladders, don't you?'

Layton grinned. 'We are pretty sure the perpetrator came through the main entrance since the vestry is always locked. This is an alternative way in, keeping us clear of the evidence trail, such as there is.'

'Can I go in?'

'Through the vestry, yes. The police surgeon has been and gone and Nesbit is on his way.'

'He will be cross I beat him to the scene again.'

'He's cross already. I had to break the news that the ambulance crew had moved the body.'

'Careless of them.'

'They didn't have much choice. Either that or leave the old dear crushed underneath.'

'I'll take a peek inside if you don't mind?' Savage said.

'Be my guest. There are some PPE packs inside the door on the left.'

Savage signed the log that Layton proffered and clambered over the ladder into the churchyard.

The blue and white tape leading to the vestry door weaved among the gravestones, and as she passed each stone she had the weird sense that she was walking over long dead bodies in order to view a fresh one.

She opened the door to the vestry and stepped out of the rain into the silence of the church. Someone had put up a written note on the door leading to the main part. The message said 'Coats off, suits on BEFORE YOU OPEN THIS DOOR'.

Savage took off her wet coat and hung it up on a peg next to a row of cassocks and surplices. Then she opened one of the PPE packs, put on the disposable suit and tied her hair back, pulling the suit hood up and making sure the elastic was drawn snug around her face. Next on went the paper face mask covering her nose and mouth and a pair of plastic overshoes. Finally she pulled on the nitrile gloves. These days you couldn't be too careful.

The heavy oak door swung open without a sound and she left the vestry and entered the church.

A harsh bright light flared up at the altar for a split second and for a moment the two white-cloaked figures there looked like angels, frozen in time as if they were on a giant canvas. The light flashed again and the angels moved about their business. The illusion was dispelled when one of them spotted her and called out a warning muffled by his mask.

'Keep to the right if you wouldn't mind, ma'am.'

The main aisle had been taped off, but she could walk up the right hand side of the pews and go behind the choir stalls to view the chancel.

As she emerged from behind the stalls she caught sight of the girl's body. It was lying tumbled on the floor, half-covered by a white sheet or cloth. Savage looked at the face; Simone Ashton, no question about the identity this time. Simone's beautiful blonde hair contrasted with the horrific mess of flesh at the mouth and Calter's earlier comment about escalation came back to her.

'Worse than last time, isn't it?' The voice belonged to Rod Oliver, unrecognisable behind the mask. No sign of his stupid assistant. 'Same cut in the belly too, but like before it hasn't bled and there is nothing else suggesting trauma.'

'The CSM said the body had been moved?'

'The casualty was underneath the body. The paramedics

didn't have a lot of choice. We believe it was on the altar wrapped in the white cloth.'

'And Foxy's mother-in-law pulled the cloth off?'

'Yes, seems that way. Under UV we might be able to get some idea of how it was positioned. Turin shroud sort of thing.'

Savage left Oliver and wandered back the way she had come. A third CSI knelt on the floor near the entrance and he beckoned Savage over, pointing to a set of muddy footprints.

'They are good prints and we believe the church was cleaned yesterday so they could well belong to whoever brought her here.'

'They are certainly too large for the flower lady.'

'Yup. And the print is something like a walking boot.'

The CSI told her they would be doing a fingertip search of the church once Layton had finished outside. In the meantime she could walk around if she didn't touch anything and kept away from the entrance, the aisle and the chancel.

Savage moved towards the rear of the church to view the whole tableau. At the back there were several stacks of chairs and a little play area with a soft rug and some plastic toys she thought would have occupied Jamie for precisely two and a half minutes. Next to the play area the font stood atop a stone pedestal. The font itself was an elaborate marble affair with many carvings on the outside. The wooden lid lay half open, balanced on the edge in a precarious position.

Savage reached to move the lid back into place before remembering she shouldn't touch anything. Then something soft and white inside the font caught her eye. Material of some kind. She peered in.

The lid cast a dark shadow but she could distinguish what

the material was now. Cotton. A pair of soft, white cotton knickers and a plain white cotton bra. Something else too, wrapped in the knickers, reddish-pink with little rivulets of blood. Something resembling a small piece of steak if you wanted a slim-line dinner for one.

Chapter Thirty

Despite the latest developments Savage had managed to take Sunday afternoon off. She had been glad to spend half a day away from the case at home with the kids. They had played some board games, romped in the garden, made a big chocolate cake and watched a DVD. The rest of the weekend had been taken up with administration. These days each case produced a mountain of tasks to complete, forms to fill in and procedure that had to be followed. Hardin had dumped the lot on her, pleading a weekend-long engagement he couldn't get out of. Golf, Savage suspected.

Monday morning brought her back to earth with a bump. The *Leash* case had as good as wrapped. Now they had seen the master bedroom at Mitchell's house it was obvious the videos had been filmed there. In addition John Layton had managed to retrieve a number of hairs from Trent's car which matched two of the victims. Amanda Bradley – Richard Trent's lawyer – was eager to cut a deal: he'd admit to the rapes if an accessory to murder charge relating to Rosina Olivárez was dropped. The decision was ultimately down to the CPS, but it looked as if Trent would be going away for a very long time.

The elation from the conclusion of the case was proving short-lived though now operation *Zebo* had another body to contend with. Over the weekend extra staff had been drafted in and the incident room was becoming rather cosy. An extra-large photograph of Simone Ashton now adorned the main whiteboard. Blonde tresses, cuddly jumper, a pout on her lips like she had blown the room a 'thank you' kiss. And startling eyes, deep blue, intoxicating. Those eyes had seen the killer when she had been picked up, when she had willingly gone with him. Those eyes had gazed upon someone who had reassured her. Those eyes had been deceived. But by whom?

The post-mortem on Simone had taken place over the weekend and Nesbit confirmed signs of freezing were present. Worse, the girl's mouth had been mutilated with a knife and Nesbit had identified the piece of flesh Savage had discovered in the church font as the girl's tongue. Nesbit had also, in his words, 'double fast-tracked' the toxicology. The results only served to further dampen the mood: Simone's hair had traces of GHB in and the segmentation analysis suggested that she had only lived for between seven to fourteen days after it was administered.

'Alice Nash went missing two weeks ago this afternoon. Time is running out. We need a lead and fast.' Savage sat at a desk with Calter and Enders, indulging in a spot of brainstorming. 'Kelly, Simone, possibly Alice. All disappeared without any sign of an abduction. No struggle, nobody notices anything, in broad daylight?'

'They knew the abductor?' Enders said.

'Thank you, Patrick, that much is obvious. But the problem is who?'

'There are so few male staff at these places. We've eliminated them all.' Enders scanned a printout of names and Calter peered over at the sheet.

'Different places anyway,' Calter said. 'We are looking for connections. Someone who can access all the nurseries and who arouses no suspicion.'

'OfSTED?' Enders said, a half-smile on his face.

'I want you to check when they made their inspections and get a list of the people involved,' Savage answered. 'No stone as they say.'

Enders groaned and now Savage went off on one. She wanted lists of cleaners, caretakers, plumbers, builders, entertainers, anyone who might have cause to visit more than one of the nurseries. She got up and crossed the room to one of the whiteboards on which she drew a checkerboard of lines.

'Names of nurseries along the top, possibles down the side, a cross where we get a result. Two crosses and we are interested, more than two and we have a definite suspect. We put the data in the system and this is what the results will look like graphically. The important thing will be not to miss anybody.'

'They'll have been CRB'd, ma'am,' Calter said.

'Good, the CRB check will make it all the easier to find them and eliminate them.'

'How are we going to be sure we get everyone?'

'We will start with the accounts. Staff and other workers will all get paid. Anyone from outside doing work at the nursery, like builders for instance, send in invoices and the details will be in the ledger. After that we can develop any other possibles. Like OfSTED.'

'Ma'am?' Enders said. 'One group of people who use the nurseries won't have been CRB checked and that is the parents.'

'You are right and we mustn't overlook them. But the

nurseries should hold accurate records so we will be able to see any correlations.'

'You think some dad took a fancy to one of the girls?' Calter asked.

'That is entirely plausible.'

'At different nurseries?'

'People move house, children are unhappy, lots of reasons to change nurseries.'

'But you think a parent could do what this guy has done?'

Savage paused. Parents killed, of course they did, but in this situation? You drop your little Jake off, wait outside and when one of the girls comes off duty you pick her up, take her somewhere and rape and kill her?

'I would hope not, but if you put a stop sign at the end of an avenue you can't drive down the road can you? We can't start with any preconceived ideas about who we are dealing with.'

At that moment DS Riley came into the incident room. He stood at the door with his hands on his hips, out of breath. He had sweat on his forehead and worry on his face, but excitement in his eyes.

'Ma'am, someone got stabbed on the terraces below the Hoe last night.'

'So I heard.' A stabbing wasn't unusual. Neither, for that matter, was a glassing, a bloody good kicking or any one of the other possible ways to hurt someone when you'd had one too many and somebody had knocked your drink over, glanced at your missus or just stepped on your toes. Late night Plymouth did violence like West End London did shows.

'The victim is one Ben Robbins. He happens to be Simone Ashton's boyfriend.' Riley pulled out his notebook, slid a finger inside, and glanced down at the page. 'And we have a witness.'

* * *

When Riley explained the witness they'd found was Done That Danny, a well-known police time-waster, Savage sent Enders off to deal with taking a statement. Danny's evening meal often consisted of a bag of soggy chips washed down with half a dozen cans of Tennents Super, so it wouldn't be altogether surprising if the lead turned out to be nothing but a drink-induced fantasy. Something to get Danny a bit of attention and maybe some free biscuits and a cup of tea, five sugars.

Enders had trooped off to the cliff-side terraces wearing the sort of hang-dog expression Savage was used to from her junior officers when put on house-to-house duties, but he called through breathless and excited an hour later and insisted Savage ought to see what he had found.

She had dutifully got in a car and driven to the Hoe to find out what Enders was on about. He stood at the gap in the wall where Simone's boyfriend had been attacked and he led her down a twisting path towards the sea.

Danny waited on the beach, hands in the pockets of his threadbare raincoat, head bowed, his greasy black hair shaking off the drizzle. He had an expression of sublime resignation on his face, a look Savage had seen many times before on the faces of those used to having the world push down on them day after day. It was a world-weary acceptance of the way things were, a humility in the face of greater powers, a perceptive understanding of the fact that although things would happen and the years would pass, in the end nothing would ever change.

'Tolds yur, dinna I?' Danny raised his head and smiled, touching his cap with his hand in a deferential manner belonging to another century, another era.

'Told us what, Danny?' Savage said.

'Tolds yur guys about the flash and seeing the knifing. I

saw a man with one of those dickable cameras. Flash, and then I heards a scuffle and fawt that's one of them poofters getting buggered, I did.'

'Sometimes used as a cruising area, ma'am,' Enders said.

'Yes, I know. So what is this about a camera?'

'Well, it wasn't one of them poofters, was it? No, it was attempted murder by camera, Mrs Savage. That's what I was tryin' to tell your boys, only they wouldn't believe me.'

'OK, let's get this straight, what exactly did you see?'

'I was sitting on my bench up there 'aving a leetle drink, trying not to get me head blown off by the fireworks.' Danny gestured up at the terracing. 'Then I sees a white flash and I thinks who's messing me evenin' up? So I jumps up and has a good look. That's when I sees it.'

'What, Danny? You saw what?'

'I sees blood, Mrs Savage. That's when I thinks that's a pretty amazing camera, something I 'aven't seen before.'

'What did you do then?'

'I runs. I don't forget me beer, mind you, but I gets out of there quick. I heads into town and I don't stop until I gets to me spot at the back of the Sainsbury's car park. Then I sleeps with scary dreams.'

Scary dreams and cardboard boxes, Savage thought.

'Ma'am?' It was Enders. 'The long and the short of the story is that Danny told me about this camera flash he saw. Now there were a lot of people on the Hoe taking pictures of the fireworks and it could have been Danny saw one of them or an explosion from a rocket or something. However, Danny was insistent and he said he could prove his story was true.'

'I did, Mrs Savage. I told Detective Constable Patrick that I knew where the killing-camera was because the man had dropped it.'

'*What?*'

'I came down to the beach with Danny and we hunted around until I found this wedged in a crevice just above the tide line.'

Enders reached into his coat pocket and pulled out a plastic evidence bag. Inside was a compact digital camera, Canon brand.

'What is really amazing is the camera is still working after tumbling down here.' Enders fiddled with the controls through the plastic and the screen on the back lit up. A hand was reaching out, partially obscuring a face. The face of Ben Robbins, Simone Ashton's boyfriend.

'Bloody hell, Patrick. Good work. You too, Danny.'

'There's more, ma'am.' Enders flicked a control on the camera and navigated through a series of images.

'Oh God, oh no!'

It was Simone Ashton herself. She was reclining in some kind of weird chair, all black plastic and shiny stainless steel, the sort of thing you might find in a hospital or maybe a prison. Her arms were tied above her head, her legs apart, her feet restrained on some kind of footrests with leather straps. She was naked and the look of absolute terror on the girl's face was something Savage would never forget.

By the time Savage got home that night Jamie had gone to bed.

'Shattered. Not him, me,' Stefan said as Savage came into the kitchen.

On the table a purple and green robot lay face down on a half-eaten potato waffle and an assortment of little monsters fashioned from Play-Doh clambered over the rest of the dinner.

'Godzilla, King Kong, the Hulk,' Stefan explained. 'Don't ask me where he knows them from though.'

'The other kids in the playground. I'm shocked at what the little ones are allowed to watch these days.'

'Our parents said the same.'

'Probably.' Savage paused. Stefan did look shattered, really shattered. For a ninety-kilogram grinder who thought nothing of hauling ropes for hour after hour on a race that was something. Jamie must have been one handful today.

'Go on, get yourself back to your place, I'll sort this lot out.'

Stefan nodded and stumbled from the room.

After a quick trip upstairs to find out what Samantha was up to – homework: no; IMing with friends: yes – she got down to clearing up. The simple monotony of tidying calmed her and contrasted with the hectic atmosphere of the incident room. Dishes in the dishwasher, Play-Doh separated into constituent colours, a wipe round and then she grabbed a cold Peroni from the fridge with the intention to put her feet up in front of the telly while the frozen pizza she had put in the oven cooked itself.

The fridge door closed and the green and purple magnetic dinosaur's eyes bobbed up and down. The tide times had been replaced by a colourful printout from Jamie's school. In the top right corner two little pictures caught her eye, one of Jamie and one of his class. The word 'Proof' ran diagonally across the thumbnails and on the left of the page a list of various ordering options gave print sizes and prices. She remembered he had talked to her about his school photograph last week, worried about a little spot on his chin. Getting him to go in on the day had been a real struggle. Examining the proofs now Savage didn't think she could even see the thing. Probably the photographer's lights had been strong enough to wash the red mark out.

278

Flash.

Shit!

She strolled across to a knife rack where a bottle opener hung and opened her beer. A quick gulp and she exchanged the bottle for the phone. Four rings and Enders's voice came on the line. He sounded weary.

'You still working, Patrick? You ought to get home and read your kids a bedtime story.'

'Ma'am? I need the overtime. You know what the finances are like with three . . . sorry ma'am, I didn't—'

'That's OK. Can you bring up the accounts for a few of the nurseries for me? Kelly's, Simone's and Alice's?'

'Sure, give me a minute.'

The keyboard clattered in the background and Enders said he had the documents open.

'We've been concentrating on trades people and looking for the invoices the nurseries have received requiring payment. The accounts have been our way of linking the nurseries to people from outside of their direct employment, right?'

'Yes, ma'am.'

'Look on the other side of the sheet. The incomings.'

'OK. I'm on Little Angels, Kelly Donal's nursery.' A pause. 'A whole load of entries, ma'am. All the monies received from the parents.'

'Yes, of course. But scroll through. I am looking for a payment from somebody other than a parent. The name might appear only once in a year's worth of accounts.'

Nothing but static for a few moments and Savage could visualise Enders running his finger down the screen. He wasn't the most competent or the fastest with computers, but he was meticulous.

'What have you got?'

279

'I've got parents. Parents. Parents. Parents. More parents. Bloody hundreds of them. Interest from the bank. More parents.'

'Keep looking.'

'Parents. Interest. Parents . . . Hang on.'

'What?'

'Oliver Photographic?'

'Bingo! You understand what I'm talking about?'

'Photograph commission the note says. That's Rod Oliver isn't it? The CSI photographer we use?'

'Yes. He does other work as well, weddings, schools, etcetera. Now check out the other two sets of accounts. Do a search for an Oliver.'

Some faint noise from the keyboard reached Savage's ear before Enders grunted with frustration.

'Control F,' Savage said.

'Oh yes. Thanks, ma'am.' There was a further period of silence until Enders spoke again. 'Got the results, ma'am. Yes, all three nurseries used the same company.'

'Patrick, can you get Oliver's number for me?'

She heard Enders tapping away at the keyboard and then he gave her the number.

'Thanks. Don't go anywhere, I'll call you back in five.'

Savage hung up. She took another swig of the beer, the liquid cold on her tongue, and thought of Kelly Donal. The girl had lain cold in the woodland over at Malstead. Frozen. Savage remembered the glade and how it had been lit up by the flash from the photographer's camera.

Photography was definitely the key. Done That Danny had discovered the camera used in the attack on Simone Ashton's boyfriend. He'd seen the flash of the camera when the boyfriend had been attacked and the camera had contained the chilling images of Alice Nash. In addition

Mitchell and Forester were both into photography, and a neighbour of Mitchell's reported the flashes coming from a window. But both Mitchell and Forester were dead and Richard Trent was in custody.

That left Rod Oliver. Was he the killer?

She looked back at the sample pictures on the fridge. Oliver had access to the nurseries, he could have scouted out the girls, marked each one down as targets. They'd have known him, trusted him.

Savage shook her head. Surely not. She'd known Oliver for years, couldn't see him as a murderer. And anyway what about the woman Riley had interviewed over in North Prospect? Julie Meadows. Her description of the man she'd seen arguing with Forester didn't match the elderly, silver-haired Oliver. But Julie had said that the man had a camera with him.

She sighed, relieved, and punched in the number Enders had given her. Oliver answered in a couple of rings and Savage introduced herself.

'Oh hello, Charlotte, not another body I hope?'

'No, Rod. Are you out on a shoot?'

'No, at home. About to clear up the dinner before the wife starts giving me earache over the mess.'

'Just a question about your assistant.'

'Sure, what's up?'

'Has he been with you long?'

'Ever since I went independent. He's not the sharpest tool in the box, but he is good with the equipment and takes cracking pictures.'

'Ever had any problems with him?'

'He is not always reliable, but he only works for me part-time so I can't expect him to drop everything and come running. Other than that I've no complaints. He's got a brilliant eye for a picture. Some people have a way of seeing things which enables them to simply point the camera at something, click, and get a brilliant photograph. He's a natural, but that's really all there is to him. He doesn't say much, just gets on with the job. That's not a crime, is it?'

'No, of course not.' Savage paused for a moment. 'Rod, you introduced him to me back at the Malstead Down crime scene. I want to confirm his surname in case I misheard.'

'Is it important?'

'It might be. Can you give me his address too?'

'His name is Harrison. Matthew Harrison,' Oliver said. Then he gave her the address. She wrote down the details, thanked him and hung up.

Savage stared down at the surname, unable to quite believe it.

Harrison.

As Mitchell had died he'd talked of a man called Harry. The team had spent time trying to track down somebody of that name. Now it turned out that had been a complete waste of time: Harry was Matthew Harrison's nickname.

Savage thumped her fist onto the work surface and then moved her hand across, sweeping her notepad away and at the same time catching the bottle of beer. The bottle clattered over and lay on its side disgorging golden liquid. She ignored the mess, grasped the edge of the worktop and swore.

Harrison had been there at the scene in Malstead. He'd taken pictures, shot a video, all while gloating over the body of Kelly Donal. The body he'd just dumped. The body he'd just had sex with. Harrison, not Oliver, was the one who'd selected the girls from the nurseries and abducted them, raped them and killed them.

Kelly Donal, Simone Ashton, Alice Nash.

When she'd stood near Harrison at Malstead, Simone Ashton had likely as not been already dead, but Alice Nash? The girl had gone missing the previous day, but the photographs on the camera found by Done That Danny proved she had survived for days after her abduction. If only Savage had known she could have done something.

She shook her head, aware she was blaming herself for something which wasn't her fault. Then she picked up the phone and dialled the number for the incident room. Enders answered within seconds.

'It's Matthew Harrison,' she said. 'Rod Oliver's assistant. He's the killer.'

'What?'

'I'll explain it fully later, but Harrison works alongside Oliver when they do shoots at day nurseries. Any girl he fancied, he took.'

'Bloody hell, ma'am. That's sick.'

'I've got Harrison's address so gather some bodies together. We are going to need a TAG team in on this as well. I'll get on to Hardin and fill him in on the details. And don't leave without me. I'm on my way in.'

Chapter Thirty-One

Harry sat in the dark in the living room at the cottage examining the pictures on the screen on the back of one of his cameras. The images scrolled by and Harry studied the faces looking out. Lovely, all of them, but none resembled any of the girls from his past. No Deborah, no Katya. Perhaps he was going to have to widen his search beyond the sweet angels at the nurseries. He chewed his tongue and began to feel uncomfortable with the thought. Other types of girls wouldn't have the exquisite qualities that he wanted, the inner qualities he remembered from long ago.

He switched the camera off and the room slid into darkness. He liked that. Safe. Then there was a noise from the ceiling, a creak of a floorboard. Emma. She must be moving around up there. Poor girl. He felt sorry for her now. The final test had taken place and the result disappointed him. Chasing her naked through the house had made him suspect that the girl was no different from Trinny or Lucy, despite the cleansing regime he had carried out. And so it proved. All that fresh fruit and bottled water had made no difference. He would have to deal with her. Tonight. Of course he would keep her for a while after she had been preserved and have some fun, but in the end that wasn't very edifying. Eventually he would have to dispose of her like the other two.

Harry felt the weight of the camera in his hands. Funny how all those girls were in there, somehow captured on the chip. He had hundreds of pictures of girls, thousands even, and it was comforting to know that they would remain living forever.

He put the camera down and moved across the room in the dark. He walked to the fireplace and groped for some matches on the mantelpiece. Finding them he lit a candle and began to lay a fire in the grate. As he crumpled sheets of newspaper and laid the kindling on top he noticed the headlines and the pictures of the dead girls, *his* dead girls. The pictures of Carmel showed how lovely she had been, but Harry knew that she didn't look that way now. Not after having been in the sea for all those months. Trinny had looked better when she was dead, he knew, but even she would be rotting soon.

He struck a match and lit the paper, watching the girls die a second time. Things were better kept alive, like Emma, but sometimes it just wasn't possible. If they didn't behave as they were supposed to, if they didn't get clean, then he had no other option. Once they were dead he knew that he should get rid of them, but then they would just rot away and he would have nobody to talk to. Which was why he kept them. At least until they lost their beauty. That was why he'd had to get rid of Trinny and Lucy. Their bodies had gone saggy and started to smell. Which was hardly surprising considering they had been frozen and defrosted half a dozen times.

Chapter Thirty-Two

Grand Parade, Plymouth. Monday 8th November. 11.17 pm

Inspector Nigel Frey was commanding the Tactical Aid Group and Savage had briefed him on the situation, emphasising the possibility of a hostage scenario.

'Alice Nash. We are pretty certain he has her.'

'Alive?'

'Let's hope so.'

'But you are not sure?'

Savage told Frey about the frozen bodies of Kelly Donal and Simone Ashton and also about the murder of Forester and the attempted murder of Simone Ashton's boyfriend.

'He doesn't think twice about killing so if he does have her we need complete surprise.'

'Two armed officers will enter first,' Frey said. 'They will sweep and clear. Then the rest of us pile in en masse.'

'We need to remember the house is a crime scene. If Harrison isn't in there we want to keep the number of people entering the building to a minimum.'

'Understood. But safety comes first. It's my call as to if and when you get in. Sorry, instructions from Hardin. He mentioned something about the Moor Vale incident.' Frey's tone came across as serious, but he was grinning at the same time. 'If you ever fancy a change of career I'm always looking for officers with a bit of backbone.'

'Thanks, but no thanks.' Savage smiled back. 'Once is enough. I'm quite happy watching you guys from a safe distance.'*

A safe distance equalled fifty metres up the street in an unmarked car. Savage, Riley and Enders waited in the darkness for the TAG team to appear. A few minutes earlier Enders had cruised the car past Harrison's place. Even an estate agent would have been hard pushed to describe the property as anything other than grotty. Paint peeled from the window frames and the railings on the first-floor balcony were rusty. On the front wall a hunk of plaster had fallen off and lay in pieces in the tiny garden. Alongside the rest of the street's smart looking dwellings the house stuck out like a sore thumb.

'The press will love this,' Riley said. 'Fits their stereotype perfectly.'

'And if it doesn't they'll make it fit,' Enders said.

Savage brooded, her own thoughts blocking out the chat of the other two officers. Had they missed something which might have led them here earlier? The house flagged Harrison up as different from his neighbours and it was surprising nobody had complained about the state of the place. Should someone else have spotted other things that might have drawn him to the attention of the authorities and prevented him being able to work at the nurseries? Savage didn't know, but she reckoned she had done her best. In the end no one could expect more.

'Ma'am?' Enders nodded towards the house. The front door opened and light washed out onto the street. Two girls dressed for a night on the town tottered down the steps and walked along the road.

'Students,' Riley said. 'Ground floor and basement are rented out. Harrison has his studio on the first floor, flat on the second and third.'

'Nice looking tenants,' Enders said as the girls breezed past the car, a whiff of perfume noticeable a few moments later. 'Don't suppose that is a coincidence. Whatever, they will be searching for new digs come tomorrow.'

'Maybe your missus would be happy to give them a room, eh?'

'Shut up, ladies,' Savage said. 'Here we go!'

The TAG van drove by and drew up alongside the kerb in front of them. The rear doors opened and six men jumped out, Frey leading the way. Black clothing, body armour, SWAT team boots and guns. They jogged down the street to Harrison's house. Two of the team now held the enforcer – a tubular steel battering ram – between them while a third peered through the letterbox. 'Clear,' he mouthed.

The two officers swung the ram and the door crashed open, splintering around the lock. Two more officers with weapons drawn now raced past and into the house. Savage heard muffled shouting from inside and the rest of the team rushed in.

'OK, we're on.' Savage opened the door and got out of the car. As they walked down the street and neared the house they heard commotion from inside. A crash as an internal door caved in and a high-pitched warble sound from a burglar alarm. More shouting. Bodies thumping up and down stairs. Now doors were opening on houses either side and a couple of the TAG team were screaming at the residents to get back inside.

'Give me CID any day,' Enders said. 'All this running around would leave me too knackered for anything.'

Frey appeared at the front door.

'Clear so far. No lights evident on the inside so seems like he's not around. Burglar alarm would indicate that as well. Give my lads another five minutes and then you can call your CSIs in.' Frey indicated the white SOC van pulling over up the road. He grinned. 'Methinks there will be plenty for them to get their teeth into.'

Layton climbed down from the van and began unloading gear from the back as Savage went over.

'I want a quick search around inside,' she said. 'And then I'll leave you to it.'

'That's what they all say,' he said, shaking his head at the sight of the TAG team members leaving the building. 'Honestly if you knew the pain that causes me. All those sweaty bodies clumping around over my lovely crime scene.'

'Want me to get suited up?'

'Ma'am, that would make my day. Your boys too, please.'

The three of them got into the garb Layton provided and padded into the house. They had the place to themselves now the TAG team had left and it was quiet.

The hallway had stairs that led up to Harrison's studio and the flat above and Savage led the way.

'Patrick, you take the studio. Darius and I will go to the flat. Prelim scout only. Leave the digging for Layton and his crew.'

The stairs and the studio area seemed neat and tidy. Bright white walls, cleanish. When they ascended the next set of stairs to the second-floor flat that changed. A stale odour of sweat and unwashed clothes invaded Savage's nostrils. Something else too.

'Darius?'

'Not sure, ma'am. Unpleasant anyway.'

The door to the flat led straight into the living area. A big bay window looked out to the Sound, lights sparkling in the distance across the water. In front of the window, but set back from the glass, three cameras on tripods reminded Savage of the Martian machines from the *War of the Worlds*. One camera had a long lens and pointed towards the Hoe. Savage went into the room, aware as she did so of something scattered over the floor.

'Huh?' Savage glanced down at her feet where sheets of paper overlapped each other, a white carpet made of A4.

Riley bent down and picked up one of the sheets.

'Printouts, ma'am. Must be a computer somewhere.'

'Interesting?'

'Jesus, no. Sick. Ranting. Nonsense.' Riley laid the piece of paper back where it came from.

'OK,' Savage said. 'I wanted to examine those cameras, but I think I'll leave it. Too much to disturb in here. Let's check out the rest of the flat.'

On the same level a kitchen didn't hold anything of interest. Old linoleum lay on the floor, sticky and smeared with grease and scraps, and a bin in the corner overflowed with fast food packaging. In stark contrast the stainless sink and chrome taps gleamed as if from a showroom and the gas hob was spotless. The black granite worktops looked clean too, but the inside of the fridge stank: a half-empty bottle of milk had gone sour.

'Not much for us here. Let's go upstairs.'

Savage led the way up to the next floor. A series of three rooms jigsawed themselves into the odd space. The master had a large double bed and inside the room a bad taste gagged at the back of Savage's throat. Acrid, bitter, just plain off, she thought. Various items of clothing lay strewn around the floor and at the end of the bed two piles of white hand towels; one pile neatly folded, the other in a jumble.

'Jesus wept,' Riley poked the jumbled mess with his foot while covering his nose with his forearm. 'This smells bloody disgusting.'

'What is it?'

'Semen I think, ma'am. The towels are absolutely saturated and the whole lot stinks as if it's rotting. Looks like he has been wanking for England.'

'This is where we need DC Calter. I'm sure she would be able to come up with something witty.'

'"Come" being the operative word, ma'am.'

'Quite.' Savage turned and left the room. 'Let's move on, I promised Layton this would be a quick scan around.'

The next room was about half the size of the master and seemed to function as some kind of storage area. There were cardboard packing boxes, an old mattress on its side, a rolled-up carpet, a computer base unit with no monitor, no leads.

'Layton will take care of sifting through this lot,' Savage said, moving to the final room.

The door opened and when she flicked the light switch she knew at once they had hit gold. 'Box room' would have been an honest estate agent's description for the space measured no bigger than Savage's arm span. A large window overlooked the road, but you wouldn't know it because heavy black card had been taped over the glass with parcel tape. Not a chink of light penetrated from the outside.

'Darkroom?' Riley said. 'Once anyway.'

With the advent of digital photography the darkroom had become redundant, but it appeared as if Harrison had elected to keep the room sealed to the outside world for other reasons. Against one wall a small computer workstation had a printer shelf to one side, a base unit below and two large widescreen monitors on the desk. Apart from the space taken by the workstation the rest of the walls were covered in prints. A4 in size, each print overlapped the next and ran up the wall in a column reaching all the way to the ceiling with no space between each column. In fact, Savage noted the ceiling had been plastered with prints as well. The prints seemed to bear down on the room, compressing the space and threatening to bury them in an avalanche. Of girls. Savage recognised some shots Harrison must have taken in the nurseries he visited because the girls sat staid and starched in formal poses. However, most of the shots appeared candid, many taken from Harrison's front room. They showed girls passing by on the street or sunbathing on the Hoe, unaware of Harrison's long lens sucking them in.

Looking closer now Savage could see that dozens of the pictures had been annotated in black marker. An arrow drawn on pointing to a bra strap showing, a flash of panties, a glimpse of inner thigh, a trio of drunken girls staggering down the street with their breasts half hanging out. At the end of the arrow a word: 'Slut?', 'Tart?', 'Whore?', 'Dirty?'

The words shocked her as much as the sheer number of images, but most of all she found herself shocked by the actual image content. These were ordinary girls Harrison had snapped outside his house and on the Hoe, not some fantasy from a magazine, but real. The message didn't need much decoding in Savage's mind. Out there, in the streets and the parks and the clubs flesh displayed itself, advertised the availability of easy sex and longed to be touched, to be consumed.

Savage saw Riley shifting his stance, his face grimacing at each new image.

'Is that what you think? Those words?' Savage said. 'I mean "you" as in "men"?'

'It's not what we think rationally, ma'am, but maybe it's how we think when we look. You are in a sweet shop, you expect the sweets to taste nice, right?'

'And nice is slutty?'

'Nice is available.'

'But possibly not to Harrison.'

'It could explain a lot.'

Savage examined the images for a second time. If so much unavailable flesh had flashed in front of Harrison perhaps frustration had made him go mad, but then again maybe the pictures on the wall comprised a mere sideshow and something deeper drove him to kill.

'Ma'am?'

Riley pointed to a row of framed prints on the shelf above the printer. Rosina Salgado Olivárez, Kelly Donal, Simone Ashton and Alice Nash. They were formal pictures, each girl dressed in her nursery uniform, smiling and looking straight at the camera. Donal and Ashton can't have realised their killer peered back through the lens at them.

On a higher shelf golden writing sparkled on a set of hard-backed notebooks. Five altogether, each with a girl's name embossed in gold on the spine: Trinny, Lucy, Deborah and Katya. None of the names matched the victims nor any of the women on the mispers list.

Savage took the first book, the one with Trinny written on the spine. Inside narrow ruled lines were filled with an almost impenetrable scrawl in black ink. Harrison had never thought of using blotting paper and the resulting ink smudges everywhere made deciphering the writing even more difficult. She skimmed through the lines of facts and figures about Trinny, whoever she was. Height, weight, eye colour, those made sense. But the rest of the text just waffled. Page after page describing, in minute detail, Trinny's clothing, her shopping habits, her food preferences. Then came other ramblings, Harrison's explanation of the love he felt for Trinny, what he was going to do with and to her. Some of it was impassioned, half poetry, half florid prose, the rest was pornographic, sick. After thirty or so pages the writing ended with a single word on an otherwise blank page: 'Sorry.'

Savage scanned back through the text. Who was Trinny? Might she be another victim they had yet to discover? Savage shuddered at the thought and skipped back through some more pages. Then she spotted it: an address.

'Beacon Park. It's Kelly Donal.'

'Trinny is Kelly?' asked Riley.

'Yes.' She handed the book to Riley. 'Read the description of her, first page.'

'My dream lovely dream with the long brown hair and that starched white shirt top buttons undone and those heaving breasts pushing outwards wishing to be free and in my hands hazel eyes with plucked eyebrows narrow lips and white teeth the cutest nose that can smell my desire you sweet for me alone and your young innocence that longs for the closeness of my lonely flesh with your purity wrapped around me so safely.'

'You've seen the shots of Kelly? The description matches,' Savage said.

'Perfectly. Anyway the address says everything, ma'am. Congratulations.'

Savage nodded. 'In the circumstances I'm not celebrating. Especially since we have two big unanswered questions.'

'Which are?'

'Where is Harrison and where the hell is Alice Nash?'

Chapter Thirty-Three

Tatershall slammed the phone down and thumped the desk. First thing Tuesday and the day turning crap already. He had called a certain DC Nikki Lees from Dartmouth nick and unhelpful appeared to be her middle name. Rude too, treating him like an out-of-town hillbilly deputy. She hadn't known the owners of Netherston Cottage, hadn't been willing to try and find out either and didn't seem at all interested in his mispers.

'Stupid idiots,' Tatershall said to Simbeck. 'A few boats, a bit of sun and some rich ponces flashing their money around and they think they are living in bloody Monaco. The likes of them are obviously too busy licking some yachtie's arse to have time to bother with us thickos down here in Cornwall.'

'A yacht, a bit of sun and a rich ponce would do me fine, boss,' Simbeck said. 'Even if I did have to lick his arse occasionally.'

Tatershall groaned at the thought and picked up a pad from his desk. Jottings, doodles and random thoughts covered the paper, all connected to the couple from St Ives. What had started out as another boring mispers inquiry had now begun to fascinate him. The couple weren't the sort of people he would usually feel much empathy for. Incomers rankled with him and rich ones twice over, but something about the couple drew a strand of compassion from him. At first glance they appeared to be not so different from the hundreds of retirees Tatershall came across in his work. Yet they had got under his skin. The husband, a cancer patient with not much time left, his wife a painter of dull landscapes, nothing unique there. But when he had read the letter from the hospital and stared out of the big window across the bay some of the emptiness from their lives washed over him. The trawl through their papers that revealed little, the sterile paintings, the flat devoid of memories, the story spoke to Tatershall of a couple who didn't want to look back but had nothing to look forward to either.

He had managed to find out that they originally came from near Plymouth, another Devon link. The wife had been born in a small village on Dartmoor where the couple had later married at the local church, but beyond those bare facts nothing. Without a trip across to Devon, he thought, he couldn't proceed further, certainly not if the local police were going to be as obstinate as DC Lees.

Reviewing the notes on his pad again brought to his attention the one nugget of information of any use so far. The location of Netherston Cottage. The place had been easy to find. A quick Google had revealed the hamlet of Netherston buried in the deepest part of the South Hams, an area of Devon which lay to the south of Dartmoor and took in the coastline from Plymouth to Dartmouth. Examining the aerial photograph overlaid on the map and comparing the lie of the land with the image on the painting he was pretty sure he had identified the exact location. The cottage lay nestled up against a wood in a valley only accessible along a mile or so of track. Even compared with places he knew in Cornwall the location was remote. Was it possible his mispers were there? Considering the health of the husband and his need for regular drugs and treatment Tatershall could think of only one reason why they would be: they had gone there to end their lives.

The thought depressed him some more. But kicking the idea around in his head the notion didn't quite make sense. The couple had moved to St Ives presumably because they liked the area. The view from the big window in the flat suggested an appreciation of the scale and beauty of the landscape and the wife's paintings, however bland, indicated some sort of affinity for the place too. The gallery gave them a social connection right into the heart of the town and meant they would be able to get help and support. Why choose to go to some isolated cottage to die? Even if the couple had planned some suicide pact it would have been just as easy to carry it out in their own home. Unless they needed help, of course.

From their enquiries they had discovered the couple had no close friends in the area and no immediate family either. Could that explain the need to return to Devon, the county where they were born? Tatershall had brought the cardboard box with all their papers back to the station and he had started to go through the material again. This time he took each piece of paper out, checking between sheets and making sure he wasn't missing anything. The pile on the desk beside him grew until the entire contents of the box had been removed. He sighed, disappointed he had found nothing new, but satisfied he had done a thorough job. He started to put the pile back in the box when he noticed a piece of paper wedged under one of the flaps at the bottom. He lifted the flap and pulled out the page of an old newspaper, which had been folded several times. As he unfolded the newsprint another piece of paper fell out. It was a birth certificate. Tatershall smoothed the document on the desk in front of him and read the details.

'They've got a son,' he said to himself.

'Huh?' Simbeck had been working at her desk opposite answering emails, but now she looked up.

'Born in 1971, registered in Totnes.' Tatershall read the name. 'Can you do a search on the PNC for me?'

Tatershall spelled out the name and then inspected the page from the newspaper. As he digested the headline and associated story the sympathy he had for the couple began to drain away to be replaced by a wave of emotion comprised of both anger and sadness. He felt sick and all of a sudden wished he was out of the force and just an ordinary bloke who could go home and cuddle his kids without having to think about this stuff.

'Boss?'

'Rape and child abuse. He got fifteen years. And there was me worrying about the cancer. Bastard.' Tatershall put his head in his hands for a moment and then sighed. 'Right, Kate. Do you know what I'm going to do? I'm going to go to the new coffee shop across the road and get a coffee and a cake. Afterwards I'm going to come back here and complete the paperwork on this case and be done with the bloody thing.'

He stood up and went to the door.

'Coming?'

'No.'

'Why not?'

'Because I've found the son.' Simbeck pointed to the screen displaying the results of her search. 'Matthew Harrison. There was an entry made yesterday. He's wanted for murder.'

* * *

So cold, I'm so very cold. And I'm going to die.

Alice Nash knew that now. For certain. For a while she had clung to the hope she had been kidnapped, that a ransom demand would be issued and some rich benefactor would pay up.

Idiot. There is no kidnapper.

No, the house belonged to Matt Harrison, part-time photographer's assistant, full-time madman, rapist and killer. The nutter wouldn't be letting her go, not now, not after what he'd done.

After. At least now was after.

She had run from him and he'd caught her, smashing her down with a horrifying violence. She'd felt him against her, his naked body all over her as she squirmed underneath, and she waited for him to rape her. But he hadn't. He had been aroused, but for some reason he stopped himself and had simply stroked her head as she had lain on the bare floor and sobbed.

'There, Emma, sweet Emma. Don't worry. Everything is going to be fine. I promise. Just you wait and see.'

Back in the little room she fell asleep and when she woke the hallucinations had started. Daytimes passed by in a whirl of colour and dizzy spells and the nights brought sweat and muscle spasms. She guessed Harrison had drugged her food or drink, but she had no choice but to consume what he provided each morning. Eat and drink or starve and die. Then one day she awoke from a deep sleep and the nightmare seemed to be over. Bright lights and white walls, not the old house she had been imprisoned in. A hospital. She had been rescued! The blurry images snapped into focus.

Flash!

'Emma! You are back!' Harrison smiled at her as he put the camera down. He wore casual clothes with a white coat

299

over the top, like a doctor or one of those people who sliced up animals in a laboratory.

She screamed and tried to move, struggling against the ties holding her hands fast and the straps on her legs spreading them . . .

Oh my God no!

. . . wide apart.

'Please no, don't hurt me!'

Harrison bent over some kind of trolley, gleaming tools of stainless steel clinking together in his shaking hands as he sorted through them.

'Hurt you?' He turned round, shocked, mortified. 'I'm not going to hurt you. You are lovely, perfect, look at you!'

He moved his hand over and touched her breasts, cupping each in turn.

'Yes, yes. Perfect. And clean. I hope.'

His hand began tracing its way down across her stomach and lower and Alice closed her eyes to try and blot out Harrison's caress.

'No, not yet my love. Soon, I promise. And the wait will be worth it, I know.'

When she opened her eyes he stood over at the trolley, holding some kind of medical device shaped something like a giant stainless steel dildo.

'But first a couple of tests, just to check. You see the trouble is dirt gets everywhere these days. Into everything. Nothing stays pure. Nothing stays untouched. You must understand I need to make sure. Yes, yes. Surety and purity. I must not be corrupted by your flesh. Desire must come later, not now. I don't want to get dirty again.'

He moved between her legs.

'NO!'

*   *   *

Now the cold slipped into her skull, deadening the memory somewhat but freezing the images too, as if to stop her forgetting.

He had examined her for a few minutes, pausing every so often to scribble in a notebook. Then his expression changed, something had annoyed him and, without a word, his coat fell from his shoulders and he tore at his clothes until he had stripped himself naked. He stood between her spread-eagled legs with his hands grasping her waist and raped her. Horrid grunting sounds spluttered from him with each thrust and he came with a gasp and shouted that name again.

'Emma! Emma! Emma!'

When it was all over he wouldn't meet her gaze. He took a cloth from the trolley, held the bitter smelling material over her face and she drifted to sleep.

She woke to complete darkness, freezing cold and the knowledge of certain death. But that was OK because she was more scared of living now. She had seen the other instruments on the table and the look of utter depravity in his eyes. Death would be a release. Except . . . except . . .?

Dad, I love you.

If she died she wouldn't see him again, would she? The thought of him grieving so soon after her mother's death, of him never knowing how much she loved him overwhelmed her and she began to sob.

No, I'm not going to die.

Calmer now, but still very cold, she reached her hands out to explore the dark space. Tiny, not the room where she had spent the last dozen or so days. She stretched her legs out in front of her, but when she tried to sit up she banged her head. To either side of her she touched some sort of wall.

Like plastic?

When she knocked her fist on the surface she was sure. She was in a kind of large plastic box.

Cold?

Yes, ice cold. A humming noise as well, like an electric motor or something.

She scrabbled around with her hands and feet, trying to find the limits of her confinement. To one side of her she discovered a small grille-like opening in the plastic. She tried to get her fingers through the grille but the openings were way too small. There seemed to be an air flow coming through the slits though, cold air, freezing air . . . a freezer! She was locked in a freezer!

She put her head in her hands and let all the air flood from her lungs in a long sigh. With the extreme cold there wouldn't be too many more breaths, and naked there was little she could do to conserve her body heat. She thought she remembered something from childhood swimming lessons where you were supposed to curl yourself in a ball so she tried that, putting her hands behind her head and pushing it down between her knees. That was when she found something.

A hairclip.

They insisted on your hair being tied back at work and she wore both a hair band and a couple of metal clips. The clip had been tangled in her hair for all these days. She pulled it out and turned in the small space to get at the grille. The clip slipped between the little slits and she poked it in farther and began to wiggle it around.

Bang! A bright blue flash and her body slamming back against the side of the box. A tingling shot along her arm and a convulsion ran through her chest and something smelt bad. Like when the toaster had gone wrong at home and

302

tripped the cut-out switch. A pungent odour reached her nostrils, a mixture of electrical components having shorted out and organic material burning.

My hand.

It hurt now, a searing pain along the backs of her fingers. She slumped down, knocking her head on the side of the box. An extreme drowsiness overcame her and in front of her eyes stars flared in a dark night sky. The sky spun round and round and round and then the stars were fading to an inky black nothing, like when the lights in the theatre went down at the end of a play. Silence, everything quiet and she was aware that even the humming of the electric motor had stopped.

Chapter Thirty-Four

Savage yawned. Bed late and up early yet again wasn't doing her any good at all. And crawling through the morning traffic didn't help either. Stop, start, green light, red light, some tosser cutting her up on the bridge. She wanted a clear road, a smooth ride, but somehow the option had been left off the menu, at least with this case.

She mulled over the possible actions open to the team now they had all but confirmed Matthew Harrison as the killer of Kelly Donal and Simone Ashton. Tracing Harrison was the force's highest priority, but the empty fridge and half a dozen pieces of mail behind the front door suggested he hadn't been in his flat for a few days. Had he somehow got wind of details of the investigation and cut and run? If so, what did that do for their chances of finding Alice Nash alive now fourteen days were up? The chilling picture of Simone Ashton on the camera Enders had found pointed to Harrison carrying out some sort of procedure on the girls. God help Alice, Savage thought.

The jam cleared and Savage got to the station just in time for the morning briefing in the Major Crimes suite. She

304

squeezed in past the overflow of officers crammed in the corridor, and when Enders spotted her entering he let out a cheer that was followed up by everyone else in the room. Hardin beamed at her and bounced across like a gas-filled party balloon, knocking into desks and causing coffees to spill and computer monitors to wobble.

'What can I say? Congratulations to everyone. Case solved. Now we just need to catch the bastard!'

To that end he detailed the liaisons he was setting up with other forces and with the port authorities. Savage reckoned a more likely result would come from the crime scene trawl which had been going on all night and would continue throughout the day. So far only the pictures linked any of the girls with Harrison's house. After Hardin had shaken hands with everyone and returned to his office to work on his media briefing Savage sat down with Riley, Calter and Enders and they began to work up possible actions.

'He must have another place, ma'am,' Riley said. 'A garage, a lockup, a boat even.'

Riley was right. The girls hadn't been murdered at the house in Plymouth. Harrison would have dealt with them somewhere else. Somewhere quiet.

Savage instructed Riley to get over to Harrison's flat on Grand Parade and try to find anything which might indicate a location he could have used. She would take Calter and Enders back to Malstead Down and see if they could dig anything up in the village.

'It doesn't appear as if Harrison had any connection to Malstead, but the evidence points to something. He dumped Kelly in the wood on the evening of the 26th October, the night the village held its bonfire party. However, Simone is left in the church. On the 26th Harrison would have found it impossible to leave Kelly in the church, but my hunch is that is what he intended. The question is, why? Now we have a name we can do some door-to-doors and maybe drive around the area and see what we can pick up.'

'The old lady, ma'am,' Calter said.

'Which one? Old ladies are not in short supply in Malstead.'

'The one at the top of the green. The little cottage with the tumbledown porch thingy. Mrs Harbersher I think her name was. She said she had lived in the village all her life. Born and bred. If anyone could remember Harrison she might. If she can remember anything, that is. When I visited she thought I had come to read the electric meter until I showed my ID.'

Calter was right about the old lady. When she opened the door to Calter again she behaved as if there had been some problem with her bill payment.

'The standing order went through, I'm sure. I checked online yesterday. We are not all fuddy-duddies you know.'

Calter tried to explain about the return visit, but it took Savage's intervention to get them an invite into Mrs Harbersher's front room, Enders made to wait outside because the cottage didn't appear big enough for the three of them. Net curtains, porcelain figures of dogs and cats, old-fashioned upholstered chairs, a carpet with patterns on and a coal fire with heat so intense it hurt to look at. Mrs Harbersher had been young in the sixties and yet the room matched Savage's childhood memories of her own grandmother's parlour.

Tea and biscuits took an age to arrive, but when they did the tea came in fine china and the biscuits in a Tesco's luxury brand tin. Savage glared at Calter as she grabbed two at a time. No wonder the electricity company aroused such suspicion if this was how they acted.

'Mrs Harbersher,' Savage began. 'You'll know we are here about the murders and the body discovered in the church?'

'Shocking business. In my time we behaved with a little more care. These days the young ones can't wait to get their knickers off and this is the result, mark my words.'

'We are trying to find out some information about a man who may have had something to do with the area at one time or another. He's called Matthew Harrison. Does the name ring any bells with you?'

'Matthew?'

'Yes.'

'That's a good old-fashioned name, isn't it? Part of the problem these days is those silly names parents come up with. I am sure that is why there is so much bad behaviour.'

'So you don't recognise it?'

'I didn't say that. I do recognise it. Matthew Harrison. Elizabeth Foulds was his mother. She came from Bridge Farm. Those Foulds are all dead, and now it's just a house with a couple of barn conversions since they parcelled the land off.'

'And? This Elizabeth Foulds?'

'Lizzy? An attractive girl, very pretty, but a bit quiet and in her own head. She was a few years below me when I left the local school. That's closed now. Not enough children in the village, you see? Everyone moves away or dies.'

'What happened to Lizzy?'

'She left too. Got married and moved to a remote little cottage somewhere over towards Totnes. She visited a few times, but as her parents got older she came less and less. When they died she inherited a tidy sum from the sale of the farm, her being an only child.'

307

'And her husband?'

'Richard Harrison his name was. A draughtsman by trade or an architect or something similar. He'd come to the farm to plan out a milking parlour and found a bride instead. Very romantic. At least we all thought so at the time.'

The information was coming, but was taking an age to arrive. Calter wriggled on the edge of her seat, itching to ask the obvious question, but Savage didn't give her a chance.

'Where did they get married, Mrs Harbersher?'

'Oh, same place as I did. Right here. In the church.' The old woman's face wore a saddened expression and she looked much older as her eyes shifted their focus from Savage and stared out the window and across the green to the church. 'I don't suppose anyone else will want to do so now, will they?'

Savage didn't think so either, but she didn't want to get into a prolonged discussion.

'What did you mean when you said you thought the way they met was romantic at the time?'

'Well, history changes things, doesn't it? When you look back with hindsight you bring the truth to bear on distant events. Everything comes out in the wash in the end.'

'I'm sorry, Mrs Harbersher, but I don't understand.'

'Don't you lot know anything? It happened over thirty years ago, but you do keep records, don't you? Richard Harrison went down, convicted of rape and child abuse. The girl he raped was only seventeen and poor Matthew, what? Nine, ten, eleven? A disgusting business, he should have been hanged, Lizzy as well, if you want my opinion.'

After they left the cottage Savage strolled across to the church, leaving Calter and Enders next to the car. She peered over the wall at the rows of gravestones. Moss and lichen covered the older ones, the inscriptions weathered and

308

indecipherable. In fifty years' time what had happened in the church and the sordid story Mrs Harbersher had told them about the Harrison family would have become just another Dartmoor legend. Today's tragedy would be tomorrow's distant memory to all but those families involved.

Then all of a sudden Calter was waving across at Savage and shouting something about Riley being on the phone. It was a crap signal and she didn't understand half of what he said, but it concerned a lead from a detective in Cornwall and a location for Harrison's bolt hole.

'Ten minutes' drive, ma'am,' Calter screamed. 'Come on!'

Enders revved the engine as Savage ran across the green and jumped into the back of the car. He hit the accelerator and the car swung sideways tearing great chunks of grass out from under its wheels before they bounced onto the tarmac and screeched away.

'Where to?' Savage said.

'Somewhere near Gara Bridge,' Calter said. 'Approximately five miles south of the A38. Riley's coming from town with a bunch of cars. Blues and twos, ARVs, the lot.'

A few minutes of driving and the country lane had become like a tunnel, cutting through the land with the trees at the top of the steep banks curving overhead and almost blocking out the light. The speed of the car gave a sort of rushing sensation like they were playing in some giant video game. Objects by the roadside shot past in a blur, only sharpening for a frozen moment, a blink of an eye, before they vanished; green moss on a tree stump, a herd of cows waiting by a gate, a startled rabbit. There was a roaring noise in Savage's ears too, but she didn't think anyone else in the car could hear the sound.

'We're here!' Calter jabbed her finger at the Sat Nav and pointed ahead. 'Into the wood.'

A forestry track curled up away from the road and disappeared behind a cluster of pine. The muddy track had deep ruts and a 4x4 would have been more suited to the task than the Ford Focus they were in.

'Do you think we can manage it?' Savage asked Enders.

'Of course we can, ma'am.' Enders seemed offended, as if Savage's question was a personal affront to his driving ability.

They left the road and headed up the track, the car yawing to the side for a moment before Enders turned into the skid and they lurched onward. They crested a rise and headed down into a small valley, soon leaving the wood behind and bouncing along between stone walls behind which the occasional sheep could be seen nibbling at the poor pasture. Up ahead a little cottage sat on the far side of the valley, nestled under a vast conifer plantation.

'Shit!' Enders brought the car to a halt.

In front of them the track forded a fast flowing stream, bank full thanks to the rain. The depth was hard to estimate, but Savage thought it could be anything up to a couple of feet.

'We ain't going through the water, ma'am. Too deep for us, I am afraid.'

Savage could see the cottage standing about half a mile away, no problem to walk to, but they would get wet crossing the stream.

'Calter and I will go on. You reverse the car back until you can find a place where you won't block the track. The others will be here by then, but if not come after us.'

'I'm not sure I like this, ma'am.' Enders hesitated. 'I mean—'

'You mean we're both women?' Savage glared at him. 'I'm aware of that. I'm also aware Jane could have you for breakfast and still eat three Shredded Wheat afterwards.'

Enders looked sheepish, but said nothing.

Savage and Calter got out of the car and tried to find a

shallow place to cross the stream, Calter peering down at her already mud-splattered shoes.

'We're not dressed for this, ma'am. Maybe Patrick is right, maybe we should wait for backup.'

'No,' Savage said, 'we're going on.'

They waded across the shallowest part of the stream, the freezing water coming up to knee height. Enders reversed out of sight and Savage thought he'd need to go all the way back to the edge of the valley where she had seen a gateway.

Across the ford the mud was even worse and Savage realised they must look a right pair of clowns slipping and sliding towards the cottage. The little windows under the eaves seemed like eyes tracking their progress across the field and she wondered if anyone was inside watching them. Curtains obscured the interior but Savage thought she saw the edge of one twitch, something pulling back from the window with a jerk.

'Did you see that?' she asked Calter as they neared the cottage. 'At the upstairs window?'

'No, ma'am. Nothing there I can see.'

Savage shrugged. 'Well somebody's at home.'

To one side of the house a large and newish looking black Shogun stood under a dilapidated car port, the modern shape of the vehicle out of place against the cottage's lumpy walls and rotting window sills.

'Forester's car, ma'am,' Calter said. 'And look at those tyres. Call me a trainspotter type but I bet they are Bridgestone D689s, size 265/70S15. The same as the ones in the field at Malstead Down. I spent half a day phoning tyre fitters so the type is stuck in my brain forever now.'

The cottage itself appeared neglected. Savage followed the mass of ivy on one gable end upward to where the dark green leaves spilled out onto the roof. Several tiles were missing and the chimney stack crumbled over at an alarming angle.

They approached the front door, a low portal with a huge stone as its lintel. The door itself was wooden and white paint flaked off revealing the dark oak behind. There was no doorbell or knocker so Savage rapped with her knuckles.

Seconds later came the sound of movement from within and they heard a bolt being drawn top and bottom. Following that a screeching and clanking which grated Savage's teeth before the door opened a crack, a safety chain stopping it from going farther.

'Yes?'

A male voice and in the gap a pale face with jet black hair.

'Detective Inspector Charlotte Savage and Detective Constable Jane Calter. May we have a word please, sir?'

The door closed and the chain rattled off, before swinging wide and revealing a man dressed in a grubby blue boiler suit which he appeared to be wearing over a shirt and tie.

'Matthew Harrison?'

'Yes, yes, yes. Of course. I recognise you from the other day. What do you want?'

'We'd like to ask you some questions. Perhaps we could come inside?'

Harrison's mouth dropped open. He clasped his hands together and then raised them to his forehead before sliding them backwards over lank hair the colour of waste oil. In contrast to his hair the skin on Harrison's face was pale, almost translucent, resembling quartz in the way it shone. In sunken sockets his eyes appeared devoid of any colouring, the white sclera merging into dark pupils with no iris. The pupils danced in circles as Harrison brought his hands down in front of him, wringing them over and over each other, the fingers dancing like spiders' legs. On his neck a huge adam's apple bobbed as he swallowed and gulped. His breathing had quickened and his eyes brimmed with moisture.

'Is this about the girls? Which one? Trinny or Lucy? Or both of them? Lord knows I have had some trouble with them. And Emma. Oh dear. Can't live with them, can't live without them. Isn't that what they say?'

Savage and Calter looked at each other and the man's eyes darted between the pair of them, his head twitching back and forth as if he had some sort of nervous affliction.

'Please, Matthew.' Savage gestured inside with her hand.

Harrison retreated into the house. Savage turned to look over her shoulder. She could see Enders at the ford now, inching his way across. She and Calter went through the doorway.

Once inside Harrison seemed a little less agitated and a sense of calm descended. He waved at a nearby door and went through into the room beyond. Savage followed but whispered back at Calter for her to check out the rest of the house. The room was almost bare and with the curtains drawn, gloomy. Harrion was bent over a tall candlestick over near the fireplace scrabbling with a box of matches. He scraped a match across the box and lit the candle.

The candle flared into life and now Savage could see the only piece of furniture in the room was a wooden wheel-backed chair. A couple of leather belts criss-crossed through the dowelling on the chair's back and behind it on the floor a fan heater was angled up to point at the chair.

'There,' Harrison said. 'Now what did you want to ask me?'

'What's that, Mr Harrison?' Savage said, pointing at the chair.

'Hey?' Harrison turned and a look of surprise came over his face as if he'd seen the chair for the first time. 'Oh, that's Lucy's stuff. She must have left it behind.'

'Who is Lucy?'

'Lucy is a friend. Or rather she was a friend. She was naughty so I had to tell her to leave.' Harrison smiled and wafted a hand towards the chair. 'Please, you can sit down there if you want. Lucy won't mind.'

'No thank you.' Savage moved a little nearer to the door and called out for Calter. 'Jane?'

There was no answer, just a creak from somewhere above.

'Wherever can she have got to?' Harrison said. 'I hope she's not looking at my private things. I wouldn't like that very much.'

'Mr Harrison, where is Alice Nash?'

'Alice? Alice.' Harrison shook his head, reached for something near the fireplace. A poker. 'No, I don't know an Alice. There's been a Carmel, a Trinny, a Lucy and an Emma. No Alice. Not here.'

'Emma then. Is she here?'

'Emma? Oh, I see. Yes, yes. The girls. Of course, I was forgetting, you've come about the girls.' Harrison jabbed the poker into the grate and a cloud of ash billowed out scattering a shower of cinder onto the hearth. He moved a foot and tried to scuff the ash away. 'Now look, you've made me make a mess. That's been the problem all along. The mess. Dirty, dirty, dirty girls. Slippery, sticky, slimy girls. I tried my best, but they wouldn't stay clean. Do you hear me? They wouldn't stay CLEAN!'

'Calter!' Savage shouted and moved to the door. 'Get down here!'

Harrison turned from the fireplace and thrust the poker towards Savage.

'And that meant . . .' Thrust. 'that . . .' Thrust. 'I . . .' Thrust. 'got . . .'

'Mr Harrison,' Savage held out her hands as she backed into the hallway. 'Calm down.'

'DIRTY!' Harrison was halfway across the room now, the poker outstretched. He jerked it one more time and then raised it above his head.

'Ma'am!' Calter. Right behind her, bouncing on the balls of her feet, her hands held up in a fighting stance.

'Matthew Harrison,' Savage said. 'I am arresting you on—'

'WAIT!' Harrison shouted and then dropped the poker. He made a sort of huffing, sighing noise and his voice dropped to a whisper. 'I think I need to show you something. Here.'

Savage moved aside as Harrison came into the hallway. He opened a small door to the left. Steps led downwards into some sort of cellar. Harrison reached in and touched a switch. There was a flickering and then a hum before a fluorescent white bathed the area below.

'Ma'am?' Calter said, sounding nervous.

Savage peered through the door and then turned to Harrison. He looked at both of them in turn again.

'Of course. How silly, how silly. Please follow me.' Harrison moved downward.

Savage followed, taking care on the steps which were rough and uneven, almost as if they had been cut from the bedrock. To one side a couple of ropes acted as some kind of handrail, although Savage doubted if they would hold her weight if she grabbed them. Calter hesitated and glanced back through the doorway.

'Enders, he's on his way now,' she said and started to descend as well.

Harrison stood at the bottom and he turned back towards

Savage, his mouth opening into a smile and his tongue flicking a wad of spittle onto his lips. Suddenly he moved forward and grabbed one of the hand ropes, snatching it with a sharp tug. Behind Calter the door to the cellar slammed shut and at the same time Harrison made a dive for a switch on the wall and the lights went out.

Black. Pitch black. Savage's heart thumping.

'Stay where you are, Mr Harrison.'

From below came a scuffling sound, something moving away from her, a metallic click that sounded like a door latch and then nothing.

'Calter?'

'Ma'am, I'm here. Trying to find the bloody door handle.'

Savage stayed still. Some distance away a chink of pale light shone out for a couple of seconds and then black again.

'Shit, he's out of here. Jane, for God's sake hurry up.'

'Got it, ma'am.' There was a creak and a rectangle of light appeared above, Enders's beaming face right in the middle.

'Stop grinning you idiot. Make sure he doesn't go off in the car. Calter, come with me.'

Savage found the switch at the bottom and turned the lights back on. Now she could see the ropes were not designed as a handrail, but rather they linked up to some sort of pulley mechanism that had allowed Harrison to close the door from the foot of the steps.

She looked around, amazed at the sheer size of the cellar. The space must have been the same dimensions as the cottage. Dotted everywhere brick supporting pillars held up RSJs and they appeared to be newish, like the cellar had been dug out and the pillars had been necessary to prevent the cottage above collapsing. A door in one wall stood ajar and must have been where Harrison had disappeared to. Savage walked over to investigate.

It seemed to be some sort of bathroom because tiles covered the floor. Savage reached in and searched for the light switch.

White. Bright white light, shiny white tiles not only on the floor but the walls too. Spotless.

Jesus!

A chair. Or maybe a bed? Except the thing wasn't full length. The monstrosity resembled something from a hospital. A reclining, adjustable bed with . . . leg stirrups.

Savage remembered the picture of Simone Ashton and a sickening feeling spread in her stomach. At the head end of the chair a set of padded restraints didn't look like anything you would purchase in an Ann Summers shop, nor did the piece of leather with a rubber ball spliced into the middle of it. More like a dog toy or something.

'Calter! Get in here!'

'Ma'am?'

Savage jumped. Calter was right beside her. Savage nodded into the room and Calter peered past her, drawing breath at the sight of the bed.

'Cosy.'

Savage pointed over to a steel wheeled table next to the bed. On a tray lay a weird metal device like a beak from a large seabird, about six inches long and with a sort of trigger grip at the bigger end. The stainless steel glinted under the harsh lights.

'What the hell is that thing? A medieval torture device?' Calter said.

'A speculum.'

'Ma'am, you know we shouldn't be in here? Forensics.'

'I want to follow Harrison.' Savage pointed to the door on the other side of the room.

'Ma'am, shouldn't we wait for backup?'

'What's got into you, I thought you had a black belt in Jujitsu?'

'I'm giving it back. This just doesn't feel right.'

'Two words: Alice Nash.'

'Bugger.'

Savage moved forward and reached the door. An inch open, a thin line of black revealing nothing about what lay on the other side. She pushed with her foot and the door swung wide. A humming filled the air now and some flickering neon lights glowed green, orange and red. Savage fumbled for a light switch.

The square room measured about four metres a side. Around the edge of the room several chest freezers stood against the walls and snake-like tails led from each to a jumble of adapters plugged into a socket on one wall. The freezers didn't look like the sort you would have at home, they were bigger, more industrial, more clinical. One, two, three . . . six.

'Bloody hell, ma'am,' Calter whispered. 'Are you thinking what I'm thinking?'

'I'm thinking how many mispers we have who had connections to nurseries or were au pairs or childminders or babysitters.'

'Exactly.'

Savage stepped over to the nearest of the freezers. A green neon light shone out from the handle. It was the locking type but the key was in the lock. She turned the key and the latch slid back. She grabbed the handle and heaved the lid up until it opened on the built-in springs. What the unit contained was unexpected and brought a gasp from Calter.

'Ma'am, please tell me—'

'No. It's not.'

The freezer was filled with meat. Regular cuts of meat

from the supermarket or a butcher. Savage had no idea what a human would be like cut up, but it wasn't like this.

'Look, half a lamb and a leg of beef. The beef has got a stamp on the side.'

Savage brought the lid down and clicked the lock shut. The next freezer wasn't switched on or locked. The lid swung up and a faint smell of disinfectant wafted out. The inside gleamed clean and bare.

'Simone Ashton could have been in here. Or Kelly.'

'Doesn't bear thinking about, boss. Gives me claustrophobia just looking.'

The next freezer had a red light that was blinking on and off. Savage moved closer and realised the temperature alert had triggered.

'Something is wrong with this one.'

'Not sure I want you to open it, all things considered.'

Savage ignored Calter and twisted the latching handle. She swung the lid open until it popped up.

'Fuck! Ma'am! The Nash girl.'

Up one end a naked body lay curled in a foetal position. A strong smell of burned out electrics mingled with a more unpleasant odour of urine. Savage leant in and more out of procedure than hope she searched for a pulse.

She touched the girl's neck and felt a tingle in the end of her finger, a faint throb, throb, throb. Almost undetectable, but there.

'She's alive!'

A little later and Alice saw light, a brilliant white luminescence surrounding her which could only come from heaven. She could feel herself floating on a wave of warm air even though her skin bristled with cold.

As cold as death.

Someone was coming for her, an angel calling her name as she floated down the corridor of light.

'Alice. Alice. Alice.'

Her mother, her face smiling and radiant, her hair a flash of vermillion, just as it had looked before she had got ill. Arms scooped her up and embraced her and it was like when she had fallen over as a kid and Mum had held her so tightly that she had known through the pain and the tears that everything would be alright.

Chapter Thirty-Five

Netherston, South Hams, Devon. Tuesday 9th November.
12.30 pm

Savage heaved herself up and into the freezer, standing inside and bending down to scoop up the girl in her arms. The girl's skin felt icy and there was no noticeable response as Savage struggled to lift her up over the lip of the freezer. Cradling Alice in her arms Savage bent her head to the girl's face. A faint movement of air from the nostrils touched Savage's cheek and she saw a tiny flicker from the eyelids.

'Get upstairs and call for help!' Savage said to Calter.

Calter was already on her way, sprinting through the door. Savage had an afterthought and yelled after her.

'Make it an air ambulance!'

Seconds later she heard Enders clumping down the stairs and he came through the door and helped Savage with the girl. They carried her out into the main part of the cellar and up the stairs.

'In here, ma'am!'

Calter was in the living room and had ripped the heavy velvet curtains down from the windows and was spreading them on some cushions on the floor.

'How long?' Savage asked as they laid the girl down and covered her.

'Flight time seven minutes. That was two minutes ago.'

'Seven!'

'Yes, we got lucky. The helicopter was already airborne on its way back to Exeter.'

Savage thought that Alice Nash deserved a bit of a break, but it would take more than luck to pull her through. Calter had done a good job with the curtains, but they weren't going to warm the girl up. Savage looked around for inspiration and spotted the fan heater next to the chair with the leather belts.

She went over and pulled the heater out, moving it across the room as far as the cable would allow. Then she switched the unit on and turned the heat setting to the highest possible.

'He would tie them to the chair and heat them up? Is that some sort of torture?' Calter wasn't getting it.

'Defrost,' Savage said. 'He'd get them out of the freezer, give them a bath and stick them there to dry and thaw out fully. Then he'd have sex with them.'

A rush of air washed over the girl now and Calter pulled the curtains to one side to let the warmth reach the skin. Savage knelt and felt the girl's pulse again. It was weak and her breath was very shallow.

'Right now would be a good time for the helicopter,' Savage said.

On cue they heard the distant thump, thump, thump of the approaching aircraft and Enders went outside to signal to the crew. Savage looked at Alice Nash again. The helicopter noise was much louder now and the windows started to vibrate and the ground beneath her feet shook. Calter was shouting something, but Savage couldn't make out what she was saying. Nor could she make out whether Alice's chest was rising and falling anymore. She touched the girl's neck and now she was sure.

'Defib!' she screamed at Calter and began to perform CPR on the girl, counting aloud as she did so. 'One, two, three, four . . .'

Calter rushed outside leaving Savage alone, the noise of the helicopter in her ears replaced by that roaring sound inside her head. The same noise she had heard in the hospital when Clarissa had died.

'Twenty-nine, thirty.'

She bent down to give mouth-to-mouth and then resumed the CPR.

'One, two . . .'

Then the paramedics were beside her, unpacking the defibrillator, readying drugs, one of them taking over the chest compressions. Calter helped her get to her feet.

'They know what they are doing, ma'am.'

Savage nodded and sniffed, aware that she was crying.

'My . . .'

'I know, ma'am. You don't need to say anything, I understand.' Calter put her arm around her and the two of them went outside. The bright blue and red helicopter stood in a field to one side of the house, its blades rotating slowly. Enders was talking to the pilot. The black Mitsubishi Shogun had gone.

'Jesus!' Savage said, pulling herself together. 'Where the hell is Harrison?'

Two hours later and the place was heaving. The Chief Constable had been on to one of his military chums and a team of engineers from the Royal Marines in Plymouth had erected a temporary bridge over the stream to allow vehicle access. John Layton and his CSIs had trundled across it in three white SOC vans and they had disappeared inside the house like kids eager to explore Santa's grotto. Hardin had arrived along with Garrett, Davies and a car boot full of supplies purloined from the canteen.

'An army marches on its stomach,' Hardin said, mouth crammed full of sandwich, the diet abandoned in celebration. 'We are going to be here for days so we have to keep morale up.'

Hardin had taken the last bacon butty so the rest of them got stuck into egg and cress and soggy cheese and tomato. Washed down with lukewarm coffee. Morale, at least where lunch was concerned, was tepid.

The air ambulance had long gone to be replaced by the yellow and blue air operations helicopter. It buzzed overhead, circling the valley taking pictures. Hardin asked about Alice Nash.

'Just took a call from Derriford, sir,' Savage said. 'She is doing OK, all things considered.'

'All things considered, I think you and your team deserve a bloody medal, Charlotte.' Hardin wiped some ketchup from his chin and sucked it off his finger. 'DC Enders for getting you here so quickly and you and DC Calter for tackling Harrison and saving Alice Nash's life. Quick thinking to call the air ambulance too.'

'Harrison got away, sir.'

'Bah!' Hardin dismissed her comment with a wave of his hand. 'He hasn't got anywhere to go now and every police force in the country is on the lookout for his car. We'll have him before long.'

'And then we'll have some fun,' Davies said, rubbing his hands together.

'Quite,' Hardin said. 'Anyway, we have weathered the media

storm and in the end the results show crime doesn't pay. Mitchell, dead. Forester, dead. Richard Trent, banged up. Harrison soon to be apprehended. There have been victims, yes, but thank God there won't be any more.'

Just then a movement at one of the upstairs windows caught Savage's eye. It was John Layton. He was waving and fiddling with the latch, trying to open it. Finally he gave up and moved back from the window. The next thing the glass was shattering and he was shouting something about calling for an ambulance.

Layton had found them in the attic. A man and a woman in their seventies, half-naked, emaciated, the sort of thing you saw on the news when there was a famine somewhere. Or maybe in a documentary about the second world war where you got those flickering black and white images of the concentration camps after they had been liberated. Except this wasn't on TV and it played before them in full colour.

Now the couple sat in the back of Hardin's car wrapped in space blankets, the engine running, the heater going full blast. They had accepted water and sandwiches, only the man had retched when he had tried to swallow his. The heavy chain that had been secured round their necks with padlocks had been removed. Layton had used a drill from his toolkit, the horrible screeching sound jarring Savage's teeth as he worked on the locks. God knows what it had sounded like close up.

Savage, Hardin and Layton were standing some distance from the car, Hardin tapping his watch every minute, probably noting the response time for the ambulance.

'Who the hell are they?' Hardin said, as if their presence was an affront to the otherwise neat conclusion of the investigation.

'They told me that they are Harrison's parents, sir,' Layton said.

'What?' Hardin puffed his cheeks out.

'It fits, sir,' Savage said. 'It was DS Tatershall who called in the location of the cottage, remember? The parents were mispers from down in St Ives, Cornwall. They used to live here years ago before Harrison senior was convicted of abuse.'

'I know where St bloody Ives is, thank you, Charlotte. What I want to ascertain is what the hell they are doing here?'

'According to DS Tatershall the father has cancer.' Savage glanced across to the car and lowered her voice. 'Maybe he wanted to see his son again before he died?'

'Fine. I can go with that. But why the fuck did Harrison chain them up in the attic and half-starve them to death? Jesus, have you seen them close up? They look like extras from some zombie movie.'

Hardin wasn't big on sympathy, especially when it didn't have tick-boxes alongside it. In this case Savage thought he was being harsh, but she said nothing. Instead she told him about the information Mrs Harbersher had given them and the planned liaison with the officers down in St Ives.

'DS Riley is heading down there first thing tomorrow and he will find out everything they know. I'll take DC Calter with me to the hospital tomorrow and get the full story from Alice Nash and the parents.'

'Tomorrow? Can't you . . .' Hardin peered at the occupants of the car, gave an involuntary shudder and then corrected himself. 'No, you are right. The state they are in it would be better to wait.'

It was getting gloomy now, dusk enveloping the valley, and when the ambulance arrived its light cast ghostly patterns amongst the trees, the shadows dancing like demons waiting to pounce. Hardin tapped his watch for the final time and muttered something about twenty-three minutes being bloody pathetic. Then he was all smiles for the paramedics, keen to get the old couple out of his car and into the ambulance so he could get away.

'It's my daughter's birthday. She's nineteen this week. Me and the wife are taking her out to dinner tonight. Late is not on the menu.'

Layton looked over at Savage and she could see he was thinking the same as her: if only. The CSI team would be working through the night and Savage knew that she would have to return to Plymouth to file some sort of preliminary report. When she would get back home she had no idea.

Chapter Thirty-Six

The clock on the dash showed close to ten before she turned in off the lane and her car crunched over the gravel drive and into the garage. She sat in the dark for a few moments, enjoying the warmth of the car and the silence and thinking about the kids. She had noticed both Samantha's and Jamie's lights had been on so she'd need to have words with Stefan again. He was great for them, but he didn't practise quite the same discipline that she or Pete might.

Tomorrow she would interview Harrison's parents and afterwards take the rest of the day off, God only knows she deserved it. She would pick the children up from school and go for a pizza and enjoy some quality time with them. It would give Stefan a rest too.

Key in lock and she opened the door to blazing lights everywhere. They must all be playing some game that took in the whole house. She sighed at the thought of the mess.

'Kids! I'm home!'

She dropped her car keys on the table in the hall and went into the lounge where Stefan sat on a kitchen chair in the middle of the room. He must be taking part in the game, she thought, because he didn't move, he just sat still, like a

328

statue, staring ahead. His eyes widened, but he couldn't say anything due to the parcel tape wrapped around the lower part of his face.

Then something hit Savage from behind, knocking her to the floor and sending the room tumbling over and over, the light in the centre spiralling round and fading to stars. A haze rose in front of her eyes with strange floaters swimming across a checkerboard of grey and white. She groaned and moved her hand to touch the back of her head. Wet. Sticky. She felt a sudden heaving in her stomach, the nausea blotting out the pain from her head, and then she vomited through her mouth and nose, coughing and spluttering sick.

Now someone had her arms and was pinning them behind her. A zipping sound came as her wrists were yanked together and some sort of binding cut her flesh and secured her hands.

Footsteps moved away, out of the room, and a few moments later returned, something being dragged.

The person lifted her now, up and onto another one of the kitchen chairs. Then the sound of tape being stripped from a roll. Not across her mouth, but round and round her body, holding her against the back of the chair.

Then he moved round to her front.

Harrison.

He appeared calm, almost normal. Apart from those eyes. They didn't look normal. They darted back and forth between Savage and Stefan, to the door, to Stefan's baseball bat lying on the floor, to the blood on the carpet where she had fallen, back to Savage.

She spat saliva and vomit and tried to breathe slowly, to stay calm. She looked at Stefan. He didn't seem hurt, but he had certainly been immobilised. A cable tie secured his arms behind the back of the chair and his legs had been bound with parcel tape too. He rolled his eyes at Savage, looking sideways, indicating something. She couldn't understand what he meant, but it gave her a glimmer of hope.

Harrison dashed out of the room and the sound of him bounding up the stairs made Savage shiver to her very core.

The kids.

'No!' she shouted, trying to wrench her arms apart. 'Leave them alone!'

'Where are you?' Harrison's voice echoed through the house as he stomped around on the floor above. There was a wail from Jamie and a scream from Samantha. 'Daddy's away, so Harry can play!'

Savage struggled on the chair, trying to rock it sideways towards Stefan, but moments later she heard Harrison coming down the stairs. He marched the children into the room. Savage could see their faces were stained with tears and their hands had been bound in front of them with cable ties.

'Mummy!' They ran across to her, but before they got near Harrison was shouting.

'Sit down on the fucking sofa!'

Jamie and Samantha cowered before him. He shoved them across the room and bundled them onto the sofa.

'Stay there!'

'Matthew, please. We can work this out, we—'

'Shut the fuck up! We're going to do things my way from now on. Harry's way.'

Harrison didn't look normal now. Anything but. His hands shook and lips trembled as he muttered to himself.

'You had to meddle, had to nose, had to interfere.'

'That is my job,' Savage said in a low voice, surprised at her outward calmness. Inside though her mind raced, trying to think of some way out of the situation. Harrison had gone over the edge. The final stage of a serial killer's madness. The frenzy at the very end. There was no way of knowing what he might do next.

'Your job. My Emma. Gone.'

Was Emma Alice Nash? One of Harrison's made-up names, like when he had used Trinny for Kelly.

'We can talk about Emma if you want,' Savage said. 'Just let the children go. Please.'

'Younger,' he said, eyes staring off into nowhere. 'Lucy was right.'

'Or would you prefer to talk about Lucy, Matthew?' Savage moved on the chair. Tried to think. Harrison was completely deranged. He would kill them all. She needed to play for time and keep him occupied until she or Stefan could somehow get free or somebody turned up at the front door. 'Matthew?'

Harrison was mumbling to himself but now he looked at Savage again, mouth opening wide.

'Don't call me Matthew!' he spat at her. He came over and leant close. 'My name is Harry now. OK?'

Savage flinched as globules of phlegm flicked onto her face. Behind Harrison she could see Samantha and Jamie huddled on the sofa, Jamie visibly shaking, both her children distraught. Jesus! Savage thought, panic all of a sudden washing over her, the calmness gone. She didn't know what to say. Harrison was in total control of the situation and there was nothing she could do to prevent him from harming the two people she loved most in all the world. She gulped back a sob, thinking for a moment of Clarissa. Lost to her forever.

'Sorry,' she whispered, turning her head away from Harrison and fighting back the tears. 'Harry it is.'

'Good,' Harrison said, moving away from her and into the centre of the room.

Stefan shifted on his seat. Savage looked across at him. He rolled his eyes sideways again. Then she heard the engine. A motorbike. The gravel crunching, the bike stopping, the ignition off.

Harrison cocked his head on one side. He marched across to Savage, the roll of parcel tape in his hands. He pulled off a length and wrapped the tape around Savage's mouth.

'One word, one squeak.' He glared at the children and drew his hand across his throat.

The doorbell rang and Harrison scuttled out of the room and into the hallway, shutting the door behind him.

Jamie jumped down off the sofa and ran across to the big old oak bureau. Savage made a noise and shook her head. Jamie glanced over but ignored her. He was struggling to open the bottom drawer with his hands tied. In the hall Savage could hear Harrison talking to a pizza delivery man. She saw Stefan nod a confirmation. He must have ordered a takeout earlier, to arrive after he had put the children to bed.

She drew deep breaths in through her nostrils, fighting the claustrophobic panic caused by the tape across her mouth. Steady. Calm. Relax. She closed her eyes for a moment and visualised herself with Pete and the children. Christmas morning, Pete back home from his tour, Jamie and Samantha playing with their presents. The four of them together as a family. Safe.

When she opened her eyes she saw Jamie had managed to pull the drawer out and was rummaging in an Airfix box. The box contained a kit he had been working on with Pete months ago, an air-sea rescue helicopter. Then he was putting the kit away and pushing the drawer shut. Coming over to Savage with a craft knife in his hand.

Savage nodded and Jamie rushed across. He went round

332

behind her and placed the knife in Savage's hands. Next he moved round to her front and laid his head on her lap. Savage heard the motorbike start up and then the living room door opened. Harrison stood with a grin on his face and a pizza box in his hands.

The grin vanished when he spotted Jamie kneeling at her feet and he dropped the box and leapt across the room in a second, lashing out at Jamie and kicking him hard in the ribs. Jamie screamed and collapsed in a ball where he lay still, a soft sobbing noise coming from him.

'Don't move again or I'll kill you!' Harrison yelled.

He moved over to Savage, ripped the parcel tape from her face and retrieved the pizza box and went and sat on the sofa next to Samantha. She cowered away. Out came a triangle of pizza and Harrison munched on the slice, chewing each mouthful over and over and staring into nothing, distracted, distant.

Savage tried to move the knife, adjusting her grip so the blade touched her fingers, trying to place the sharp edge against the cable tie. She moved the knife, sawing up and down, careful not to drop it.

'My mother used to buy second-hand school clothes for me,' Harrison said. His voice calm and passive with no trace of the anger from a moment ago. 'She didn't need to because we had plenty of money, but she did. They had stains on or they were faded or ripped. Preloved, she called them. The boys at school used to tease me about it. They said I wasn't even that. They were right. I was dirty and used. My father told me so each time he fucked me.'

Savage jerked the knife now, picking at the hard plastic while trying to keep her shoulders still and her expression blank as Harrison continued his rant.

'My good friend Lucy informed me that younger is better.

333

All the older ones are dirty these days. That is the way of the world. Squalid. Used. We have been stained by our very existence. Everyone is doing it, existing I mean, and no one clears up the results. Shit, spunk, spew. That is what we are walking around in. Soon it will be up around our nostrils and we will have to recycle the stuff orally. Maybe then people will understand what we have become.'

Harrison put the pizza box to one side, shook his head and smiled.

'Listen to me. I sound like Mitchell and look what happened to him.'

'You went to Mitchell's parties,' Savage said. 'You took pictures. You enjoyed yourself. Seems to me like you are part of the problem, not part of the solution.'

'No! I only attended to observe.' Harrison spat the sentence out. 'Mitchell was sick, but he made me realise that you could get away with things.'

'But you haven't got away with anything. We know about Kelly. We know about the other girls.'

'Kelly was an accident. Believe me the last thing I wanted was for her to die. That was Forester's fault for soiling her. Mitchell got to him too. Used him to shoot the videos after I had gone. Drugs, sex, poor Kelly couldn't resist and in the end she turned out to be dirty too, they all were. They made their choices before I ever met them.' Harrison's eyes rolled upwards to the ceiling and he placed his hands together as if in prayer. 'Dear God I wished they hadn't, but that is the way of things. Like I said, the world is decaying. My only wish is to find somebody like my girls. They were clean and I loved them and there was nothing dirty about my feelings. Lust is evil. I learnt that long ago, but it seems impossible to escape because there is so little left that is pure.'

He suddenly reached out across the sofa and grabbed a

handful of Samantha's hair, dragging her down onto the floor.

'Mummy!'

Harrison pulled her across the room towards the door and she scampered along trying to keep up. Her eyes pleaded at Savage with desperation.

Savage felt a surge of anger sweep up from deep inside. Harrison wasn't going to do this, he wasn't going to take Samantha away from her, she wasn't going to lose her baby girl. She made a final effort, levering the handle of the knife on one side of the tie and the blade on the other. She would either break the blade or make the cut. Harrison reached the hall now and he looked straight at Savage with a wide grin as he took her car keys from where she had dropped them. He put them in his pocket and opened the front door, dragging Samantha behind him like a sack of rubbish.

Snap!

The cable tie parted and Savage had her arms free. She flicked the knife upwards, slicing through the parcel tape, and jumped to her feet. Harrison stood at the front door and met her eyes again, but this time there was no grin. She leapt at Stefan, cutting the tie and the tape. Harrison ran out the door, Samantha screaming as he pulled her by the hair. Savage rushed after him. Through the front door and Harrison was halfway across the driveway. He saw Savage and let go of Samantha, sprinting down the drive and into the lane.

Savage reached Samantha and knelt, embracing her. At the same time she heard the sound of an engine start up and in the lane headlights beamed out into the night sky.

'I'm OK, Mum,' Samantha said. 'Don't let him touch me again. Please.'

'He won't, Sam,' Savage said. 'I promise.'

335

Stefan was at the door and Savage ran back to him.

'Help Samantha inside, shut yourself in the house and dial 999.'

She pushed past him and grabbed a single key from the bowl on the table. She rushed out of the house again, across to the garage and jumped in the little MG. Fumbling to get the key in the ignition and then the car was firing up with a roar. The car shot forward as she floored the accelerator, wheels spinning and spitting gravel.

The car skidded as she turned hard into the lane, the lights of Harrison's car not far ahead. The heavy 4x4 struggled to get up to speed and its width meant the vehicle took up most of the road. Once it was moving it lurched along, Harrison fighting for control as he went faster; the MG was much more suited to the switchback run towards Plymouth and the main road. Harrison slammed right at a junction into a smaller lane, the Shogun crashing into the hedge, but ploughing back onto the road and hurtling onward. Savage flicked the handbrake as she took the turn, slid round and accelerated out of the corner. She was gaining by the second and Harrison increased his speed as they plunged down into a valley.

Fifty, sixty, seventy miles an hour on a road no wider than the car. Then Harrison reached the bottom of the hill where the road crossed a stream and Savage remembered the humpback. The first Harrison knew of the bridge was when the Shogun left the ground. It landed on two wheels, bounced back onto four and rolled, crashing onto its side and flipping onto its roof. Two tons of upside down car screeched along the lane spinning in a circle before colliding with the corner of an old stone barn.

Savage braked hard to stop and jumped out of her car and ran across to the upside down 4x4. The roof had crumpled and the windscreen and side windows had shattered. Inside the airbag had exploded, but the white balloon hadn't prevented the seat from deforming, crushing Harrison and trapping him against the steering wheel. He groaned and Savage crouched down to peer into the car, her heart pounding. Little sparks began to jump from the dash as some of the wiring shorted out and the plastic started to burn with a fierce, sooty flame. She thought she had better reach in and remove the ignition key to cut the electrics. She'd also need to phone for an ambulance and the fire brigade to cut Harrison out.

Savage put her arm in the window and groped for the keys. Her hand brushed against them and they jingled, *ding-ding, ding-ding*. The noise made her pause for a moment. Then she smelt it.

Petrol.

Petrol? The car was a diesel. She had noticed the letters TDI on the back and remembered the data Riley had obtained from the DVLC. She looked in again and now she saw a green plastic container on the roof, a spread of liquid seeping into the headlining. What did Harrison want with a can of petrol?

Harrison's eyes darted back and forth, manic and then she knew. And could see that he knew she knew. She left the keys where they hung and withdrew her arm.

'You bastard!'

'Please, help me,' he said, sucking air in and out with sharp little breaths, blind panic in the eyes now. 'I only wanted someone to love, someone to love me. None of this is my fault.'

Harrison shuddered, his body quivering, and he appeared all of a sudden fragile, human even. Savage smelt something else now too, something strong enough to overpower the petrol odour. Urine. Harrison had pissed himself.

She looked again at the keys dangling in the ignition, they danced in motion, swinging back and forth like a little pendulum on a clock counting down the passage of time. Every second marked a moment that could not be lived again. Every second offered new possibilities. That was what life came down to in the end. Choices. Harrison had made his long ago. Now it was her turn.

She stood up straight and looked around. A house stood a little way down the road and a dog barked somewhere way off in the distance, but there was no sign of anyone coming to investigate. Savage turned and walked back to the MG, climbed in and closed the door. She sat still, trying to think. Her heart was beating fast, but she took slow, deliberate breaths and after a few seconds she felt calmer. Mind made up she reached for the key and started the engine. She reversed into a gateway and turned round, driving back up the hill. Then there was a sudden flare of light in the rear view mirror and an orange glow flooded the inside of her car. She never heard the explosion, only the roaring in her ears again, the volume subsiding until all that remained was the noise of the little car flying along the lane, its headlights slicing a path through the blackness towards home and Samantha and Jamie.

Epilogue

Two weeks later.

Rain. It never seemed to stop in Plymouth and right now the deluge came down as heavy as ever. The wind had returned with a vengeance too and the crowd of people waiting on the dockside struggled to hang on to their hats and umbrellas and their banners and flags. Everybody seemed in a good mood though, every last face painted with a wide smile. The weather might do its worst but nothing could dampen the high spirits.

Savage stood at the front of the crowd and she felt elated too. Jamie bounced up and down on her right, holding her hand in a clam-like grip and Samantha was to her left. For once she had ceased texting and put away her mobile. Savage noted with some pride she had even switched the damn thing off. Instead she fiddled with her hair, trying to keep it neat under her waterproof hood.

A shout went up from somebody on the dockside and all eyes turned to look down the estuary. Through the driving rain a huge grey shape was coming round the bend beyond the Torpoint ferries. The warship sounded a horn and Jamie jumped with fright and squealed with delight all at the same time.

339

'Mummy, he's here!' He held Savage's hand even tighter and she hoped he wouldn't wet himself in all the excitement.

Now they could see the crew lining the deck, standing to attention in their crisp uniforms, as oblivious to the weather as the waiting crowd. The boat was slowing and Savage spotted a group of officers outside on the starboard bridge wing. She couldn't see Pete yet, but he was there for sure.

The vessel's movement forward seemed almost imperceptible now as it stemmed the tide and ferry-glided sideways towards the dock. The ship had been gone nine months and sailed to the Falklands and then circumnavigated South America, returning via the Panama Canal. Tens of thousands of miles lay in its wake and yet the final few minutes seemed to be taking a lifetime.

Savage thought about the past month. It was two weeks since Harrison had died in the car crash and the investigation was winding down. Much work remained to do, of course, but the major part of the inquiry was over. Harrison's parents had been taken to hospital and his mother had recovered sufficiently to be discharged. Because of the fury whipped up by the press the Chief Constable had decided the good people of Devon and Cornwall posed a real threat to her life and her safety could only be ensured by moving her to a safe house. The father remained in intensive care and in a terminal condition. In private the doctors told the *Zebo* team that he wouldn't ever be leaving.

Donal had been charged with the murder of Everett Mitchell, although his brief was trying to get him off on an admission of manslaughter. Savage should have been pleased the law was being upheld, but the events at her home made her more sympathetic towards Donal. He had broken the law, true, and Hardin saw Donal as just another crime cleared up, another point on the score sheet. Somehow that didn't wash with Savage. Few people would be worried about the death of Mitchell. Many more would be lining up to congratulate Donal for what he had done. Savage understood the sentiment. She had killed Harrison after all.

When the newspapers dredged up all the stuff about Harrison's parents she had questioned her actions and her judgement. The father had served his time for the abuse of his son and the rape of the nanny, and on his release the couple had moved to London. Many years later they had returned to the West Country and settled in St Ives. Harrison knew nothing of this, but on his eighteenth birthday he had been given the cottage near Gara Bridge and a sum of money, as if that was reparation enough for his suffering. Harrison had been a disturbed young man, but somehow he had managed to control himself until the encounters with Mitchell and the return of his parents pushed him over the edge. The abused went on to abuse, it was a common story and a sad one.

So did that mean Harrison deserved to burn to death in the car? She didn't know even now. But at night, when she closed her eyes to sleep and lay in bed thinking about the petrol can and Harrison's plan to torch the house with her, Jamie and Stefan inside and to kidnap Samantha and do God knows what to her, she knew the choice had been right. Just like Donal had made the right choice for himself when he shot Mitchell.

Jamie tugged at her coat and brought her back to the present. He jumped up and down some more and pointed at the ship.

'Look, it's Daddy!'

Pete stood high on the bridge wing, a microphone to his lips as he issued instructions to guide the vessel the final few metres. He was too busy to wave, but he caught her eye and smiled. Savage squeezed Jamie's hand.

'Not long now,' she said.

Read on for an exclusive sample of

Mark Sennen's next novel,

publishing in September 2013.

Prologue

The pain always came when Ricky Budgeon least expected. Right now a wave swept from within and hit him between the eyes like a needle pushing hard into the bridge of his nose. He put his hands up and gripped his scalp, pulling and clawing at the burning sensation which spread across his forehead to his temples. The last attack had had him writhing on the floor, but this time the jabbing ceased after a few seconds and he merely needed to steady himself. He moved his hands from his head, clasped them tight around the cool metal bar of the gate, and stared across the field into the night.

A scan had showed nothing but the old scarring, afterwards the doctor muttering reassuring words about migraine and mentioning therapy, maybe acupuncture.

Crap.

The idiots must have missed whatever was in there, whatever was causing him such misery. Some sort of mutation of the cells, a cancer or a tumour, the latter growing fat on bad memories, enmity and bitterness.

When the doctor disagreed with his self-diagnosis and said surgery was out of the question he'd thought of taking a drill to his own skull, imagined placing the bit against his head and pressing the trigger. The whine of the motor would come first, followed by agony as the drill ripped into the skin and bone. Then the spinning metal would seek out the tumour and chew it to a pulp. The pain would be gone forever. He had even gone so far as to go to his workshop and set up the equipment. With the drill in its stand all he had to do was press the switch, put his head beneath the bit and pull down on the lever. Eventually though he had decided against it. Whatever the thing inside there was frightened him, but it motivated him too. Remove the pain and what would drive him forwards?

Budgeon stood in the darkness, gulping air and then biting his lip until he tasted blood. The throbbing in his head subsided and ebbed away. He bent and picked up his fag, a half-smoked roll-up dropped as the agony had come on. Drawing on the cigarette he looked out again and took in the landscape spread out before him, the vista which had quickened his heart and brought the misery sweeping in.

Close at hand, the hedges and trees appeared black against the sky. In a nearby field, the occasional sheep bleated, and from a copse off to his right the hoot of an owl rang out. But beyond the empty countryside lay the city, a corona of brightness where a thousand glittering lights promised excitement and danger, their individual pinpricks of heat coalescing like a mass of stars at the centre of a distant galaxy. Moving outward from the core white dots crawled between avenues of static orange: cars heading for the soft radiance of the suburbs and home.

A twinge in his forehead caused him to screw his eyes shut. Home.

He opened his eyes again and took another drag from the roll-up, pinching the end between the tips of his thumb and forefinger so he could extract every last piece of worth without burning himself. The way he had smoked in prison.

Years ago, before he had gone down, he'd had friends in the city. Friends who'd grown up on the same street as him. As kids they'd pinched sweets from the same shop and sworn at the same old ladies whose flowerbeds they trampled across. Later on, as young men, they'd thrown bricks at the same police cars, shared the same cells and sworn vengeance on the same enemies. They had been like brothers. Blood brothers.

Those days seemed so long ago now. As if someone else had lived the time for him.

Budgeon took a final drag from his fag and then dropped the butt to the floor, stamping the orange glow into the mud.

Everything had been fine until she came along.

Why did it always come down to a woman? Almost biblical. Garden of fucking Eden and all that shit.

In the end, he had been the lucky one, sliding around on silk sheets, relishing how sweet she tasted, promising her everything. But afterwards, as they shared a cigarette, he realised things weren't going to be the same. Not with the others wanting her too. Even among friends you couldn't reconcile a contradiction like that.

He shook his head and took one last look at the distant lights before moving back to the van and clambering in. The thin, pale man in the driver's seat grunted and asked him a question. Was he ready to go?

Was he? Peering down on the city and reminiscing about his childhood, thinking about the group of them as little boys without a care in the world, had made him reconsider for a moment. Now, as the warmth of the van slipped around him, he felt cocooned and cut off from everything but those memories. He could easily get misty-eyed again. Half a lifetime later perhaps it was time to forgive and forget, move on.

An ache flickered across his brow.

No, life didn't reward that kind of thinking. He'd gone soft over the girl and when his guard had been down he'd been betrayed. There were rules, unwritten maybe, but rules all the same. If you broke them you paid and some debts took more than money to settle.

Much more.

Of course he was ready to go. And the sooner they got the show on the road, the better.

Chapter 1

The noise carried through to Savage in the kitchen. Laughter. Samantha and Jamie's high-pitched squeals layered over her husband's voice as he sang an inane song in a mock Swedish accent. The cause of the frivolity was Stefan, the family's unofficial au pair, who had just returned from his home country laden with chocolates for the kids and two matching sets of stupid-looking knitted gloves and hats for Savage and Pete. Pete had shoved the hat down on his head, pointed out the window at the daffodils in the garden, and teased Stefan about being a little late with the winter gear. Stefan responded in kind, putting on a thick West Country drawl, muttering something about pilchards.

Savage had retreated to the kitchen to make a pot of tea, thinking Pete was right about the change of season. Mid-January, Christmas not much more than a few weeks ago, and already the east side of their garden a swath of gold, ochre and lemon. Other changes too: Pete arriving home at the back-end of November after nearly nine months away.

The celebrations of his return had run on into the Christmas period, the result one long spell of parties, relatives, more parties and more relatives. Now the holiday season was over Savage was pleased for life to settle down a little. Pleased too the spring had arrived early in Devon. The forecasters had spoken of a hard winter, but despite some snow in November, so far they had got it wrong. Out of the kitchen window the sun hung low in the sky, a cool yellow rather than the deep red of a summer sunset. Below the sun the Sound lay placid, only a hint of a swell disturbing the surface. A yacht, black against the light, motored in past the eastern end of the breakwater. The crew on the yacht waved to a trio of dinghy sailors struggling to catch a zephyr of wind to take them home before the chill of nightfall. Last night the frost had returned, but the first two weeks of January had been unseasonably warm, pushing the temperatures close to the mid-teens. Weather more suited to t-shirts than to a gift of hats and gloves.

A couple of days earlier Savage had received an altogether different type of Christmas present. One of the best ever, although Pete hadn't seen it that way. He told her in the kitchen, as she prepared a pizza, her hands floured with dough. The news stunned her and she could hardly take his words in.

'Scrapped?' she asked.

'Yes,' Pete said. 'Decommissioned. Mothballed. Sold-off. Cut up and made into plough shares for all I know. Seems as if I'm to be based ashore now. For good. Bloody stupid cuts.' Pete's face looked ashen and his eyes brimmed with emotion.

'I'm sorry.' Even as she said the words she knew she wasn't. Pete might be losing his ship but for the past fifteen years and more she had lost her husband – and the kids their dad – for months and months on end. It wasn't as if she hadn't known what she was getting herself into when they got married, but back then heart very definitely ruled head and the day-to-day practicalities of juggling a job and young children appeared to be years off. Pretty soon though Samantha and Clarissa had come along, unplanned, and mid-twenties she'd found herself with two babies and an absent father. Later she'd had Jamie and then the tragedy of Clarissa's death to cope with, Pete around for what seemed like mere fleeting moments.

'You're not,' Pete said.

'No.' Savage moved over and hugged him, pressing her face into his neck and kissing him, aware of her floury hands making prints on his jumper. 'I'm sad for you, of course, sad for your crew too, but I'm not sorry. Have you known long?'

'Before the last voyage I got an inkling of what might happen. At least the old girl went on a grand final trip.'

Pete had taken the frigate on a circumnavigation of South America, cruising down to the Falklands, through the Straits of Magellan and up the Pacific coast of Chile, using the Panama Canal to get back to the Atlantic. Before that the ship had been on patrol in the Gulf and seen action in pirate alley. As with every warship returning to Devonport after active service, she had steamed into the Sound to a hero's welcome, although one unnoticed by anyone living outside the city.

Now, as Savage poured water into the big blue teapot, she felt a warmth from knowing Pete would be in Plymouth and bound to a desk for the foreseeable future. With a more normal job perhaps they could have some sort of existence like a normal family. For years she'd coped on her own, but combining her job and home life was almost impossible. Having her and Pete's parents living close by helped, and more recently they'd employed Stefan. It still wasn't easy though, and with Jamie being six and Samantha thirteen there was hardly ever a time when she could relax.

The steam from the pot curled upwards and she chinked the lid in place, watching the final wisp of vapour dissipate along with her thoughts as the phone rang. DC Patrick Enders calling from Major Crimes.

'Don't you ever have days off, Patrick?' Savage said.

'It's the overtime, ma'am. Worth its weight. If there's any available I snap it up. I can always take a day off in the week when the kids are at school. So much more peaceful.'

Enders was late twenties, already with three children and a mortgage, designs on a four bedroomed place in Mannamead where his family could spread out and not live cheek-by-jowl. But then when she'd been that age, Savage thought, she'd had the same aspirations. When the twins were born, she and Pete had been lucky enough to find a large wreck of a house on the coast before prices sky-rocketed and such properties became unaffordable to all but the very few.

'Well, what can I do for you?' Savage said. 'I'm just about to sit down with my own kids and have cake and tea so you had better not have something for me.'

'No, just a reminder, ma'am. The DSupt says not to forget about the *Sternway* meeting tomorrow. He's sending you a bunch of stuff, so check your email.'

'Great,' Savage said without much enthusiasm. She already had a mountain of papers to read concerning *Sternway* – the force's long-term drugs operation – but she promised Enders she would check her email, hung up, and gave a silent 'thank you' she didn't have to rush out. The irony, given her recent talk to Pete about how much his job had taken over his life, wouldn't be welcomed.

The call from Enders reminded her there was other paperwork to complete too: notes for an upcoming PSD inquiry. The Professional Standards Department wanted to know why she had left the scene of a car accident in which a man had been killed. No matter that the man was a serial killer who had tried to abduct her own daughter, Standards wanted answers. Over Christmas and the New Year she had pushed all thoughts of the inquiry to the back of her mind, but now, with the interview looming, she knew she needed to spend time preparing.

She sighed and then went back to the living room to find Stefan teaching the kids some toilet humour. The scatological references sounded twice as funny in Swedish and soon all five of them were conversing in a mixture of languages interspersed with prolonged periods of giggling. Savage turned from the mayhem and looked out through the big window. Shadows crept across the lawn, painting black shapes on the grass which glistened with silver moisture in the fading light. Beyond the garden, the cliff fell away to a mirror which stretched to the horizon where the sun was just kissing the sea somewhere out past Edison Rocks. Sunday afternoon bliss.

Chapter 2

On any other Monday the three builders cradling mugs of steaming tea and sitting on the low brick wall outside seventy-five Lester Close might well have been discussing the weekend's footie. Plymouth had gone down three nil at home and the handful of points the team had collected in their last ten games wasn't enough to appease the fans. A demo had been arranged and there were calls to sack the manager, the players, the board, the boot-boy; anyone who could conceivably be to blame for the team's recent abject performance.

On any other Monday.

Jed Rammel was the oldest of the three builders, twenty years the oldest, and he'd never seen anything like it. Except, of course, when he'd been over in Iraq, but that was different. You expected things like that there. Not here, not on a Monday morning when all you'd come to do was dig up somebody's back yard to put some concrete footings in, preparatory work for a new conservatory. Jed guessed the owner would be cancelling the work now. Nobody in their right mind would want to be sitting out the back any more. Lying bathed in sunlight, relaxing, dreaming, and sipping a beer. Thinking about what had once been buried there. Give over.

Jed scratched his head, slurped another gulp of tea, tried to forget the toothy smile showing from behind the dried up lips and those empty eye sockets which he knew sure as hell couldn't see and yet seemed to be staring right out at him.

They'd started that morning at seven thirty with barely enough light to work by. Carted picks, crowbars, sledgehammers and shovels round the back. Jed had checked the instructions and marked out the limits of where they were to dig with lines of chalk powder and a couple of stakes. Young Ryan had first dibs, lifting the broken paving slabs with the edge of his pickaxe and then going ten-to-the-dozen with the crowbar on the old concrete beneath.

Youth, Jed had thought, all now-now-now, no care for the future. And so it proved. Ten minutes later and Ryan was knackered so Jed and Barry took over, breaking the concrete while Ryan shovelled the residue out the way.

They'd found the bones of a small dog soon after. Nothing to get excited about, Jed said, even as Ryan began to lark around. The larking ended when they found the box nearby. Plastic, buried in the soil under the layer of concrete about two feet from the dog. Jed wondered if the thing wasn't some sort of drainage sump, but when they took off the lid and saw the contents they realised it wasn't. They'd thought the thing inside was a doll at first. A big doll, sure, but a doll nonetheless. Jed's granddaughter had one, a large, life-like thing he and the wife had bought the kid the Christmas before last. But no, it wasn't a doll. They'd known that when Ryan's spade pierced a hole in the chest where he poked it. Crackled like parchment the skin had and through the split the three of them had seen the bones of the ribcage.

Definitely not a doll.

Jed sipped his tea again. Thought about Iraq. About things he'd never told his work mates nor his wife. Things he'd only shared with the men he'd served with. The type of horror he'd thought belonged thousands of miles away in another country.

'Losing three nil,' Ryan said. 'At home. You can hardly fucking believe it, can you?'

No, Jed thought, you couldn't.

Savage drove into the car park at Crownhill police station a little after eight fifty-five to see DC Jane Calter jogging over, her breath steaming out in the cold air. She pulled the passenger door open and collapsed in the front seat.

'Off to a property in Efford, ma'am. Right next to the cemetery. Handy, because there's a body under the patio. And I'm not joking. Wish I was.'

'Right,' Savage said. 'You sure you're OK? You don't look so good.'

'Bad weekend, ma'am.'

'Oh?'

'Brilliant, I mean.' Calter pulled the sun visor down to shield her eyes from the glare as they headed back towards town, the sun still low in the south east. 'Too much booze, not enough sleep. I never learn.'

The DC leant back in her seat and ran both hands through her blonde bob, pulling at a couple of tangles and squinting at the vanity mirror on the back of the visor.

'I barely managed a shower this morning, let alone a hair wash, and these clothes are the first ones that fell out of the wardrobe.' Calter indicated her rather crumpled grey skirt and jacket.

'I hope you didn't get into too much trouble.'

'No,' Calter grinned, 'unfortunately not. But I am seeing him again next week.'

As they drove to Efford Calter sat quietly, fumbling once in a pocket for some painkillers, dry-swallowing them and then closing her eyes. Only a dozen years or so difference in their respective ages, Savage thought, but Calter's lifestyle a world away from her own. Not that she was beyond getting drunk herself, having a good time, partying – Christmas being a case in point. But there was always the knowledge that the next morning any hangover would be punctuated by a seven o'clock visit from Jamie wanting to be up and at the world, Samantha needing a lift somewhere and Pete feigning his own hangover as near life-threatening.

Efford was an innocuous part of Plymouth sandwiched between the A38 and the Plym estuary. A mixture of older social housing, now mostly owner-occupied, and some newer but smaller properties, made the place out to be working class. Really though, Savage thought as they negotiated streets still busy with school-run traffic, you couldn't tell anymore. Even the tiniest flat cost a small fortune these days.

The web of crescents and avenues which made up the area was interspersed with plenty of green space, the largest being the twenty acre cemetery which Lester Close backed on to. The close itself had been cordoned off, already a number of people hanging round the junction with the main road. A dustbin lorry stood to one side, the driver leaning out of the window and arguing with one of the two PCs on duty, his language blue: 'Fuck', 'wanker', 'tosser'. The PC's face remained calm and expressionless as he informed the dustman there'd be no collection today. Heads turned as Savage was waved through by the other PC and drove into the close. The road rose in a gentle slope, the houses on each side post-war semidetached, pebble-dashed, uPVC windows with net curtains. The front gardens neat little patches of lawn with a shrub or two for good measure.

'Pleasant,' Calter said opening her eyes, 'but I'm more of a penthouse flat type of girl myself.'

'Rich is he?'

'Forces.'

'Don't go there,' Savage said, smiling. 'And as you know I speak from experience.'

Calter laughed as they reached the far end of the narrow cul-de-sac where a patrol car on the left hand side marked the property, a house in need of some TLC, the front garden full of clutter stripped from inside. Behind the patrol car a Volvo estate straddled the curb, the rear door up, a jumble of plastic containers and toolboxes crammed in the back.

'Layton,' Savage said. 'The sooner he gets to a scene the happier he is.'

John Layton was their senior CSI and where crime scenes were concerned he could be labelled a misanthrope, believing that only himself and his team had any right to be present and hating all other invaders. Especially interfering detectives. Savage got out and retrieved her PPE kit from the boot.

'You might as well start with them, Jane,' Savage said, pointing to the builders sitting on the front garden wall as she suited up. 'I'll risk Layton's wrath.'

At the house the youngest of the builders nodded a greeting as Savage went down the passage to the side. The other two stared into their mugs, one of them shaking his head and muttering something under his breath.

Round the back a patio stretched the width of the plot. Or rather it once had because one end was now a mass of broken slabs and concrete, the spoil from a large hole creeping across the postage stamp sized lawn beyond. Beside the hole Layton and Andrew Nesbit, the pathologist, knelt, peering down into the mud. Layton stood up as Savage neared, tipped his battered Tilley back with the finger of a blue-gloved hand and pointed at the brown goo.

'Bloody mess.' Layton scratched his roman nose with the back of his hand and shook his head. 'Builders don't wear ballet shoes, do they?'

Nesbit glanced round and smiled, his eyes sparkling behind his half-round glasses. He raised his bushy eyebrows, looked at Layton and then turned back to the hole.

'Mondays, Charlotte,' he said. 'What is it about Mondays?'

Savage walked over and peered at the puddle forming down in the excavation, a grey sludge-like liquid which oozed from the surrounding soil.

'The thing on the right is a dog,' Layton said. 'The builders found the animal first. But that wasn't why they called us.'

Savage could see a set of tiny bones and a pointed skull. A leather collar had rotted to almost nothing but the buckle and a little brass name tag. Next to the skeleton a large translucent plastic storage box, the kind you shoved under the bed or stacked up in the garage full of junk, lay close to the concrete foundations for the boundary wall. A snap-on lid concealed the contents, something pale and indistinct pushing up against one side promising nightmares for weeks to come.

'According to the ID disc the dog's name is Florence,' Layton said. 'Don't know if she is named after the place or the character from the Magic Roundabout. Whatever, I'd say the animal was buried a good few years ago. The crate was probably only buried within the last few months.'

'The lid?' Savage asked.

'The builders removed the top of the box. I put it back so the photographer could take some pictures. Andrew?'

Nesbit reached down, long fingers inside his nitrile gloves feeling around the edge of the lid, clicking the plastic back, lifting it off.

Savage gasped at the tangle of flesh and bones inside, the tiny hands clutching at a red house-brick, the torso curled round in the box, foetal-like. The child's skull had plenty of skin left on, hair twisted in long, curly strands, teeth bared in a mocking grin. The flesh on the limbs and body hung loose, looking stiff and like starched clothing or light brown paper. The child was naked, but there was a bundle of rags up one end of the box. That fact alone spoke volumes to Savage. Unlikely this was a terrible accident, somebody trying to cover up an RTC for instance. Not when the infant had been stripped. She considered the skin again, gone tan, the colour and consistency of filo pastry. The corpse reminded her of mummies she had seen in a museum and she said as much.

'Desiccated,' Nesbit said. 'The body was kept somewhere hot and dry after death and that caused the effect you are looking at.'

'So how long?'

'Very difficult to know at this stage. Maybe we will find some entomology or something else organic to help us establish the time the death. All I can tell you for sure is that she was buried here a good while later.'

'She?' Nesbit's confirmation of the gender chilled her, not that 'he' would have been any less horrific. It was the fact an identity was even now beginning to take form, a life created from the sad heap of skin and bone. Something solid to mourn over. Something solid to try and seek justice for. If possible.

'The hair looks like a girl's and then there's that.' Nesbit pointed down to one side of the plastic box next to the rags.

A patch of pink flashed out, vivid and incongruous alongside the bone and flesh. 'It's a trainer. I didn't want to disturb anything too much, but I managed to note the size. Twelve. Children's that is.'

Twelve. Which would mean the child would be half that: five, six or seven. Savage peered down again at the body in its makeshift plastic coffin. Once the girl would have snuggled up to her mummy or daddy, perhaps clutched a teddy to her for comfort as she fell to dreaming. Now she only had a brick to cuddle.

'We'll move the box and all to Derriford,' Nesbit said, standing and nodding to the two mortuary technicians who had come round the corner of the house. 'It will save disturbing her. Better that way.'

'Yes, better,' Savage said, wondering how anything could be much worse.